Michael Grant Jaffe

SKATEAWAY

A BRILLIANT NEW NOVEL FROM THE AUTHOR OF *DANCE REAL SLOW*

Skateaway chronicles three stages—preteen, late teen, and early adult—in the lives of Clem, Garrett, and Samantha Boone, who try to lead a conventional childhood in a small town somewhere in the Ohio River valley, in spite of their unconventional parents. Their father, Kendall, is an artist battling mental illness; more important, their mother, Mercer, is an OB-GYN who performs abortions. Many of the more difficult moments in the lives of these children inflate to disproportionate size because they occur against the backdrop of a conservative, blue-collar community. Often the Boones are forced to confront the taunts of schoolmates, the rumors spread by neighbors, and the threats of violence from anti-abortion protesters. As hard as they try to lead normal lives, neither Clem, Garrett, nor Samantha can resist the impulse to escape, each in his or her own way, because their lives are anything but normal, as the harrowing climax of the novel demonstrates. They're as cool and slippery—and as brittle and breakable—as ice.

MICHAEL GRANT JAFFE is the author of *Dance Real Slow* (FSG, 1996), which was made into the movie *A Cool, Dry Place*. He lives with his wife and daughter in Cleveland, Ohio.

5½ x 8¼ / 352 pages
HARDCOVER 0-374-26571-2
$24.00/$38.95 CANADIAN

ALSO BY MICHAEL GRANT JAFFE

Dance Real Slow

SKATEAWAY

SKATEAWAY

MICHAEL GRANT JAFFE

FARRAR, STRAUS AND GIROUX / NEW YORK

Farrar, Straus and Giroux
19 Union Square West, New York 10003

Copyright © 1999 by Michael Grant Jaffe
All rights reserved
Distributed in Canada by Douglas & McIntyre Ltd.
Printed in the United States of America
Designed by Abby Kagan
First edition, 1999

Library of Congress Cataloging-in-Publication Data
Jaffe, Michael Grant.
Skateaway / Michael Grant Jaffe. —1st ed.
p. cm.
ISBN 0-374-26571-2 (alk. paper)
I. Title.
PS3560.A3134S58 1999
813'.54—dc21 99-15204

Special thanks to John Glusman, Georges Borchardt,

DeAnna Heindel, Bertis and Katherine Downs,

and, of course, my family and friends.

FOR JANE, FOR SCOUT . . .

Too much has been disfigured in the name of symmetry.

Our lives were the shortest distance between two points,

birth and chaos . . .

Americana

Don DeLillo

SKATEAWAY

Here was home. Pitched behind the swish and swagger of life's motion tripping past. The way familiar things appeared at easy angles. Distant visions of landscapes in which smokestacks resembled a crooked row of incisors, sharp and rusted with age. The hillside above squeezed into cheekbones and, abruptly, a shortened forehead which vanished beneath a brush cut of evergreens. Then any stillness swung closed as if on whiny hinges. There was no more mouth or teeth or nose, only an apron of soot and coal dust. A mewing that grew louder and louder until, finally, it escaped into a yelping siren blast. The ache of steel against hotter steel.

Sometimes a hidden face, fuzzy without perspective. Mostly, though, the town was built of chipped brick and chimneys and iron and chicken wire set between the panes of thickly cut glass. Where one might expect to find calves and ankles and feet, instead stood houses with rubbery lawns and motes of black-tarred roadway. The smell drew the neighborhoods close to the smack of industry, breathing through screened doors and loosely rigged windows. A rancid cocktail that never faded, similar to spoiled cole slaw or turpentine.

The days braided together in a rope of noise and cooled cinder. Everything swallowed by the same foil of naked gray, like the wintery skin on poplars. Two years after Garrett was born, when Sam was still a baby and Clem was only four, his parents moved the family to a parcel of land in northeastern Ohio, slightly below the place where you'd affix a postage stamp if the state had been some squat-shaped envelope with edges worn furry.

The house, a large ivory Georgian, was hard by the southern line of their property. Each window had heavy black shutters tacked back at the sides—working shutters of narrow slatted pine which they'd used, twice, to protect the glass from high winds and blowing debris.

On the left side of the house was a pressed dirt and gravel driveway. Angled off behind the garage sat an enormous, silt-colored warehouse. From the moment the Boones moved onto the lot, the warehouse had been in a terrible state of disrepair. There were times during fierce weather when Kendall, who used the warehouse as his studio, braced its walls with four-by-six boards and weighted steel hinges at the corners. Some nights when rain was expected, he climbed to the roof and hammered reams of tar paper into the spongier sections while Garrett stood below, aiming a spotlight to his directions.

Besides two apple trees growing on the quarter-acre plot beyond the driveway, there was nothing especially remarkable about the house, though in the early primary grades of their schooling, the Boone children achieved a certain unexpected celebrity because they each had their own bedrooms—something of an oddity among the small, well-stocked homes in Lukin.

From the window of the second-floor bathroom Garrett shared with his sisters, they could see in the distance large smokestacks from factories huddled on the shores of the Wayonga River. As the children grew, their eye levels coincided with a peeling socket of frosted glass, a clear smudge that expanded with the massage of each thumbnail. Out there, above the horizon, seven chimneys, straight as pencils, loosed inkblots of black and gray against the sky. Sometimes at night, when one of the children had awakened from sleep too logy for lights, the smoke seemed almost white. Phosphorescent.

But that initial viewfinder etched into the window, dime-sized, appeared mysteriously one morning after the first protesters came—Clem or Sam or Garrett, though none had any recollection, wheedling a tunnel to the outside world. A place where they could see things they weren't allowed—an eyelid folded back. If they kneeled on the toilet seat, from the proper angle, they could peer almost directly down at the street. There were days, when the protesters returned and the kids had been sent to their rooms, that Sam and Garrett imagined crosshairs had been painted along that hole. The two of them pretended: each making clicky shooting sounds with their mouths or the snapping of fingers until they got bored. They could hear their mother's voice inside their heads urging them to stop; this desire made them no better than those people chiding her from beyond the property line.

Most of what mattered in their young lives seemed set into motion that autumn their mother was tapped with recognition. Everything around them suddenly labeled for change. And they understood, even as children, that they'd been pulled in another direction, one they weren't likely to have chosen themselves, set apart from the normalcy they saw shared by schoolmates. Not much affected them in tangible ways, not in ways they were forced to deal with on a daily basis other than the occasional argument or fistfight. They were bent and buffed into three tiny moons, orbiting each other, constantly, for protection and ease, because they retained a similarly queer source of gravity. They knew this *thing*, rarely discussed, powdered like prickly steel grinds, impossible to scour away. Each of them, desperate for stations of relief, took turns fumbling into freedom. Always, though, came a familiar, whispery tug that brought them back home.

HARPOONS OF LIGHT WRIGGLED loose from the sky, or at least it appeared that way behind squinted eyes. In truth, Sam was tossing silver batons which caught the sun when they rose above the torn line of treetops. She let them roll off her shoulders, across the nape of her neck, coming to rest, briefly, between the doughy-humped flesh at the base of her palms, before throwing them upwards once more.

There had been rain, nearly three solid days. Saucers of tobacco-colored liquid pooled on the front grass, greasy and dark. She knocked the instep of her sneakers with one of the batons as if she were a batter flossing spikes of dirt.

They expected strangers; they had been warned. So when the van pulled to the curb, she only glared, crossing the batons near her waist. Not once did she back herself to the porch, where the rest of the household was standing. She watched, she dragged her sneakered toes in an arc as if drawing a border. Something invisible to keep danger away.

They had come to march, her family had been told. Gum-soled boots belching in the muddy pathway. Most of the signs were hand-lettered and dripped runny ink like juice pressed from a blood orange. *Baby Killer* or *No Death* with a small, plastic infant doll hanging by a noose of wash-line cord. Parked behind their van was a navy-and-white squad car. Two police officers drank coffee; they held the Styrofoam cups between their hands, steam climbing across their cheeks. *To Serve and Protect* read the emblem stenciled to the car door, below the metal keylock. They simply watched to see that none of the protesters stepped on private property.

The new lawlessness of civil disobedience was accepted by these picketers. Discovering where their quiet world smeared into something else.

A cresting wave of hair, auburn losing to white, was tugged clean of Mercer Boone's face by bobby pins and aerosol sprays. She looked bloaty, tired. The engine of her life was clotted by stress. Running down the left side of her neck was a vein that inflated whenever she spoke.

Recently, she'd caught herself massaging her hands with regularity—turning them over against each other in knots of pink friction. Another new habit born of anxiety: she pet the hinge of her right hip, in quick, tappy strokes, as if assuring herself the bones hadn't exploded beneath the weight of her torso. From a distance, this practice made her seem like a gunfighter in the sticky moments before he was preparing to draw his weapon.

What she wanted, most, was a single day when the cogs that moved the traffic of her family trundled along without interruption. Nothing to provide a pause of alarm—for Mercer, for her husband and children. The filmy screen of uneventfulness, belonging to other families, hopefully slipped over the lens of her life.

It had been a long and taxing week. On Wednesday, a woman ran into the clinic screaming, "Got vines comin' outta my ginny! Got vines comin' outta my ginny!" She was from rural Caledonia and some weeks earlier she'd inserted a small potato into her vagina for birth control. Early Wednesday morning while urinating she'd noticed thin white tentacles sprouting from beneath the lips of her vagina, twisting their way through the coarse, dark hair of her groin. On Thursday, Mercer had a patient with two uteruses, something she'd seen only once before. The woman had come to her, like others, for an abortion, only now she needed two. And the following day, in her office, a patient's water broke while she reached for a Kleenex—bathing Mercer's desk with a gritty, gelatinous solution it took three amonia-strong buckets to clean.

"Come inside for some breakfast," Mercer called to Samantha.

The rest of her children were standing near the doorway in various states of morning dress: T-shirts, jeans, ratty oxfords. Garrett wore his father's old Ohio State sweatshirt flapping down below his kneecaps.

"Sam?" said Mercer, again, holding open the door.

All would have been fine if the protesters had simply stayed quiet. But one of them cast a quick, patronizing glance at Sam and, in a barely audible voice, as if his mouth was stuffed with sausages of dental gauze, said, "Run along, little girl. Listen to your murdering mommy."

Letting one of the batons fall to her feet, Sam clutched the remaining baton in her tight fists and carried it, a headless three-iron, toward the man.

"This is *my* house," she said, cocking the baton behind her right ear. "*You* leave!" She swung it, hard, into the bony edge of his shin. When he hunched down to massage away the pain with his fingers, Sam cracked him flush in the face. Even from where Garrett was standing, behind Clem, he could see the smudged redness against the curve of the man's temple.

"Fucker," said Sam, walking to where her mother was now waiting on the bottom step. Flanking Mercer, Garrett and Clem studied Sam's movements as she approached. She had acted from anger, not knowledge. She was defending a thing she didn't yet understand. Only, to each of them, a pack of unwelcome guests.

Once inside, they sat around the kitchen table eating sugary bowls of cereal while Mercer explained why they mustn't stoop to the protesters' level. Buttering slices of rye toast, she said, "We're above this."

"Well, I'm not," whispered Sam.

And even then, at the age of eleven, Garrett thought that Sam was right, she was not inclined to turn from trouble. Large or small. When Clem walked past Sam carrying two jars of preserves, strawberry in her left hand and apricot in her right, clucking her tongue against the back of her gums, Sam responded by trying to stick Clem in the butt cheek with the tines of a fork.

There was a crookedness to Sam's character, scaley and black, that bared its teeth at the oddest times. Garrett might be talking with her, say, underneath the shelter of a blanket fort canopied between twin beds with pillows holding down the corners, bonding over how much Clem's faux-prissiness bothered them both. Suddenly Clem would wander into the room, dressed in a frilly, high-necked nightgown. The shape of Clem's face, slender as a shoe print, made her features seem distorted in size. First to catch a newcomer's gaze were her lips, shiny pink against the vanilla of her skin. When she walked, it appeared her limbs, bony and angular, might cause damage to some other part of her body: immature joints or flaccid rib cage or certain organs lacking a fragile space. And once Clem had entered the room, Garrett was sure Sam was going to let loose with some meanness, some*thing* that would send Clem off crying into the night. But then Sam would aim the insult at him. Quick and unexpected, like walking into a glass door.

That morning, after Sam's altercation, they all sat in the front window while Mercer discussed things, reasonably, with the police officers and protesters. The children's breath left moist paw prints of fog along the glass. A few times Mercer raised her arms above her head, the way she did when she was trying to explain something to one of her kids, something she was pleading with a higher power to help them understand. It was silent inside the house, only the draw of air being taken into each of their lungs and then spit back out. Finally, Sam said, "I hope they take me away to jail. I hope they do."

Clem responded in a sharp, clear tone, letting each word break off under its own weight: "For once, Sam, would you please just shut your mouth."

It seemed to Garrett, standing beside Sam, watching her face warm and contort, that she might poleaxe Clem, too. But she didn't. Instead, she placed the baton down carefully at their feet, some delicate offering of peace. Then she walked to the back of the room and sat facing the wall, her bottom resting on the stiff wooden floorboards. She waited only for her mother to return.

SAM CALLED GARETT into the garage. She led him around back where the workbench was pressed against the corrugated siding. The slope of her cheekbones was so severe, half valentines, that sometimes when she smiled they appeared nearly to obscure a portion of her vision. Seeded across the bridge of her nose, in a delicate, inverted-crescent pattern, was a constellation of freckles. She had a narrow, elegant chin that lent a sternness to her face, making it seem as if she were always deep in thought. Her hair was flopped across her shoulder, tied loosely with a band of blue elastic. She motioned to something blurred in the wheat-colored strands below the curve of her neck. She had drawn a line onto her hair with black indelible marker.

"Do this," she said, pointing with her thumb.

She cranked her ponytail between the brailly mouth of a vice, stretching the cable of hair straight by pulling her head away from the workbench. Then she handed Garrett a fine-toothed hacksaw and made a chopping motion against her thigh.

"No," he said, retreating. "Not me."

"Yes . . . "

"Sam," he started, looking for something to hold.

"It's *my* hair. Shouldn't I get to keep it the way I want?"

"It's just . . . "

"If you don't help me, then I'll do it myself. You want it to come out all messy?"

And for whatever reason, this seemed to make sense to a boy Garrett's age, to a boy of twelve. If she was committed to lightening her head, well, then who was he not to lend assistance, to make sure she did it correctly?

At first, the hacksaw had difficulty finding a groove in her hair, cutting, nay, yanking a few pieces at a time, snapping them off one by one. But soon it moved easier and Sam, who had begun to cry from all the pulling, no longer needed to bite the underside of her lower lip to take attention from pain. When finished, she gathered the feather duster of hair and bound it with a short measure of kite string.

"It's not so straight," said Garrett, pointing to her head.

Peering at her reflection in a silvery hubcap hanging from a Peg-Board, she answered, "Good enough."

She had not provided a reason for the sudden change in hairstyles. Simply, a control exerted against the recent rise of disorder in her young life.

Later, Mercer sat Sam down on the center of the newspaper-covered kitchen table and evened out the ends of her hair with angled medical scissors. If she was angry, she didn't show it. She let Sam chatter away, attempting to distract Mercer with a series of inane questions. One concerned their dog, Barley, a thick-nosed yellow Labrador retriever. Sam wanted to know if Mercer would be attracted to him if she were a female dog.

AT THE FAR END OF THE TABLE, Sam sat with a cotton dish towel for a place mat. In her right hand was a rubber mallet. To her sides, Garrett held a wood-handled knife, and Clem fingered a serving spoon. The night before, Sam was awakened by a strange nightmare about one of the factories down by the river. There was nothing especially frightening about the dream—only, a young girl (not Sam or anyone she recognized) wandering a catwalk beside yards of hard-moving machinery. There was also noise and light steam and the hoarse sputter and clank of hidden workers. But none of these things, in the clearheaded moments of daytime, would've caused Sam to be afraid. The catwalk wasn't even suspended from a terrific height. Still, Sam had risen with a panic—retreating to the safety of the ottoman in her parents' room.

When Mercer heard the fractured breathing of her daughter, she rubbed tiny ovals into Sam's shoulders and, later, when she convinced her to return to bed, she sat humming a childhood lullaby in Sam's ear.

Now, as if to humanize the "disruption" (Mercer's word), Mercer gathered the family in the kitchen. She spilled shelled almonds onto Sam's cloth; she told Sam to cover the mess and begin busting the almonds into pieces with the mallet. Garrett's job was slicing dried apricots into narrow strips; Clem was instructed to use her spoon to spread gingerbread dough into flat cookie sheets. Their father, Kendall, was running an old cotton-candy machine he'd bought for parts, blending sugars and colored syrup in the whorl of tweedy paste to achieve a grayish mix of blue-and-pink.

Mercer wanted to hike the thoughts of her daughter, youngest child, into a pleasant direction whenever Sam again considered what had kept her from sleeping.

"You've heard of a gingerbread house," Mercer had said after first bringing them together around the table. "Well, we're going to make a gingerbread *factory*."

When the sheets of dough had been cooked and cooled, Mercer and Kendall fastened them with a tacky glaze of egg whites and strawberry licorice whips they tied at the corners in bows. Garrett's apricot strips were laid into squares for baked-in windows. The almonds, crushed by Sam, were sprinkled along the surface of the half-cooked dough for texture. Crumbly tubes of cannoli, bought creamless from the Italian bakery, were plugged into the roof for chimneys—spitting lopsided scarves of cotton candy set to appear like smoke.

There was a childishness to every facet of the project: the way Garrett and Sam and Mercer, even, flicked loose gumdrops across the table at one another; the sloppy edges to the factory failing to meet in a flush seal; the roof sagging desperately at the center and two sides. But, in truth, this was exactly what Mercer had wanted for Sam, for all her children: a wonderful distraction to spill across worrisome thoughts, to drown them away.

"We're going to eat this?" asked Garrett.

"Later," said Mercer. "In a day or two."

Beneath the ceiling lamp, Kendall fumbled with some of the supplies. He was building tiny people (and pets!) from miniature marshmallows and toothpicks. He dipped the end of a fine quill into food coloring to draw detail—facial hair, neckties, workboots—against the soft, puffy pebbles.

Once the three children had readied themselves for sleep, Kendall carried the gingerbread factory into Sam's room and cleared a place for it on the dresing table—directly in Sam's line of vision were she to open her eyes from bed.

"Other things I can understand," said Mercer, removing her shoes, her socks, while seated with a slivered view of Sam's room down the darkened hallway. "Maybe a bad dream about someone at school or one of those protesters or—"

"—an awful haircut," said Kendall.

They both smiled.

Wearing a white V-neck T-shirt and boxer shorts, Kendall disappeared into the bathroom, reemerging with wings of toothpaste poking from the corners of his lips.

"You know," he continued, his words climbing above the scrubbing sounds of the toothbrush, "I wonder if kids from other parts of the country have nightmares about, say, farms or shipyards or skyscrapers."

Mercer shrugged and then so, too, did Kendall. They both sat on the bed, nearly naked, only a foot of space separating them from each other. Their thoughts forked in opposite directions: Mercer considered whether she should again check on Sam; Kendall had a desire to knead the tight rope of muscle along his wife's shoulder, which, peculiarly, gave way to recollections of a magazine article on his bed stand.

In another day, the bad dream would carry less weight. In a few days, the only reminder would be the crummy shards of gingerbread on Sam's dresser.

MORNING BROKE behind an orange chemically light that left the kitchen walls a husky shade of pumpkin. The photographs, taken years ago, were Scotch-taped into a scrapbook, four per page. The idea had come to Kendall the evening of Clem's birth: he would chronicle the first year of his first child's life by taking a single Polaroid each day.

Some were perfect—sharp, mirthful: Clem caught in unexpected poses, crawling from beneath a couch or dirtied by a former neighbor's flower garden. Others were too dark or streaked with motion.

Now Mercer, first awake, leafed through the book. She'd remembered the photographs while lying in bed, hopeful, still, she'd lose herself to another hour of sleep. But the scrapbook skipped through her head; she finally found it beneath a world atlas in the den. Thinking hard, coffee cup at her side, she could not recall why she and Kendall hadn't put together similar books for their other two children. More complications had filled their lives, she allowed, crowding space between the second and third births.

But she felt guilty. This obvious lapse in parenthood could be triggered, simply, with a glance across the spines of a bookshelf: *Clementine's First Year* in rub-on decals, and nothing else.

"Is anyone up?" she asked, suddenly, as Kendall appeared in the doorway.

"Don't think so."

She turned the page and attempted to wipe something small from Clem's cheek, a meal worm of red thread. When it didn't move, she turned to her husband.

"A scratch or cut," she said. "Do you remember how she got this?"

Leaning down, he took a closer look and shook his head.

"Nothing serious," he said, reaching for the coffee pot. "Maybe we'd forgotten to trim her fingernails."

To Mercer, years later, it seemed unfathomable that she and Kendall didn't know the details—*every* detail—of their children's past. We should have this answer, she thought. We should be able to re-create whole long-winded tales about each of them—Clem, Garrett and Sam—with no more to jog our memories than a near-invisible scarlet stripe, the size of an eyelash, against the skin of their cheeks.

Other days, perhaps, Mercer would not have been pricked by the immediacy of needing a response—the *correct* response. But she was feeling like she'd begun to lose hold to things that mattered. She was again seized by a guilt that came, this time, from knowing that she'd brought trouble to her family's doorstep. Here, maybe, were the seeds to her daughter's bad dream distorted into something else.

She'd discovered another space in which she could not watch over her children. Even with the swift freedom granted them, some worries would never be completely their own.

LATE IN THE DAY, balancing himself on a cleaved section of railroad tie, Kendall lowered the Plexiglas visor over his face. It was tinted dark green, like the rear windows on a limousine. He was wearing stone-colored chinos tucked into a pair of black-and-yellow Wellingtons; his T-shirt was speckled with paint, mostly hardened into squiggly hang-nails of random punctuation: periods and semicolons and twisted exclamation marks. He lit the torch, narrowing its bluish flame to a manageable width. A tongue of sparks, spiky and fat, lifted from the hood. The mangled body of the truck appeared coppery behind the glow of the torch. Abandoned at roadside, the truck was towed home on the bumper of the family's Country Squire station wagon so their father, Kendall, could dismember it; singe and slice apart prongy hunks he could shape into sculptures.

Rock and roll music played from a clock radio that had been duct-taped to the door of an old refrigerator where Kendall stored some of his supplies: paints, bricks of film, beer, and a hard kosher salami. In the corner, Garrett sat on a wire stool and assembled a plastic model battleship. He had the pieces spread on an overturned gasoline drum.

Kendall came up behind his son, boots clopping on the cold cement floor. In his left hand, the torch, now quiet, blew papery claws of smoke toward the lamp. He examined parts of the model from under his mask. It seemed he wanted to help put the thing together. But instead he reached for the tube of glue and screwed off the cap. He slid it beneath his visor, near his nostrils. Garrett could hear his father take several long breaths—measured, consistent, like a hunched sprinter, hands knotting the fabric of his shorts, sucking heady gulps of oxygen after a race.

"I'm just trying to see if you should be using this kind of glue," said Kendall. "I'm not sure it's safe. Maybe it'll give you a headache or something."

"I don't have a headache," said Garrett.

"Well, not yet." He kept sniffing; he walked across the room to one of his work drawers. "What about using some of this glue instead?"

He held out a white bottle of Elmer's.

"That's the wrong kind," said Garrett, pushing back from the drum. "It'll look all gooey and ugly."

"Oh, relax," said Kendall, sensing panic in his son's voice. After another whiff, he returned the tube to its place beside the barbed pieces of battleship. "If you start feeling shitty, put the stuff away."

Humming with a toxic high, Kendall went back to his work. Garrett walked to the steel-lined sink, looking for paper towels. His father had inadvertently rubbed phlegmy glue onto the tube's cap. Garrett hadn't yet grown into the long, beefy profile of his nose, which, until he turned seventeen, would appear as if it belonged on a boy many years his senior. The elongated frame of his shoulders, much like Kendall's, made him travel at the fractured pace of someone being guided from above by string.

Above the water spigot was a shelf heavy with art books and frayed cardboard boxes. There, jammed between two empty milk cartons, was a dusty Tupperware container, the corner of its lid peeled back, partially damaging the seal. Curious, Garrett climbed on a stepladder and brought the container to the floor. Once opened, it revealed a Popsicle-sized tool with a delicate needled at one end and a long, black electrical cord at the other. It almost looked like the wood-burning set his friend Bryan Foster got for Christmas the previous year. As Garrett started fingering the ribbed handle, his father stopped working, again, and made his way to Garrett's side. This time, he removed his visor and wiped the perspiration drooling from his hairline with a wadded bandana.

"It makes art," he said, suddenly. "It makes art on people."

Garrett stared up at him; Kendall continued:

"It's for drawing tattoos." He paused, scratching his left ankle with the toe of his right boot. "You know about them?"

As Garrett nodded, Kendall reached down and rolled the cuff of Garrett's trousers above his calf.

"See that?" he asked, pointing to a black dot, the size of a pencil eraser, located below the hollow of Garrett's right kneecap. "When you were almost two I was gonna draw your zodiac sign—a Taurus—right there," he said, tapping Garrett's skin near the black spot. "But just as I started, your mother came into the room and threw a fit. I only got as far as touching the needle to your leg."

"You mean this is a tattoo?" he asked, pressing the dot between his thumbnails as if squeezing a pimple.

"Yep . . . But you're unfinished."

For nearly all of his short life until that moment, Garrett, like most everyone else, believed it was simply a birthmark. Even so, he was less surprised to learn that the blackened pupil on his leg was a tattoo than he was to learn his father had not completed the work.

Later, when Garrett asked his mother about it, she steadied herself against the banister bending upwards to the second floor. She set a pile of newly folded laundry upon one of the carpeted stairs.

"For a long time, I hid his tattoo needle," she said. "I was convinced he'd try and finish whatever it was he'd started . . . A bull or something."

"Taurus," said Garrett, sitting between his mother and the laundry. "My birth sign."

She didn't want to discuss this, he could tell. Her fingers, slender and flaky dry, removed a cloud of lint from her sleeve.

"What child—what *infant*—wants a bull tattooed on his leg?"

"Me, maybe."

"Oh, yeah? And remember when those kids teased you about your baseball glove last summer?" His father had made Garrett use a four-finger vintage model from a rummage sale instead of buying something new. A sensitive child, Garrett was razzed so mercilessly—over nothing—he quit Little League after two practices. "How do you think you'd have fared with a *tattoo* on your leg?"

And so Garrett's skin remained blank, stretched over his bony frame until it favored a swatch of lightly stained canvas. Gummy, washed-out pink. Tattooless.

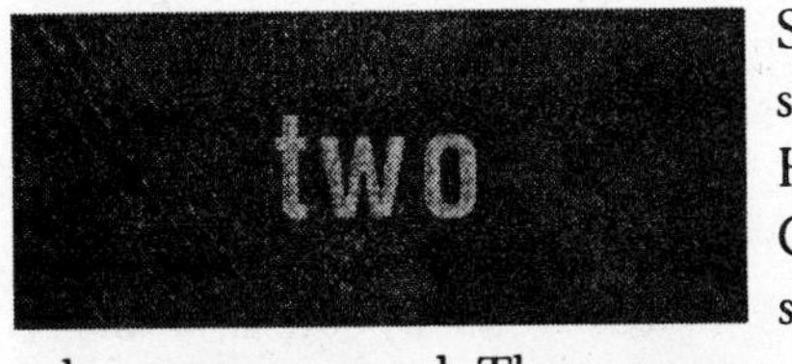

Stacked on the counter like dark, stubby cord wood were eight Ho Hos snack cakes. Beside them, Clem smoothed out the pocket-square-sized tinfoil in which the cakes came wrapped. There was no more wax paper in the house and Clem was trying to pack peanut-butter sandwiches for lunch. She didn't have any immediate plans for the Ho Hos, so Garrett took one to the table and picked loose the crunchy chocolate skin; he carefully unrolled the cake and scraped away the white frosting with the back of his index finger.

"Put this on my sandwich," he said, tapping the thinly pressed cake.

She glanced over her shoulder, squinting, as her mother sometimes did. Soon the three of them assembled at the back door, pausing to make sure they had everything.

Waiting for the morning bus, they each stood ankle-deep in wet earth; spears of grass curled into the laces of their boots and shoes. Clem was rigid—the insides of her puffy knees sheathed in navy-colored tights, pressed against each other. Occasionally, she looked down quickly, as if simply an extended blink, and adjusted the pleats of her skirt.

Closer to the street, Sam rocked her head to the rhythm of her corduroy slacks as she shuffled her legs. She ignored Garrett, who'd asked her twice, nicely, to stop prancing around.

He began waving a springy stick near Sam's waist. To one side, Clem moved only her arms, purposefully, to create space between several books whose wire binders were threatening to interlock. The tip of the branch caught the outside of Sam's hand, above the spidery knuckle of her left pinkie. She looked startled, not because it hurt, but because she didn't think Garrett possessed the skill to make contact, the deftness to graze her skin. For a moment it seemed as if she would ignore this action. Her attention was drawn to the paper sack containing lunch, making sure no harm had come to the sandwich or pear or cookies. Then Sam eased herself toward Garrett and stomped her heel, sloppily, into a puddle of brown water. It sprayed his khakis, from shins to hips, with soupy mud.

"Oh, jeez," said Clem, who stepped back and then, after following the school bus breaking from behind the trees with her eyes, forward again.

Before Garrett could respond, the bus had stopped, its accordion-style door yawning open with a high-pitched, chesty squeal. Looking downward, the driver motioned the three kids onto the first step. Garrett was last. When he reached the aisle, Danny Mills, who was seated in the second row, asked if Garrett shit his pants. The hate came an instant later. From the back. Soft, so soft Garrett almost didn't hear it, Win Carter asked, "Helping you mama dig a grave for all them babies?"

This Garrett knew: everything would now be different. It was the first time anyone Garrett's own age had spoken against his mother's work at the clinic. Even back then he had the presence to understand those weren't Win Carter's words; they belonged to his parents. Also, he realized that if Win's parents were talking, then so were others. The children of those parents would bring their beliefs to school. Always, Garrett and his sisters must accept that some nastiness could sting them from a lightless place. There was a new collection of rules, hastily assembled, for which the Boones must now be prepared to interpret. A very public knowledge of a family secret that wasn't a secret at all.

THE NEXT DAY WAS COLD enough so the puddles turned crusty with ice. Splashes of mud along the sidewalk had dried into brittle, distorted waves. Inside, awaiting his turn in the bathroom, Garrett pulled off his T-shirt, stopping once the neck hole caught at his hairline: he flung his head backwards so the shirt resembled billowy red hair. He touched the cottony wig with his fingers, delicately, the way he imagined a woman might stroke the ends of her own shoulder-length tresses. No one was watching him, so he gathered the T-shirt at the back of his neck, pretending to bind it like a ponytail. Letting the moment take hold, he began walking in little circles, throwing his hips from side to side and fluttering his eyelashes at an exaggeratedly rapid pace. When he placed his hands against the sides of his rib cage, thumbs forward, and shimmied up close to the wall blowing movie-star kisses, the bathroom door snapped open. The noise froze him.

He expected Clementine or Sam. Instead, it was his father, who, incredibly, appeared in a more peculiar state than Garrett. He held his arms like a scarecrow and at intervals (wrist, forearm, elbow) hung a variety of brassieres.

Both could feel their faces brighten with blood. What they wanted most, really, was to let the other pass; Garrett to walk, head down, into the bathroom and his father to wherever his destination. Forget all this. Kendall not needing to wonder whether his son wished he was a daughter and Garrett not worrying that, indeed, the things he'd overheard townspeople say about his father were true: that he was not settled in the brain. But too much time had already expired. So one of them started, simply:

"Your mother was drying these against the shower curtain," said Kendall, his arms remaining straight. "I'm bringing them to our bathroom so you kids can get washed. They're still wet." On the word "wet" his voice dropped, as if, suddenly, he'd found some anger. "They gotta be kept apart or they'll turn moldy."

Garrett moved, finally, letting his arms fall tight to his sides. He wanted to tell his father that he was only fooling around, his mind caught on some way to kill the boredom while he waited to take a piss.

His imagination offered a place to follow. But he chose a lie, something pale.

"I was looking for Sam." And then, swallowing hard, trying to keep truth from what's nearly believable. "I guess I was gonna tease her."

"Unacceptable." At first, Garrett wasn't sure whether his father was talking about his excuse or the teasing part. "Leave her be." He paused, again. "Remember what happened the last time?"

Garrett nodded. They both remembered: Sam had twisted the index finger on Garrett's right hand so severely that it tore tendons loose from the bone. He had to wear a soft cast for six weeks.

"Okay, then," said Kendall. "Will you reach over here and help me? Just push that black lacy job up a little farther, it's slipping down."

Extending himself, Garrett adjusted the bra strap against his father's arm. He let it come to rest in the hollow of Kendall's elbow. Then he stood in the door frame, fingers picking at pulpy splinters of wood in the lock socket, watching his father walk away. Before Kendall disappeared from view he dipped, slightly, so his arms could remain outstretched. He looked like a kite, Garrett thought, or some low-flying dirigible dragged near-vertical by the wind before striking power lines.

SEATED IN THE SHADOWS behind the warehouse, Sam dug a trough in the frozen soil. She was using a dulled lawn-mower blade like a hand shovel, gripping it near the middle. The ground was firm. She slashed away layers of earth before patting dirt into piles with the side of the blade. Every so often there was a tinny chime when she struck a stone, ringing off the metallic hide of the warehouse.

Here she was alone; Mercer had office hours, examining patients at her obstetrics and gynecological practice in downtown Lukin. The rest of the family was inside the house. Sam was burying one of her mother's cigar boxes, emptied first and then filled with a shaggy log of her hair tied with the same kite string and a greened spool of fishing line.

She wanted to sink her hair beneath three feet of land, hide it someplace where she wouldn't be reminded—not stumbled upon at the back of her underwear drawer or the top shelf of her closet. What she wanted was to forget about things, shake off the discomfort of not belonging in a family that itself didn't belong. In the roll of common days, she knew, there were few connections she shared with schoolmates. Rarely did her family operate as a unit—together visiting restaurants or museums or taking warm vacations. All pieces fitting snug. Sam, too, couldn't imagine anyone else her age understanding how it felt to be awakened by hostile noises coming from their front yards and, worse, hearing those epithets directed at their own mothers.

What's it like, they might ask.

She didn't have easy answers. Not about *that* world—or about the often strange behavior exhibited by her father. Only there appeared lasting scabs on young people. *Three* young people. A longing by each of the Boone children to evaporate.

So now, once Sam had finished, she tore away handfuls of grass, cold and spiky, and sprinkled them across the sealed hole. Still, there was a lump, so she positioned her feet together, insteps touching, and stomped down. After the second time she heard a creaking from the cigar box. But she continued until the mound had been flattened so it nearly matched the height of the other ground.

The year before, in school, Sam's class had buried a time capsule beside the gymnasium. For that, she'd contributed a collector pin Garrett had given her from the Football Hall of Fame in Canton. But here, in her own yard, she was leaving behind an actual piece of herself. This, she imagined, would be found someday by a person she didn't know, maybe even by somebody who hadn't yet been born. She wondered what they would think of her, the little girl who owned all the hair. Mostly, she believed they would be wrong about who she once was.

WHEN SAM RETURNED to the house, Garrett was lying stomach-down in the den. His mathematics homework fanned out at his side, radiated by the blue light of the television set. She'd caught him raising his arm toward a battered corduroy chair against the back wall.

"See, I know they're yours," she said, framed by the doorway.

For as long as the Boone children could remember, disgustingly, the hindquarters of the chair had been flecked with dried nose offerings, boogers casually tacked or smeared to the ribbed burgundy fabric when no one else was watching. They called it the Boogie Chair, to each other.

"It's a piece of paper," said Garrett, rising to his knees. "My notebook is shedding." He held up his books and shook them, but nothing fell free.

One time, after Mercer had stumbled upon a crackly swatch of chair while vacuuming, below its left armrest, she'd threatened to have it reupholstered. But, in truth, you had to look closely to see anything and, even then, it seemed like fraying, toothless corduroy. If you felt it, though, ran your hand across its shingled surface, then you might begin to wonder. The ones that were obvious, long and branchy, usually passed dried to the carpet beneath their own weight.

"You're nasty," said Sam. "People *sit* in that chair."

"This isn't me," said Garrett. He tapped the wooden leg, which drew the dog's attention. Barley nudged close and began licking the offending section of chair. Both kids groaned. Garrett tried to yank Barley away, slipping his fingers under his collar and leaning toward the couch.

"That's really sick," said Sam, walking into the other room and then scaling the stairs, two at a time.

Now Garrett knew Sam had something on him. He would stay quiet for a couple days until, hopefully, he could find her in the throes of her own suspicious act. They'd barter, exchange chits. This was how it was with Sam, always forcing others to play from a position of weakness.

THE WEATHER BROKE for two days, turning warm, warm enough even for shirtsleeves. But finally it was winter and the snow came in flakes that seemed as large and fangy as pinecones. On the weekend, neighborhood children appeared behind the house with their skates slung across their shoulders, or else they dragged them by the laces. They waited; they tested the yard with the toes of their boots, if only to make certain. And when they realized it wasn't yet time, they returned home.

First was Buzzy Page. He'd known Sam since age four when the two of them attended a children's traffic school together called Safety Town. The concept was to teach kids the right and wrong way to cross the street, the meanings of the various traffic signs, and where they should avoid playing. For whatever reason, though, Sam had a violent reaction to the school, perhaps because it was her first genuine brush with authority; she nearly bludgeoned one of the junior policemen with a hard-plastic stop sign. The cop was Buzzy. All was forgiven when Mercer invited Buzzy over for chocolate phosphates and peanut-butter sandwiches.

On this weekend, Buzzy was first to examine the yard. Soon after, he was followed by David Klein, Perry Niles, Lois Sandrift, the Gandley twins. And there were more. They were waiting for Kendall to build his skating rink, something he'd done each of the previous three winters. He'd been struck by inspiration that first December when a burst water pipe sprayed the patio and he'd allowed water to flood the yard until it froze solid.

Over time, it was commonly accepted that the neighborhood children were at the Boones' because of the ice rink. Rarely did anyone ask for admission to the house, for warmth, or drinks, or to use the restroom. This proved a comfortable "truce" for both parties: Garrett and Sam, especially, were most at ease when skating—a window in which they were judged for themselves; their schoolmates had little desire to peer beyond the family's fence. They were content to remain a safe distance from the truths behind any gossip they might have heard.

Eventually, the Wednesday after Buzzy's visit, Kendall carted his tools and loose plywood and fastening brackets onto the lawn. He had developed, even in the brief time he'd been building the rink, a favored way of doing things. First, he spread flat a waterproofed tarpaulin that had once belonged to a nearby college; it had been used to protect the school's baseball field from rain. Then he laid the two-by-fours end-to-end so they formed an enormous rectangle over the tarp, converting the yard into a sandless box. He clamped the two-by-fours together with steel brackets, saving door hinges for the corners. In a few places, along the sides, he stapled the rubberized canvas to the wood so it wouldn't tear loose.

Placing his thumb over the mouth of a gardening hose, to build pressure, he showered the tarp with water and left it to freeze. Again, in the evening, he repeated the process. It usually took three or four days before the ice was thick and firm enough to support a person's weight. Then Kendall poured warm water from a bucket across the surface and smoothed away the dimples and ruts with a long-handled squeegee.

One evening during dinner—franks and beans—he announced that the rink was ready. Beneath illuminated floodlights strung from trees and bolted to the outer wall of the warehouse, Garrett and Sam retrieved two goals from the garage; goals which had been built with packing crates and plumber's piping and knitted fishing nets.

Close to bedtime, the first night of the season, Garrett and Sam skated in pajamas and overcoats. They used a stale pumpernickel bagel, hardened solid, for a puck. Mostly they practiced their stickhandling, holding the makeshift puck against both sides of the curved wooden blade, skating to the far end and back again before passing it off to the other.

Once they'd begun perspiring, now skating only in blousy pajama tops and bottoms, they took a few shots, snapping the puck into the nets with their wrists and a tight swivel of the hips. After some time, Sam uncorked a slap shot from mid-ice; she'd raised the smile of the stick close to her ear and followed through with all her muscle and torque. When she connected, the bagel exploded into three hunks, each of which landed in the webbing at the back of the net.

After they finished, Mercer bundled them in blankets and wool socks. She fed them butter cookies and hot chocolate prepared with milk, whipped in a blender. Clem, too, sat nearby with her hands spread out like dried flowers against the table. As she moved, light zippered above the cuticles of her fingernails. While her siblings skated, Clem manicured her nails with the tools from a red leather pouch her mother kept at bedside. She shellacked each nail with two even coatings of clear polish.

Sam had minimal interest in Clem's nails, but she found herself staring at them from across the table. Uncomfortably, Clem curled her fingers into fists and, when that only called further attention to her hands, she crossed arms so either fist could find port behind the opposite elbow.

Despite Sam's age—youngest of the three—she still inspired fear in her brother and sister. From the time she was old enough to walk, to talk, she'd not been equipped with any *off* switch. She was occasionally reckless, unable to tighten whatever valve supplied a body with adrenaline and grit and a guttural caw to retreat. Were she a distance runner, she'd collapse before slowing to pain. She expected the same hard-pressed diligence in others. So she felt compelled to display disappointment in ornery fits, both vocal and physical.

Even in the kitchen, after skating, Clem and Garrett could feel a tenseness once Sam had focused on the freshly painted fingernails.

"That take you a long time?" she asked Clem, who, though she knew what Sam meant, feigned ignorance. "The nails. Did it take a long time to get them that way?"

Clem simply shook her head, waiting for the rest.

"Maybe, could you do mine sometime?"

Now Clem nodded. Garrett raised his eyebrows as if to say, "Go figure."

"Tomorrow?"

"Yeah, I guess we could do it tomorrow," said Clem. "Whenever."

Once Sam and Garrett had left the kitchen and gone upstairs to bed, Clem examined her hands, blowing loose some fuzz that had stuck to her thumb.

A WITNESS COULD SEE THE BABY from three blocks away, its head as large as a rubber tire. It took two people to lift the sign past the clinic—an oversized photograph pasted to heavy cardboard with the words *Choose Life* stenciled across its bottom. Sometimes, on Saturday mornings, the Boone children would wander into town while their mother worked half days. She forbade them to come near the clinic, even when there wasn't much commotion. Instead, when it was almost noon, they waited across the street in a window booth at Kunkles' restaurant.

Perhaps, early in their lives, this was how the resentment learned to crest. Nonsensically, to a child, they were held at arm's length from the part of their mother's world that wielded the most authority. People had disrupted their home—strange people who on random weekdays would picket and holler near their doorstep, wave banners in the same air space occupied earlier by kickballs and Frisbees. A violation only Clem, of the three kids, could begin to understand.

And always Clem and Garrett and Sam were shuffled away. Left to consider, with their own immature minds, what their mother (and father?) had done that was so terrible as to inspire adults to rise from morning beds and take positions, curiously offensive, outside the residence of others.

Months before came an answer, unsatisfying, when Mercer explained to her children, in a painfully clinical manner, that these people who made regularly animated visits to their property did so because they objected to a "medical procedure" she sometimes performed. Back then, there was nothing else. Not even a pause for questions.

Hidden by what they *could* picture—a low-rise of cinder blocks, near-windowless, surrounded by the same wire fencing used on ballfield backstops—was a surplus of shadowy visions inspired by what they could not focus upon. To Sam, the hollow-blade casing of a device used to core apples found beside the house had suddenly become a tool—misplaced by her mother—to extract brain tissue from behind the earlobe. Occasionally Garrett wondered if electrical currents and heavy fluids were employed.

On this day, Garrett and Clem ate waffles with butter and maple syrup. Sam had a grilled-cheese sandwich. Drinking warm tea and milk, seated beside Sam, was a large, light-skinned black man whose cleanly shaved head was protected by a lime-green bandana tied front. Beneath a topcoat, unbuttoned, he wore a sleeveless pink turtleneck and high-waisted gray trousers. Sticking to the lashes of both eyes, at the corners, were clumping beads of mascara. Twice a week, sometimes more, he helped clean the Boones' home. If needed, he also watched the children.

"Do you think those policemen would ever shoot somebody?" Garrett asked their companion, whose name was Tiff.

"They got guns."

"Yeah, but they're only for emergencies," said Garrett. "Like if there was a robbery or something."

"I don't think they would," said Clem.

Tiff removed a wedge of lemon from the saucer beneath his cup, shielded it with his hands, and squeezed juice into his tea. He'd begun working for the Boones shortly after the family had moved to Lukin. While waiting for a bus, he'd volunteered to assist Kendall in loading an abandoned couch—to be used vertically in a sculpture—into the station wagon. Kendall offered Tiff a ride home if Tiff would be willing to help carry the couch into Kendall's studio. That same evening, Tiff showed Mercer the "proper" way to season a baked ham, and, three weeks later, he quit his job at a florist's to work for the Boones after Mercer had been won over while watching him play dominoes with Clem on the back porch.

"Don't fool yourself," he said. "They shoot people all the time."

"Bad people," said Clem.

"Naw, they shoot people just like you and me."

Smashing a slice of banana garnish with her fork, Sam said, "Last summer, Craig Wilde got shot in the head."

"That was with a BB gun," said Garrett. "It didn't even break the skin. When I saw him, there was only a little red mark on his cheek."

"He still got shot."

"It's not the same."

"I know," said Sam, spooning ice from her water. "But it's still getting shot."

Afterwards, the four of them stood in the cold and waited for Mercer to pull the station wagon to the curb. Sam had removed her gloves and was flicking her cheek with her middle finger. She continued to ring the skin in the same spot.

"Hon, what're you doing?" asked Tiff, rubbing his knuckles across the scarlet blotch on Sam's face.

"Seeing what a BB feels like."

"It hurts more than that," said Garrett.

"What about a bullet?" asked Sam.

"Don't even think about those things," said Tiff.

Sam reached into her coat pocket, grabbing for a yellow pencil. She popped loose the eraser with her thumb and pushed the tiny metal cup into the slope of her palm. Letting it dig and twist, she used the coat's seam and her fingers for leverage. Surely, now she had drawn blood. But upon examination, she only saw a petite, circular welt. This was nothing like a bullet wound, she thought. Just a young girl's displaced fantasy and some school supplies.

A FEW YEARS AFTER MOVING his family to Lukin, Kendall accepted a job teaching introductory art courses at a nearby community college. Not surprisingly, he lacked the patience and desire to excel at this new post—more than anything, he became resentful of his students because he believed they were keeping him from focusing on his own work. Still, during the four days a week he spent at the college, over nearly five full semesters, it became necessary for Mercer to sheer down her own schedule so she could devote more attention to raising their children.

Many of the strongest memories Clem, Garrett, and Sam had of their mother were cultivated during this two-year period. There was a softness, a gentle grace she possessed which helped to guide her children. Though the kids always knew this was a part of her character, in the passage of time, Mercer became stingier with what she offered—as if she had only a defined number of kind exchanges before they might run dry.

But each child held fast to certain remembrances, an afternoon or event when their mother seemed most accessible. Once, while Sam was cleaning her bedroom, she came across a book Mercer had read to each of the children during their infancies called *Where-oh, Where-oh is Eric Tombow.* It was the tale of a young, lost Viking who was searching for his crewmates. While passing in the hallway, Mercer caught a glimpse of Sam, who was about four years old, seated on the floor with the book spread across her little thighs.

Moving cautiously, Mercer knelt behind her daughter and began reading the text aloud. Then, struck by inspiration, she gathered her other two children and they all descended to the basement.

"Remember this book?" she asked.

Both Clem and Garrett nodded.

Following their mother's direction, the three children sat in a semicircle while Mercer carried various items in from the laundry room.

She fastened a clump of red yarn to Sam's head, tying off both pigtail ends with string. She used a silver pail as a Viking helmet, clipping on safety pins to resemble horns. A broken broomstick, wrapped in gray gaffer tape, was converted into a sword.

Collecting a few more things in a box, she took the kids to the back yard and stood them within arm's distance of each other.

"O.K.," she said. "We'll do this like a play. Sam gets to be Eric the Viking." She pointed to her youngest daughter, who was struggling to keep the yarn and pail from falling over her eyes. "Clem and Garrett will take turns being everyone else."

Mercer began reading, slowly at first, pointing to a designated child when his or her time came in the story.

"It was a long and lonely journey for Eric," she read, looking toward Sam.

Slightly befuddled, Sam turned to Clem and then Garrett before locking eyes with her mother. Instead of speaking, Mercer acted out the motions of a person—presumably Erick the Viking—trudging across great distances. Sam nodded; she mimicked her mother.

"The first person he met was a farmer named Willie," read Mercer, choosing a British accent for the farmer's voice. She picked a piece of lemon grass and stuck it in the corner of Garrett's mouth. She showed him how to bury his thumbs beneath his armpits, pretending to stretch a set of imaginary suspenders.

As she continued the story, her children became more animated, their interest growing with each turn of the page. Clem flapped her arms to depict a bird of prey; Sam swung the makeshift sword to imply cutting through heavy brush; and Garrett pawed at the sky while portraying a bear. Slowly, the words coming from Mercer contorted into a dim echo in her children's ears. The specifics of the book faded to background music. The three kids were only paying attention to each other, their mother now resembling a distant lawn jockey. Garrett wrapped his arms around Sam's shoulders and playfully wrestled her to the ground. Nearby, on her knees, Clem tugged handfuls of grass and tossed them at her siblings. She then joined Garrett in pinning Sam, who was laughing so hard her face had begun to match the color of the yarn.

Once they had all separated, Clem started to roll away in a series of somersaults; Garrett and Sam, backs pressed together, copied their older sister by tumbling in opposite directions. From above, the three of them must have looked like scattered billiard balls.

Though Mercer had not finished—Eric was about to be reunited with his compatriots—she let the book come to rest against her chest. And now, her voice suddenly gone quiet, she studied each child. Garrett was in possession of the broomstick and he was boring small holes into the lawn. He was humming something to himself, loud then soft, while his narrow wrists flexed with every twist.

The sun had begun to sink; across the yard it cast salmony streaks of orange in Sam's hair. She had dropped her face into the grass and, without explanation, was teething on a sprinkler head. Her sneakered feet were pedaling in a freestyle kick. It reminded Mercer of the way Sam used to sleep when she was nine months old; she would drift into dreams while sucking her thumb and, unconsciously, bounce her footsie-pajama toes against the mattress of her crib.

The memory made Mercer think of Clem, who, very distinguishable from Sam or Garrett, needed complete quiet when put to bed as an infant. The slightest disturbance—a creaking closet door or the sound of sink water—would trigger her awake. Seated on a hump of dirt, Clem was building something with loose twigs and broken sticks. From where Mercer was standing, it looked like her daughter was making a cabin or a wooden castle.

Despite the fact that these children had all been raised by the same sets of hands, in a common environment, they were each so very different from one another. As they grew older, thought Mercer, and as their paths, in all probability, skewed into separate directions, they would continue to kindle unique personalities. A twinkle of emotion began to rise within Mercer once she started to consider what might become of her children in ten years. In twenty. How one of life's small details might register outsized importance in the shaping of character. The late-night fear of walking through a questionable neighborhood could lead one child to generalize about the types of people who lived there; a fender bender in icy weather might foster a phobia of driving.

Beside a sagging storm fence near Kendall's warehouse, she watched

Clem and Garrett come together over something. They stood side by side, their faces pitched at similar angles. Words were exchanged. Garrett nodded; he prodded a gray, trapezoidal object with his foot. He rubbed his chin in a way that reminded Mercer of his father. Desiring human touch, she reached for one of her children. Whoever was closest. She held Sam's head, free of pail and yarn, against her waist.

They could take this afternoon with them into sleepless nights and extended plane rides and conversations with future spouses. Their only regret, looking back, would be that they didn't have enough of an appreciation for things while they were happening. Too much taken for granted. But while the images scurried past Mercer's line of vision, with urgency, she had the wisdom to know she needed this to last a little longer.

Mercer released Sam from her grip with a delicate shove, allowing the girl to skip across the yard to where Clem and Garrett were now each attempting to balance on an overturned bucket.

"Be careful," said Mercer.

When Sam almost lost her footing, Mercer raised a hand, instinctively, to lend assistance even though her daughter was a good length away. In the same motion Mercer folded her arms across her chest, which had inflated with satisfaction, and continued watching her children until it grew dark. Until it was time for bathings and night clothes and a snack of home-baked corn muffins.

A FEW NIGHTS LATER, blackness drained from the sky like motor oil. It was nearly dawn and Kendall hadn't seen his wife or children in three days. He locked closed the door of his warehouse studio. During afternoons, he'd hear the voices of kids on the ice rink, the slushy whisper of skates and the tock-tock of the new rubber puck being batted by wood sticks. If he listened closely, let his mind exhale all else, he could even distinguish between the slight muffle of those who'd friction-taped the curved end of their sticks and those who had not. He knew, invariably, when the clopping stayed longest and loudest that Sam was handling the puck.

He'd run out of filters, so Kendall used newsprint in his coffee machine. He hadn't bothered to exchange old, soggy pieces for new ones; he'd even dumped fresh coffee over the muddy, squeezed grounds. Now the heap spilled from the cone, and more water dripped onto the counter than found its way into the heated pot. He ate salami from the stick, peeling back shrink-wrap like the skin of a plantain.

He was disgusted with his work, some oversized, elaborate surgical fixture with fenders. The night before, dressed only in boxer shorts and reversed baseball cap, he'd scrunched himself inside the piece to gain another perspective. Still, he was not happy. He'd even considered folding one side in on itself with a sledgehammer. Instead, he'd put on clothes and backed the car softly into the darkness.

Late that morning, a scraping noise entered Clem's head from beneath her jaw as if a dentist was scratching at plaque with a silver pick. She couldn't see anything from her window or from the bathroom, so she came into Sam's room and climbed over Sam's still prone body.

"Don't you hear that?" she asked.

The two of them raised the shade and watched as their father dragged the eagle, seemingly stiff with rigor mortis, by its left wing into his studio.

"Jeez . . . " said Sam, exhaling loudly so spittle met with the fine hair on her arm, which rested beneath her chin. "What *is* that?"

"A bird," said Clem. "A big one."

"He killed a bird?"

"I don't know . . . but it's something huge like a chicken hawk."

Together, they descended to the kitchen, where they expected to find their mother. Tiff was standing beside the stove, stirring a skillet of scrambled eggs.

"Y'all need to get dressed."

"Where's my mom?" asked Sam.

"She had to leave early. You both need to get yourselves ready for school."

Sam pressed her finger onto a piece of bacon and watched it bleed warm grease into a squared paper towel.

"Do you know what my father's doing?" asked Clem.

"Does anyone *ever* know what that man is doing?"

"It's just that, well, we—"

Leaning close, Sam kneed Clem in the thigh; she breathed, "Don't say anything."

"Get on," said Tiff. "Quit worryin' about him—you got five minutes till breakfast."

Seated at the table, Garrett was fixing a sandwich with triangular-cut slices of toast. He piled on egg, bacon, and spoonfuls of raspberry jam, peppered with seeds. When Clementine and Sam returned, clothed, they were talking softly. At first, Garrett pretended to be uninterested; he took some orange juice into his mouth but didn't swallow for a moment, not wanting to block his ears and miss any words. Finally, when he could bear it no longer, "What?"

Sam pushed away from her plate and walked to the back door, parting the curtains to peer out at the warehouse, past the narrow patio and iced yard.

"Sit yourself down and finish breakfast," said Tiff, drinking coffee from a wineglass because he liked the feel of its stem between his fingers.

"I'm not hungry."

"You better find a way to *make* yourself hungry."

On her way back to the table, Sam kicked at one of the legs to Garrett's chair. When he turned to respond, Sam slid her face close to his and said, "He *did* something."

"Who?" asked Garrett.

"Dad," said Clem. She craned her head across the table. "We think he killed a bird. We saw him dragging it to his workshop."

"So . . . It's only a bird."

Glancing at Tiff, who was filling the skillet with soapsuds and water, Clem said, "Not just a bird. This was really long—it was almost as big as Dad."

And then, suddenly, Tiff turned from the sink and announced it was time for school. When Clem tried to finish what she was saying to Garrett, Tiff rapped the counter with a wooden spoon, making a noise like rolled powder caps being struck by a hammer.

From the front window of the house a parent, if inclined, could see the three of them walking to the bus stop. Garrett slowed, then sped up to catch his sisters. Once, when they had nearly reached the corner,

Sam raised her arm and it looked as if she was brushing her teeth. In truth, she only had a small itch above her lip.

For these three, rare was the day that folded without incident into the rest of the calendar. Always, they knew, something would announce itself, some queerness with a burly weight their schoolmates were forced to deal with only once or twice a childhood.

Best were the mornings, like this one, when the damage came early. The Boones understood about probabilities; their lives moved easier when the troubles were bared before school, before Clem and Garrett and Sam were pushed into contact with others. Too often, they were deposited into a posture of defense—desperate to bring back a normalcy they almost reached when things were quiet, nearly settled.

But invariably the Boone children had to watch events unhinge. A week earlier, it was their bird-killing father who had seemed the stable parent as they'd seen their mother buckle behind a load of unexpected stress. Beside the cash register at the grocery store, Mercer had become acutely aware of a man staring at her; she thought she remembered him from outside the clinic. Maybe he was only shopping, maybe she had his features confused with those of somebody else. But, heart racing, she began to believe this man had followed her—and the rest of her family—into the store. She started to tremble and, before Kendall could intercede, she shouted in a hysterically high tone for the man to leave her *children* alone. Soon, she—and the very children she wished to protect—grew more frightened by the pitch and unrecognizableness of her voice. Had she lost it? (In fact, the man in question was carrying a jar of B&M baked beans and some dish-cleansing powder.)

Sam and Garrett both took a step back. Kendall tried to lay a soothing hand against her waist. Moments later, the three children sat silently in the backseat of the car, behind their mother, while Kendall returned to the store for the groceries. Afraid, they listened cautiously to the heavy breathing of their mother—a wheezy inhale followed closely by a wet, spittly sigh.

"I'm sorry," she'd said, finally. "I don't know . . . I don't know what happened."

They were all quiet, again. The children watched the back of their mother's hair as it brushed the headrest, then pulled free.

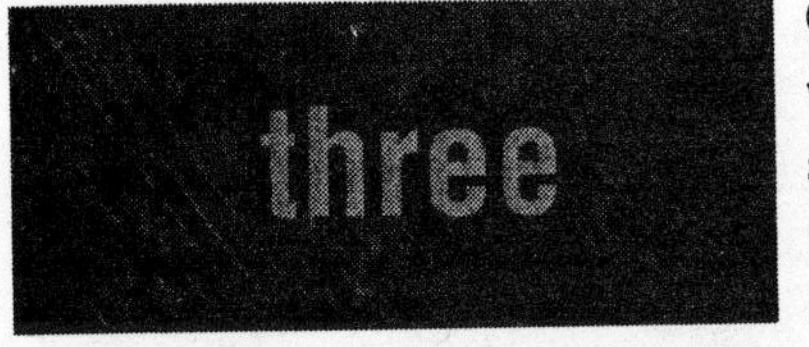

Clem liked to kick things. You wouldn't expect this of her—surely Sam and even Garrett, but not Clem. It seemed out of character because she behaved (and dressed) like a mannered lady from nearly the instant she'd been coughed from the womb. To her, though, it was a release; she enjoyed striking objects with her feet. Best was something light and loud that would travel a respectable distance when booted correctly: a plastic Clorox jug or pop can, or once, discovered at the mouth of the Packards' driveway, a dried gourd with seeds.

When she wore open-toed shoes, in warmer months, she chose to punt softer objects or, if she couldn't resist, she used the inside ball of her foot as if a field-goal kicker.

On this day, in ankle boots, she walked home carrying books against her chest. Behind the crosswalk, half hidden by leafless shrubbery knotted into arthritic claws, were dark spines poking from beneath scattered sticks, dead grass, and wood chips. Abandoned, perhaps by accident, was a perforated chrome hairbrush with quills matted like badger fur, fiercely bent and misshapen. Nothing about this brush would hold your interest, nothing would make you stop at its side, unless, of course, you were Clem and considered this find the ultimate good fortune. She had something exceptional to kick during her way home: new sounds, new ricochets and angles off the cratered sidewalk.

She had left school early, by ten minutes, to retrieve a package from the post office. She'd volunteered. Wrapped in brown paper, the box was the size of a cloth-bound dictionary but significantly lighter. In the upper left-hand corner the return address was written by hand in black marker; the postmark was foreign, Brazilian. The parcel, Clem knew, was from a friend of her mother's in Rio. Clem also knew there would be a letter, mailed separately, for which she would have to sign.

Because these were cigars, hand-rolled in Cuba, they were illegal in the United States. Earlier, Mercer had mailed a check to Manny Ballante, one of her lab partners from medical school, and he was filling her list of requests. Oddly, she'd acquired a taste for the cidery nicotine in fine cigars while studying for exams with him. The cigars came bandless; the envelope would contain the colorful rings, pressed flat, which Mercer and Clem would carefully slip back over the naked brown fingers. This way, if the box was inspected at customs its contents were no more unlawful than a carton of Dutch Masters from the corner drugstore.

Clanking, scraping along sandpapered cement, the hairbrush led her home, books and boxed cigars balanced on her forearms. Beyond, the horizon's gray turned deeper, as if someone were shading the earth's roll with crumbly charcoal pencil. The walk was not long and Clem's thoughts drifted to, of all things, automobiles.

On Thursdays, her mathematics class became a human diorama, of sorts, depicting a make-believe town, with each student responsible for his or her own business. There were two telephone companies, two bankers, two of everything as to inspire free trade. They called it *simulated economy*, and Clem had been selected to run one of the car dealerships. Recently, her competition, Alex Russo, had unexpectedly slashed prices on inventory. Four classmates, including Clem's only close friend, Lindsey Simon, had gone to Alex for new or second cars. By whatever means, Clem needed to figure a way to sell off three of the previous year's models from her own lot, or she'd be overstocked when she took delivery on the new line next month. More important, if she didn't move those cars it would affect her semester grade.

There was a shift change at one of the mills—paper, thought Clem—and a stuttery air horn sounded. From across the street she watched some of the workers, soiled and slow, pass from the mouth of a chain-linked fence. Most were carrying lunch boxes with tunnel-shaped roofs to accommodate thermos bottles of coffee or juice or ginger ale. In the waning afternoon light, each man's face had the lifeless complexion of nickel plating. If she closed her eyes, which she did, briefly, she could hear the heavy *whop* of steel-toed boots meeting asphalt. There was also the higher-toned slapping of shoes with overworn soles, the ones with heels no thicker than the folded cover of her composition notebook.

The men all looked the same, mostly, except for a distinguishing jacket or knitted cap. Several summers ago, Kendall worked two mornings a week for a silk-screen sign company, assisting the art director. The majority of the signs were large and long and fitted for grooved slots on the sides of city buses. They advertised alcoholic beverages and political campaigns and hosted events, like the sportsman show, at the convention center. Some days Clem had met her father after school at the truck bay of the sign company. No matter the temperature outside, her father would be damp with perspiration. The signs were dried on a heated conveyor that turned Kendall's work station into a furnace. Often, until he saw Clem or Sam or Garrett, his face had the same ashy emptiness as these workers, as if a turkey baster had extracted his blood in a single squeeze.

Clem angled hard to the right while crossing the street, steering clear of a couple of millworkers who looked particularly intent on finding the closest bar. Then it occurred to Clem in a sudden but reasonable thought: she needed to bridge the gap between what was pretend in the world of simulated economy and what was real. She had to entice her classmates with more than simply a reduction in the amount of Monopoly money they were going to spend. She knew these classmates, she knew what they wanted. If they could only get something tangible with their new "car": homemade chocolate-chip cookies or a sandwich bag filled with jawbreakers or decals to stick against their notebooks. Obviously, it couldn't be something elaborate or expensive—she wanted to avoid the appearance of trying too hard or, worse, she didn't want to be accused of "buying" customers (which, of course, was exactly what she intended on doing).

A single-story building of dark red cinder block, shadowed by factories, faced the intersection. Even now, during winter, the garage door was propped at half-mast to allow an escape for the hot air. Clem paused for a moment, tightening the grip on her belongings before crouching to crawl beneath the door. Inside, to her right, sat a small office with a rectangular slide window where someone could hang out their hands to sign for deliveries. Down a narrow hallway was a large, open room. An industrial-strength dryer stood bolted to the concrete floor. Sign after sign emerged on a conveyor belt of chain mail, their surfaces warm and smooth to the touch. A canopied hood tapered into exhaust pipes extended through the ceiling and beyond the roof. A worker then loaded the signs on to wire racks, which were wheeled against the wall for storage.

The noise was loud, irritating, but most of the men standing at various locations around the room seemed oblivious to it. All except one guy dressed in dark blue coveralls, who kept raising his voice, nearly shouting, at another man. As Clem made her way toward the back, the smells turned familiar; she remembered them from her father's clothing. Fastened to the wall was an enormous trough of brushed steel, bowed along its sides, with a drainage hole in the middle. There, two more men, wearing disposable plastic gloves, sprayed used frames of silk screen with kersosene, then rubbed wet rags against the fine fabric gone clotty with paint.

"Can I help you?" said the man in coveralls, startling Clem, from behind.

"My father used to work here," she said, for lack of better words.

"He doesn't work here anymore?"

She shook her head.

"Did he forget something?" said the man, whose name, Les, was stitched across his left breast pocket.

"Oh," said Clem. Suddenly she realized how misplaced she must've appeared. "No, I'm here for school. Actually, um, I'm trying to . . . "

Les led Clem to the art department, where it was quieter and they could talk. He listened as she told him about simulated economy and

Alex Russo and automobile inventories and the importance of grades to fourteen-year-olds. After she'd finished, after she'd explained to him what she wanted, they just stood there, the two of them, waiting, breathing, both thinking of other things: Clem considering the ingredients of several chocolate-chip-cookie recipes; Les reminding himself to buy rock salt for the front steps on his way home.

"Let me see," announced Les, if only to break the silence. "There're a bunch of discards we use for scraps. Cleaning ink spills and stuff."

He began rummaging through an assortment of vertically stacked cardboard signs. While looking, he asked, "What're your cars called, anyway?"

"Huh?"

"What kind of cars are you supposed to be selling? Buicks? Fords?"

"CleMercuries," she said. "They're named after me."

He nodded, unfurling a sign and tacking it to pieces of corkboard above a drafting table.

"How's this?" he asked.

Written in thick block letters across the top of the sign: Seventh Annual Auto Show. Below, there was a collage of photographs featuring a variety of cars—mostly prototypes which appeared to be lifted from science-fiction magazines. A space had been left blank, white, where a sheaf of tear-away cards could be fastened for individual removal.

"Right here," said Les, pointing to the empty box, "you could write in the name of your cars. *CleMercuries.*"

She smiled. It was exactly what she'd pictured. Les wrapped the sign in newsprint and rolled it into a tube, binding the ends with tape and string so it would be easier to carry. He led her to the garage door, which he pulled higher so she didn't have to stoop, and made her promise that someday, when she was running a real dealership, she'd cut him a discount on a new pickup truck. After she turned away, walking to the bend of the block, she heard the metallic squeal of wheels as Les tugged the garage door down to its original height.

CLEM AND HER MOTHER SEPARATED THE CIGARS by size at the kitchen table. Because there were only four brands, of significantly different sizes, it wasn't difficult to match the rings with their corresponding cigars. Harder to delicately slip the bands onto the soft cigars without peeling loose any of the tobacco leaf. It worked best, Mercer found, if you wet the cigar with saliva to hold any anxious veins from catching on the paper and tearing away. They would touch their fingers to their tongues and rub them against the glued flaps of envelopes; the tackiness gave them some control, some grip over the rings.

Sam and Garrett, meanwhile, fussed with their homework. Clem had baked cookies for school, for simulated economy, and she promised the broken ones to her brother and sister. They waited.

Days had passed without anyone seeing Kendall except, briefly, Sam, when he came into the kitchen the night before, late, for a drink. She glanced at her father as he took three pears and a heel of rye bread back with him to the warehouse. She didn't say anything; she wasn't actually sure he'd seen her. Once the door closed and Sam could hear her father's feet shuffling in the gravel beside the house, she waited until she was sure he hadn't forgotten something, until she was sure he wouldn't return. Then, quickly, she poured herself some cranberry juice and pattered off to her room. For the first time she could remember, Sam was afraid of her father or, perhaps, more so, afraid *for* him. In the last few months, he'd become stranger and stranger. And though Mercer had explained to them, from a very early age and again last week, how artists operate to their own sometimes peculiar rhythms ("Like the way only a dog can hear certain pitches," she'd said), Sam and her siblings were beginning to believe it was more. The other afternoon, while she was talking with Garrett and flipping television channels, they paused on a documentary about van Gogh. When it was revealed that the artist had hacked away one of his ears, Garrett, without slowing for thought, said, "Our father would saw off *both* his ears." Sam nodded. So did Garrett.

Still, there remained another less obvious piece to Kendall's character: the desire for attention. As with most artists, much of his day was spent alone. This isolation only served to amplify the importance of those brief blips of time in which he found himself in the company of others. Deep down, he had an overwhelming longing to be appreciated and, even more, to be *noticed.* Both Kendall and Mercer recognized the irony of their needs when juxtaposed against those of the other: one wanted less of the spotlight's glare, one wanted more.

Most of the attention brought to the family—good and bad—by protesters and pro-choice activists and curious neighbors, was inadvertently set into motion by Mercer's work. Even when all eyes fell to Kendall there came a reason, sooner or later, to turn their gaze to his wife. A month before the cigars arrived, a young couple traveled from Columbus to buy a painting of Kendall's they'd seen in the back of an art-house catalogue. While they were drinking red wine and nibbling on cubes of cheese offered by Tiff in the warehouse studio, the sounds of protesters came again from beyond the front lawn. The couple, undaunted, purchased the artwork despite the interruption. But the disturbance was painful for Kendall; he couldn't completely enjoy what should have been one of the rare moments of pure pleasure resulting from his creativity. Instead, he was forced to raise his voice above the rhythmic shouts—they were using Mercer's *name*—while he helped the couple bind the canvass to the roof of their car.

Given the circumstances of this lifetime, Kendall understood, he was unlikely to achieve the fame (or infamy?) of Mercer through his art. So he let his focus fall to smaller arenas. He curried favor with neighborhood kids by building the skating rink each year. He'd spent three weekends repainting the elementary school's playground in fiery, comic-book colors. With his own children, on occasion, he would halt whatever they were doing—homework, board games, sometimes sleep—for squirrel-chasing expeditions or pumpkin carving or drawing murals onto a nearby quarry with bright chalk. One of the more memorable activities came on a warm evening a few autumns ago, before bedtime, when Kendall gathered the family in the back yard and passed out swimming goggles he'd purchased from a sporting-goods store that was going out of business. Then he surrendered compression-top seltzer bottles to his wife and kids for a boys-against-girls water fight.

Regrettably, these types of interaction were irregular. Waiting beside a seldom-used landing strip for the approaching lights of a plane. The expectation of a starry blink that took forever to arrive.

STANDING NEAR THE SCHOOL'S SIDE DOORS; fiddling with the tumbler on her locker, Clem listened to the conversation of two classmates. She wanted to be sure they weren't talking about her; she wanted to *know* the class thought her cookies were nothing more than a fine marketing tool. In fact, they were discussing a pair of shoes one had loaned the other.

Originally, Clem had fastened sandwich bags with wire ties, each holding three cookies, and contemplated passing them out to everyone thinking about purchasing one of her cars. This, even to Clem, seemed too obvious. So she set out the cookies, debagged, on her notebook beneath the sign that read *CleMercury*, in red felt-tip marker. She was successful, to a degree, selling-off two of last year's models and receiving a promise, from Kyle Wallach, after he'd taken four cookies, that he would buy either her remaining car or something new once next season's stock was delivered.

The bulge of insecurity affected all kids, Clem understood, whether curious about boys or gossip or the perceived intention of home-baked cookies. But for her, too, she always considered—*over*considered—if perhaps she was carrying another load. Opinions cloggy with a residue, over which she had no control.

She rode home in a window seat near the rear of the bus, with Sam and Garrett across the aisle. When they'd been released, walking the remaining few blocks from the bus stop, something caught Clem's eye from behind the strained webbing of bare trees. As they moved closer, Clem could see a series of lights: red and white and orange.

At the corner, Sam began to say something but stopped. Police cars, two of them, parked in the pawed space at the back of the driveway between the house and their father's studio. They had seen police cars before near their property. Together they wandered slowly to the side of the house where their mother was standing with Tiff. Embarrassed, they feared catching the eyes of passing classmates or a neighbor. Mercer was speaking to one of the officers in a stern tone, and she slapped the palm of her hand with the fingers of the other. When she saw her children, Sam first, then Clem and Garrett, she pulled away and tried to lead them toward the house. But she paused to whisper into Tiff's ear. And in that moment, with Mercer's back turned, the large delivery doors on the side of the warehouse were shoved apart by an officer on each handle.

Two more officers had been in the warehouse with Kendall, and they emerged into blurred lightness dragging ropes, taut, fastened to a flatbed cart. There, standing almost ten feet high, was the sculpture which had been consuming Kendall. Dropping from a contoured dome at the top were rough-cut slats of iron as thin as yardsticks. Soldered inside, sprouting from the base, was a large bronze-cast sculpture of a bald eagle, wings raised, carrying an illuminated lantern in its beak. Bolted between its claws was a narrow nameplate which read, "go bite yovr art." On closer examination, though, you could see that many of the engraved letters had been filled with smudges of grease paint. The nameplate originally read, "A good book is the best of friends, the same today and forever (Martin Tupper)," and beneath that, "Lukin Public Library."

The police struggled to wedge the sculpture into the trunk and then, when it wouldn't fit, into the backseat of a squad car. They stepped away, perplexed, and one of the officers announced what seemed apparent to everyone else, even the kids. "We're going to need something bigger to haul this off," he said. "A truck, or maybe the paddywagon."

As they radioed for assistance, Sam stepped closer and began touching the sharp metal, lightly, with only the tips of her fingers. "It looks like a birdcage," she said quietly, to no one in particular.

One officer, dressed in a regulation bomber jacket, walked over to Mercer and asked what Kendall's relationship was to the children.

"He's their father."

"Well, it might be a good idea to take them inside. We're going to have to drive him to the station . . . and he's cuffed."

"You've got him in *handcuffs?*"

"Ma'am," started the officer, adjusting his squeaky leather belt, "he committed a crime. Several crimes."

"But really . . ."

"It's your decision. I just thought you'd want them"—he motioned with a slight wave toward Clem, Garrett, and Sam—"out of the way."

"We do," said Tiff, speaking from a place behind Mercer's neck. "Thank you."

Tiff called out to the children, herding them rapidly through the side door of the house.

"I wanna watch," said Garrett.

"Me too," said Sam.

"No one's gonna watch." Tiff pushed them past the kitchen and dining room, into the study, where the only window faced a lonely alley. "You'll sit right here and study something."

"Well," said Sam, "I wish I could study what they're gonna do to Dad."

Once Sam and Garrett had fanned open their books, along the gutters of their laps, not bothering to look down at the pages, Clem moved to the door. Tiff was seated straight, his back refusing to find ease in the couch. He filed his fingernails with an emery board.

"I need to get my compass," said Clem.

"Where?" asked Tiff, keeping his eyes focused on his hands.

"In my room."

"Hurry, then."

Clem ran up the stairs, taking them in twos, knowing any time she saved on the front end she'd have moments later. Quickly, she grabbed the compass from her desk and then ducked into Sam's room, peering out the window as they opened the door to one of the police cars. She saw her father being guided by a gloved hand buried in his armpit. The officer then held Kendall's head and lowered him onto the backseat of the car, behind the thick shield of Plexiglas.

"*Clem!*" said Tiff, loudly.

"I'm still lookin.'"

Before she returned downstairs Clem took a final peek at the yard, at her father sealed in the squad car, grinning, his skull thrumming the headrest. In the distance, she could make out a figure walking precariously across a corner of the ice rink. She didn't know if it was another officer or her mother or just one of the neighbors coming to watch.

Several nights earlier, Kendall had driven from the steel and mill smoke, past Dinker Drug and Dairy Freeze and Kunkles—all closed—to a band of houses, mostly gated, at the western property line of the county. Behind, on a low grade hill, sat the Lukin Public Library. Centered near the double-door front entrance was a fat concrete slab holding the bronze casting of a majestic eagle, speckled with oxidation.

Kendall had lowered the propane tank from his back, set the flame of his torch, and begun cutting the eagle from its perch. He burned carefully away, using his left hand to guide the fire in a straight line below the talons, below the nameplate. As he neared completion, he braced the eagle against his torso so it wouldn't fall; the bird's sharp feathers sawed into the spongy skin above his collarbone.

Once the last of the amoebae-shaped bronze burned apart, Kendall balanced the sculpture along his hip and thigh and yanked free the lantern wire. He carried his gear to the car and then went back for the eagle, hoisting it sideways over his right shoulder so one wing pointed forward and the other behind. A drunken weather vane.

Now, gathered around their parents' bed, Clem and Garrett and Sam waited for their mother to speak. What words would she offer to make sense of this night? In Mercer's own head, ringing like a cowbell, was the risk of hypocrisy hitched to any explanation. How could she apologize for this humiliation brought by their father when, in truth, she'd long ago aimed klieg lights at all of them?

She was delicate, providing her answer in a slow, broken voice that sounded as if she were deciphering Sanskrit.

"How unexpected," she said, straight-faced. She adjusted a notepad and pencil on her nightstand. "Well," she continued, "this should teach you each a valuable lesson: *Never* forget your library cards."

They all smiled.

"Here's something . . . " She stopped; she took two attempts at starting again before, finally, "Your father had a lapse in judgment."

"I'll say," Clem interjected.

"But this will be fine. I promise."

It was not a guarantee she'd ever offered with respect to the unrest her own work had carried their way.

"So much of this life must seem strange and difficult to you three."

The language she was choosing made it sound as if she were speaking to someone older, someone unrelated. Sam adjusted herself on the floor, ankles beneath buttocks. Each child watched her intently as Mercer's hands traced cones into the fabric across her thighs. She couldn't give them an answer for their father's actions, so, she reasoned, she would attempt to give them a piece of an answer to something else.

"There are times when people just want to hear that everything's going to be all right. I see this when I'm with patients. But along the way, I can't anticipate certain difficulties."

She loosened the top button on her blouse.

"I came to a part of what I do by accident. The hard part. The part about performing abortions. I was in my residency, working four nights a week at a free medical clinic." She stopped to take a breath, to measure what she was preparing to say against the maturity of her children. "I saw so many women damaged by poor medical care, so many babies simply abandoned a day—an *hour*—after birth. I guess I just didn't want to see that happen anymore. I got sick of the sameness to these tragedies, day after day. Can you understand that?"

She asked the question without expecting a response. Still, Clem, Garrett, and Sam each nodded.

"But now, the difficulty I didn't anticipate was all the crap my *own* kids were going to face." Garrett's eyes got wide after Mercer said the word "crap." "No mother—no good mother—wants to see her children have to deal with . . .

"I worry about you at school or walking home or, some days, even when you *are* home."

Once Mercer was quiet, Sam, who had been staring into the stalks of the carpeting, looked up and exchanged glances with her brother and sister. After another moment of stillness, it was Clem, not Mercer, who exhaled a loud, watery sigh.

THE MOON APPEARED so perfectly round and white hanging against the sky it seemed die-cut from a sheet of black Lucite. It had taken three days for Kendall to relent, allowing his wife to post bail. Filled with a prickly wave of excitement by her father's stay in the county sheriff department's lockup, Sam insisted on repeating to anyone who'd listen, "My father's a convict," or, from an old movie, "He's in the big house." At first, Clem or Tiff would raise a finger to their mouths, trying to hush Sam. Eventually, though, they just tossed back their heads, deflated, and surrendered to some odd passion that pushed young girls to the brink of ecstacy because their father had been imprisoned.

Maybe the charge in Sam came from what had suddenly become tangible. There now existed a label for her father—for *one* of her parents—that, however crude, was something she could understand. No longer must she hear cloaked insults breathed by neighbors and schoolmates in a language she had trouble deciphering. She knew exactly what types of people belonged in jail cells.

Once Kendall had been bathed and put to sleep early, Mercer stepped onto the back porch and lit a cigar. She wore a heavy fisherman's sweater beneath a coarse wool blanket. Great clouds of smoke, as on a steamship, burst from Mercer's lips and nose.

"Mom hates this," said Clem, seated on the floor of the dining room.

Behind half-closed doors earlier that afternoon, they'd heard their parents arguing. This was uncommon. Over the years Mercer and Kendall had worked the appropriate push-and-pull of their relationship to a keen balance. But now, suddenly, too many stones pitched on the scale by Kendall.

"We've given you all this space," said Mercer. "For creativity, for a different way of living." She was pacing across the den. "These children—*our* children—need a ballast I can't always provide. There's too much shit they've got to deal with already—"

"—Then quit your job."

His answer, so simple, was something none of the children had considered until that moment. They each let the idea hang in the air, like a pleasing smell, until their mother finally responded.

"Really? And you'll cover the lost income by . . . ?"

Obviously, there was a greater impetus behind Mercer's work at the clinic than financial. Here, though, she'd figured this angle of attack was the quickest way to quiet her husband.

"Please, Kendall," she continued. "They have enough roadblocks to a normal way of living. The last thing they need—*I need*—is to worry about another."

Sam, also in the dining room, lay on her stomach by Clem's side, and removed a photograph of her father from a family album which she taped to a blank piece of paper in her notebook. Using a dark marker, she connected the borders with vertical lines so they resembled prison bars.

"I wonder what they fed him in there," said Sam.

She rose and crossed her legs.

"It seems like this kind of thing never happens to other people, to other families," said Clem. She was not speaking to Sam or Garrett, who'd moved into the doorway, but instead simply to herself. Another blink of attention these children could do without.

"What about Mr. Glentini?" asked Garrett.

He was talking about the father of one of his friends, Chris Glentini, who the previous March had fallen from a scaffolding at work, impaling himself through the chest. When they removed the body, hacking apart a six-inch pipe, witnesses said the blood began spraying so wildly it resembled one of those handicraft sets where you squirt paint into a whirling dish.

"Different," said Clem. "That was an accident."

And then there was silence, save for the squeaking of Sam's pen and, finally, the slap of the back door when Mercer returned to the kitchen.

PLAY GOD. For a moment, Clem thought. Maybe longer. A way to repair all the pimpled edges that weren't laying flat. Places where she could attach herself without awkward seams. No longer would she feel anxious passing certain classmates, fearing appraisal. She would not be the girl seated alone in the lunchroom or library or on bus trips. Let her become one of those cliquey field-hockey players in tartan skirts. Let her have "wicked" crushes to share with friends. Beside her bed, of course, a personal phone that would always seem busy. Invitations to parties that might not exist without her presence. Rides from school in cars belonging to popular boys—older and handsome and more interested in her than she was in them. Other students asking her opinions on insignificant matters ("Can you *believe* she wore that top?").

A control that previously did not exist. Some way to peel loose her infamy and, among those qualities most important to a teenage girl, the ability to gain the right kind of notice. She allowed similar thoughts to enter her head during ripples of quiet: as she drifted to sleep; when she'd completed an exam before the rest, pencil down and eyes riveted to the chair in front; on the long walks home she sometimes shared with her brother or sister. Granted a month of days in which she didn't seem irrelevant. Such hopes were hardly fantastic: the ease of acceptance. A normal conversation with other kids between class bells was distant from a desire for terrific speed or beauty or pails of cash. She only wanted the glide of all things reasonable.

She let her thoughts catch on these daydreams as she worked her way along the meady riverbanks. Below the clutter of refineries were several silo-shaped tanks for storing oil, short and squatty like half-smashed pop cans. Even closer to the Wayonga River, standing on legs flaking with scabs of rust, were two Hueletts a few hundred feet apart—enormous girdered skeletons hunched across the waters, once used to remove iron ore and lumber and coal from passing ships. Winding beyond the most difficult stretch to navigate was a tight and busy corner followed by a narrow straight. Above, one after the next, sat hollow buildings of brick and cinder block and aluminum and corrugated steel. Abandoned spaces soiled with graffiti and broken glass and the film of sooty air. Twisted American cartilage.

A crooked path of worn-pressed dirt led to splintered wood shucks fitted for stairs that climbed to the rear of a renovated building. Nearly windowless, it resembled a military bunker. A four-sided antenna, straight and tall as a rocket ship, exploded from the middle of its roof; scattered beside the antenna were a series of satellite dishes. Painted above the front door, facing the parking lot, in red block letters were the initials WZBI-TV.

The town's largest television station, affectionately known as ZB or ZBTV, had recently moved its studios to the industrial epicenter of the county because it could deliver a cleaner, stronger signal to people in the lowlands. Like many small-market stations, ZB filled its broadcast schedule primarily with network programming, syndication (7 p.m. weekday offerings of *The Honeymooners* was a ratings favorite), and a variety of locally produced stuff (news, important high school football games, lottery-induced game shows).

Clem waited to be called, seated on a Naugahyde couch in the studio's lobby, leafing through a trade magazine. She had been recommended by Marjorie Pressey, her English teacher, for a part-time job several afternoons a week. Mostly, she'd been told it was a gofer position with room for advancement.

The smoked-glass doors parted and Clem walked down a thin hallway with framed posters of local newscasters and television personalities and larger, slicker ones featuring network stars. Magazine in hand, she was left alone at the head of a rectangular table in a wood-paneled conference room. She had dressed this morning in a dark skirt and white blouse. But at school, in fourth-period history, someone had placed gum in her chair and it stuck to the side-stitching of her skirt. At lunch, she iced it and later spread the fabric over a bench in the girls' locker room and tried tweezing it away. Seated here in the conference room, she was conscious of the sticky pink nib at the roll of her left thigh. She shielded the spot with her arm and then the magazine. When a man entered she rose, quickly, keeping the magazine in place, before returning to her chair.

He introduced himself as Larry Willick, an associate producer for many of the local programs. What they needed, said Larry, was someone eager, intelligent, and hardworking who was willing to be on the set of a new show for "young people" four days a week. That person's responsibilities would consist of everything from "retrieving" coffee to copying and collating scripts to running errands for staff members. For the duration of Larry Willick's discourse, he flipped through a set of papers attached to a clipboard, making marks, occasionally, with a green felt-tip pen. Not once did he look up to see if Clem was listening. In fact, if Clem had been so inclined she could've left the room, pumped a fistful of change into the candy machine, taken a drink of water from the cooler, and returned to her seat without the hint of a pause in Larry's cadence.

The program, from what Clem could glean, was some peculiar hybrid of a teen dance hour and academic quiz show. There would be dancing, of course, but at the conclusion of each song the dance teams would be peppered with questions from a variety of subjects: mathematics, science, history, music (!), pop culture, sports, etc.

"Do you know Mickey Gott?" he asked, suddenly, pushing Clem from her trance into a full-body shrug. "Well, he's done a bunch of things for us here: *Saturday Afternoon Theater* and voice-overs, and sometimes he does the weekend weather. He's going to host this new show . . ."

It seemed to Clem that Larry had now lost what little desire he had of speaking with her. More, he was chewing on the cap to his pen, head raised, hoping he'd heard someone around the corner call his name. This was beneath him, interviewing a *fourteen-year-old* girl.

"So," he started, moving to the door. "Are you interested?"

All Clem could manage was a slight nod.

"Swell."

He turned to leave, banging the clipboard nervously against his belt buckle.

"Do you . . ." began Clem, swallowing the first words of her sentence. "Do you mean I've got the job?"

He smiled and told Clem to return on Monday, ready for work. As he walked away, down the hallway to his office, to one of the sets or the bathroom, she could hear him muttering to himself, though she didn't think it had anything to do with the show.

ALMOST SINCE BIRTH, Sam breathed peculiarly in her sleep. She held her breath for two or three counts—fatty, pregnant pauses—and then rapidly exhaled and inhaled, a swift stroke with a wood saw. It used to scare Mercer or Tiff when they passed her in bed at night or found her tuckered out on the couch. Initially, they were convinced she was suffering seizures. They would shake her awake, holding her, frightened, in their arms. Once, sure this was not like the other times, certain this was truly something dangerous, Mercer jimmied a spoon between Sam's teeth to prevent her from swallowing her tongue and drove to the hospital. Though the tests were negative, Sam did need a butterfly bandage from where the spoon had cut her above the lip.

On this particular morning, Garrett stood beside Sam's night table and listened to the delayed *chuffing* of his sister exchanging breaths. It was nearly five, still dark, and they were beginning their first season of youth-league hockey. He knocked the butt end of his stick against her headboard. After a moment, rolling to her side and back, Sam left her bed, sheets tangled into a sloppy rope, and got dressed in the bathroom.

The walk to Thurmer Park ice rink was long and cold. Every few blocks Sam or Garrett would stop, setting their duffels of equipment onto the hard ground to rest. Late the previous summer, Mercer had purchased much of their hockey gear from a yard sale near the town of Fowler. The pads seemed enormous, circus-sized, especially for Garrett, who was a goalie. They were frayed, spitting wiry thread like pubic hair, and stained with leaf-patterned patches of sweat. Helmets of scuffed white plastic, which they both wore, listed from side to side as they moved. Garrett had a mask, which he tied to his chunky stick.

Some of the houses were lighted, but only the kitchens, where mill and factory workers ate soft-boiled eggs and drank coffee and smoked one last cigarette before leaving for the day. The final few hundred yards, behind Thurmer Park, was a deep incline that during snowy days was used for sledding. Often, the older kids stole molded fiberglass trays from the school cafeteria and tried riding down on their bellies or standing upright, knees slightly bent.

Sam, the only girl, used a separate locker room for dressing. The floor of the building was coated in a rubberized carpet so people could walk in their skate blades. The boys' changing room was drab, rank: wadded balls of athletic tape and yellowed T-shirts were scattered among dust bunnies and curious puddles. To Sam, the girls' room appeared as though Clem had been consulted during decorations. It was stocked with the trappings of young and gentle figure-skating ballerinas. On one wall, a series of photographs of all the top skaters in Thurmer Park's history and some of their assorted blue and red and white prize ribbons. Most of the important awards were in a glass case near the main entrance, beside the turnstiles. Several costumes, glittery and pink, were strung from hangers below the lights. Stapled to the back of the door was a poster of Peggy Fleming accepting her gold medal at the 1968 Olympics. Someone had written in pencil, across her left calf, *Peggy Phlegmball.* Lying in a pile beside the sink, like kindling, were dirty white skate-guards of various lengths.

Sam slipped on her underclothes and padding, adjusting the straps across her chest, armpits, and smoothing down the swelled hip-sleeve.

She used a hook to pull tight the laces of her skates. She could hear the voices of her teammates, muffled, as they skipped through the heating ducts like the sound of a radio beneath wooden floorboards. When she was finished, dark green jersey pulled over her head and soft-armored body, she wobbled toward the ice.

It was still early, not quite six. The suspended ceiling lights, wide trays of blue, buzzed so loudly that Sam thought someone had pushed open a fire exit. She climbed the boards, hitting the ice with a *punk*, before easing her slight weight from foot to foot. She pushed herself, all grace, in a loopy oval. Threaded through her elbows, behind her back, she kept her stick parallel to the ground.

Sam was a significantly better player than any of her new teammates. There had been some question, initially, about whether she would be safe playing in a league with only boys. But when the coach, Ray Kyler, called her to the rink for a tryout two weeks earlier, he watched his doubts dissipate once she skated with the others.

"I'm not worried about her taking a hit," he said, to some of the more skeptical parents. "To put a body on Sam, they've got to catch her . . . and I just don't see that happening a whole lot."

After they had finished practice, that first morning, one of the boys from across town, from the other school district, said, "I'm not sure I wanna play with a girl."

From across the locker room, wiping the slush from his skates with a towel, Buzzy Page said, "Then don't."

And though it wasn't much of an exhange, it was the last time anyone at Thurmer Park spoke out against Sam.

LATER THAT AFTERNOON, Mercer and Kendall took the children on a shopping excursion to a local strip mall. So rarely did the family travel together, all five of them, that it caused the kids to question their parents' motivation. What the children had surmised—Clem leading the discussion—was that, with the threat of protesters, their mother feared leaving them home alone. Maybe she also questioned the stability of their recently paroled father.

Six pieces of collapsible lawn furniture were weighted with bricks against strong gusts of wind. Weatherproofed belts of fabric, woven between the tin frame of a lounge chair, were sagging under the strain of concrete that had been poured to dry in the bottom of a bleach bottle. Along the front wall was a sign announcing sale prices on various out-of-season items: charcoal grills and beach umbrellas and plastic wading pools for toddlers. A week ago one of Garrett's classmates had visited this hardware store with an uncle and returned home with an air rifle. It was the kind of pump-action gun in which a shooter could clot dirt in the mouth of its barrel and cock, repeatedly, for pressure, before firing off the muddy debris.

Near the hardware store, where Kendall was buying spray paints and rubber plunger-heads, was a pharmacy, a dry cleaners, a Woolworth's, and a supermarket. Clem, Garrett, and Sam sat on the ground waiting for their mother to finish stocking her grocery cart. Kendall had given each a dollar to spend. At Woolworth's they'd purchased candy and a hot-rod magazine for Garrett; pop, a superball, and wax lips for Sam (she liked to chew the lips into a cud-like bulb, pretending it was a ballplayer's wad of tobacco); and for Clem, the practical one, some hair ribbons and colored pencils.

Now, killing time, Garrett and Clem watched Sam play soft-toss with the ball against the face of an overturned picnic table. After leaving Sam's hand, the ball found odd, skittery angles, and leapt off cracks and pebbles into unpredictably small then large parabolas. Inspired by boredom, Garrett rolled a coupon flyer into a hollow tube and spat M&Ms like blow pellets.

"You're wasting them," said Clem of the candies, without looking in her brother's direction.

He launched a few more near Clem's crossed legs. She scooted from his range.

Let them tease, she repeated in a silent mantra, let Garrett shower her with tiny chocolates, for in truth, she had the power to ignore what she could not accept. From here she bore a strength. The ability to stand alone, no matter how displaced or geeky she might appear to others.

Four teenagers drove past in a green Buick. Crooked gaps of rust lifted from above the car's wheel wells, spreading with the uncertain patterns of bacterial growth. Great clouds of whiskey-tinted exhaust trailed in its wake, rising slowly, remaining for several beats even after the boys had departed. The Boones only noticed the car because its gargle and clink had interrupted the low-level strum of silence. Once the engine noise had subsided, the kids, blocked to the right by a camping tent, heard the talk of two strangers caught in midconversation.

". . . not that I'm passing judgment," said one woman, arms pinched beneath shopping bags, to another. "But Margaret Donnell lives only a few houses down from them. She says it's happening now almost weekly."

During the stitch of empty time it took the second woman to retrieve her car keys from her purse, Clem peeked around a ripple of tent bunting. She followed the women's sight lines into the spot where they met. A queasiness twittered its way above the lonely well of her stomach. Sam gripped tight her superball; Garrett allowed his makeshift peashooter to find rest against his lap—when the first woman used the word "protesters."

"A group of protesters is coming regularly to march along the sidewalk," she'd said, her eyes, like those of her friend, locked on Mercer loading groceries into the parted tailgate of the Boone's station wagon. "Complete with big, graphic signs."

"What do you mean, graphic?" asked the woman with the keys.

"Oh, terrible stuff. Margaret Donnell told me one sign had a picture of a baby being fed into a meat grinder." Both women exhaled loudly. "She has to keep her children inside. She's afraid they'll have nightmares."

Clem's greatest fear was that Sam would jump to their mother's defense; that she might breath more trouble into an already awkward situation. But she quickly saw that Sam and Garrett were both, much like herself, wrenched by embarrassment. The three huddled together, elbow to elbow. They were not eavesdropping; they weren't even sure these women knew who they were. Still, they wished to remain concealed. Away from anything that would bring them attention. Or spread further damage.

"What about *her* children?" asked the second woman, motioning toward the parking lot with her head. "You'd think she'd worry . . . "

"I certainly would."

"Keep quiet," hissed Clem, mostly to her sister.

"What am I gonna say?" whispered Sam.

"Nothing."

She was only making sure.

Garrett was crouched into a sprinter's stance, so it appeared, as if he were readying himself for a quick dash to freedom. Here, pinned to the Boones, was a similar crowd of symptoms: clammy sweat, light-headedness, scratchy throats.

"Imagine your kids waking up to that," continued the first woman, prattling on. Clem and Garrett and Sam only wanted the discussion to end. "I mean, really . . ."

And then, curiously misplaced, a voice they could distinguish squeezed between the other two.

"What do you know about it?" asked Kendall.

He'd been standing a few paces behind the women, for long enough, hidden by angles and tent siding.

There was no response. Only, from the three children, a desire that their father not make things worse.

"We, uh, were just saying . . ." stammered the second woman.

"Don't just *say* anything."

For one of the few times they could remember, the Boones had seen their father pushed openly into a defense of his family. Of his wife. It had happened, too, a couple of months before when he'd walked the kids to their bus, halting, briefly, to threaten some especially aggressive protesters with a raised fist.

His eyes turned from the women to a perch above his children.

"Oh," said Clem, defeated, scrunching her head into the dunes of her shoulders once she'd seen Kendall acknowledge their presence.

"Come on," he said, as if there was nothing unique about spotting his children pressed low in the dirty shadows of a strip mall with this hurtfulness lurking nearby.

Reluctantly, they rose under their combined power to their father's side. A community of mutual humiliation: the discovery by both women that their words had found inappropriate ears; the acceptance by Clem and Garrett and Sam that they'd been privy to information they hadn't wanted to hear, revealed to them in a place they didn't belong.

Red-cheeked, planted curbside, the women could manage little more. Now they watched the Boone children, staring hard into the black asphalt, on their way to the parked car.

Kendall remained speechless until Mercer got back from returning her cart to the supermarket. "Some folks you just can't figure," he said. He could have been talking about anyone; he could have been talking about himself. It was the most he could provide for his children—a common witness to some abridged patch of discomfort.

Once their mother started the wagon, uninformed, they began fiddling with their new purchases. Kendall held Mercer's hand against the steering wheel before she shifted into gear. Then came a thoughtful rub with his thumb. To Kendall, their father, this amounted to a territory of outsized affection. It was intriguing enough for Sam to knock her brother on the knees with her superball, right left right, in recognition.

MERCER HAD RUINED BARLEY'S STOMACH, his taste for the kinds of food he should have been eating. She knew better but, unlike authoritative moments with her children, she couldn't help herself. When Barley was only a puppy she began feeding him a mixture of dried and canned, kneading the two together with her bare hands beside the kitchen sink. Soon she was warming the concoction for a few minutes in the oven; she spooned in leftover meat loaf and breaded turkey cutlets and broiled chicken. By the time Barley was seven, the winter Sam and Garrett had begun youth-league hockey, she was, on occasion, ordering restaurant takeout for him: low vegetable dishes from Golden Dragon Chinese (beef subgum, pork fried rice), cube-steak sandwiches from Kunkles', and, worst of all, cheesy, veal parmesan from Antonio's. The dog seemed fine, healthy even, save for the random bout with gas.

Seated at the dining-room table, each with a set of schoolbooks horseshoed around his or her place, Clem and Sam and Garrett puckered their noses. Beneath, Barley lay sleeping, oblivious to flatulence caused by two orders of scrod baked in a raspberry-garlic vinaigrette.

"That's so foul," said Clem.

"He can't help it," said Garrett, craning his neck to get a better look at the dog. "How can he be expected to know any better?"

"I'm not saying he should. It's still disgusting."

Hands flat, Clem patted the table to draw her siblings back to their homework. She had been helping them—Sam, mostly—learn to memorize. When Clem was younger, maybe six or seven, her parents believed she bore the tendencies of a prodigy, of genius. She had been quiet, pensive for much of her early life. One evening, beside Mercer on the porch swing, Clem suddenly began to recite random statistics and events: "Lou Boudreau fielding a ground ball in the 1948 World Series; Bee Bee Bee racing to a one-and-a-quarter-length victory in the 1972 Preakness Stakes; Gregory Peck winning the 1962 Academy Award for *To Kill a Mockingbird.*"

Surely, thought Mercer and then Kendall, she had read about these things in books and was regurgitating the information in a rapid-fire manner, a ticker tape of historical happenings. Soon after, they took Clem to Oberlin College, about seventy-five miles west, to have her IQ tested to have her mind examined. Waiting in a university classroom, Mercer watched her husband draw figures in a spiral sketch pad while Clem answered questions down the hall, for nearly two hours, both written and oral. Once finished, the professor who'd put Clem through a laundry list of obstacles surmised that she was not significantly more or less intelligent than the average child her age.

Refusing to believe this "laughable" hypothesis, Mercer spent the months that followed coddling Clem, keeping her homebound on weekends surrounded by literature and foreign-language tapes and flash cards filled with formulas from the worlds of science and mathematics. She sat in bed at night copying selections of problem sets from textbooks she'd borrowed. Eventually, Clem, and Mercer too, grew tired of what amounted to mostly fruitless labor. Clem showed few signs of having processed the information.

The following September, on a warm evening, Mercer sat with her children in a semicircular booth at Antonio's restaurant. Sam complained about the vinyl seat sticking to her thighs. To appease her, Mercer was trying to lay two cloth napkins, side by side, beneath Sam's legs.

"Primo Carnera knocks out Jack Sharkey in the sixth round of their 1933 title fight," said Clem, strangely, to herself. "Replaces President Franklin Delano Roosevelt."

"Huh?" said Mercer.

"There," said Clem, pointing with her fork. "That boxing picture of Primo Carnera was moved to the space where it used to say, 'President Franklin Delano Roosevelt conducts a fireside chat with the nation.' "

Mercer's head swiveled on a tight axis, like a jammed doorknob. Indeed, there was Primo Carnera, padded fists frozen in a left uppercut to Jack Sharkey's chin. Beneath the photograph was a caption, just as Clem had read it. Then Mercer's eyes followed the line of the wall, through the rest of the framed pictures. There was Lou Boudreau and Bee Bee Bee and Gregory Peck and even President Franklin Delano Roosevelt, inexplicably moved.

Queer as it seemed, no one had bothered to press Clem about where she'd culled the information. She'd been asked and her response, a dismissive shrug, seemed enough for excited, hopeful parents. She was guilty of nothing more than a keen memory and too many listless visits to Antonio's family restaurant. Later, when she was tested in sixth grade, it was discovered she'd been reading at a somewhat advanced level. But only by a grade or two. Still, it provided enough for Mercer to draft a letter, typed and stern, to the professor at Oberlin College. See, announced Mercer to her husband while she tapped away, he *had* been wrong.

Now Clem was trying to explain how she used her memory, slightly photographic in nature, to her brother and sister.

"You just picture the words—or whatever it is you're trying to remember—against your brain," she said.

She pressed her eyelids closed, tightly. Her brow crunched into a knot of creases and fine, short hairs. Near the corner of her mouth, her tongue pawed at a dried crust of milk from dinner. To her left, Garrett watched, intently, his own eyes seeming to focus on whatever was inside Sam's head.

"Can you see it in there?" asked Clem.

"I'm not sure."

"What're you trying to remember?"

"Some stuff for history."

"Like . . . "

"Like what the Townshend Acts did," said Sam, keeping her eyes shut. "How, in 1767, the Acts placed taxes on glass, painter's lead, paper, and tea."

"Good."

"Not good." Sam rubbed the inverted question mark of skin between her lower lip and chin. "I can picture it now; I *can't* picture it during tests when I've got a lot of other things to remember."

"Yeah," said Garrett. "That's my problem."

Taking a blank sheet from her notebook, Clem made a list of historical dates and beside them wrote a line or two about what happened in each year. She told Sam and Garrett to prepare study guides cf their own before each examination, so they could picture, in their own handwriting, which events followed others.

Together, the three of them sat scribbling, their soft lead pencils ticking against the paper and the polished wood of the table. Once, Sam began breathing funny, nub-nub-nub in the back of her throat, until Garrett alerted her with a finger to the side of her nose.

This was how the parts of the Boone childrens' lives locked into a larger wheel, turning, slowly sometimes and quickly others. Rarely did their fights, about small things, bleed into the following morning or the day after that. Never did it occur to them, not even to Clem, that they wouldn't always be together, living beneath the same roof. The slip and slide of their connections to one another—Sam to Clem, Garrett to Sam, Clem to Garrett—seemed natural in the way of an expectant response: the racing of a person's heart after strong coffee. Mostly, they each needed to remember, as if written in their own handwriting on loose-leaf notebook paper, what the other two had provided during this unordinary adolescence.

Silently, the great wheel spun through another revolution.

"Try," began Clem, again, "to give everything you put into your brain the same importance."

This seemed impossible. Especially to these children. How to conjure the details of Thomas Paine's life with the same speed as a remembrance, several weeks old, of someone in gym class making fun of Mercer before launching a battle ball at their knees.

"This will take a while to learn," she continued.

This will take a lifetime to learn, they each thought, in their own way. Finding some ability to let the good gain equal balance with the bad. Each tiny joy—a kind word at school, a wonderful hockey practice, a mouthful of blueberry pie—meaning just as much as anything either parent could trail to their doorstep.

It was an amusing picture: the three of them seated around the table, faces stern, trying to squeeze things they were hoping to remember—and forget—into bundles of similar size.

Black or white or gunmetal gray. Usually the limousines were black. Parked beside Missy Reeler's house, long and wide, sinking into the soft grass after being driven by her father. Part of the company *belonged* to him, Missy would say, unprovoked. Some days, when Mr. Reeler had come home late the previous night, she was allowed to sit in the cars with her friends before the limos were hosed down. When younger, they pretended the cars were submarines or spaceships; they would raise and lower the Plexiglas window behind the driver's seat and open the sun roof, disembodied heads yanking in all directions. Sometimes, taking turns, someone seated at the wheel would wear Mr. Reeler's cloth cap, excess fabric tied in a tail with a rubber band, and make believe one of them was chauffeuring the others.

Always, there were heavy glass decanters, cut to resemble crystal, emptied and turned on their sides. Squared tumblers, boozy with fingerprints, were squeezed between seat cushions or underneath floor mats. The ashtrays, tops sprung back, spit tiny white logs, mashed so hard that cuticles of tobacco peeled free like mustache hair. Once, stuck to the armrest, a used condom. Lois Sandrift knew what it was, immediately, and they all shot from the car as if chased.

Waiting, on this day, were Sam and Garrett, who'd been promised a ride to Thurmer Park with Missy. It was a Saturday afternoon and Mr. Reeler had a customer to pick up at the airport, in the same direction as the ice rink. If Sam and Garrett and Missy, who was coming to watch, remained silent, motionless, they would be given a lift. During the drive, Sam and Garrett sat with their duffels rocking across their laps, sticks laid flat on the floor. From the corner of his eyes, Garrett saw Missy fiddling with a bag of Lorna Doone cookies and was petrified her father would spy them, in the rearview mirror, and, incensed, toss all three for this breached agreement. But Missy was only shifting the bag from one pocket to the other.

At Thurmer Park, Sam and Garrett and their teammates lined the hallway between locker rooms, nearly dressed for their first game. They were each assigned a number and given dark purple jerseys with white silk-screening across the front. A hollow gear wheel with a number in its socket was centered at the sternum. Ben Briar had agreed to sponsor the team with his tool, die, and gear shop. His only commitment was financial: purchasing the uniforms and paying for weekly beverages and a post-season pizza dinner.

Not surprisingly, there were not many people in attendance for the first youth-league hockey game of a new season. Some parents and friends, like Missy Reeler, with nothing better to do on an early winter's Saturday. Play was slow, sluggish, except for a few slick maneuvers by Sam and one of the guys from the other team. In his three (truncated) periods in net, Garrett stopped all but four shots; the other goalie missed six. In celebration, Sam and Garrett and their teammates drank Hawaiian Punch and ate seven boxes of Fig Newtons.

Afterwards, riding precariously on the backseat of Mr. Reeler's limousine (he'd already completed his "run"), Sam and Garrett and Missy were permitted to watch the tiny black-and-white television mounted to the driveshaft hump along the car's floor. Even after they'd arrived, they remained in the car, three sets of eyes transfixed to the pocketbook-sized picture tube flickering a chemically light. For several weeks, Sam and Garrett had waited for Clem to return home, in time for dinner, from her job. They had missed the show's first broadcast, the previous Saturday, because of a hockey scrimmage against a team from Portage County.

The program was, as Clem had mentioned a few nights earlier over lamb chops and boiled potatoes, in the words of its producer, struggling to find a voice. Things began with a darkened screen and a sudden burst of music, some twangy blend of folk and pop, followed by tumbling, multicolored question marks like those sewn to the Riddler's costume on the old Batman TV series. The words began small, in a half circle, spinning around and around until they were large enough to read. A stilled record label beside several textbooks. In fat cursive and in other, lighter fonts on the spines of books—*The Answer Dancer*.

Clem watched the show herself from beside the director, chewing a tube of red licorice, notes and scripts laid neatly across her knees. Dressed in a brown three-button suit and white, open-collared shirt, Mickey Gott winked into the camera (as he had done less effectively on early incarnations of *Saturday Afternoon Theater*) and then shimmied toward a fragile-looking podium erected in the center of the dance floor.

He opened the show with customary disclaimers regarding the rules, the schools represented among the Answer Dancers, the folks who provided the questions ("This week, teachers from Bethel High slipped us our crib sheets"), and the prizes (encyclopedias and savings bonds). Music played and Mickey Gott backed away, allowing two shoulder-mounted cameras to bounce freely amid the kids, shaking, twirling, jerking in spastic conniptions.

"Cards . . . " said Mickey Gott, loudly, from above Clem.

Knowing exactly what he'd meant, she reached into one of her manila folders and handed him a think stack of blue question-and-answer notecards. Nodding, in agreement of nothing, Mickey Gott raked the cards against his cheek as if challenging his face for razor stubble, and then walked to a masking-taped X on the linoleum floor.

"All righty," he said, as the music faded with song's end. "Let's see what *we* know."

Two students, preordained, stepped forward while the rest of the Answer Dancers sat on stadium bleachers near the edge of the floor.

Mickey Gott asked the students for their names (Gus Wiley and Michelle Banks), schools (Evergreen High and St. Albans), ages (seventeen and sixteen), and extracurricular activities (swim team and drama club).

"Fantastic . . . really fan-*tas*-tic."

Nervously, Mickey Gott thumbed at the index cards, forcing the cameraman to pan upwards, away from Gott's twitching hands. Viewers were left with a bust of Mickey Gott beside the disembodied heads of two high school students. The director, now lifted free of his captain's chair, motioned for Gott to settle his arms.

"Use the podium," he whispered, pointing to the stand at Gott's left.

Nearly tripping, Gott managed to find his place behind the podium and then guided his contestants to the side.

"Christ," said the director, quietly, so only Clem could hear. "He just led those two kids across a live camera . . . The audience got a swell shot of the backs of their heads."

Then came questions, three each. They were devised to be challenging but not overly difficult. As the show progressed, the toughness of the questions would increase and, appropriately, the amount of the savings-bond prizes would also grow. Unfortunately, it became evident from the initial show, the previous week, that there was no direct correlation between a young person's ability to learn dance steps and his or her ability to learn in the classroom. In fact, the results, if graphed, would likely resemble mirror images of each other. "This kid is dumb as a post," said Lester McCaw, flagship sponsor and owner of a string of northeast Ohio convenience stores, watching the first broadcast from side stage. He was responding to a high school junior from Bath missing three straight questions ("A goddam trifecta of ignorance," said McCaw) in his self-described favorite subjects of Civil War history, American lit., and geometry.

On the second broadcast, the questions were to have been even easier. Still, except for a fortuitous piece of word association by Michelle Banks when asked to name two of Christopher Columbus's three ships ("Pinta, like the beans, and Nina, like my friend—though she spells *her* name differently"), the students struggled. Fortunately, before the final break, another junior steered the show from the jaws of complete disaster by nailing three mathematics questions without pause. This so startled Mickey Gott, who had grown accustomed to shaking his head, as if fighting bowel cramps and reciting the correct responses, that he began to read the answer just given him . . . until the director clapped his hands, lightly, as if waking Gott from sleep.

Shifting on the seat of the limousine, Garrett leaned closer to the television and said, "This stinks."

"Who do you think's gonna watch it?" asked Missy.

"Not me," said Sam. "Maybe the parents of the kids on the show."

"Well," started Missy, kicking one of the hockey sticks from beneath her foot. "I wouldn't even watch it if they *were* my kids."

When the broadcast was finished, Sam and Garrett lugged their equipment home; Missy turned the battery-powered TV louder, for the closing music, and began dancing in the snow-covered driveway. She did this alone, to a beat in her head, even after the show erased into one commercial and then another and, finally, into the talking voices of something else.

FOR THE FIRST TIME in a long while, Mercer was filled with fear. Parked in a white Oldsmobile, outside the clinic, two men waited for the day's end. She had called home, for Kendall, and when he couldn't be found, she sent for Tiff. During much of the afternoon, the clinic's phones had been ringing with hang-ups and heavy breathers and, lately, a threatening voice that promised "all things right will prevail."

Dressed in a secondhand tweed sport coat and low-cut V-neck sweater, Tiff met her at the back door. Together they walked to the station wagon, barely visible from the curbed Oldsmobile. Mercer wondered aloud why she felt so rattled.

"It's only natural," said Tiff.

She nodded, watching Tiff close the door behind her and then move around the front hood of the car to the driver's side. When they departed, they were not followed; there was no honking or shouting. Only the sounds of Mercer breathing and Tiff sucking food turned pasty from between his teeth.

On the rear porch, Mercer drank peppermint tea and smoked a

cigar. In the darkness, nearly alone, Sam skated, stickless, her hands held locked against the small of her back. She didn't see her mother standing behind the house, smoke and cold tea breath pushing from Mercer's face. There were some nights when Sam, tightly wound kinetic twine, would wear herself out by skating laps around the yard; she would lurch through the back door, damp and steaming, barely able to kick loose her skates before collapsing on the couch. Sam knew, herself, what it took to shut down until the next day. Many evenings, even as a young child, the price was too great and she'd remain awake, thinking, until just before the sun slapped itself over the horizon. To be elsewhere, she considered. Not necessarily another city or state but even, she would accept, a different house on a different block. The longing to exchange her problems for those of someone else. A mother with a normal job—teacher or nurse—and a father who was simply normal.

Once the snow came, carried on a soft breeze, Sam sat on the black ice and let flakes catch on her eyelashes. She flopped onto her back, staring skyward, pushing herself in crooked circles with the blades of her skates. From where Mercer was standing, Sam looked like a sea lion slinking toward a rush of water. The first winter Kendall hammered together the back-yard rink, Sam would lie on the ice, like now, and listen to the national anthem being played on television whenever the U.S. won an Olympic gold medal. She never thought about winning medals herself; she just liked to hear the music, dulled through the study's window, while she rested in the clean night air.

Mercer spilled the rest of her tea over the railing, and Sam let her gaze turn to her mother. She watched the end of Mercer's cigar brighten and dim. It occurred to Sam, with her mother standing guard behind the house and her father in his studio, that, despite her parents' intentions, they had nudged their children onto a busy highway. Dozing caretakers. From unexpected angles, hidden to their eyes, Mercer and Kendall had become interstates for trouble, opening the gate to harm's way. Early, Sam and Clem and Garrett had rubbed against things too sharp for the hands of the young. They'd been spittoons for words of terrific cruelty, they'd felt the sting of noses turned bloody.

Awfulness that usually began in defense of things they didn't completely understand: their mother's work or their father's mind. Only a few days ago, Sam, angered because a classmate confessed to unleashing an obscene gesture at Mercer's clinic while driving past, tore her shirt cuff as she wrestled the boy to the ground.

"You need to come inside," said Mercer. She offered the tangible. "You're going to get sick."

As Sam inched backwards, away from the house and away from her mother, she could see the branches of two sugar maples waving above the line of the roof. She could hear her mother's feet against the creaky porch: walking from the swing; wiped against the furry mat; clipping the aluminum door guard as she stepped into the house. And then, only herself and a sharp wind that made her flesh turn crinkly with goose pimples.

DURING THE WINTER before Kendall quit his job teaching community-college art, the entire family became violently ill with some type of virus. Mostly, the children were logy with symptoms of the flu: nausea and body aches and noses oozing mayonaisy snot. But in Kendall doctors feared a more serious bronchial ailment and they kept him hospitalized for a night.

There was some part of Mercer that suspected her children were afraid they, too, might join their father away from home. The sicker the kids became, the more they pretended to be aimed toward recovery. So Mercer attempted to distract them; she moved to fill their time with busy work—anything that would occupy their minds during the hours between sleep.

Mercer supplied board games and coloring pencils and comic books from the drugstore. She allowed them long stays before the television set, each taking a turn with the remote control. It was difficult for her to witness them battling the illness—especially when Clem would unknot from her fetal position on the couch to vomit in a nearby bucket or when Garrett would suffer long, loud bouts with a hacking cough that was so severe it made him light-headed. Worse still was the clothing Sam layered and shed depending on her body temperature: she looked pathetic wrapped in wool blankets or, soon after, dressed only in cotton underwear, which turned sheer with sweat.

They all had trouble sleeping; their sinuses were clogged and their chests were heavy with mucus, as if someone had placed a giant can of tomato paste against their sternums. The only thing Mercer wanted was for her children to feel better, to feel anything besides miserable.

She let them watch the late news in her bed; she brought them tangerine Jell-O and root-beer floats on a service tray. Mercer had even found flexible straws she'd once hidden in the back of a kitchen drawer.

"How come we don't get to do this every night?" asked Garrett.

"You're not sick every night," said Mercer.

Later, Garrett and Clem played war with a deck of cards while Mercer dabbed a cool compress along Sam's forehead. Then Mercer retired to the bathroom to rinse the washcloth. As she stood over the sink, she saw one of Kendall's drawing pads peeking out from a magazine rack beside the toilet; sometimes he liked to sketch during spells of constipation.

The sight of the pad gave Mercer an idea. She tore loose several sheets of the nearly transparent paper and made her way back across the bedroom. Her children watched, intently, as she used Band-Aids to tack three pieces to different spots along the window. She slid a steamer trunk, in which she stored clean linens, to the base of the windowsill. There was also a wicker ottoman that came paired with a rocking chair.

"You can sit on these," she told her children, gesturing with her palms facing upwards.

They each rose, reluctantly, leaving the blankets in a crumpled heap across the bed. Once they'd found comfortable positions at the window, Mercer tapped the squares of paper obscuring each child's view.

"With these pens," she began, handing felt-tip markers to each of her children, "we're going to trace the stars."

"How?" asked Garrett.

Mercer turned off the television and the bedroom lights.

"See the stars?" she asked, crouching to look at the sky from the same angle as her children. "Make a dot on your sheet of paper at every place where a star is visible."

"I'm not drawing a dot," said Clem. "I'm drawing a *star*."

"That's a good idea. Let's all do that—draw tiny stars to represent the real ones."

They each pushed their faces close to the window, bracing the heels of their hands against the cold glass.

"Some I can't tell," said Garrett. "They look like stars but they're really airplanes."

"Watch them for a few seconds," said Mercer. "If they don't move, they're probably stars."

Then there was silence, interrupted only by the sound of pen against paper against glass. When finished, the three children sat back while Mercer used a red marker to label each picture—Clem's Constellation and Garrett's Galaxy and Sam's Milky Way.

"Very nice," said Mercer.

After a moment of pause, she filled her hand with aspirins and Vitamin C tablets; she dispensed them to the children along with several small cups of water. Together, they squeezed into bed—the four of them—and took turns talking to Kendall on the phone. He was feeling better; he told the kids that the hospital had brought him soup for dinner that tasted like something from Barley's water dish. He promised he'd be home the next day, as soon as the doctor would agree to discharge him.

In the darkness of the bedroom they all drifted to sleep. Mercer, on the far left, remained awake last, listening to each of her children swallow and spit breaths. She tried to differentiate between the three—Sam, who held oxygen longest, was easy; Clem and Garrett were more difficult.

How wonderful, she thought, lying there with her children at her side. Only the gentle noise of their breathing and the occasional rustle of sheets. She wanted to kiss each of them, again. Square on their germy mouths.

She remembered another time when she'd slept with her children, years earlier. Sam, still an infant, had turned rashy with roseola. The other two kids were fearful their sister's skin would always be splotchy and pink. Before Mercer retired to bed that night, she checked on Sam; when she pushed open the door to Sam's room, she found Clem and

Garrett sitting together against the toy chest. They were worried, they'd said.

In an effort to ease their concern, Mercer decided the three of them—Kendall was already asleep—would camp out on Sam's floor. Quietly, she set up pillows and blankets along the throw rug beside Sam's crib. Whenever Clem or Garrett began speaking, Mercer would raise her finger to her lips. "Hush," she'd said, pointing at Sam.

As they let sleep come to them, their buttocks and bellies pinned to the floor, Mercer made sure some part of her body was in contact with both children: her knee against Garrett's foot, her elbow touching Clem's shoulder. Together, they formed a human chain—needing only a hand reaching to Sam, another directed down the hall at Kendall, to be completed.

While sinking into slumber, only a nod or two from a deep REM cycle, Mercer was suddenly aware of something stirring in the room. Though no longer awake, Garrett was clinging to the fabric of her nightgown. But above him, staring silently at the three figures on the ground, Sam knelt on the stiff mattress of her crib. She was holding the wooden bars loosely in her fists. Instinctively, Mercer smiled. Her daughter responded in kind, waving her hand before, briefly, losing her balance. Maybe it was only the darkness, a trick of shadows, but Sam's condition appeared considerably improved. The red bumps that filled her cheeks were less severe, shrinking into recovery.

"Hi, honey," said Mercer, so softly she wondered if the words had actually left her mouth.

Another wave and then, as if the whole exchange had been dreamed, Sam lowered her head to the fitted sheet, her legs tucked close, so her heinie raised into the air, and she shut her eyes.

That was everything.

Again, in Mercer's bedroom, surrounded by sick children, she whispered that she loved them. It was the final thing Mercer remembered until late in the night when she inexplicably rose to a seated posture and opened her eyes. (As Sam had done years before.) While touching the floor with her feet, she rubbed a chalky pebble of aspirin between her fingers. Across the room, the three pieces of tracing paper glowed soapy-white in the moonlight—except for a collection of black marks, which crowded the sheets like water bugs. This was the work of her children, she thought, her head still filmy with sleep. They had created a tiny space of their own.

She wanted to remind herself in the morning to save these pictures, to place them in storage for the kids to see when they were older. Maybe, decades from now, the drawings would jog one of their memories. Bid them to recall the taste of root beer and melted ice cream against the back of the throat. The warm bodies of their siblings, their mother. A single evening when being sick didn't feel so bad.

ONE WEEK'S EPISODE stumbled into another. Though lifted by the occasional promise of intelligent life (twice, Answer Dancers from Cleveland's West Side ran the table: winning five-hundred-dollar bonds and a wheelbarrow's worth of reference books), there was still a surfeit of airtime choked with stammering "*Uhhhhs*" and "*I means*" and responses so ill informed they sucked loose the collective breath from the production staff. Thumbs hooked through the belt loops of her slacks, Clem stood beside Wendall Crue, the director, who was shaking his head dejectedly as a senior from Delvin High incorrectly placed the Yellow Sea off the southern coast of Greenland.

"Christ," said Wendall. "He's not even in the right hemisphere."

As the show continued, Wendall watched from the corner of his eye, while Clem mouthed the appropriate answer to each question when it was read. She knew them all: geography, algebra, *human* science.

"You're awfully smart," he said.

"Not really," she said, dropping her chin in embarrassment at being noticed. "I have a good memory."

"How do you mean?"

"I see all the cards . . . before I give them to Mr. Gott."

She explained how each week she rifled through the index cards on her way from the offices to the soundstage.

"You can remember all those questions and answers and categories from a two-minute walk down the hall?"

"Pretty much."

"That's impressive." From the way Wendall was massaging his

hands, anxious heat tugging each knuckle, Clem could tell he was digesting this new information, letting it sail around in his brain until he knew what things meant. "Very impressive."

She thanked him and walked away, toward the second camera, where she'd been told to remind one of the handymen to fasten the bleachers to their cable so they could be rolled off the floor for the next dance segment.

Later, at home, she sat at the kitchen table eating a bologna-and-cheese sandwich. Chewing on a plastic fast-food straw, Garrett announced, almost to himself, that his shoulder was sore because he took a slap shot between the pads. He told Clem that after the game, which they'd won, his coach taped a Ziplock bag of ice to his clavicle, like they do with professional players. Clem exhaled, sarcastically, and congratulated her brother on his injury. On occasion, Clem had the capacity to become overly dramatic: wandering the halls in a sibilant haze late at night when she couldn't sleep or draping damp washcloths across her forehead and sucking cough drops when she felt ill. She liked to dab at her eyebrows with the back of her palm, a silent movie actress, to demonstrate concern. Even Garrett, spooling the straw into a serpent's tongue, could see that Clem wanted to speak; she longed to breathe away her troubles.

"Do they pay a lot?" he asked.

"Who?"

"At the TV station . . . Do they pay you a lot of money?"

Again, Clem sighed. "Enough, I guess," she said, taking a strand of her shoulder-length hair, bright as beechbark, and wrapping it around her index finger.

"What can you buy?"

This, of course, was what concerned a boy treading near teenage: what types of things—dart guns, motorized boats, replica football jerseys—his sister was capable of owning.

"It's not about what I can buy," said Clem. "There's nothing I really want, anyway. Except maybe some clothes or something."

"Clothes?" said Garrett, his mouth turned sour.

"Or maybe I'll save for a car."

"Yeah. Save for a *car*. Get a Mustang or Camaro."

She shook her head and then offered, "They don't ever speak to me."

"Huh?"

"All the kids on the show," said Clem. "They never say *anything* to me."

"What're they supposed to say?"

She shrugged. "I don't know." She pressed her thumb print into a corner of orange cheese. "But they could say something . . ."

Garrett didn't know how to answer his sister, what words would make her feel right. Instead, he chose silence. The two sat there, across from each other, listening to the sounds of their saliva swallowed.

"Every week there are all these kids," said Clem, "from all these schools. And they're only a grade or two or three older than me. Just one time, when this girl with really red hair asked me for a hand mirror, did any of them even look in my direction. The people who talk to me are adults—and that's to tell me what to do."

Removing the straw, curled and crinkled with teethmarks, Garrett slipped it over his pinkie like a ring.

"We have someone like that in my class," he said, without thinking. "Ronald Perry. His name is Ronald Perry the third, but everyone calls him Ronald *Fairy* the *turd*."

In an instant, once Garrett realized he'd compared his sister to the dorkiest kid in school, he scrambled to shift directions. "I mean, most kids think it's hard to talk with him," said Garrett, straightening in his chair. "But he's a pretty good guy."

None of this was reaching Clem. She'd only heard the word *turd* banging against her eardrums, a quarter flipped into a tin can. It was, truthfully, exactly how she felt: something grotesque to be avoided, to be scraped from the heel of every other young person she encountered. She knew as a girl nearly fifteen, seated at the kitchen table of her house, what it takes others a lifetime to discover: she was slowed by the gummy hinges of limitation. She would never possess the careless popularity of some, or the simple tools to blend where necessary, like others. Not Clem, who, despite her smarts and fine intentions, could not draw people close. She'd realized how ironic it all seemed—the harder she pulled, the faster they ran, whereas the more Sam pushed, the nearer they wished to be.

Closer to morning, in the quiet of her bedroom, Clem read through a stack of fashion magazines she'd found abandoned beside the trash bins at the television studio. A brisk wind squeezed at the frame of the house, causing boards and nails to swell and peep. For some time she stared at a photograph of three men and two women knee-deep in aquamarine water, until, eventually, her eyes grew tired.

A portable black-and-white television was balanced on the slick hood of the washing machine. As the washer hummed through its spin cycle, the TV shook, filling the picture tube with compressed hills of static. Wrenched and crippled coat hangers sprouted from the top, behind a retractable carry handle, serving as makeshift antennas. Tiff stood over the basement sink, warm water running slowly into his hands. He was rubbing Mercer's underpants clean, using a washboard and Woolite. (Delicates were rarely surrendered to the machine, old and suspect.) Every few moments he would stop, cock his head, and squint in the direction of the television; he'd then cluck his tongue and mutter something disagreeable to himself.

Between several other piles of clothing, separated on the floor by color and fabric, Sam sat massaging the blade of her skates with a sharpening stone. It sounded like the stiff bristles of a new broom catching on concrete, again and again. When he'd heard enough, Tiff turned, purposefully, and said, "Not during my *stories* . . ."

Sam knew, immediately. Each day Tiff watched three soap operas back to back to back, whether working or not. He kept the televisions running, loud, from each room so he could listen to the conversations even when he couldn't see them. Sometimes he turned the volume high so he could follow what was happening above the drone of the vacuum cleaner or, as now, the washing machine.

Framing Tiff's head, near the jawline, a horizontal window exposed curb-level flower beds rough with ice. The snow and slush had faded to such a consistent gray the entire town appeared to be sprayed by ash. From her place on the floor, linoleum bloated and buckled with water damage, Sam watched her father's booted feet wander past the window. She leaned comfortably into a hump of bed sheeting and began spitting her gum—two pieces of Juicy Fruit—into the air and catching it again with her mouth. Once, the gum missed and bounced from her cheek into the laundry. She blew it clean and continued until Tiff kicked her on the leg.

Sam's thoughts drifted: she imagined her father ridding other public buildings of valued possessions. The Natural History Museum kept a marble triceratops in its lobby; the post office had an oil painting of Teddy Roosevelt riding horseback; the Dairy Freeze was marked by a two-story statue of some jowly youth, red-and-white apron covering his crotch, with his arm raised skyward, supporting two burgers (one with cheese) and a Pontiac-sized milkshake. Best, she wanted him to pry loose a bayonet-wielding soldier from the war memorial. If someone was sneaking around their property at night, she reasoned, the soldier—bulbous eyes, hands slithering with aggressively carved veins, rifle gripped like a harpoon—would send him racing away in terror.

Rolling to her belly, Sam crawled crab-style, the way Marines shimmy beneath barbed wire, until she reached the storage room. She parked herself between the legs of a partly folded Ping-Pong table. There were boxes of things belonging, mostly, to her parents. Old yearbooks and photo albums and souvenirs from fairs and vacations and their lives long ago. For Sam, it was strange to think of her parents having a world that didn't contain children. Always, to Sam, there was Clem and Garrett.

Brittle with age, loose photographs of her mother in high school and college and then, once she'd begun medical school, paired with Sam's father. They looked like pictures from a catalogue, thought Sam, fingering the peeled edges. These people could be anyone, really, except for her parents. She wondered, seated crossed-legged beneath the green table, how her mother and father had found this life for themselves. When did it all change? Where does promise drain to reality?

Spied before the other prints was one of Mercer on her parents' farm in western Pennsylvania wearing soiled overalls and a sleeveless T-shirt. She was tanned, windburned, and her thin arms were pulled taut across a burlap sack of horse feed. Her hair, darkened by sweat, was short and tousled and resembled Sam's most recent cut. Drawing the photgraph close to her nose, Sam sniffed it two, three times; she was hoping there would be a smell, something to tell her how her mother was feeling in those days. What it meant for Mercer, at that precise moment, to be young.

In another box, for files, Sam found a lab notebook with journal entries written between photographs taped down on four sides. Most of these words, these pictures, took away Sam's breath. She had to slide from beneath the table for better lighting. The book chronicled the nearly two years Mercer spent working in a veterans' hospital. Penned in tight, thoughtful cursive were accounts of caring for patients whose bodies had been raked and tugged into something different . . . into a soldered collection of human parts, unfamiliar, both working and ornamental; useless legs still attached, dead arms and fingers, glass-eye sockets. The worst for Mercer and, reading about it here, for Sam were the burn vicitms; many left with hides marbled and swollen and directionless. Living candle wax peeling loose in crumpled shingles. "A painted balloon," wrote Mercer, "suddenly infused with more helium so its hardened crust cracks away." For one man, James from Allentown, the doctors had sewn his arm into the lining of his stomach so the skin would regrow. Though there was no photograph, Mercer described James awakening to find his body swallowing itself, contorted past logic. "What do you tell this man?" she wrote.

Near the end of the book, in red felt-tip, there were several pages about a volunteer who was helping some of the patients fill their time with arts- and-crafts busywork: stitching together pigskin wallets, watercolors on flimsy cardboard from dry-cleaned shirts, tin-working for the more adventurous. He was an art student from the university who was, according to Mercer, "kind, gentle and respectful of every patient." Clearly, in the final days of Mercer's journal, this man, Kendall Boone, whom she would later marry, filled many of her thoughts. They would sit together, beneath the cement stairwell, sharing coffee and bear claws from the cafeteria, talking until one of them finally had to leave.

Besides an almost immediate attraction for each other, consistent in all of Mercer's entries, the most meaningful passage, marked with stars and underlinings, concerned Kendall's reasons for spending two afternoons a week at the hospital. He told Mercer, seated on the hood of her car in the parking lot one warm evening, how he'd missed out on the war. Kendall's father, a man who hadn't lived to see any of his son's children, was strict and, more often, mean. He had enormous hands and feet and hated having his toes stepped on in crowds, so he wore, always, boots with steel shanks and toe plates. Sometimes, when he'd been drinking, he would kick Kendall with the boots, hard and swift, in the legs or ribs or once, even, the neck. As Kendall got older his father used to yell, loudly, whenever there'd been a disagreement, "Wait till the army gets hold of you! They'll fix things right!"

On the day Kendall returned from the draft board, when he was only eighteen, his mother was standing over the sink washing the dirt from a bowl of potatoes and his father was sitting at the kitchen table drinking beer. Leaning against the back door, Kendall announced, as some boys might say their carburetor had quit running or they'd just torn a hole in their best pants, "I failed my army physical." (His skin turned violently rashy when he perspired.) For a moment his father remained still, letting a frothy tongue of bubbles creep down the neck of the bottle and across his hand. Then, in a clear, low voice, staring straight into the wall, he said, "Good . . . " Like he'd never meant anything this much before in his entire life.

When Kendall began seeing his friends and the brothers of friends coming home from fighting, mangled and distant, he decided to give back something . . . even if that only meant balsawood or model kits (never tanks or fighter planes) or vinyl rope for braiding lanyards.

None of this had been mentioned before to Sam. She only knew her parents had met when they were in school, studying art and medicine. They were a peculiar couple, Sam and Clem and Garrett had always thought, when discussing their parents or letting things turn over in their own minds. But, strangely, they belonged together. It was difficult to imagine one without the other. Whether separated by a few feet or miles or time zones. They fit: the screw-down lid on a thermos bottle.

Sam stood, kicking the boxes back beneath the table. She wondered if other children had these thoughts about their parents—believed father and mother were right for each other even as they chafe apart. Sam flicked a dented Ping-Pong ball, listening for the slapping sound of water coming from Tiff in the next room.

AFTER WORK one Thursday, Wendall Crue called Clem for a talk. In his office. There were no other people around, only Clem and Mr. Crue. She never sat, choosing instead to grip the back of a chair for support while he spoke. Several times, clapping his desk with the heel of his palm, he used her full name: *Clementine.* What he asked ("Between us . . . *just* between us," he kept saying) was for Clem to assist him "in raising the intelligence level" on *The Answer Dancer.* It took Clem only a few moments to realize that what Mr. Crue really wanted was for Clem to help him cheat.

She would become a regular, *on the show.* Though she would still retain many of her other gofer duties, now she would also be a member of the weekly cast of Answer Dancers. Most important, she was to use, in Mr. Crue's words, "her talent" for memorization while she delivered the index cards to Mickey Gott. Having spied the correct answers, she was to whisper them to certain contestants during the commercial breaks between the announcement of the category and the actual playing of the game. "I'll give you some type of high-sign to let you know when it's all right," said Mr. Crue. "Maybe I'll rub my nose or forehead."

That evening, alone, she roamed the house, searching for some place to get comfortable. She moved from her bedroom to the den to the kitchen and then back to her bedroom. Nothing about this was right, Clem knew, despite what Mr. Crue had said about saving the show from ever-worsening ratings. Still, part of it appealed to her; she was involved in something important . . . and she would be *on* television. Best of all, she reasoned, she'd be helping the other cast members, making them look good.

At every turn, though, Mr. Crue's idea imploded with splendid force. A chain reaction of catastrophic buffoonery. First, there was Clem's inability to clip together even the most cursory combinations of dance steps. She was, truthfully, such an awful dancer that her partner, Mark Weiner, remained at a distance for fear of injury. She moved *against* the music so often it appeared by design; she flung her arms, windmill-like, at awkward angles, suggesting she might be knotted with seizure. Midway through the second song, once Clem's contortions had created a mote between her and the rest of the cast, Mr. Crue told the cameramen to pan clear of her whenever possible. "Keep her out of view!" he hollered into their headphones.

Worse, during quiz breaks, the other students seemingly ignored Clem's advice. They preferred responding with incorrect answers to listening to a younger, annoyingly yappy girl. During one exchange, when a boy from Solon paused to consider the names of the islands where Charles Darwin gathered much of his evidence for his theory of natural selection, Clem, positioned in the first row of the bleachers, repeated *Galapagos* with such pitch and frequency ("Gloppa-giss, gloppa-giss, gloppa-giss") it caused Mickey Gott to scan the floor for an overturned pop can. Pleading with the boy to concur, Mr. Crue nodded his head even as the buzzer sounded, as if he, too, recognized defeat.

The following Monday, in school, Clem saw any remaining celebrity rub apart when classmates mocked her dancing skills. "Hey," announced someone from the back of biology class. "You should keep a pen between your teeth so you don't bite your tongue." She spent her two free periods—lunch and study hall—reading in a bathroom stall, feet pressed against the door whenever somebody knocked. Afterwards, she skipped work, telling them she was sick, and returned a dress she'd purchased for the next show. Part of this will remain with me forever, she considered presciently on the walk from the mall, cold pricks of snow hitting her in the face. Part of this will pass by week's end.

TOWNSPEOPLE WORN AND PALE with age stared down from the window. Butcher, fireman, a physician listening through his stethoscope. Old cast-iron figurines that Garrett had unearthed from his back yard; collectibles belonging to the folks who had lived on this property before his family, or the people even before them. There were seven, but Garrett had searched for more. His favorite was the policeman, right arm raised to direct traffic, left arm painted to his side. Illuminated by moonlight, he'd watch them from bed before drifting to sleep. Some nights he imagined a separate universe in his head, each tiny statue playing its part away from the windowsill, away from Ohio.

When he was younger, he would remove one of the figures and place it on his nightstand, rubbing its chipped and rusted skin with his thumb and forefinger while his thoughts carried him into a make-believe village where he was king. Depending on his mood, he would allow lawlessness to rage or rest for Officer West (from a television show), giving him some way to fill his time. Other evenings, like when one of the real-life patrolmen sent to watch protesters told Garrett's mother to shut her mouth, he pictured the butcher sinking his meat cleaver between Officer West's shoulder blades.

During school the previous winter he wrote a theme paper about a weekend he'd spent with his Uncle Roy, a carpenter, who in actuality was a creation inspired by the figurine toting a hammer. His teacher believed him; she suggested he take photographs of the porch they had built together for an illustrated booklet that was to be part of the next class project. Fearful, allowing the lie to inflate and distort, Garrett found some construction workers, one of whom agreed to pose for photographs beside a neighborhood roof he was reshingling. In the introduction to the book, nearly three-quarters of a handwritten page, Garrett explained that the porch was too far away for pictures . . . "in another state, in Tennessee."

His self-styled universe was a way to still the mind. He was, like everyone, groping for some sliver of escape, some warm greenhouse in the winter cold where he could be alone, undisturbed. There were difficulties, he knew, growing up the middle child in a house filled with three women and a father who disappeared to his studio or on scrap runs for days at a time. But here was a place that he owned. Where, despite all else, his words and imagination represented authority. Certain moments, say, after he'd retreated to his room for a long Sunday, the line brayed fuzzy; he was less capable of separating the truth from the fantastic. Never did he consider them lies: he was simply speaking of another part of his life. The intent was not to mislead. He was never malicious.

But as with the tale of his "Uncle Roy," the door to trouble was fastened like those on old cowboy saloons: spring-hinged, unobstructed, easily nudged apart. He was, even into his late teens, confronted with inconsistencies: "I thought your mother's brother was a carpenter" or "Didn't Sam spend a week last summer farming in Arkansas?" or "Wasn't your cousin a minor league shortstop?" (He had later found a baseball player—the *eighth* figurine—while weeding his mother's flower beds. Though it was larger and newer and made from a different metal than the others, he'd cleared a place on the windowsill.)

Sometimes it all seemed natural: the active mind of a young boy. Other times, however, it buzzed like an annoying tremolo. His parents or sisters would find him lying on his bed or floor, in darkness, the figurines scattered at his sides. Usually, music played softly from a small clock radio he'd been given for his ninth birthday and he was outstretched, near-motionless, resembling a surgery patient tumbling into the late throes of anesthesia-induced rest. Most alarmed was Sam; she nearly walked into him while retrieving some books from his desk. She stomped her foot, twice, beside his head to yank him toward reality, flipping the toy figures from their flat bases. She screamed from surprise and anger. "You're *so* queer," she said, repeating the remark until she'd reached the hall again.

Seldom could Garrett predict the path his imagination would follow. The day after Clem's embarrassing episode on television, he retreated to his room, having grown tired of hearing her warble to Mercer and Tiff and Sam, even, about how her life had been ruined. The only light, pressed narrow between the door frame and floor, shone from the hallway. Garrett fell across the bed, intending to read his English homework; he turned the radio so low he had to strain to hear it, remain perfectly still or the moan of boxsprings or rustle of sheets would drown away the music. Suddenly a song, something rough and clinky, played first from his nightstand and then louder in his head. It continued after the disc jockey announced the weather and station contests and disappeared behind a wall of commercials. For Garrett, he began to consider a rock band belonging to Officer West's son . . . Did Officer West even *have* a son? When did he get married? The band, Electrolyte (Garrett was learning about body tissue fluids in science class), practiced in the West family garage and J.D. (Officer West's son) played the drums. Of course, it wouldn't require a tremendous stretch to discover the smoky glow of Garrett's own personality reflected in his fictional characters. In some, obviously, his imprint burned clearer than in others. For weeks, part of him actually believed he *was* J. D. West the drummer. He imagined conversations with magazine critics, similar to stories he'd read in the school library periodical rack. Expensively appointed tour buses, record-store appearances where his proud father (Officer West!) joked with colleagues sent to protect J.D. from overanxious fans. He even wandered into a music store to price a drum kit, though his only previous experience with percussion instruments was the annoying rap-a-tap-tap of chopsticks against Formica restaurant tabletops.

Great troughs of art supplies were at his disposal. Kendall allowed Garrett and Clem and Sam to help themselves: newsprint, ribbons of canvas, colored chalk and pencils, tubed or panned paints of acrylic and oil, bottled dyes, metal shivs shucked from sculptures. Most appealing to Garrett were the reams of simple white paper and soft-lead pencils. It was here, on these sheets, that he would give form to his pretend world; he'd sketch much of what was in his head. When not daydreaming, he was hunched over an old drafting desk, bringing two-dimensional life to Don the Butcher (who, later, after Garrett had read about Chicago's underworld, became a crime boss) and Fireman Bob and now, closest to his heart, J. D. West, the drummer.

Rarely did Garrett let others see his drawings. Only when classmates stumbled upon him doodling in a notebook at school, or when Clem or Sam crept in from behind, breathing quietly, did they glimpse his work. In fact, he did his best to keep people away from this private piece of his life. One time Mercer happened upon an intricate sketch of a crime lab the carpenter was building for Officer West beneath the police station, while she was straightening Garrett's room. She was so impressed by the scale and detail in the drawing she brought it to the dinner table to show Kendall and Clem and Sam. Hot with astonishment, violated, Garrett snatched the picture from his mother's hand, tearing a corner, and ran upstairs. Some part of him felt so ashamed his family had seen into this secret world that he couldn't bring himself to draw again—couldn't even allow his thoughts to spill back to his land of fantasy—for nearly three weeks.

He wondered, during deeper moments, whether other people created places to seek refuge from reality; whether they, too, needed a pocket of pretend, no matter how small, where they could be in control.

CONTEMPORARY-SHAPED PLASTICS in purple and orange were molded to form couches and coffee tables and receptacles for trash. Seated alone, Garrett paged through hospital literature while waiting for his mother to complete her weekend rounds. She was visiting one patient on whom she'd performed a difficult cesarean-section delivery a day earlier, another patient was eager to be discharged after the removal of an ovarian cyst.

Garrett had already consumed two candy bars and a can of ginger ale. The gift shop held little interest: cutesy bunnies and potted flowers and music boxes which tinkled, with optimistic songs. Once his mother had finished, she would take him for a new pair of dress shoes. He'd outgrown his old black lace-ups and needed something to wear with a gray suit when his class sang for a nearby nursing home the following week. Like most boys, he detested shopping for clothes and before breakfast he'd tried to shimmy and plow his feet into the shoes he owned. They might have passed for one final run had his mother not decided on dropping into a three-point stance—mimicking a football lineman—to feel for his hunched toes.

He liked hearing the hospital paging system—especially when his mother's name was called: "Dr. Boone, Dr. *Mercer* Boone . . . " He'd caught it before, on the few visits he'd made with his sisters, and today, by himself, he repeated other names—his own, J. D. West's—with the prefix "doctor" fastened for posterity.

He allowed his mind to wander again, imagining what it might be like to roam these bright, sterile hallways in a white lab coat while regurgitating medical terminology similar to phrases his mother spoke into telephones or that was written in the pamphlets at his side. So immersed was Garrett in picturing himself—aged, taller—parting the doors to an operating room that he didn't notice Sean Wiley until he was only several feet away.

Though Garrett and Sean were classmates, it still took them both a moment to lock into mutual recognition. A familiar face in a shifted context; the unlikelihood of two healthy boys meeting in a hospital lobby. They waved, awkwardly, neither raising his hand much past his waist.

Suddenly self-conscious, Garrett ran his fingers through stiff brown hair gone ragged with a Saturday's neglect; the ends were curled upward, along his ears and in back, as if he'd recently removed a ball cap. He was wearing blue jeans—dungarees, Tiff called them—and a plaid flannel shirt. To compensate for eyes set deeply, lost in angles and shadow, he'd developed a habit of opening them unsettlingly wide. The blinking away of bad dreams. Twice, he wiped his mouth with his sleeve, fearing the remaining grains of an English muffin or smudged chocolate.

"Hey," said Garrett, before anything else.

They sat across from each other, uncomfortably, talking about school and cars and disruptive construction that forced everyone to enter class through a side door. Until, finally, the truth behind their thoughts:

"What're you doing here?" asked Sean.

"I've got to get new shoes," began Garrett, reluctantly. And then, because more was needed: "My mother sometimes works at this hospital."

They both nodded.

"What about you?"

"My sister," said Sean. "She's older."

The two of them watched an orderly fish out cigarette butts from a sand ashtray, using a miniature net.

"She came here last night," continues Sean. "She lost her baby . . . "

Flushed with a sudden embarrassment, unfairly rooted, Garrett directed his vision toward the ground. Though no detail of the exchange suggested Sean had made a connection between whatever happened to his sister and Garrett's mother's work, Garrett began to squirm. He and his sisters now understood what their mother did at her clinic. The talks had come, not so many weeks ago, when on the night Kendall was arrested Mercer described her reasons for performing abortions, and later, when she told them more.

The rest of the explanation, the sanitized particulars she believed them now ready to hear, were offered, again unexpectedly, on a Sunday afternoon. The night before the talk, Kendall had drawn hollow outlines of neighborhood scenes—the skating rink, a factory on the riverbank, their house—to lift the spirits of a friend dying of prostate cancer in northern California. The children were lying stomach-down in the living room, rug peeled away, the drawings flush against the wooden floorboards for firm backing as they used colored pencils to bring dimension to their father's sketches.

Clem was deliberate, careful to remain inside the lines and select appropriate colors; Garrett and Sam were simply anxious to finish the project. Against the far wall, Kendall was building a rigid mailing envelope from corrugated cardboard and packing tape.

"Where *is* the prostate?" asked Sam.

"Beside a man's dinky," said Clem, quickly.

Sam nodded, as if this vague answer was all she needed to satisfy her curiosity.

Sipping warm tea, Mercer smiled at the exchange. She had several patient-history folders stacked against her lap.

"Have you ever seen a prostate?" Sam asked her mother. Then, because she knew Mercer's patients were now only women, "In medical school or something."

"Yes," said Mercer. She wrapped the string of her tea bag around the spoon. "A long time ago."

The children thought that was all.

"Back when I was thinking about practicing general medicine—maybe in a small town, smaller than Lukin—I knew about lots of other things." She squeezed more lemon into her cup. "But now I take care of women and their bodies. I bring babies into the world and . . . " She paused. "Well, sometimes I don't."

Like static beneath her breath came the sounds of Kendall's box cutter tearing through the seams of pre-scored cardboard flaps.

"You understand what I do at the clinic?" she said, her eyes meeting each of theirs. She asked the question as plainly as if she'd posed a query about the cleanliness of their respective rooms. "I use surgical instruments—a machine, mostly—to terminate unwanted pregnancies."

She had lapsed, with certain words, into the comfortable crutch of medical jargon. A place where arms were upper extremities, a place where her children—too young?—were still held at proper distances. So she continued, pulling low the final scrim.

"Pregnant women come to me to remove their unborn fetuses. To dispose of them."

"Babies," said Garrett, suddenly.

"Not yet," said Mercer. "This is where some doctors, like me, differ from the people who protest outside the clinic and our house. I don't believe the fetus, at the time most abortions are performed, is a life. Certainly—and again, this is me speaking—it's not a living person as we recognize one."

"Some people think so," said Garrett.

"Some people do, Garrett."

"We *don't*," said Clem.

"Maybe you do," said Mercer. "It's not so easy. For me, I've come to believe women should be allowed to make this choice. Freely. As you three get older, maybe you'll think differently."

It was hard to know if Kendall was listening to the conversation and choosing to remain silent, or if the noise of ripping cardboard and stretched tape was simply too loud.

Of course, as each of them sat with their thoughts, this was what worried Mercer most: someday, intelligently, one or more of her children might come to the decision that their mother had placed them all in harm's way for a belief they did not share.

Garrett looked across his knees at Sean.

"A miscarriage," said Sean, referring to his sister.

Both boys nodded, though it was unclear whether either knew exactly what the word meant. Guilt climbed through Garrett from some tamped-down place. The swift panic that all unsuccessful pregnancies—unwanted and *wanted*—would find blame in his mother.

Excusing himself, Sean followed a yellow line painted to the floor that would purportedly lead him to the cafeteria. Despite Garrett's best intentions, he couldn't think of the right thing to say: a true and tested sentence to make them both feel better. His mind punched to selfish territory where he wondered, with immediacy, how he'd registered in another boy's judgment.

DAMP KIDNEYS OF MOISTURE pulled at the fabric of Sam's shirt, below both armpits and in the valley between her stomach and chest. Wisps of steam lifted from her face. Beside her, Garrett rocked in the porch swing, feet hooked on the handle of his duffel. To keep warm, Sam rose and began dragging snow into piles with her hockey stick. They had won again. Having been driven home by one of their teammate's older brothers, they found themselves locked from the house. Someone was supposed to be there: Mercer or Tiff or Clem. They knocked on their father's studio, but the window was dark and no one answered.

A squeaking—boots in snow—came from the driveway. It was Clem returning from her final afternoon of work. She stopped, taking in the view of her brother and sister, one seated, one standing, in the muted darkness, before continuing toward the stairs.

"No one's home," said Garrett.

Often, the back door was left unlocked, or sometimes Sam or Garrett would climb through the window above the kitchen sink. But there had been ice the previous night and the windows were either frozen closed or latched.

"Dad's not there," said Sam, turning in the direction of the warehouse before Clem could speak. "Just us . . ."

Garrett spat over the railing into a swelled drift of snow. From her spot on the walkway, Sam began chipping stones of ice and volleying them with the face of her stick. The cold whistled through the alley between the edge of the porch and the beginning of the warehouse. Garrett moved faster to keep his blood pumping in his toes and fingers.

Clem watched her siblings, in the blurred sepia of early evening, trying to hold heat close to their bodies. Tightening the collar on her coat, she sat with Garrett and matched the rhythm to his swaying. The bench-swing chain, dropped from above, was pulled taut; it whined with each tug of chain link against chain link. Heads cocked, they bounced on the stiff pine beneath their bottoms. Sam hacked at the yard, wildly, with the elbow of her stick, waiting for motion from the black beyond the ice rink and hurricane fencing. She planted the stick, butt end down, in the snow and walked to join her brother and sister on the porch. She squeezed close, between the two, and let her feet drag, toes splayed, with the pendulum arc of the swing.

In the distance, from across the street or down the block, came the sound of glass breaking, followed by a reedy voice. None of the three could make out any words. Then, only the metal joints grinding above their heads and the flapping of the handle on Garrett's hockey duffel. Six hands, six feet. There was numbness they needed to warm away.

Five years later . . .

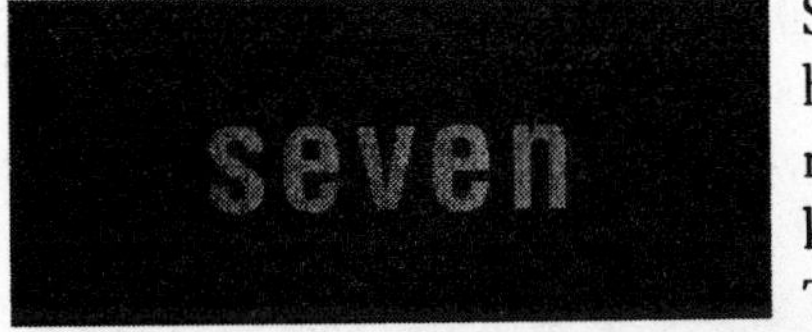

Smoke filled the windshield. Sam had been lighting cigarettes, their remains poking like broken monkey fingers from the ashtray. Turned low, the radio played from a single speaker beneath the perforated dashboard near the glove compartment. She watched him behind the haze, eyes reddened and irritated. By then her hair had turned thick and coppery, ragged against the line of her shoulders—longer and darker than when she was young. The skin of her cheeks was the fine pink of conch shells. She adjusted the strap of her overalls, faded and frayed, against her left breast. There was a tiny vertical slash colliding with the right corner of her upper lip, still freshly purpled and moist. It stung when touched with tobacco. She drank cola, all syrupy and tingles along the tunnel of her throat. The empty cans, squeezed once, were tossed on the floor behind her seat.

After seeing her car's reflection in the plate-glass window, he walked through the electronic doors and stood on the sidewalk. To his left, vending machines for beverages and candy and newspapers from three counties. He lit a cigarette and held the smoke in his lungs for a count, two, before letting it spill from his mouth, following the seams of his face and climbing away. He said something, quietly, knowing she couldn't hear him, and kicked at the car's bumper.

When she opened the door, on the driver's side, he asked, "Who hit you?" patting his own lips with the wrist of his cigarette hand.

"Got tripped," said Sam, swiveling so her feet touched the pavement.

"You should buy a pair of figure skates," he said. "The white kind."

She nodded, smiling slightly so the wound now pointed toward her nostril. Removing a yellow rubber band from the car's gearshift, she pulled back her hair and fastened it loosely, above her neck, in a puffed ponytail.

"I thought you were gonna come watch," she said.

With his head, he motioned to the convenience store behind him. "I got called to work," he said. "Someone didn't show."

"That sucks . . ."

He wore a long-sleeved thermal shirt, gray, beneath a short-sleeved button-down in the store's colors, lime-green and white. His hair, blond and bleachy, coarse like a swimmer's, gathered into cowlicks that swirled toward gravity-challenged knots. Clean, smooth, his jawline broke at hard angles, making him appear larger and older. He dragged his boots, scuffing fat crescents into their outer heels. He kept his wallet fastened to his belt loop with a long silver chain that banged against his thigh when he moved his legs. Resting heavy in the stitched breast pocket of his shirt was a Zippo lighter, which, on occasion, he removed and snapped open and closed to emphasize certain words in the course of conversation ("Didn't you buy any pretzels . . . *clink-clock-clink-clock* . . . to go with that beer?).

From behind, the doors spread with a *shush*.

"Hey," said another guy wearing the same lime-and-white shirt. "Hey, Doak. Something's wrong with the Swishy machine. The blueberry side is coming out too wet. It's not icy enough."

"Yeah . . ."

"I don't know how to fix it."

"I'll be right in," said Doak.

He balanced a bottle cap on the car's antenna.

"Some girl wants one," said the other boy, sounding slightly exasperated. "She wants one *now*."

"Tell her to have lemon instead."

"She doesn't want *lemon*, she wants *blueberry*."

In a single motion, Doak whirled and fired the bottle cap, with his right arm, into the glass storefront beside the boy. The noise, a slight, toothy ping, caused the boy to jump and, without removing his eyes from Doak, back his way through the doors.

"He's such a dipshit," said Doak.

Sam unwrapped a stick of chewing gum, folding it in half and then folding it again before dropping it into her mouth.

"When're you done?" she asked.

"Nine," he said. Making a fist, he kneaded the stiffness at the top of his shoulder. "Want me to come get you?"

"No. I've got a chemistry test tomorrow that I should probably study for."

"Sure?"

She nodded and then so did he. Knocking twice on the roof, he leaned down and kissed her, dry, on the forehead before disappearing into the store. She sat motionless for a few more moments, letting the remaining smoke drain from the car until it was time to leave. She touched the thickly taped tail of her hockey stick, wedged against her leg, when she grabbed for the gearshift. She pushed the stick away, letting it rest between the dimples of the passenger seat cushion.

CROOKED NOW, HIS BACK CURVED from a car accident two years earlier, Tiff held a hot iron against the collar of a white cotton shirt. Near his elbow was a glass of water which he sprinkled across the shirt with his fingers to remove creases. There was not much light, only from the television and a small desk lamp behind the ironing board. Seated Indian-style on the floor, Sam ate peanut butter and saltine crackers, then wiped her mouth with the sleeve of her sweater.

"That was just cleaned," said Tiff, refusing eye contact. "*You* gonna wash it next time?"

Sam shook her head; she picked crumbs from the thin-weaved cuff near her wrist. The ceiling gasped beneath someone's footsteps.

"Who's here?" asked Sam.

"Just your mother."

When she chewed, Sam could feel salt in the cut along her lip. After she dabbed it with a paper towel, once, twice, checking for blood, Tiff asked if she'd been injured.

"Not really," she said, turning away.

As Sam walked back toward the kitchen, she heard Tiff calling for her to leave things alone unless she wanted it to start bleeding again. Sam stood over the sink and peered into the window. She rinsed her glass, sticky with apple juice. Headlights bathed the porch and part of the driveway in whiteness. Sam and Garrett shared a car, and after hockey on this evening, Garrett went for a burger with friends. They were all talking, parked, with the engine humming so fiercely it shook the side windowpanes of the house. She was staring, eyes puckered to slits, concentrating hard on the mouths of her brother and his friends, trying to figure what they were discussing. There was a *maybe* and one of the boys in the backseat, Jake Boyle, said *fuck* a few times. But that was all she knew.

When Garrett stepped from the car, Sam moved quickly across the kitchen to the table. She opened her books and pretended to be reading as her brother shouldered his gear through the door. She feigned disinterest as he removed a box of Frosted Flakes from the cupboard and poured a bowlful across from where she was seated. He ate noisily, crunching the cereal before it had a chance to turn flaccid with milk.

"Didn't you just have dinner?" Sam asked.

"Not enough."

These thoughts he could not avoid: he wanted to know what had happened. Forever, to them, Sam and Garrett had skated together, played hockey on the same ice. In all that time, only once, earlier that evening, had Garrett ever seen his sister appear uncomfortable, awkward, in skates. She had scored twice in the first period and, not unusually, dictated play among her male teammates and counterparts. Then midway through the third period, Garrett saw her follow the puck behind the other team's goal, at the opposite end of the ice from where he was standing. His view was blocked by other skaters, and once the whistle blew, he turned to take a drink from the water bottle resting in the webbing of his own net. There was some noise and another trill of the whistle, when he heard someone shout his name. Shuffling slowly, in his clunky goalie pads, he moved from blue line to blue line. Just as Garrett worked his way to the scrum he heard the guy, a big defenseman, say, "Wanna go? Huh?"

Near where Garrett had skated there was a cross-hatching of arms and hands twisted in the fabric of other jerseys; the linesmen were pulling people loose and pushing them to different sides. The noise came first: a soft double-thump as the big defenseman's gloves hit the ice. His left fist caught Sam flush in the mouth, driving her hard into the Plexiglas curtain surrounding the rink.

"I don't give a shit if you're a girl," he said.

Seated, her back pressed against the boards, Sam spit blood down the front of her jersey. There was little movement as one of the officials held the big defenseman back, steering him in the direction of the penalty box. Shaking off hands lowered for assistance, Sam rose under her own strength and continued, silently, not missing a shift for the remaining minutes of the game. Too much space and not enough time for Garrett to involve himself. Also, the newness of his sister—*this* sister—in need of security.

"Hitting him back . . . " said Sam, trailing off, arms folded across her chemistry textbook. "I don't know, it seemed like something dirty. Not *cheap* dirty but *wrong* dirty. I didn't want anything to change."

What she'd meant, what Garrett understood over milk oily with cereal and sugar, was that she couldn't lose this. She knew only grace for the sport. Hockey ice had belonged to her for all these years . . . and she was afraid of seeing it grow different, turn apart in places she could not reach. She would, one day, sooner or later, not play this game again. At least not with boys, at least not in ways that mattered.

Once he'd finished putting away the cereal and bowl and taken a long drink of tap water, Garrett said, "He was big."

And Sam only nodded. On his way upstairs, Garrett paused, briefly, to remove his dirty clothes for the laundry. He listened to his sister turn the page of her book, sigh, then turn the page again.

SHE HAD NOT WANTED THIS PART, EITHER. The next day someone told Doak what had happened. Some kid who'd been at the game came into the convenience store and started talking, blathering on about Sam and the beefy defenseman and how the guy sucker-punched her in the mouth.

"Let it go," said Sam.

They were beside one another, Sam at the wheel and Doak in the passenger seat. She licked her lip, trying to hide the damage with her tongue. He continued to stare through the windshield, pointing with his fingers as they slowly rolled into one intersection and then the next. These were poorly lighted side streets, two towns over.

"The next block," he said, glancing down at some oozy scribble on the back of a napkin.

Before, there had been a light, icy rain and puddles filled the street like spilled change. It was quiet and Sam could hear the scored rims of the car's brake shoes as she flexed her foot.

"There," he said, removing from the backseat two hockey sticks that had been duct-taped together. "When I give the signal, hit the gas."

He lowered the window and hung his torso out, hockey sticks braced against the door frame. As the car gained speed, he made a sound, from deep in his throat, and Sam pressed the gas pedal. Passing the house, Doak caught the mailbox with his sticks and caved in its side. He nodded for her to reverse. She backed up and this time he held the post of the mailbox in the curve of the sticks and pulled; the box snapped loose. Relieved, Sam began driving away.

"Go back," he said. "There's more . . . "

She turned, reluctantly. He unwrapped something from a plastic bag.

"That reeks," she said.

He smiled; he was holding an old hockey helmet, overturned, stuffed with crinkled wads of paper and, carefully centered, a sealed sandwich bag of dog shit. Spraying the insides with lighter fluid, he set the helmet afire and dropped it beside the tumbled mailbox. Black, stinky fronds of smoke lifted upwards, following the car's path until it broke into transparent ellipses.

Once they were gone, flaming helmet long vanished from the rearview mirror, Sam lowered her own window and fanned away the remaining smell with her free hand. She had told Doak before that she thought mowing the mailbox was childish and unnecessary. But she went along with him because she saw this as a moment in her youth, finally, to be the bully. To lash out in some expected way. Still, she'd been prepared for all but the dog shit.

"Where did that come from?" she asked in a voice hard with anger.

"Inspired, huh?"

A dizzying strangeness, perhaps from the lighter-fluid fumes, forced her to coast for a couple blocks. She could feel Doak staring at her, his eyes, unblinking, fastened against the side of her face. Not so alike, she thought. Even for teenagers.

Later, they sat across from each other at an all-night doughnut shop near the interstate. Doak was stirring packets of sugar into his coffee, already muddy with milk. They had met half a year earlier at a fair. He lived with his uncle, who, on occasion, would drink malt liquor from quart-sized bottles and beat on the hollow walls with a lamp stem or doubled extension cord. Collecting money from friends, his uncle had bought into a "skill" booth at the fair. For a dollar, visitors were given three tennis balls to knock down three fuzzy dolls stitched to spring rods. (Sam was told, afterwards, that only about half of the dolls would release when struck.) There were prizes, of course, and Sam had wandered to the booth while sharing a box of popcorn with Dawn Hudson. She'd spied a straw boater to wear as they walked the grounds.

"Give it a try?" said Doak.

He was standing to the side, twirling a toy whistle around his index finger.

"No one ever wins at these things," said Sam.

"Are you kidding? We just had some guy win three times in a row . . ."

"*Right.*"

Still, Sam laid a dollar bill on the counter and lifted the first of her balls. She tossed it, quickly, and then threw the other two. Each caught some part of a doll, but only one, the third ball, snapped a figure back.

"So it goes," she said.

He let her try again, for nothing, but she still could manage only one solid hit. As Sam and Dawn began to leave, he told her about the rigging.

"See," said Sam, smiling. "I knew this was *fixed*."

It was then, seeing Doak fight to keep the corners of his mouth from rising, that Sam knew she could like this boy. His crooked nose pushed sloppy to the left of his face, long eyebrows nearly meeting below the pinched skin of his forehead. The way he talked, almost as if speaking was a chore. He tried to rid himself of words, squeezing them together rapidly.

She saw him the next afternoon, the final day of the fair. Sipping from a bottled Coke, she watched while he helped disassemble his uncle's booth. He wore tight, faded Levi's that showed the dimples of his ass when he reached high. In the pitted fairgrounds, nearly closed, hollow and rideless, Sam and Doak sat on the bench of a Ferris wheel cab resting in the dirt and shared a cigarette. When he reached to wipe something from her cheek, she saw a scar, shaped like a waning moon, on the middle knuckle of his right hand.

Again in the doughnut shop, she watched him fondle a salt shaker, her eyes transfixed to that same scar. Though he'd never said, she imagined he'd gotten the cut by wrestling in the gravel of a parking lot or falling from a friend's motorbike.

"Some people deserve better," she said, not knowing herself whether she meant the big defenseman or Doak or her own family.

He nodded and then let his gaze follow the lights of a car leaving the gas station across the street.

Much of the attraction, she reasoned, was because both she and Doak perceived themselves as misfits. Sam, surely, had no great desire to bring others close. She and her siblings had always felt they were hiding something—parents, a home life—from people. And their relationships with friends, with suitors, suffered deeply. Interactions remained on the surface, broken immediately loose if they dipped much beyond that level. Any news that mattered was shared only among themselves: Sam and Garrett and Clem.

At home, night smudged to morning, she lay clothed upon her bed watching the shadows from the blowing tree branches cast against the ceiling. She heard Garrett take a piss and return to his room. Then there was only more silence.

CURTAINS FROM CLEM'S ROOM, burnt orange, were missing. No one knew for how many days because, with Clem away at college, her room remained empty. Abandoned. Tiff had noticed the naked window when he'd made his rounds watering plants. A jade tree, heavy, scrooched, was now fully exposed. It took Tiff a moment, stock-still and pondering, to figure out what was different about things.

He could not find resolution at breakfast and, given thought, neither Sam nor Garrett could remember if the curtains had left the house with Clem.

"Why would she take them?" asked Garrett.

"Goddam *curtains*," said Tiff, removing fried eggs from a skillet with a plastic spatula.

Once they'd eaten and were in the car, a bruised Chevy Nova, Garrett muttered to himself. Then he asked his sister why the car smelled so terribly. "Like someone took a dump," he said, contorting his face. Sam opened her window to the cold, slightly, and shrugged.

"Don't you smell that?"

"Not really," she said, lying.

At school, Garrett spun the tumbler to his locker. He worked slowly, diligently, pausing even after he'd found the final number. He read the hallway with the corners of his eyes before lifting the lever to store some books and remove others. At first, he didn't see her—she was hidden on the staircase by two other students. Stepping back, after changing the lead in his mechanical pencil, he caught the green of her canvas sneakers. Now he refused to move, unable, his hands moist and, until she was nearly behind him, squeezing tightly the cap of a yellow highlighter. She passed without greeting and Garrett, considering rationalizations, imagined she was deep in thought for some exam she surely had later in the day.

Though he had known Jessy Wicks ("A real movie-star name," he'd announced to friends) since grade school, he'd only recently found himself attracted to her in "other ways." In fact, if one was looking for a single, galvanizing moment, it was not difficult to unearth: seated across from her in English during a warm afternoon the previous fall, he'd stared dumbfounded at her knees, dark and smooth as cherrywood, as she'd parted and pressed them, revealing a fang of white panty above the hemline of her short dress. That night, alone, he'd squirmed in bed while letting his mind race to a disjointed amalgam of (vaguely) real and make-believe. His fictional world, which had matured with him, cleared sites for a federal agent (she liked danger, he'd reasoned) and his wife. Other evenings, he was a financier living overseas or, with band mate J. D. West, a famous rock musician faithful to his hometown sweetheart.

On this day, he followed Jessy Wicks from one wing of school to the next, risking tardiness for a few minutes longer, watching the motions of her body. What he liked most, as she walked away from him, was how her hips seemed to rock, hingeless, from side to side with the ease of lubricated ball bearings. A girl on flat earth, freed of wasted motion.

At lunch, only twice weekly did their breaks coincide. He sat in the auxiliary cafeteria, where he could follow her through a greasy glass portal punched into the wall. He ate a sandwich of lettuce and cured ham, taking bites without looking down. Beside him, two boys were discussing quotes they were considering for beneath their senior yearbook photographs. The first Garrett missed; the second came from something the boys were studying in class: " 'Time is dead as long as it's being clicked off by little wheels,' " said one boy. "What do you think of that?"

"Not bad," said the other boy. "What's it mean?"

"I'm not really sure. I just like it."

They both nodded knowingly.

Feeling a hand on his shoulder, Garrett turned to find Nick Briar searching for a place to sit. He chose a space across from Garrett, directly in his line of vision.

"How's your sister?" he asked.

For years, Nick had played on the same youth-league hockey teams with Garrett and Sam. It was his father, Ben Briar, who had sponsored the squads from beginning.

"She's fine," said Garrett.

"I think that guy's getting suspended for their next game."

Garrett broke the seal on his carton of orange drink. He liked Nick

Briar fine. He'd always respected the way Nick refused to make issue of his family name. A decent third-line player, he never complained about losing ice time to others when, really, he could bitch about the fact that his father's money ran the team, paid for the uniforms and coaches' salaries. There were times, even, when some of the other kids had spoken against Mr. Briar in the locker room or rented bus, grumbled about crappy sandwiches or ill-fitting jerseys, and Nick, quiet, kept his distance. Then, when the words had ceased, he returned as if nothing had happened. He did not expect more than he'd earned, which, considered Garrett, was a pretty good policy to extend toward other aspects of life.

As Nick continued to speak, Garrett watched Jessy Wicks's blurred figure stand and dump the remains of her lunch into a trash bin—empty Baggies that had been filled with carrot sticks and browned wedges of apple and pear. Though he wanted to follow, he knew her schedule and she was leaving to sit with friends in the student-activity center and drink Diet Cokes until the bell sounded. The most he could expect was a tiny finger wave or nod when he passed for his locker. Maybe, if all was right, she might ask him about something from a reading assignment. And always, no more.

Even then, in his waning teens, Garrett recognized it unlikely (impossible!) that he would ever become more than friends with Jessy Wicks. He listened, halfway, letting the sound of Nick Briar's voice drone into a single note like snapping fingers behind the ears.

After blueberry there was grape. Always, it seemed, the other was lemon. Once or twice weekly, Doak changed the second flavor on the Swishy machine: cherry and cola and strawberry and birch beer. From the nozzle, a stream of finely minced ice and colored syrup poured into wax cups, which were then covered with transparent, plastic-domed lids. The largest size, amazingly, was a bladder-bursting *thirty-four* ounces. Fat as hose straws fanned into flimsy spoons at the bottom.

Waiting, darkness down, Sam slurped on grape. She placed a cellophaned Moon Pie (vanilla) into the microwave for only five seconds. Across the room, crowded with stock, Doak spat the cracked husks of sunflower seeds into a paper bag. He had nearly an hour remaining in his shift. Spread open on the counter was a magazine with full-page photographs of motorcycles, bellies in coiled chrome holding bikini-clad models tanned the color of pinewood. He watched as, between bites, Sam wandered to a rack of cheap sunglasses and began trying them on while studying her reflection in a small mirror. Her favorites, oddly, were enormous white-rimmed ovals similar to those made famous by Jacqueline Onassis. Practicing various looks (elated, sultry, tough), she stepped away from the mirror and walked, exaggeratedly hippy, toward a camera mounted to the ceiling above Doak's cash register. Unsheathed from near the small of her back, leaking against the waist of her jeans, she removed a squirt pistol and fired water, straight as string, into the camera's lens. She stopped, suddenly, and tucked a strand of hair behind her left ear.

"What're you doing," asked Doak.

"Boys could be watching."

"Forget that."

"*Cute* boys."

"No one's watching you," he said, turning his attention again to the magazine. "No one but me."

She removed the stopper from the back of the squirt gun, rubbery, tiny as a dripping of candle wax, and began chewing it between her side teeth. Moving, bored, she slipped behind the counter, a place where she was forbidden, and held the gun beneath the spigot of the Swishy machine. Pulling the lever on grape, she allowed the sticky concoction to bleed into (and across) the gun's refill hole. More, of course, spilled into the collection trough. Eventually the gun turned heavy.

"It's too thick," said Doak.

"Gimme a little credit."

Again, she punched a short series of numbers into the microwave and allowed the gun and its contents briefly to heat. She held the barrel to her lips and squeezed the trigger, pumping purple liquid down the back of her throat.

"Not bad," she said, aiming the gun at Doak.

She nailed him with two blasts, in the cheek and chin. The juice dribbled loose, beading along the counter, collecting in dime-sized pools.

"This is a *great* idea," said Sam. "We could market these, call them something like Swishy Squirts."

"Big sellers," said Doak, wiping his face and the counter with paper napkins from a dispenser to his left. "Another *Pop Rocks* or *Wacky Packs* . . ."

"*Please.* You've got no imagination. Think about selling specially equipped guns that would keep Swishys cold and icy . . . They'd have bigger mouths, though, so we wouldn't have to nuke the stuff to make it shoot. Little kids love this shit."

"What do you know about it?"

"Enough . . . "

They quieted as a customer entered. A man in his early thirties to purchase disposable diapers. More people for ice cream and light beer and sandwich meat and toilet tissue. And then Sam only waited, silently, sucking on the pistol to the sounds of the cash register's bleeping.

THERE WERE DRESSES, old ones, hanging plastic-wrapped in Clem's closet. Sam was another size: leaner and harder than her sister. Still, some work with a needle and thread by Mercer or Tiff would fix things. Sam had seen her mother tighten her own clothing for Clem; it could be done for her, too. She flipped past each dress, like pages in a book, some forgotten more quickly than others. Her arms were nice, well defined she'd been told, so something sleeveless might work. Also, most comfortable: no loose, blousy fabric with which to fidget. Nothing too tight, either; she didn't want her calves, thick from skates, to chafe. Behind her, framed by the doorway, Tiff stood watching.

"What about that white one?" he said, finally, his voice gritty and low, startling Sam.

"I hate it," she said, pushing the dress to the side. "It looks like something a nurse would wear."

"Nonsense."

The next dress, deep blue so it resembled crushed velvet, had some appeal. Sam removed it from the closet and pressed it near her chest, turning with the hanger running along her collarbone.

"How 'bout this?"

"Pretty," said Tiff.

Sam made her way to her sister's vanity table, where a mirror, kneecapped, only showed her from mid-thigh upwards. When she moved, the dress, unattached, swayed against her torso like a grass skirt.

"What kind of shoes?"

"Well," started Tiff, hands on hips, "we could dye something to match."

"Or I could play it cool and wear a pair of high-top sneakers."

Tiff exhaled, loudly, his lower lip peeled down.

"There's nothing cool about dressin' sloppy."

Sam stepped away, garment tossed across the curved wicker of a chair, and moved toward the window so she could gain perspective. This, she figured, needed further examination. Leaning back, ass touching pane, she crossed her arms and sent her mind drifting through a series of imaginative scenes in which she was wearing the blue outfit: in the car; at dinner; dancing beneath looped crepe paper in the gymnasium.

As if the words were tugged past her face on a TelePrompTer, she spoke: "There's a zit behind my left ear."

Tiff nodded sympathetically. "Use a hot compress to draw it out," he said, tapping the lobe of his own ear.

She pushed across the wooden floorboards in her stocking feet, pausing momentarily above the trash can to hawk a wad of bubblegum.

"Wrap that in paper," said Tiff.

Wedged into the frame of her sister's mirror was a postcard of Vancouver, a place, strangely, that Clem had always wanted to visit. Sam tore the card in half and squeezed the gum, pink as Silly Putty, between the folds. She knew Tiff would disapprove. When she turned back in the direction of the door, Tiff had already departed. Still, she could hear his tongue *tsk-tsk-tsking* against the gilly roof of his mouth.

That evening, after dinner, Sam wore the blue dress into the kitchen and stood on the table while her mother and Tiff tacked fingers of fabric away from her rib cage and waist. She twirled, slowly, some enormous whiskey cork guided by her mother's hands. It was time to rotate a quarter revolution, she knew, when her mother, lips parted by straight pins, released a grunt.

"More from the top," said Tiff, head cocked.

Sam had narrow hips, like those of a boy, and tight abdominal muscles; she was also less bosomy than her sister. While being fitted, she sucked on hard candies, two at a time (watermelon and cherry, apple and lime). When her mother was almost finished, Sam, standing stiff as a sunburned child, fearful of pinpricks, watched Garrett enter and remove something from the refrigerator.

"We need more orange juice," he said, from behind the smooth aluminum door.

No one answered and so, shielded, he took three quick bites from a slab of cheddar cheese. There were other foods, of course, but truthfully, he was not hungry. He was only looking for some way to occupy his mouth. Upstairs, reading history homework alone in his room, he'd filled part of a cola can with tobacco juice from leafy Red Man chew. Later, he would switch to sand-cut snuff stored in pucky tins. To Garrett, it seemed peculiar: not four days earlier, Sam had shared his dip, dirty and brown, squeezed tight as aspirin tablets beneath her lower lip. It burned, peppery to the exposed blood vessels. They had read somewhere that grated tobacco was ground together with glass to score the tender skin of the mouth. A way to trip the nicotine into the body quicker.

He watched, now, this same sister in a thigh-length dress holding poses against the dull white walls. Her hair was slicked back, wet from shower water, combed away from her forehead. There was a sadness, he thought, in her eyes and, most apparently, to her mouth: low at both sides, bent crooked like a mangled paper clip. You would guess, glancing upon this teenage face for the first time, she had experienced a roughness to life: wisdom in the slope of her temples; the start of wire-thin lines tucked toward the break of her hairline; the feint imprint of a crucifix-shaped crease between her eyebrows. Top lip, still punctured and pawed, made her appear even more vulnerable.

"This reminds me of something," said Mercer, gently taking hold of her daughter's hand. "Something I want to show you." She turned toward Garrett. "To show both of you."

Mercer disappeared. Sam remained stoic, flexless, while across the room her brother kneaded scraps of cheese into tiny balls and flicked them into the trash can.

When Mercer returned, she was carrying a large cardboard box, the kind department stores used for holiday gifts. As she removed the lid, both children craned their heads forward for clearer views. Inside was a layer of tissue paper—pink, white—covering a plastic garbage bag. It was still difficult to see what the packing material was keeping protected.

A photograph came loose, followed immediately by another and another. A string of photographs. Mercer kept one hand gingerly beneath the stack of pictures, as if she were lifting a tray of hors d'oeuvres. Then she placed her other hand on a wire hanger sprouting from the middle of the pile. The photographs spilled with purpose against Mercer's side to form, from jumbled madness, a thigh-length coat of snapshots that had been stitched together with fishing line. The common bond connecting each photograph, other than tiny knots of transparent string, was that they were all pictures of newly born babies.

"What *is* that?" asked Garrett, slightly bewildered, running the tips of his fingers across the photographs' tily surface.

"A jacket," said Mercer. She carefully slipped the sculpted topcoat, stiff as cornstarched denim, over her shoulders. "I delivered each of these infants."

"That's a lot of babies," said Sam.

"It's only a handful," said Mercer. She sighed; she lifted her arms into a scarecrow's T. "There are more."

Mercer described how each of the pictures had been taken, by Mercer or one of the nurses, shortly after the birth of a baby. The few they had missed over the years—lacking film, complications—arrived a week or month later, usually accompanied by a note of thanks.

"I was feeling very blue about something or other," said Mercer, taking a small half turn so the jacket caught the light. "You were both very young. Clem, too. It was late at night and I was lying in bed watching Johnny Carson. Strangely, I started to get misty-eyed during a song by one of Johnny's guests. Your father, who was reading beside me, huffed and got out of bed; I heard him leave the house for his studio before he returned ten or so minutes later."

Mercer inched the jacket delicately down her arms and spread it flat across the box. She took a drink from her water glass.

"When he came back into the room he was carrying this box." She pointed. "He told me he'd planned to give it to me for my birthday, which was still maybe three weeks away, but he thought I needed it more now. At that moment."

"He was right," said Sam.

"Yes," said Mercer, turning her attention again to Sam's dress. "He was right."

Sam rolled her shoulders forward, ever so slightly, and the dress fell into a gauzy pool at her ankles. Mercer focused on repacking the jacket. In the cool air, now wearing only undergarments, nipples pressed rigid against the nylon of her brassiere, Sam swung her hips to nonexistent music. Garrett could see, even in these brief movements, that this was where his sister's gift was generated: great golfers and hitters in baseball produced power in their strokes from the hips; opening their torsos as if on greased runners. And Sam's slap shot was born in the wink of her hips—in a shutter speed all was complete. It's the kind of thing a parent doesn't want to remember. Mercer would push the thoughts from her brain whenever she felt them rising beneath the day's innocuous clutter. The project was meant to entertain the children on a rainy afternoon. Mercer had recalled Kendall showing some veterans at the hospital how to make place mats for their girlfriends or wives or mothers. So, imagining it might be a constructive way to kill this sloppy Saturday, she gathered the kids in the kitchen.

Clem, who was only seven, sat at the head of the table between her brother and sister. The idea was to take leaves they'd scavenged from underneath the porch, ones that hadn't been soaked by water, and lay them on a sheet of wax paper. Each child, using a dull butter knife, shaved unwrapped crayons across the leaves and paper. Then Mercer would lay another piece of paper against the surface; she'd run a hot iron over the picture to melt the wax and colored crayon and leaves into a stiff collage.

Mostly, they all had a good time. They learned to talk with their faces turned away from the table so their breath wouldn't blow loose the leaves and crayon chips. Garrett became excited when he realized he could sign his picture in the lower right-hand corner, as his father did on paintings. Clem, neatest of the three, arranged her leaves and chip piles in symmetrical designs.

When each child had completed his or her first piece, Mercer stuck it to the refrigerator with a dinosaur magnet. As they continued to work, Mercer took a phone call from her office. She stood behind the kids.

While she spoke, half paying attention to a nurse who was discussing a list of prescriptions, she decided to make the children some hot chocolate. She removed the milk and a tin of powdered cocoa and a saucepan.

"Mine's done," said Clem, leaning back from her position at the table.

What she'd meant was that her second picture was ready for Mercer to press with the iron.

"Okay," said Mercer. "I'll be over in a minute."

Cradling the receiver between her ear and shoulder, Mercer guided the phone cord across the counter—lifting it over a juice glass, a jar of coffee beans, some cooking utensils. The next part was where Mercer had trouble squeezing things into focus. After she'd begun heating the milk, stirring whirlpools into its surface with a wooden spoon, she crouched to remove a few clean mugs from the dishwasher. The phone cord was stretched straight; she was sure about this because when the sound came the cord snapped back across the counter, knocking over a tumbler of pencils. It was Clem's voice, Mercer knew instantly, chased into unrecognizable octaves.

Once Mercer had risen, once she had made her way back around to the table, she saw Garrett and Sam standing to the side, frightened at their sister's screams. By then, Clem was curled against the floor: a writhing ball of tears and squeals and sweat.

Mercer placed her hand on Clem's shoulder. She asked her what had happened and then, before another question, she knew the answers. Tiny wires of smoke were lifting from the table beside where Clem had been seated. To avoid fire, Mercer raised the iron. It had been tilted down; its flat, stainless-steel face was soupy with wax and bleeding colors and the blackened remains of paper.

"Let me see, honey," said Mercer, kneeling over Clem's body.

When Clem wouldn't respond, Mercer walked across the room to remove a tray of ice from the freezer. She wrapped the ice cubes in a dish towel.

"We've got to put this on the burn," she said.

It took another few minutes for Clem to allow her muscles to relax. The sobs were so forceful, so overwhelming, they sucked away her breath. But finally, once Mercer convinced her daughter to unclench, she was able to see the damage: a bright red cauliflower welt across the first three knuckles and fingers of Clem's left hand.

"This will make it feel better."

Mercer sat on the floor with her daughter between her legs, as if they were riding a toboggan. She held the ice pack against the wound, combing Clem's hair from her face with her free hand. Mercer could feel her daughter's tears striking her along the forearm. And then, suddenly, Mercer also began to cry. She was upset, of course, that Clem was in pain. But there was more: she was seized by a guilt that this had all been her fault. She'd neglected to warn the children about the hot iron; she could easily have moved it away from the table or not taken the phone call or saved the hot chocolate for another time.

She should have been better prepared. An afternoon, she thought, when all good intentions were turned into something else.

Having taken a step or two backwards, Garrett and Sam were staring at Clem and now, mostly, their mother.

"This is nothing," said Mercer. "She's going to be fine."

But when she realized the two of them were more worried about her than about Clem, she raised one arm.

"Come here."

She held the three of them, against her rib cage and thigh and loin. She tried to fight the tears by tipping her head upwards, toward the ceiling, as if it was a pitcher of liquid. The prospect that all her children might remember this day for the wrong reasons was nearly too much for Mercer. How could she carve a place in their memories away from Clem's burned hand? Away from the sadness?

She gripped them, awkwardly, in a bear hug of high elbows and narrow waists. "It was only an accident," she said, softly, into the zigzaggy parts of their hair. "And it made me feel bad."

First to break loose was Garrett. He walked to the garbage pail, nodding, as if he understood everything, and posited a crumpled leaf he'd been squeezing in his fist. Sam was next; she climbed back onto her chair at the table. Finally, there was Clem. The skin under her eyes was pulled taut by dried tear salt. She shrugged off the ice her mother was holding and looked down at her hand, puffy and pink.

"It feels hot," she said. "But not like before . . . "

She kissed Mercer, briefly, on her damp wrist and then left the room.

Later that night, Mercer sat beside Kendall on the porch. Both were drinking tea. She had already told him what had happened.

"Things are never how you expect them," she said. "I mean, they might be. But they also might end up totally different."

He nodded.

"It's better that way," he said, poking at the tea bag with his forefinger. "Would you want to know how everything turns out?"

"No." She was staring into the dark; she wasn't looking at anything but, instead, she was letting her eyes rest against the blackness. "Only with the kids. Only if it was something bad, something that maybe I could prevent."

He smiled.

"We don't get to choose."

She took another sip of tea and then the two of them were quiet until, before heading to bed, they both whispered good nights into the doorways of their sleeping children.

INFORMATION OFTEN CAME to Sam and Garrett and later, to Clem, as if by medicinal drip: slow and measured. News of clinic protesters—rogue bands who clung to wire-link fences, kicked up loaves of dirt—reached them in the whispers of friends, townspeople, or, occasionally, a small notice in the back pages of the newspaper.

Over time, they had grown less awkward about things. Perhaps because they'd been led into a certain acceptance, the way a lame man might finally surrender to his limp. But a self-consciousness remained: these three children placed *on display*. It was a difficult way to live—always wondering if they were being judged, assessed, for something over which they had no command.

They secretly considered if escape, however fleeting, was plausible: maybe a town, an outing where the families of those who worked at abortion clinics could meet for some relief, where they would no longer tote around the label of outcast.

A breed of closeness knotted them in adolescence. Harm would be less effective, they figured, if challenged by three rather than one. Incidental thoughts entering their heads, they believed, were never shared by teenaged classmates. As in the serious hours of a recent morning, when Sam asked her brother, "Do you ever feel like you're being watched?"

SHE WAS NOT BEING COY, Clem insisted, armored pay-phone cord between her fingers. It was his *whole* first name.

"Z," she said. "Only the letter Z."

"Like, Z period?" asked Sam.

"No. Just the letter Z . . . no period, because it doesn't stand for anything."

"How'd he get that kind of a name?"

"Well," began Clem, turning to see if anyone was waiting to use this shared phone in her dormitory hall. "He's got an uncle named Zeb . . . and his parents are big Zorro fans. They didn't want to name him after either. So, I suppose, they felt Z was a decent compromise."

"Z what?"

"Huh?"

"Z *what?* What's his last name?"

Clem could hear her sister exhaling. From the sound alone, she knew Sam was lying stomach-down on her bed. There was the noise of rustling paper: Sam leafing through a magazine or mail-order catalogue.

"It's Z Churnip."

"Turnip? Like the vegetable?"

"No. *C-H*-U-R-N-I-P."

"God, that's weird."

"Yeah," said Clem, jabbing at a clover of loose plasterboard on the wall with her pencil. "But it's cool, too. He's got this baseball cap from some minor-league team, the Zephyrs, and above the bill is the letter Z stitched to the front. And it's his *name*, his entire *name* right there."

The two spoke for a time longer, taking turns explaining what had suddenly gained importance in their lives: for Sam, a dance and Doak and, of course, hockey; for Clem, a new school in a new town away from Ohio, Z Chirnup, and, for everyone back home to know, friendships. When considering colleges the previous winter, Clem randomly selected one school on each coast, along with several universities in the Middle West. After a fine weekend visit and a considerably generous financial-aid package, she chose Brown University, mostly, she believed, because of two hours she spent drinking cappuccino (which she'd never before tasted) at a coffeehouse near the ocean. There were so many different types of students, she remembered thinking, people unlike those she'd ever found in Lukin. There was also distance from everything she had known to that day. She returned home the following afternoon, decision made, wearing a heavy gray sweatshirt with the Brown school crest in raised lettering across her chest.

Finished, hundreds of miles apart, each sister let the other's words root in her head. They studied how the shapes were taking from hidden from view, in the care of strangers. Sam wondered about a world without curfews where beer and boyfriends and schoolwork rustled for position behind self-tethered lines. To Clem, there was concern over what she'd left behind: safety her mother lacked walking the driveway to retrieve the morning newspaper; new threats from those who'd begun circling their block late-night in darkened automobiles; lower window shades, stronger door locks; a suspicion of those moving too near on crowded thoroughfares. Or, odder still, ever more cryptic appraisals of her father's health. In her absence, Kendall's peculiarities had been filed to a sharpness that couldn't be ignored. His hours had become even more sporadic: some weeks he worked nights and slept days, other weeks he didn't rest at all or, when the caffeine had been pissed from his bladder, he collapsed until the desire for food or drink shook him awake after nineteen or twenty-two hours. Things missing, mysteriously, were attributed to him: the drapes and an oversized roll of aluminum foil and one of the trays from Tiff's sewing kit.

Mostly, Sam had told her sister, the rest of the family felt Kendall pulling further away. Even in those rare moments when he was present—occasional meals or watching television or digging through drawers and closets—he'd begun behaving like a boarder. No longer did he speak in specifics only, his concern came in wide strokes. "How was school?" he'd ask, hands busy tearing the heads from a book of matches, never listening for a response. "We dissected a human in biology class today," Sam or Garrett would announce for effect, without fearing reprisal from their father. "A *live* human. Some guy we pulled off the playground and split down his gut like a three-pound trout."

None of them, not Sam nor Garrett nor Mercer, could expect Clem to understand, even in the short months since she'd been at college, how Kendall had seen his already precarious hold on reality slacken. Other troubling episodes: stabbing a fried chicken breast so fast, so numb, the fork splintered bone until marrow, gritty as peanut butter, leaked to the plate; two evenings spent with tiny lightbulbs screwed into his ears while he pawed at the carpet in his stocking feet, trying to draw electrical currents. Hearing something after they'd gone to sleep, Sam or Garrett would cover their heads with pillows, hoping to lose the sound, forget about whatever their father was doing. There were no tools to make it better. Or rather, perhaps the tools did exist—therapists and pharmaceutical cocktails—but Kendall was unapproachable. He was, now, a man who so abhorred outside contact that he chose to pry loose a rotted molar with a hammer's claw rather than visit the dentist.

Their phone conversation ended, Sam continued paging in old catalogues past items she neither needed nor wanted. (The exception was a night-table clock that, triggered by the press of a button, cast time against the ceiling behind an illuminated funnel of light.) In Providence, scratchy stereos humping against half-closed doors, Clem walked the hallway to her room. She had, for most of her nearly nineteen years of life, been painfully neat: socks balled tightly and arranged in the drawer by color, darkest at rear; creams and health elixirs placed like the pieces to a board game on the bathroom counter, manila folders for each school subject and, saved, slots for returned (and graded) homework assignments and exams.

No longer was she inflexible about the proper place of things. On the windowsill of her room there was a cardboard box filled, maraca-like, with the hardened crusts from pizza. Beside the leg of her desk, near orderly, were two mugs with dried pillows of tea, ticketed strings curled limply to the cups' handles. There were loose papers and textbooks. Some belonged to Clem, some did not.

Seated on one of the twin beds, dressed in low-slung jeans and baggy tennis shirt, Clem's roommate, Sarah Elliot, whom everyone called Siv, was carving a point to her pencil with a Swiss Army knife. She greeted Clem with a small nod before, head lowered, blowing a palmful of wood chips into the potted soil of a hibiscus plant. Clem straddled a chair, her forearms crossed against the high maple slats bowed for the curves of a human's back. She needed someone here to tell her all things at home were right; someone who knew of her life in Lukin and, reassuringly, would squeeze away this emptiness. Also, to tell her things were wrong. For as much as she wanted to leave her childhood, it remained, in part, stuck to her like a thorn in the combed fibers of a sweat sock. Her ego, tiny always, lacked some boost: that her family, her town, her place of old, could survive without the piece she provided. Not only her father or mother, sister, brother, not the high-school or almost-friends, but even Carl, who sold her packaged barrettes and spiral-bound notebooks at the drugstore, or the woman, nameless still, who sacked baked goods. They continued, daily, thinking rarely of this girl. Whether she'd moved with finality, or maybe had simply gone to visit a sick aunt. Who tells them of her life, Clem thought, nibbling the fringe around her thumbnail.

Finished, knife closed, Siv took one of the pencils and laid it between the backs of the bony fingers of her right hand. Then she snapped her arm toward her face, quickly, some half-Nazi salute, lifting the pencil skyward until it lodged in the perforated skin of the foam-core ceiling tile. There were already two pencils, red and regular, from another day.

"Sometimes you wonder why anyone ever leaves home," said Siv, knowing Clem had been talking to her family. "Other times, you wonder why you didn't leave a long time ago."

Clem nodded, only thinking of what Siv understood about these issues. They'd known each other for just a few months and, she felt, Siv was not simply speaking in generalities. Her own family, Siv's, lived in Rye, New York, on an expensive plot of greened land near a train station and Episcopal church and golf club. They "summered," as Siv described it, on Martha's Vineyard. Once, Clem had been told, Siv and a friend, before they'd turned sixteen, drove Siv's mother's Volvo into the neighbor's swimming pool. Naturally, the two had been drinking—Jack Daniel's and Cokes. It was the third time somebody had landed a car in that particular pool.

From the window, between the crooked lashes of the blinds, Clem watched the lights of a taxi and then those on a squealing bus. Behind her, fiddling with other attachments to the knife—bottle opener, tweezers, magnifying glass—Siv continued talking about families, others she'd known.

"There was this guy, Mason something or other, who'd gone to grade school with my brother. God—" said Siv, taking a breath, letting the words come whether Clem was listening or not. "I remember the whole group of them would just behave like such *boys*. They'd pile onto each other while watching football on the couch, punching the legs and arms of whoever happened to be at the bottom. Then they would turn against someone else—maybe the guy in the middle of the pile, or someone who'd returned from the bathroom or kitchen. It was all in fun, though. Just roughhousing, my mother called it."

Siv closed the knife and placed it in the drawer of her nightstand.

"So this guy, Mason . . . Mason"—Siv fell back, eyes locked to the tilted triangle of pencils hanging above her bed—"Sax! I think that was it. Mason *Sax*. Anyway, his parents had started him on tennis when he was, like, two or something. The older he got, the less time he was with his friends. He'd get picked up from school and taken right to a tennis club, where he'd practice until dinner. Eventually, he was sent to Florida or California, where the weather was nice all year long. Once, I remember my brother telling me, Mason came home during Christmas vacation, when they were all in high school, and he met some of the guys at this deli near our house. They were all eating sandwiches and french fries and shit like that, talking about things, when Mason's father comes in, all red in the face, and starts yelling at him for cutting a practice session, like, twenty minutes short. He yanked the kid, by his arm, off his chair and out the door. Just like that. One motion."

For a moment Siv was quiet, allowing her thoughts to order themselves. Half paying attention, Clem turned from the traffic, a sense of purpose washing past as she scanned the room for a textbook from her sociology class.

"He went to Stanford, I think, on scholarship. Maybe it was Berkeley. In the summers, he played a few of those small tournaments, but, really, never beat anyone good. At least not anyone we would have known." Finding a soft spot in her pillows, blanket now pulled to her chest, Siv appeared weary. She sighed, a final charge, before letting the last of it come. "The point, I suppose, is that the place we least expected to see Mason again was back in Rye. But amazingly, after college, a couple years ago, he returned. Teaches tennis at the country club, eats dinner with his folks once or twice a week."

Out of politeness, Clem raised her shoulders in a shrug to match the one delivered by Siv.

"I mean, *really*. With his father being such a dick, my brother guessed Mason would move as far from his old life, his friends and family, as possible."

"Hmmmm."

That was all. The roommates sat in silence before, struck by inspiration, Clem found the book she was searching for beneath the disengorged innards of a campus newspaper. When she departed, Siv's eyelids were heavy, her thoughts, Clem believed, stuck on other memories, meaningful and not, from her past.

WRITTEN ON RED CONSTRUCTION PAPER, in large black letters, was the letter Q, followed by a colon and the sentence: Who was Alger Hiss?

"He was a former State Department official," said Clem. "In the late 1940s, he was accused of being a secret agent for the Soviet Union."

"Impressive," said Z.

In smaller print it told all who read the flyer, tacked to a bulletin board in the student union, for the answers to this and other "compelling" questions, to join the American history club on Tuesday evenings at nine.

"Now you've got something to do on Tuesdays," said Z. "That's more than most."

"Right."

"How'd you know that?"

At first she didn't say anything. Then, "From another life."

"Very mysterious . . . and smart."

"No," she said, looking for a table where they could sit. "Think answers before questions. Common misconception: A powerful memory means a powerful mind."

Before them, remarkably, a corner booth cleared and they slid into opposite sides. The space was illuminated, mostly, from the orangish light of a jukebox. After settling themselves, arranging their textbooks and notes and chubby yellow markers, Clem removed a few quarters from a zippered case and wandered to the jukebox. There was much to choose from, old and new. It was the finest collection of music, updated monthly, of any jukebox she'd ever seen. (A hand-painted sign taped to the glass corroborated Clem's opinion: "World's Best Juke." She selected Steve Earle and Cannonball Adderley and someone's cover of "Mule Skinner Blues." Another song, a dirge from The Smiths, wouldn't play.

She paused, swaying to the jangle of room conversation and, softer, music spitting from Frisbee-sized speakers cut from the walls. She steadied herself after, for a brief passage, having turned queasy from the stink of dark beer and burnt, oily kernels of popped corn. Spun around, buttocks pressed to glass, she looked at Z and, unconsciously, her lips lifted to a smile. Then she peered back toward the song list. Something for everyone, she thought. Degrees of pleasure right in this box of steel and wire and wax. For Sam and Garrett, her mother and, even, for Kendall. Something.

The moment remained isolated in time. Tumbled so clean it would shine, always, above nearly every other memory they attempted to hide it behind. Garrett was at the kitchen window, filling a glass with tap water until he stopped, faucet still running. On the top floor and in the basement, Sam and Tiff, respectively, were unhinged by the sound. Wind from a blowhorn, the belch of an eighteen-wheel truck, changing lanes on the highway at night.

The three of them found each other, without words, at the back door. They walked to the porch and waited for more. There was the sudden flash of color and then nothing, until, from the ceiling of their vision, they saw him moving on the slick roof of the warehouse.

"Clem's drapes . . . " said Sam, which was about the most intelligent thing anyone could think to say, considering the circumstances.

The burnt-orange drapes, once missing, had been stitched into tightly formed coveralls worn by Kendall. He was also dressed in a Stars-and-Stripes Speedo swimsuit fitted *over* the crotch of the outfit. There was a hockey helmet spray-painted gold and, similarly, rubber dish gloves and Wellington boots painted gold. Over his eyes was a pair of filmy-green aviator sunglasses. Tucked into his collar, cape-like, was a red beach towel cut to fringe at the bottom. Last, sewn across his chest in silver lame, were the interlocking letters *S* and *B*. In his right hand he gripped a gas compression horn which he wielded like a weapon.

It took an extended buckle of time for each to process the information. Let it run through their fingers like a fluid. If they weren't *this* close, family, it would all seem humorous. But they were too near the man, they smelled the sourness of his teeth, felt the gravel of his unshaved chin, so now there was only a stiff sharpness behind the warp of their chests. More than funny, Kendall was being led toward tragedy. A degree or two measured against the edge of a protractor: smile or frown.

Coming in the swallow and release of air, Tiff managed to speak a broken "*Oh.*" It served, for both children, as a leash to sobriety. Fearing movement, they let everything conjoin with arms held close to their sides, feet squared to floorboards. What must it have felt like? Think. Their father dressed like a comic-book character, a clown, shuffling on the rooftop. Two cars passing stopped, then a third and fourth. One man took Kendall's photograph with a camera he'd kept stored in his glove compartment. For Garrett, the discomfort made his skin itch, turn flaky at the calves and forearms. Sam's tongue inflated to something foreign, unusable, exploded against the wetness of jaw. The desire to be in another place, thought Tiff, thought all of them.

"What's he doing?" said one of the women who'd parked her car at roadside.

Before a response, Kendall again squeezed the trigger of the blowhorn. This time the sound, something crippled at seaside, lasted longer than a single beat or three. It continued to ring in their ears once the noise had ceased. They watched, voyeurs each, those who knew him and those who did not. A live-action Zapruder film busted across the network feed, waiting for the next rapid-served memory.

He spoke, but his words came too lightly, too lost, and none of them could hear what was said. He flapped his cape, vacationers ridding an afternoon of sand; he steadied his ankles on the tipped grade of the roof. When his head lurched back and forth in a repeated whiplash nod, another person, the man with the camera, suggested they call the police or fire department. Either will do, posed Sam. They both know the way.

Behind them all, car wobbling slowly, Mercer turned the engine off and walked to the foundation of the warehouse. She was carrying her medical bag and it remained in her hand, arm pulled straight, because, you could tell, she did not think this would take more than a few moments. The oxygen came to her in several nostril-spreading gulps. Then, coat buttoned low, scarf unknotted, she told her husband in a voice of reason, in the only voice she owned, to climb down. There was quiet after that except, if you listened closely, the muffled *ting-ting* of an open car door at curbside.

Instinctively, in the quick-twitch second hand before Kendall moved a muscle, the others began to depart. They'd seen it all, more than expected. This home spilled loose, again gutted to public. A slight fold came to his legs, as if he might coil for jump, the looped string to his bathing suit wagging below his waist. But no other surprise came. Instead, Kendall turned away, paused, and then walked to the ladder down.

Once Mercer had guided her husband, hand to gloved hand, into the house, disrobing him in the privacy of their bedroom, Sam and Garrett took seats at the kitchen table while Tiff shelled sweet peas for dinner. Both were listening hard, trying to hear what their mother might be saying to fill the afternoon with perspective. But to their ears, only the delicate footsteps of stocking feet. Garrett inched his chair to the wall so he might catch something from the heating duct.

"Get away," said Tiff, having spied Garrett's reflection in the darkened window.

They had each been struck by the new queerness, involving now their father, letting static tumble in their brains until it found a place to settle. The exchanges were practical: Help your father with his boots; Tiff can start supper; or, from Sam: My pen is leaving blots of ink. Finally, from Garrett first, the question: "Do you think Dad's crazy?"

Feigning disinterest, Tiff turned his attention to quartered chicken parts that had been left soaking in warm water. Sam crossed her arms; she tipped her chin toward a hanging light fixture.

"Shea Reynolds can't think of a man's penis without smiling," said Sam, seemingly apropos of nothing. "She says they *all* look just like little boys wearing those yellow rain hats, the kind with low flaps in the back."

"So . . ."

"To me, that's kind of crazy."

"What's your point?" asked Garrett.

"There's all kinds of craziness. I mean, remember that kid from Boardman who used to make those chugging noises, like a freight train, each time he got *near* the hockey puck?"

"For Christ's sake, Sam." Garrett let his eyes find the arch of Tiff's neck, waiting for his face to rise across one shoulder or the other. "It's *not* such a fine line—some girl laughing at a guy's dick isn't the same as Dad climbing onto the roof dressed like a . . . a . . . fucking loon."

"Enough," said Tiff.

"Well, he is."

After more talk, more to help it all register, Mercer passed through the kitchen to use the phone in the den. She offered, unprovoked, that he had been given a mild sedative and was now resting.

"It would be nice," said Sam, wiping dark ink from her hands, "if we could have Sloppy Joes every once in a while."

To that, Garrett scrunched his face and dropped his forehead to the edge of the table as if, by appeal, wondering where he could turn.

HE LAY WITH HIS BACK ON THE FLOOR, bared toes kicking at the wooden nobs to his dresser. Beside his head, in a paper cup, were the splinters from a bag of pumpkin seeds. Garrett used an old tie clasp, one that had belonged to his maternal grandfather, to pluck away the nutty draggle between his teeth. He was waiting for Sam to finish in the bathroom. The water would run and stop and then run again. Wind from the north came in anxious waves, rattling the window frames, pinning steel smoke flat to the horizon. Still, Garrett was waiting for his mother to call him and Sam to a room downstairs for reassurance. He wanted to hear in her words, in her familiar pattern of speech, that things were not so bad. That perhaps Kendall had simply been weakened by the stress of his work and long hours without sleep and, maybe, something less obvious, like dehydration.

But in truth, Garrett knew there was more. When it was all finished and the passersby had departed and his mother was leading his father into the house, Garrett saw a deadness to his father's eyes. Behind the tinted glasses, twin chips of coal. And though his mother remained calm, he could also sense worry in the way the skin of her face fell slack.

Evening heaved into night. Sam and Garrett prepared for bed, procrastinating with repeated trips to the bathroom, to the hall, for a chance listen or peek at whatever might be happening. Desperate for the explanation that would ring with sense: Of course, they might respond, in unison, *that's* why.

"She's been on the phone for a while," said Sam, standing in the doorway to Garrett's room.

Then came a sentence or two of Mercer's, pushed together. The bite of something serious. "I'm afraid," she said. Her voice sounded strained, an octave away from collapse. Then, reasonably, "I've got children."

This seemed enough for Sam, who, deflated, moved to her brother's bed and took a seat. Breath sugared from toothpaste, they sat leafing through old magazines. When Sam happened on a photograph of a car her brother liked, a 1967 Pontiac Firebird, she lifted the magazine and held the picture aloft. Garrett nodded, speechless too, and then returned to his article.

Long into the night, Garrett was awakened by sounds. He saw by the fleshy glow of the closet light across the hall only his mother's feet moving surely from one side of the room to the other. It took a moment for it all to return. None of this dreamed away, he thought. Images again rising from murky water at their own measured pace. There would be no simple answers to his father's behavior, none that would announce themselves to the mind of a teenage boy at night.

In other rooms of the house his sister and Tiff also had trouble finding rest. Everyone except, of course, for Kendall, whose own infected thinking had been dulled with drugs. At his side, still standing, Mercer folded the last of the laundry. Then she sat in a wicker rocking chair in the corner of the room surrounded by fresh-scented clothing. I'm helpless, she thought, until the creaky wag of the chair offered distraction.

Alcohol was forbidden on school property. Still, Sam and Doak sat in his car taking turns with a quart-sized bottle of beer. Not enough to bring drunkenness, only a pleasant warmth. Between pulls they munched spearmint lozenges, three at a time, to hide the rummy stink of breath. Light squeezed through the glass-block windows of the gymnasium reached them, in their quiet corner, laying kudzu-shaped shadows across Sam's face. Her dress, the velvety blue one from Clem, was crunched above the bend of her knees. She wore dark tights and flat-soled shoes, once white, that she and Tiff had dyed midnight blue in the basement sink. To battle the wind, she had her rarely used hockey-team letter jacket, wool with sleeves of leather. The high school didn't have organized hockey; in Lukin, it was a club sport. But over the years the team was loaded with talent, and it meant more to play hockey than, say, baseball or basketball or even football. A club, indeed. Stitched onto the left breast, connected, a furry L and G. Patches sewn to the sleeves trumpeted various league, tournament, and state championships.

As in many towns where the sport of young people took on disproportionate meaning, wearing this coat had value. There was a time, a couple of years earlier, when Sam had made the varsity, while Garrett was still a season away. She had been presented with a jacket which to her was simply another wasted item to store in her closet. One day, though, she stumbled upon Garrett, alone, modeling the coat in the mirror of her bedroom. From her position in the hallway, looking through the gutter crack of the door, she could see how important this *object* was to him, to others like him. He'd buttoned the jacket tight, spun, and then, half closed, buried his hands in the pockets of his jeans and leaned against Sam's dresser, casual, as if waiting for some girl he'd like to push from the ladies' room after a game.

Carelessly jacketed, chocolate stain kneaded to the collar, Sam wobbled along the pathway from the parking lot. Doak cupped a cigarette, hidden, holding the smoke until all was clear. He blew it hard into blackness from the corner of his mouth. Inside, streamers of orange and black crepe paper were looped to the ceiling, braided through iron rods soldered against open support beams. Themeless, this dance. Only leftover decorations from Halloween and last spring's graduation ceremonies, where, now used, enormous teal and pink flowers of papier-mâché hung from the walls in cellophaned vases. There was also shiny Mylar stapled to mortarboards dangling from the windows like oversized confetti frozen in mid-toss. The band was a group of local kids who called themselves Tenderfoot. Five boys, stock-still, stood on an elevated stage beneath one end of the gymnasium. Above them was a collapsed basketball hoop jackknifed into the rafters. They played cover songs, mostly, of loud, tinny groups like Led Zeppelin and Pink Floyd and Bob Seger and Foghat. Except for the lead singer, who had shoulder-length hair and wore denim painter's pants and a sleeveless oxford shirt, the rest of the band was surprisingly clean-cut. The bass player was dressed in a vested sweater and chinos.

There had been trouble before, when two boys from another school, musty from bar smoke and bourbon, were stopped at the door. They departed, abusively, escorted from the building by two gym teachers.

Seated on a roll-away grandstand, against the far wall, Garrett and a friend took turns monitoring the progress of Jessy Wicks as she bounced between various cliques of students. Dressed in chinos and a black turtleneck, Garrett nervously rubbed the bud of a pimple on the rise of his chin. There would be a slow song, he knew, late, the time to cauterize his nerves and, such a natural desire, to ask for a single dance. Realistically, there would be no howl of laughter, no tremor of disgust. Simply a *yes* or, at worst, the low whispered *no* followed by some words he would not hear. It held improper weight, this thing he wanted so badly. Only two people, he thought, brushing the skin of hands, bumping shoulders and waists for three minutes of music. Four minutes, maybe, but no longer.

It appeared to Sam, standing at the mouth of the double doors, that the twitchy-paced shaking of each couple resembled one of those vibrating toy football games where the players jiggle aimlessly across a thin sheet of metal painted turf-green. Doak, though not a student at Lukin High, had been permitted admission after prolonged discussions with one of the chemistry teachers because he was "dating" Sam. When Sam's eyes caught those of her brother, they exchanged short nods.

"It seems so *forced*," said Sam, dipping a cookie into a bowl of watery red punch. "All these islands of kids—here and in school—with no overlap. Just stuffed together for a Saturday night and told to have a good time. Play nice."

"Don't they?" asked Doak.

"Sure, until, say, that guy"—she was pointing toward a pudgy, bespectacled boy standing near the free-throw line—"sits in your seat during English . . . "

"Then?"

"Then you tell him to get lost or sock him in the arm or, most humiliating, simply stand over him, wasting no words, until he gathers his books, rises, and finds another desk."

"What about you?"

"What *about* me?"

"Do you let him stay in your seat?"

"Sometimes," said Sam, adjusting the seams along the front of her dress. "And sometimes I just sock him."

THERE WAS HONEY CAKE, for those in need, cut into fat brown slabs and arranged in whirlpool designs on three serving plates. One song was inhaled rapidly by another, making it difficult, unless you listened with promise, to know what the band was playing until, finally, a familiar guitar lick or refrain. During breaks, someone routed a long-running cassette tape through the public-address system. In truth, the prerecorded music was easier to talk against.

For Sam and Doak and, across the room, for Garrett, there was limited movement. Conversations of little relevance with others. Garrett's socks were new, binding, and he tugged their elastic mouths away from his calves with his fingertips, massaging the dimpled skin. The closest he'd come to actually dancing was during a fast song, while standing to stretch his legs and back, he'd shuffled his feet and winked his hips, side to side, nearly twist-like, arms hooked into pincers.

Not much else, until near the end. There was perspiration, as Garrett knew, which ran along his hamstrings and beneath the stocky wings of his shoulder blades. Head down, up, then down. She rested against a wall of painted cinder block, index finger trolling through the hard grid of negative space. Someone was talking at her side and, half interested, Jessy Wicks politely nodded. In his chest there was a choppy tumbling, like when a puck skidded near a goal he was tending.

Ten feet away, he checked his voice, speaking *hello-hey-hello* into his clavicle. The path he took, parabolic, broke around the hairy edges of her vision. He intended to remain concealed until he came within arm's length, so, he hoped, there would be no moment of strategy, no quickly devised excuse.

A tired revolution, body opening to a slow welcome when he spoke her name. It seemed he was more surprised by their proximity, their swapped greetings, than she. Filtered light from above turned her eyelashes, briefly, to turquoise quills. *She* reached for *him*. Almost, this was enough. He had to pause, take some time to remember why he'd stopped here. A breath, another.

"Good time?" he asked, swallowing the first part of his question.

"Sure. Isn't it always?"

He couldn't tell, now, whether she was being sarcastic.

"Did you drive?"

This, he knew, was a ridiculous thing to ask: If yes, would she think it mattered to him what kind of car she had; or was he just trying to jump past everything else and offer her a ride home? Too soon, he blurted out more:

"I mean, did you come with people?"

Still, not a way to save or sink him.

"Yeah," she answered, unaffected. "Layney and Jill."

When she said their names, both girls, who had been standing beside Jessy Wicks, smiled.

And then what he'd been waiting for this night, other nights. It had bunched inside him, warming and cooling, until finally, in a spot where he could choose action, he needed to rid himself of the spin-wrapped ball of lute string, ever living, so attention might fall elsewhere. Better to let fly with these decisions of import than allow them to rot.

"Dance?" he said, again losing what was supposed to come earlier.

"Uhh . . . " Two-beat count, lasting long enough for the expressions on Layney's and Jill's faces to register with Garrett. Neither girl, none of the three, was prepared and, sense lost, they each instinctively took steps backwards. "Yeah," said Jessy Wicks in a voice not devoid of pleasure. "Sure . . . "

Away they walked, together, far enough from each other so if you had been watching from a distance you might surmise at any moment they would part company on separate courses. But once a hole was found on the dance floor, they pushed close, tentatively, hands finding hands. A smell, citrusy, like mashed peaches, from Jessy Wicks', hair or skin or maybe even her warm breath against his cheek. This would carry him, he had the presence to know, for some while.

In the time it took to swallow, even against long dryness, they swayed in measured, ratchet-turn rhythm until, heavy-eyed, busy with thought, Garrett saw the start of everything from across Jessy Wick's, trim shoulder. A noisy scuffle near the tables of food beside the double doors. He could see two teachers, four, moving in rapid steps, arms high, to a tight crowd of students and, in a moment of wonder, he thought it had all passed. It had not, of course—the voices soon raised to shouts. More people jockeyed for better positions, truer views. The band halted mid-song, except for the drummer, who was late and slapped out an extra few notes.

The tug of curiosity gathered in Jessy Wicks, too. She twisted to face the action, craning her neck above and between the backs of her schoolmates' heads. Unprepared for this brevity, Garrett tried to nudge her toward the middle of the floor. When she dropped her arms to her sides, Garrett, struggling not to lose contact, ranged for the fingers of her left hand; he wanted to lock pinkies the way he'd seen couples do while walking the school's hallways between classes. Like so much here, he was balanced, precariously, along the fine crest of what was real and what he'd only imagined. His toy-figurine world brought again to life. She shrugged him loose, awkwardly, their knuckles dry and rough colliding in a quick sting. Embarrassed, running after too much, he watched what he'd hoped for melt into something different. Now there was only a desire to keep them on the same plane of thought—reciprocity in speech or pursed mouths or eyebrows lifted into lucky horseshoes.

Another loud voice led her into the pinstripe of bodies. All he could do was follow and pretend these final steps were taken in tandem.

Nearer to the scrum she moved around its wavy folds counterclockwise. Garrett was less intent, dragging behind. The punchy armor of elbows and heels shifting for space. Teenage moisture, pressed close, in a sour glaze of tangy secretions and cologned skin. Once he could see, unobscured, he locked onto the dark fence-post bangs of a boy he knew or, at least, remembered from another place, beneath the padded brow of a hockey helmet, the one worn by the guy who'd slugged Sam.

"You're *not* welcome here" said Mr. DePetro, who taught European history. "We warned you before. I can promise, if you don't leave immediately—for good—we'll call the police."

There was room hollowed from the crowd, expanding and contracting. To one side, the boy from the hockey game and his friend were being restrained by teachers and parents; to the other side, Doak, dangerously serene, who would have reached for the hunting knife holstered in his boot and, with a word from Sam, filleted both visitors. More worrisome to Garrett, who had worked his way to the front, was his sister. Already she appeared wounded; she stood uncharacteristically slouched, hunched, letter jacket yanked low on her shoulders. Earlier Doak had placed a cardboard Burger King crown on her head and now it was knocked askew, tilted so its painted gems wandered down the left side of her forehead.

During the sudden chew of time, Garrett, forming a crooked axis between his sister and Jessy Wicks, no longer had the ballast of wits. He hadn't considered things this way. Really, it was the freebie crown that moved him to "protect" the one person whom he imagined would never need his protection. The crown's gold and red and green, colors for a child, hung above Sam's fist-squabbed lip. Before Garrett stepped forward, he glanced to his side, longingly, for a final look at Jessy Wicks, who, by this time, had moved even farther away. She had again found her friends.

He was saved from speech. The boy from hockey, Mitch Pepper, pointed his index finger at Sam, at Garrett.

"It figures you'd do something fucking crazy," he said, tongue heavy and slow. "I mean, our *mailbox?*"

The squeak of shoes against the wooden floorboards behind his silence.

"I guess I should have expected that from *you,*" he continued. "It's like, with your mother and all, it makes sense this would run in the family. Go after something that can't fight back."

And in both Garrett and Sam, relief that the insult had come directed at Mercer. They had been steeled over the years against further damage. Relief, mostly, that there was not ammunition from the new lunacy involving their father. Garrett moved forward with no one reaching to halt him. A hot coin of anger twirled against his rib cage. He found himself, unexpectedly, inches from Mitch Pepper's face. Nearly a kiss, it might have seemed—breathing each other's breath, flecking spittle back, forth. Nothing else to save his sister or, for that matter, himself.

A Benzedrined heart thrumming so fast he considered, for an instant, the organ might have actually tightened around itself. But, of course, this was still a school with students and teachers and parents and a doughy assistant principal, Mr. Gally, who grabbed Garrett by his belt loops and pulled him away. Then, in another wave of hands, the crowd was spun apart and, resembling the strained *whuff* of a furnace, the music again started.

Before leaving, Garrett took a long drink from the water fountain near his locker. All this, said Assistant Principal Gally, would be discussed in greater detail on Monday morning. Though, reassuringly, he told Garrett his concerns were mostly about keeping the other boys away from Garrett and Sam and, of course, the school.

"Well," started Garrett, wrists pressed crooked against the car door, "that sucked."

Both Sam and Doak nodded, sharing another cigarette. While waiting for the engine to warm, they sat silently—Sam and Doak in front, Garrett stretched straight in back—watching the shadows move along the glassed ceiling of the gym. They began to drive, aimlessly, with the radio, AM, turned low. Occasionally, the scratch of someone's voice with news updates or weather for the next day. They tried to remember things about the boys, Mitch Pepper and his friend, wishing for a few sprinkled grains of Clementine's mind.

"I couldn't stop staring at his lower eyelid," said Garrett. "Here, right by the corner"—he was touching his own eye. "There was this black thing and I couldn't tell if it was, like, a pen mark or part of his skin."

"What a weasel." said Doak. "And his buddy. He kept turning his head to see, I guess, if someone was sneaking up on them. Hey, fuckhead! If I'm gonna kick your ass, I'm gonna do it from the front so you can watch."

Jimmied into the corner of her seat, armrest cutting along her hip, was Sam, breathing slow, clogged. So much of this, it seemed, belonged to the life of another person, someone un-Sam. Humping past her in crippled motion: Mitch Pepper and the decapitated mailbox and Doak and all of what she did and didn't understand at home. A text before her face so near she couldn't focus on the separate words, only letters, singled and paired, like puggy symbols.

Even in darkness the trees, soon-wintered, moved with fat yellows and crimson and a few, tucked back, with Popsicle orange. The blacktopped streets, tarred newly the previous summer, were traffic-less. Instinctively, the three drifted away from town; they followed roads that landed them where the weave of things unraveled, to the steam-punched end of factories and mills and refineries, to a softness that began with twin salt heaps the height of telephone poles. More driving while, from the rear left wheel, the clippy whine of something wiry shaken out of position. Rain-ulcered fields, specked with half hooks of broken wheat and cornstalks, framed both sides of the roadway. Farther from Lukin you could see, even on this weathery night, the sky busting free from the soot and chimney smoke. Then came snow in wet, nut-sized flakes which, on contact, turned to skittering beads of water against the windshield. All three of them had grown tired and, it was mutually decided, should stop for something to eat or drink.

They huddled in a windowed booth of a diner. It remained open always, it seemed, for passing truckers and weary travelers not unlike themselves. They drank colas and coffees and shared from plates of french fries and pancakes with thawed strawberry topping. What they needed most, really, were warm beds and undisturbed hours for sleep. Hands to cheeks, Garrett pulled at the tensile skin of his face, sodium-colored, resembling the shaded gray of his napkin.

"Did I tell you this?" said Doak. His voice was tired, raked with too many clouds of tobacco. "That beanbag chair in my room exploded. I sat on the damn thing funny and one of the seams popped. It, like, squirted pellets or beans or whatever that shit is inside all over the place. I got most of it, but some must have kicked into the hall. My uncle slid on a few kernels—I thought he was gonna put my face through a door."

Neither Sam nor Garrett responded other than, almost in unison, bobbing their heads. Outside, the light would break soon beneath a moist sponge of fog.

"You'd think he'd have mentioned something about the fire," said Doak, now referring to the burning hockey helmet he and Sam had left at Mitch Pepper's house.

Then only the sounds of dishes and flatware against flatware and the griddly sizzle from a window cut in the plasterboard wall of the kitchen. They drank more coffee and quick glasses of iced water and each, in turn, visited the restroom. Hunched over the porcelain urinal Garrett took a long, caffeine-hawked piss, the kind that came with such speed and abandon he wondered if it might blow off his pecker like a bottle rocket. Most of the time, Garrett chose to pee sitting down in a closeted stall. Standing for relief made him nervous. Not for obvious reasons: having some older guy beside him making conversation or peering down in judgment of dick size. For Garrett, in truth, it was about the mess of things, the mess *he* was capable of creating. When he was four or five, he'd had a surgical procedure to widen the pin path of his urethra. To a great extent, the operation was deemed unsuccessful. Before, and now after, the urine shimmied through a not-quite-right udder, a passage, scarred, only a fraction of a centimeter (*millimeter?*) too narrow. And awkwardly for Garrett, the result was a misty spray he could not fully control, his thumb over the brass mouth of a garden hose. Finished, he was often resigned to wrapping his hand in toilet paper, mittened, so he could wipe away the yellow drool and save embarrassment in other people's homes or one-toilet public bathrooms. He discovered it was easier to simply squat down, let the piss skitter, angled, from between his thighs like a woman.

Once, not so many months earlier, he'd missed the bowl in the upstairs bathroom of Will Baker's house. The floor was wood and, dejectedly, he laid swatches of toilet paper in jagged footprints to soak away the wetness. Simply a boy longing for his piss to dry while his friend, in another room, watched football on television.

BACK AT THE TABLE Doak had poured a fist of sugar onto one of the plates; he spooned a divot from the top, spilling in muddy coffee.

"Looks like mashed potatoes and gravy," he said.

Struggling for speech, the three watched a car pull into the lot as day broke behind the woodsy edge of the road.

"That's something I just never understood," said Sam. "The roof of that car—*see* it? Half is leather or vinyl or whatever material they use."

"It's called a Landau roof," said Doak.

"What's that mean?"

"Don't know. Maybe they're named after the guy who invented them."

"Christ, they look stupid." She was straightening her butter knife. "The worst is when they have tiny portals in the sides. The slanted or round ones like on Cadillacs."

"Or Lincolns."

They paid the waitress and wandered into the cold morning air. Doak pumped the gas pedal a few times, started the car and exited to the left, in a direction farther from town. After they'd gone another fifteen minutes or so, Doak turned the car onto an unpaved road which bit against the side of a small mountain. Eventually they reached a slight clearing, exposed space between forest, where they parked with the front bumper of the car kissed to an old fence.

"What's here?" asked Sam.

From Doak, no answer. He only stared into the windshield, moving once to wipe away smudge marks.

"It's too hard from inside," said Doak, finally.

He then sat on the hood of the car, boot heels locked to chrome grillework, and the others followed. Peering down the incline, you could see, in the near distance, a wooded field with tiny treeless pockets of white where fresh snow had found its grip. The three remained quiet and still for a while, maybe ten minutes, maybe longer. Until a bright orange flash, like a mirror hit with sunlight, and then the noise of dried kindling snapped into amplifiers.

"Hey . . . " said Sam against her cupped hands.

"Guns," said Garrett. "Rifle or shotgun."

It was the second day of deer-hunting season. Below was nearly seven hundred acres of land where Doak had once hunted, using a bow, with his cousin. A few years earlier, while they were practicing in the yard, his cousin's bow slipped and the arrow jumped back and skewered his ear. A knotty scar as long as a wood screw remained.

There was something horrific about watching the firecracker burst of light from the hill. They wondered, each, whether the animals had survived or been killed or, worst of all, had limped injured to some icy riverbank to collapse and die. Each time, the light and sound made Sam's stomach turn weak with the sickness of life lost.

Deeper into the rural landscape, another forty minutes away, the deer population was denser and, in truth, that's where most of the serious hunters spent their days. But from nearly the place where Doak had stopped, the roadside was lined with the parked cars and pickup trucks and campers of men (and some women) who hoped to land a meaty buck, head tall and thorny.

Soon, Sam grew tired of feeling the lump along the back of her throat climb and dip. She lay flat on the backseat of the car and rested, covering her eyes with the turn of her elbow. If she listened closely she could hear Doak's and Garrett's voices; she also imagined the cappy snap of gunshots, though, inside, it was difficult to make out their true sound. At last she drifted to sleep.

When she awakened, both Doak and Garrett were fitted into opposite corners of the front seat, eyes closed and mouths parted slightly. A thread of dried drool reached the break of Garrett's jawline. Propping herself against the door, Sam kicked high on the back of the front cushions.

"Get up," she said, repeating the phrase twice.

In a single motion, Doak started the car and pushed the heat fan to MED. Each of them wiped a hole in the moisture of their windows.

"I didn't think I was that tired," said Doak.

"Well, you were." Sam tugged at the waist of her tights, which had hiked into the small of her back. "We all were."

They let the car descend slowly, tires finding rumps and pits in the frozen mud. At first, again on the main road, they saw only abandoned vehicles and the spokes of dirty footprints leading away from civilization. When they spotted people, three men in orange-and-brown camouflage, they let the car ease nearly to a halt. The men were dragging a large buck by its antlers, twisting the head awkwardly against the grain of its body. There was no regard for the animal, dead or near-dead; they kicked it into position with the hard toes of their boots. A few yards down, two other men were fastening a tarpaulin of clear plastic across the trunk of their car to protect its paint from blood and the rough scratch of hooves. Beyond, where the land gave way to a planter's valley near the line of expanding timber, more men were pulling on the carcasses of other freshly killed deer. From the road you could see feathered streaks of crimson in the snow, spilled loose like toppled drums of waste. One man, crouched beside the tires of his truck, used a hunting knife to saw apart the belly on his buck. When the incision lifted from the blade, swollen cables of intestine slopped to the gravel and earth. The warmth of opened skin and muscle and kidney pushed a trail of steam into the air like tailpipe exhaust. Sam looked closely, her face pressed to the damp glass, and was able to spy the deer's eye, brown as cigar leaf, beneath the hazy ribbing of lashes.

On the roof of a station wagon two teenage boys were binding the feet of another deer with burlap packing rope and then wrapping the rest of its body against boxy aluminum support strips meant for skis or bicycles. Window lowered, Sam leaned out over her arm as the car rocked past the husk of another gutted deer. Then came the milky stink of chowder, sour and wet.

"This is making me sick," said Sam, refusing still to hide her face.

"Just meat," said Doak.

"No . . . "

Who was this boy? Other thoughts fought queerly for distraction in Sam's head. The Boone children shared a reasonable fear of sex, she knew from conversations with Garrett and Clem, based partly on the shadow cast by their mother's work. Despite information suggesting other truths, too often in their past they'd wondered whether babies—and *abortions*—were the natural outcome of intercourse. Later, armed with the knowledge of birth controls—varied, graphic—they also understood the fallibilities of even the best devices, through leaflets and overhead discussions involving their mother. Always, it seemed, their worlds were infected in places they'd imagined the harm would never seep. Basement couches, darkened movie theaters—not even safety coupled in the bed of a pickup truck. For each of them there had been, over time, extended intervals of pause when they drew near someone, like Doak, with whom they wished to kiss or cuddle. A closeness reconsidered.

Even after Sam and Doak had made love for the first time, she was apprehensive about allowing it to happen again. Only a few nights ago, both of them naked on the backseat of his car, she'd been lifted from the flurry of passion—body grinding against sweaty body—when she remembered having seen a familiar face, one of the protesters, while waiting at a traffic light. The blink of a memory, charging through her brain, proved enough to make her shove Doak away. And once again she didn't have the words to explain her discomfort. Maybe another night, she'd said, slipping into her jeans.

She was bumped to the present when her brother coughed. Then there was silence, mostly, for the remainder of the ride back toward town. Rounding the final crest into flatland, they could see through the front windshield rooftops of houses, snow-dappled, all the same height and angles, resembling with distance a cobblestone roadway. Once at the Boones' there were no words, only the light slapping-closed of car doors and, for these three, the common ground of having spent a long night together. In each, something different, moments they were likely to clutch into the loneliness and static of other days.

Both Sam and Garrett retreated to their rooms. At the end of his bed, Garrett made the box springs crunch as he removed his shoes, his clothing. For Sam, the effort was too much; she remained dressed, lying widthwise against the headboard. She tried to swallow her thoughts quickly, one after the next, so the shear act of thinking might this night tire her to sleep.

She considered larger issues: not simply that she and Doak weren't so much alike but, really, would it matter if otherwise. Were the troubles she (and her siblings) faced in romantic relationships normal for young people or, in fact, were they only magnified by the peculiarity of this home life?

eleven

She waved apart the cigarette smoke of others. Then, a nervous itch. Clem scraped her fingernails along the pebbly skin behind her bicep. She needed him, now, in this moment, more than he needed her. There was trouble, she'd been told by phone. She would test him with these words, nonsensical to her even.

"Do you want anything else to drink?" he asked, Z asked, surprised by how rapidly Clem had swallowed her coffee.

"No, thanks."

A familiar booth in the student union; their thumbprints on the saltshaker and sugar dispenser. Clem wiped her lips with a napkin, firm enough so they briefly lost color.

"Strange things are happening at home," she said, while she was still able.

"What do you mean?"

"My father is"—she paused, picking at unglued linoleum curling from a corner of the table—"he's losing his . . . mind."

"I thought you told me he was just kind of eccentric. In an artsy way."

"Now it's something else." She made herself breathe, slow and easy. "Once there was charm to the way he behaved."

"And?"

"And now he's, well, crazy."

She steadied her ass against the stretched vinyl seating. The only manner in which to do this, she had surmised earlier, was to let it all spill forth in rapid succession the way it had been told her by Sam and Garrett and her mother. Any stoppage meant lost momentum and a chance for Z to put his own spin on things, which, inevitably, would be tame by comparison to what had actually taken place. After a tiny *pop*, Z breaking the seal on a thimble-sized container of cream, she reached to the wall for reassurance.

"Remember I said he'd been disappearing for long periods of time?"

A nod.

"Well, he believes he's got some kind of *powers*. A couple of bottles of supplies busted open in his studio—nothing dangerous: mineral spirits, industrial hand cleanser. Obviously, he'd been headed down a bizarre path for a long, long while. But suddenly, from the noise of breaking glass or the smell of the stuff in the bottles, he just went into another orbit." She looked Z full in the face. "Something sometime would have made him snap. Now, though, he fancies himself a . . . a superhero. Or maybe a supervillian. They're not sure yet.

"Sam says he's been dressing in this costume, beneath his street clothes, and carrying around one of those blow-horn cans of compressed air. He's been aiming it at people—"

"Compressed air?"

She was trying desperately to finish, to let the story collapse beneath its own weight.

"I guess he's calling himself Sonic Boone." Here she paused for further reaction, but when his mouth parted and closed again, she continued. "Which, if nothing else, is clever. They haven't been able to talk much with him. And, really, he hasn't put anyone other than himself in harm's way. I mean, people—the *neighbors*—get scared by the noise. But that's it."

"Can he fly?" asked Z. And then, quickly, "Does he *think* he can fly?"

"Jeez," said Clem, caught by the peculiarity of the question. "I don't know. Maybe, because they told me he keeps climbing onto the roof."

She tried to gauge the sweep of Z's concern. Ultimately, would these odd circumstances be what scared away her first real boyfriend? Or would it be something that came later?

"He'd been creeping into danger at his own pace," she said. "Long before I left, even. But sometimes, when you're right on top of things, you can't gain perspective. You can't see the mess. Your face is pressed too close to the screen—and there's only the fuzzy blur of dots."

She sounded too dire, she realized. Also, too profound. She changed tacks.

"It's kind of like leaving home. I thought so much of this place would be different. And lots of it is. But really, some days I think it's nearly the same. That Providence is a larger version of Lukin, except with an ocean."

He smiled; he tapped a plastic stirring stick against the side of his cup.

"The doctor told my mother he thinks it's a chemical disorder," said Clem. "He doesn't know for sure because my father won't be tested. He won't even visit the doctor's office. Maybe it can be treated with medication, maybe it can't."

"And maybe it's nothing."

"It's not *nothing*. Have you been listening?"

"Sure," he said, a little too quickly. The speed of his response made Clem think, in truth, if he had been listening it was not closely. "But we all want to hide from something. We all want to slip on another identity every once in a while."

"Christ, this isn't about a man—my *father*—wanting to play comic-book hero. I'm telling you he's not normal"—she knocked at the side of her head with a finger—"and he needs help. He hasn't been normal for . . . well, maybe for*ever*."

A set of papers, folded and official, were removed from Z's notebook. He pointed to a line near the top, beneath a stamp from the registrar's office, requesting a name. It read, Alexander Churnip.

"What's this?" she asked.

"Me." He waited. "I always hated the name Alex, so when I got here, I decided to have people call me Zander . . . which begat Z."

"All that stuff about your parents and Zorro . . . "

"Made it up."

Confused, she leaned away. She had meant for this to be about *her* life; she'd been prepared to uncloud some mistiness in *her* world. To remain honest, true, for the sake of them. Him and her. Now he was wiping clean the window to a deception he had carried. Something as small as dropping a few letters to his name, something as large as not knowing his name.

"And you wouldn't even tell me?" she said, voice brittle and low.

"I *am* telling you," he said. "In the beginning, when I said all that shit, I didn't think we'd, you know, be together. Like a couple. Dating."

Everything had mashed around. She'd been shoved away, a half spin of the bottle. In the catch of a breath, gone from fragile to fire. No longer did she shield herself but, instead, she plowed forward.

"What else?" she asked, strength gained from a wrong place.

"About?"

"About you? What else don't I know?"

"Probably a lot."

"Probably."

They sat across from each other, letting the anger grow. From him, a lie unfurled in the bull's-eye of a delicate moment; from her, the irony of not showing compassion in the time she most needed some. Whipsawed, she thought, having come up empty on both sides. Perhaps the same for him.

IF ONLY A WEAKNESS. A vampire's garlic, Superman's kryptonite. Some way to corral Kendall's Sonic Boone into the car, into the doctor's office. Lead this man, father and husband, away from the jumble of disorder. On the living-room phone, Mercer spoke with a medical specialist, the friend of a friend, swapping terms that sounded disturbing, unwieldy to Sam and Garrett seated against the far wall. For dinner, there had been fast food from Dairy Freeze. Between her blue-jeaned thighs, Sam used a straw to dig at the remaining ice chips of her Coke. On the couch, Garrett dragged onion strands into a smear of ketchup on the paper of his hamburger. They believed, all three, that Kendall was in his studio.

It seemed that between incarnations of his alter ego Kendall had been working. On recent afternoons when Mercer had gone looking for her husband, she'd discovered, instead, the wet debris of time spent actively. Torn sheets of yellow legal paper masking-taped to canvases and coated with the glaze of shellac; heavy applications of paint, thick as hot fudge, drizzled with a soup ladle or long barbecue fork so the colors would mix along its tilted tines. She saw he'd used body parts still fresh in paint: India ink rubbed with eyelashes; indentations left by ears, nipple, tongue.

Other enormous canvases, larger than humans, against the front wall. Departures for Kendall. One seemed almost kitschy: a collage of photographs snipped from old movie-monster magazines that had belonged to Garrett. (Not so many years earlier, Garrett would buy the magazines and keep them at his side while watching late-night horror films on a chargeable TV in his closet. He liked to read about how the creatures were invented, using makeups and prosthetics, so he'd be less afraid. Proof in the pages they were not real.) In the upper left corner of the canvas, a papier-mâché head dipped in muddy green pushing outwards, 3D-like, resembling some hybrid Frankenstein-*slash*-vulture face. Mercer could see the filmy words of newsprint peaking through along the cheeks and eye sockets.

Another frame, wobbly, situated so one side formed an open corner with the "monster" piece, right-angled, was as clean and simple as the others were cluttered. Fat black strokes against stipply white. Then, near the painting's bottom, the watery bleed of gray. Inspiration here, Mercer knew, came from an exhibition she and Kendall had visited on the works of artist Franz Kline. Years ago, before children even. For days afterwards Kendall fingered a postcard replica of a painting called *Mahoning*. The name, too, of the county in which they now lived.

To Mercer, studio contents inventoried, it seemed her husband had condensed a lifetime of work, of style variations and changes, material choices, into only a few months. Eating a sectioned grapefruit over the kitchen sink, days before, she allowed an uncomfortable smile to break across her face while imagining that her husband's "special powers" might involve speed. Perhaps, she considered as she dumped the leathery rinds into the trash, he knew his hold to this life was turning flaccid. So much left to slide between the vents of his fingers.

The talking continued, Mercer's voice into the telephone, now distant and uninteresting—a transistor radio through a single earpiece dangling at the neck. Sam and Garrett carried laundry that had been folded and stacked on a table in the hallway to the second floor. Each had a few items that belonged to their parents and they piled them on Mercer's dresser. Garrett fiddled with the TV remote control resting on his mother's night table; it was an older model, one of the first, a Zenith which used metal cylinders to send acute sound waves toward the set. He liked to hold the remote to his mouth and punch the buttons, feeling the ring against the fillings of his teeth. Across the room, Sam snooped through her mother's closet. Shoes and sweaters and slacks and little that caught her interest. The thought coming to each of them, in a slightly different manner, was that no one else on the planet—not even Clem hundreds of miles away—knew what this felt like except the other. Brother and sister.

"They might give him electrical shocks," said Garrett, half joking. "Maybe they'll bring over a home kit."

Every five hours or so you could hear a whistle sounding a shift change at one of the nearby mills.

"This'll be weird," said Sam. "Weirder than normal. Weirder than anything else."

Garrett nodded, no longer playful. He watched his sister try on a few hats hanging from an antique coatrack in the corner. She modeled them briefly, in the mirror, before coming to rest in a wicker rocking chair with a view of the window. A sudden taste on the back of her tongue, vaguely familiar, sweet like roasted vanilla beans. Her senses were instantly rewired behind a waft of unboxed mothballs.

"It's not so easy," said Sam, chair squeaking under her buttocks. "Not like at school, say, if you fail a test and the teacher decides to give you a makeup exam or extra-credit project. Nothing like that for Pop." She rarely called her father "Pop"—only when she was feeling muzzy with sentimentality. "This is gonna be brutal."

"Uh-huh," said Garrett, and then, "What about Mom? How do you think she's doing?"

"Mmmm." She swallowed oxygen. "You know, not terribly. I think now she's busy taking care of things, getting him better. At least she's no longer in that gray area. Wondering why he's behaving so strangely. She knows he's *not* fine. This—"

"—ain't just his personality."

Motionless, together, until Sam scratched her elbow and Garrett again spoke.

"How do we know when it all began?" he said. "Like, tracing it back, where does the line of stuff that's just Dad end and the real craziness start? It kinda gives you the willies. Thinking about shit that happened with him—when he took us to fly kites on the roof of the Durax Steel warehouse or taught us to paint with our toes—it's hard to shake loose what was *really* him."

Distilled to its purest condition, this, ultimately, was what mattered to Garrett and Sam and Clem far away: What were the honest details of their father? Which of his characteristics could they rely on? Similar to time spent with an addict: What part of the cocktail was symptoms and what part was simply natural behavior?

It would have been wiser to relieve the regular pressures with tiny gasps instead of infrequent, but seismic, explosions. Several months earlier, Sam, seated on the porch, had been sharpening her skates when her mother called to the studio from the kitchen window; Kendall had been fiddling with some electrical wiring, which resulted in the blowout of two fuses. Though he didn't answer, moments later he could be seen connecting three scavenged antennas to the warehouse roof.

"Enough!" shouted Mercer.

This seemed a wonderfully appropriate word to describe so much of the nonsense hovering around her parents, thought Sam. Against the gnaw of stone rubbing steel blade, Sam wondered why her mother tolerated the eccentricities—the *lunacy*—of Kendall. But as Mercer yelled out again, Sam lost the path of her anger—she turned the hot impatience on her mother.

"You're screaming in my ear!" said Sam, in a tone she'd used only once or twice before with either parent.

When Mercer failed to respond, instead standing in the door frame, elbow braced against the wooden molding, Sam's temper only grew. There was a surplus of ammunition—nights awake, recently, filled with the guilt of a teenage girl feeling at last comfortable with the rustle and spill of her own body. How could she reconcile these triggers for creation with the finality that came from her mother's hand? And what if, ultimately, Sam decided, after this antagonizing wait, that her way of thinking didn't coincide with her mother's? How to choose the other side against this parent, against these siblings? Hadn't she already witnessed too much, been led too far down the river?

As Sam prepared to speak with some flare of anger positioned for damage against her mother, the great geyser of hostility seemed to close around itself. Simple and quick. A vision had come suddenly into Sam's head: how much pain would this bring Mercer? To know with reasonable clarity that Sam had begun to question a belief at the very heart of Mercer's existence. And so, stealthily, Sam let her concern break loose in a less confrontational manner.

"I'm not sure," began Sam, letting the skate rest on her lap, "I could ever have an abortion."

"That's fine," said Mercer, sounding surprised by the new weight of their conversation. She took a step closer to her daughter. "That's good."

"Good?"

"I meant, it's good that you're thinking for yourself—though I hope you're never put into a position where you have to make that decision."

After another step, Mercer sat down beside Sam. Together, the two of them watched Kendall wrestling with the antennas and a spiral of loose wire.

"It's harder after giving birth," said Mercer. "Now, with three wonderful children, I can't imagine having an abortion myself."

Sam nodded, though, in truth, she couldn't possibly know what it felt like to be pushed to the brink of such a choice. All this—the prostesters, the insults of strangers, the moral dilemmas—was only a yeasty haze hiding a fear twittering through some cold, lonely girl seated in a blousy hospital gown while she waited for her life to change. As she waited for the pieces to a memory she would keep for a long, long time.

There was more Sam wanted to say, but before she could organize her clutter of thoughts, a loud noise came from across the yard. It was Kendall, of course, who had dropped a plank of plywood. Then, to Sam's left, Mercer rubbed the back of Sam's hand with her warm fingers.

Again, months later in her parents' bedroom, Sam felt for the phantom touch of her mother's thumb for reassurance. She left her brother, briefly, before returning from the kitchen with a jar of peanut butter and Ritz crackers. Sam sat in the floor, Indian-style, digging into the box for the ones that remained unbroken. She spread choppy waves of peanut butter on the crackers and stuffed them, full, into her overcrowded mouth. When she spoke, clots of oozy cracker rose and lowered in the corners of her lips.

"More," she managed, between huffs and bites. "She was talking about *satellites.*"

"What about them?"

"He thinks they're being programmed to control him."

"As Principal Freeman might say, 'That's *rich.*' "

They both smiled.

These two, marching nearer adulthood, had been hitched to independence sooner than most. They had grown accustomed to a certain chaos that would find them in the mock-safety of . . . *home.* A quick, funny word which to the Boones sometimes invoked degrees of doubt and mistrust. Where, truly, could they find comfort but in the company of one another? For some families, reasonably, the inadequacies of one parent unloosed a compensation in the other. But here they were left to seek a hopefulness that existed elsewhere.

On this night they watched television without the sound. It was the best way, really, because it seemingly made things move at an exaggeratedly fast or slow pace. ("Hasn't that guy been on for a long time?" asked Sam about a man selling cleaning supplies.) Moving comic strips, flickery in blue light. Occasionally, they provided speech for those on screen.

"Your money or your *wife?*" said Garrett, filling in the voice of a pistol-wielding tough.

Near-malaprops coming from both with each channel change, though it was unlikely either knew what the word actually meant.

"But . . ." started Sam, pretending to be a teary-eyed woman on a soapish serial. "How could you be dating her, too? I thought we were in a *monotonous* relationship."

"Nice one." And then, watching a father put his young child to bed, "Good night, sleep tight and don't let the *big birds* bite."

She shrugged and dropped a couple naked crackers onto her tongue. They could no longer hear their mother in the room below. Things lingering to be settled in the next few days. A family meeting, another. Decisive choices for Mercer, punched off rapidly, until alone one night in her bedroom, all completed, she would let the easy quake of emotions seethe loose. Then, perhaps, she'd be called from the kitchen by one of her children with a question about the expiration date on a carton of milk, or something equally innocuous, and she would tumble onward.

THERE WAS ICE the night before. Enough so it appeared the entire town had been grabbed by its furry roots, dipped into a bowl of water, and forgotten in a meat locker during darkness. The branches of trees hung low and heavy into power lines and rooftops. One half expected a strong breeze would bring the tinkling of wind chimes. Seated at the kitchen table, Garrett ate a brown-sugar-frosted Pop Tart while leafing through the morning newspaper.

"Do you ever read *Blondie?*" he asked.

Sam, who was scratching the black from a piece of rye toast, shook her head.

"It's so messed up," he said. "I mean, everyone is dressed normally except Dagwood. He's gotta wear some goofy bow tie and a shirt with this single button the size of a manhole cover."

Sam shrugged. She was spooning strawberry preserves from the jar.

"What's fair about that?"

Chewing toast while she stood, Sam held her hand near her neck to catch crumbs.

"Garrett," she said, "if you're trying to sound like Dad, you're on your way."

He made a noise like a steam shovel and then pushed the paper away, folding it awkwardly, against the crease. The night before, besides ice, Garrett had found sleeplessness. He'd wandered downstairs to a place on the couch. After rolling himself in a throw blanket, burrito-like, he listened to the ticking of freezing rain against the windows and side paneling. From above his head, in an ashtray on the end table, came the smell of burnt tobacco. He reached to finger the stubby tail of a cigar his father had been smoking before he'd gone away. It was still moist with his saliva, deformed by the craggy shifts and banks of his teethmarks. Beneath stale ashiness, in the palm of Garrett's hand, the brown turd reeked of his father's breath. They had taken him, earlier that afternoon, to be examined for a few days. At least that's what their mother had announced. Mercer and Tiff guided him to the car, balmed with medicines Mercer had slipped into his orange juice. In his hair, still, dried scabs of paint.

"So," began Garrett, crinkling the Pop Tart wrapper into his napkin, "what do you think he's doing now?"

"Dad?"

He nodded.

"Wondering where they hid his costume and horn."

"Really."

She took a seat across the table from him, resting her chin against her knuckles. The whole of her face constricted with worry, as if, during this exact blister of time, she'd begun thinking about the entirety of her father's life.

"I don't know," she managed, finally. "I have no idea what he's doing."

"Do you think . . . " said Garrett, refusing to look upwards. "Do you think he's in any pain?"

"No." She shook her head for emphasis. "Mom wouldn't let that happen."

"Maybe she doesn't know. They could be sticking him with needles or something."

She tightened her eyes.

"Shit, don't you think he's scared?"

She shrugged. To her, it seemed what he was really asking was if *she* was scared. After a creaking behind the wall, their mother rose from the basement door. She managed a smile, quick and low, more from the surprise of catching both children in the house before they'd departed for the day than anything else. Although a gameless Saturday, Sam and Garrett had hockey practice; they'd stacked their duffels and sticks against the porch.

"Well . . . " began their mother, bracing herself against the countertop with both hands.

But before she could continue, the interruption of more sound as Tiff let himself in through the back door. Recently, he'd been sleeping in Clem's room. The previous night offered a rare reprieve; he stayed in his apartment.

No voices, the only greetings came in nods.

"It's good you're here," said Mercer, watching Tiff unfasten two buttons on his coat. "I should probably only struggle through saying this once."

The cuticle-shaped pouches beneath Mercer's eyes had grown so dark it appeared she'd been struck or, maybe, she'd been sloppy with her fingers and charcoal pencil.

"There aren't any answers yet. And really, I'm not sure as time passes they'll be presented to us in ways we can understand. He was"—she slowed—"he was not doing well for a while. You could see that. But there was more you didn't know. He had tried to remove our entire savings from the bank. He had also tried, for God knows what reason, to buy a *wheat thresher* using two of my credit cards."

Into Sam's head, divinely, came the distraction of recent moments she could lock along her sights. Nothing to do with anything. The fibery strand of repetition: the tugging of elastic as she slipped on her elbow pads, shoulder pads, kissed Velcro against itself. Taping still shin guards above stockings. Then, only two days earlier, the cable of something finally good to bend free after the time when she'd been punched: she'd skated, alone, before the others reached the ice; she'd executed a parlor trick, one she'd been doing her entire life. But it was nice. The face of a friend gone away. Moving faster, from rink's end to end, she'd lifted the puck with the curve of the stick; she'd kept the puck aloft by tapping it with the sides of the stick blade, front then back. All eye-hand coordination. The glimpse of long hours of practice or, instead, the gift of talent.

"I'd like to believe—for *all* of us to believe—he will get better. But also, I don't want to mislead you. Maybe he will only get worse."

She then used an analogy that seemed overly simplistic to everyone in the room. Perhaps she wanted to continue speaking, not lose them in medical jargon or tears. She compared Kendall's condition to a sheet of damp rice paper. "Once it begins crumbling apart," she said, "there is no paste to make it whole again."

Garrett responded with the only thing that made sudden, unblinkered sense. "He's not coming back."

And then, together, they realized that the prospect of seeing Kendall under comfortable, recognizable circumstances seemed remote. Their lives, here, had been slapped to yet another course.

"I hope you're wrong," said Mercer.

She'd been treading carefully around the plain truth her son had, in a blow, rubbed clean. If abandonment, in one of its many forms, was to find this family, she had reasoned earlier, then now was as appropriate a time as any. These two, and Clem, had strong ankles. They could carry the weight of their young bodies.

"It's all so confusing," she said. "I'm not sure what he's capable of doing. Whether he's a danger to himself, to us."

She let the air come and go. She described Kendall's first hours away. Hospitalized. How, initially, he seemed equipped to creep back to normalcy. He was courteous with the medical staff—helpful, even. Until a sudden sting by this anthem of disorder caused him to erupt into violence. He attempted to skewer one of the nurses with a floor lamp; a doctor nearly had his jaw smashed with the lid of a disconnected toilet seat.

"I cannot . . . " She searched for a delicate means. "It's so hard. For everyone. Waiting and wondering. What space would he need to reach for it to be right again? What gauge would we use? Who decides?"

Beneath the table, Garrett allowed his knees to unlock.

"I need a cigarette," said Sam, though in the room only Garrett knew she snuck an occasional smoke. "Not even a whole one. Just a drag from something unfiltered. A Pall Mall or Lucky Strike."

After passing through a few moments of silence, Tiff finally removed his coat. "I've got a *lucky strike* for you," he said, finding an empty hanger.

A shrug from Sam, then her mother.

"If I only had a better sense of things," said Mercer. She ignored her daughter's hand, cupped against an invisible cigarette. "I wish I could impart some wisdom that worked. Like keeping a swollen foot elevated. Advice that would promise results down the road, no matter how strange it might sound."

At her side, Tiff surrendered a mug of hot water and sliced lemon.

"Later it may all seem obvious."

"Or not," said Garrett.

"Or not," she repeated.

Even as she spoke, they knew the results of this puzzle. None of them could imagine a pleasant ending. Only Kendall in another place.

CLEM HAD DECIDED, earlier, not to return home until school broke for spring holiday. A self-imposed exile. After eighteen years she needed, for her own good, the discipline of distance. Trust your instincts, she repeated during this time of unrest with family. Similar to words she'd once been told by a teacher about multiple-choice answers on an exam: When in doubt, go with your initial guess. All trouble in Lukin would be resolved with or without her assistance in tiny chores, like packing bologna sandwiches against the kitchen counter. Over the previous few days, she'd been mashing coins into the pay telephone in her hallway. She spoke with her face buried deep in the phone cubicle, shoddily soundproofed with plaster- and corkboard that had been picked and cut and graffiti'd by dorm mates. Twice, she was awakened with a kick at her door to get calls from Sam coming after midnight.

No repairs, she knew, would rise from her hand. Only to wait. There were few here in whom she could confide. In conversations with The Boy, to his face, she insisted on calling him Al-ex-AND-er instead of Z or Zander or anything else. Once, under her breath, she even caught herself saying, "There's not even a Z in your name." She hadn't been able to sort through the debris: was he making things worse or better?

The betrayal, keen or dull, had served as a shiny object to distract her thoughts from spilling toward what truly mattered. Home. A big hoop burning in gasoline as she pedaled her bicycle in, imperfect circles, faster then slower then faster again, preparing a circus jump.

Sleep found her in petite bundles, mostly in the early evening and in the late, late night. At sunrise over the past couple weeks she'd made a habit of walking to a nearby bakery for a scone and fresh coffee. Bound in heavy overcoat and muffler, she then wandered to the shoreline and watched as the men's crew rowed past, nine at a time, in long wooden racing shells that whistled against the water. Comfort arrived in the muddy waves and in the rowers, who were dissimilar to anyone or anything in the town where she was raised. Her nerves were sated by the new sounds of creaking oarlocks and heavy breathing and the even tenor of the coxswain's voice announcing stroke counts. She knew these men only by sight, not by name. Sometimes on her way to class she would pass one of the rowers, dressed in street clothes, and it would take her a moment to put the face to a place. She almost wanted to say hello, ask them what it was really like out on the water with the sun lifting higher and cold beads of perspiration welling behind their ears.

Soon there would be snow that stayed. The crew would move practices inside its boathouse until early spring. Then, maybe, she would come back. She imagined by March or April so much in her own life would have changed. Surely, she would have grown tired of the blandness of scones.

Returning to her room on this morning for a warm shower and schoolbooks, she passed a second-story porch where students, all male, were cooking coiled sausage on a charcoal grill. There was bottled beer but, she figured, it was from hours earlier. One of the boys smiled, his eyes gummy and dark. He was wearing only a sweatshirt, the bottoms to a pair of long underwear, and sandals with tube socks. She had these periods, especially now, where she felt as if she'd stepped away from everything close and was watching it click past on a child's View-Master. Each experience was a small square of film on the circular card to be peered at from binocular sockets. She could stare for as long as she liked but, once the trigger was pulled, there was no going backwards. One direction only.

She saw herself plodding along, waiting for someone to take hold and lift her onto their shoes as a father does when dancing with his baby daughter.

On the walk to her dorm, she smashed her feet into puddles only three or four temperature degrees from ice. In the lobby, one of her suite mates, Terri Howard, was reading the school paper and drinking grapefruit juice from a pint-sized carton. They rarely spoke, Clem and Terri. Not because they didn't get along but, in truth, because they hadn't spent more than thirty minutes in each other's company since the school year began. What Clem knew about her came mostly from things she'd overheard or been told. Terri was from the South, a small town near New Orleans, and the first day of inclement weather, in late September, she bought herself two winter coats with money she'd saved from summers waiting tables. She was supposedly a terrific clarinet player, though, remarkably, she had refrained from even removing the instrument in her room. She practiced in small band carrels at the university's music department.

Clem decided to take off her boots before ascending to her room on the third floor; her socks were sopping wet. She sat across from Terri, listening to the pages of the paper wave from one hand to the other. Finally, Terri heard the sticky struggle of Clem, hunched over, unlacing her boots, and raised her head.

"Where're you coming from?" she asked, her r's rolled with a nasally twang.

"Just walking." She massaged the coldness from her bare feet. "Got a cup of coffee."

"You have early classes?"

"Not too. Today at nine-thirty."

"This is my early day," she said, folding closed the mouth on her grapefruit juice. "I've got psych at eight-fifteen."

A nod of acknowledgment from Clem. Then the two exchanged long glances in sleepy silence, waiting for the other to speak or smile or adjust a piece of clothing. Right before Clem prepared to stand, Terri coughed, lightly, suggesting she might have more to say.

"My brother lives in Alabama," she announced. She stopped, scanning the area around where she was seated as if she'd suddenly become aware of an object she had lost. "He's not really there by choice. I mean, he is and he isn't. He can live wherever he wants. Mostly, I think, he wants to live back in Louisiana. But it's too hard for him."

Terri was making eye contact. Clem began feeling self-conscious and busied herself by straightening her boots and socks against her lap.

"A few years ago my brother went fishing with this buddy of his in a swamp not far from where we were raised. The two separated late in the afternoon. The next day they found the guy face down in water, drowned, with a fat red welt against his forehead. Though he probably just caught his waders against a vine or something in the dark, tripping himself and hitting his head, lots of folks thought there might have been foul play. That maybe my brother hit the guy.

"Afterwards, people looked at my brother real strangely. You could see doubt in their faces at restaurants and stores and movie theaters. Wondering if he'd killed the guy or not. It was silly, really. Of course he *didn't.* But there was always that hint of a question. He just couldn't deal with things anymore. So he finished college—at L.S.U.—and moved to Alabama. Now he's working sales for a food distributor." Here she took a few easy breaths. "It's not so bad now. When he comes home, for holidays or visits, the tension seems less. But I suppose it'll always be there in some form. For the rest of his life."

Clem could only manage to purse her lips.

"I don't know why I told you all that," said Terri. "I guess I heard you were going through something with your father."

A warmness filled Clem's cheeks.

"People talk. That phone in the hall isn't so private." Terri drank more of her juice. "It gets better and worse and better and eventually people find another thing to stick their noses into."

Neither of them had anymore to offer. Clem told Terri she hoped that one day, soon, she too would be able to look back on this time with a sensible perspective. She then thanked her and scaled the stairs to her room.

You never know the place from where hope will announce itself, she thought. Some girl from a state she wouldn't recognize on a map.

twelve

A head-high fence of blighted steel wire ran the entire length of the block. Wintered vines, dried stiff, knitted themselves through the gaps between comb-straight fence posts. There was a coldness to the air so genuine it bid the trees to speak, pushing creaky sighs from their torsos. The taste of moisture came from snow of early afternoon or, perhaps, more that was expected later in the night. A brick pathway began at the entrance gate, which had been strapped closed with padlock and heavy chain. Near the bend of the corner a trough had been carved beneath the fence. They needed to clear the snow with their gloved hands so they could wedge themselves into the other side. First went Garrett, then Sam. On their left was a gigantic tin-encased generator for those times when the town's power would collapse or, here, if eager protesters had severed the outside lines.

The snow was damp, sticky, and Sam fussed some into a tight ball as they walked past rows of naked shrubbery. So still was the night they almost expected to hear words spoken from their mother across town; she could simply wander onto their porch and, in a normal, unstrained voice, call them both home for rest. In his right hand, Garrett carried a weathered black medical bag that had once belonged to Mercer. She'd given it to him when he was six or seven to tote around his toys.

"My toes are freezing," said Sam.

"Try wiggling them."

"Yeah," she said, almost sarcastically.

They skewed off the pathway, lifting their feet nearly to their knees to avoid abandoned humps of shoveled snow. A tall, narrow light spire, similar in appearance to the Washington Monument, stood beside a collection of low stone markers with flood bulbs screwed into their faces.

"Maybe ten more minutes," said Sam, before her brother could speak.

A night earlier, Doak said he'd try to meet them if he could get off from work. They were supposed to wait until ten-thirty.

"Do you have heartburn?" asked Sam, watching her brother clear snow and ice from the ledge of one of the larger markers with the hacked-off handle to a hockey stick.

"No."

"That chili was too spicy." She rubbed her coat at her sternum. "There should have been more beef or beans or sauce or something."

"I like it spicy."

"Me too. Just not that much."

She burped and then, playfully, blew it toward Garrett. He waved his hand past his face as if scattering fruit flies. This was their first shared visit to Mercer's clinic, close enough to touch its walls, in maybe a lifetime. Slowly, he began unpacking the goods from his medical bag. Against the granite surface of a decapitated pillar, Garrett laid out six tubes of red cardboard the size of a paper-towel roll. Raking snow with the insteps of her boots, Sam formed small towers and curbs; she buried sticks perpendicular to the ground in a random pattern.

"For trees."

She dropped to her knees, using the fingers of her gloves to push out details: windows and swimming pools (with bark chips for diving boards) and palm prints to clear parking lots. A jagged crust of ice, unbroken, lowered carefully behind an L-shaped mound to depict a skating pond. Stones were placed side to side, tightly, creating a driveway into one of the pinched hills.

Afterwards, she lay back with her head in her hands and stared across what she'd sculpted. Her eyes caught on a row of decorative stones near the fence.

"Remember when we used to have ice cream in Mrs. Cullen's class?" she asked, referring to a third-grade teacher she and Garrett had shared a year apart.

Standing for warmth, Garrett nodded.

"See those stones." She gestured with her elbow, from the ground. "Don't they look like the ice cream they gave us?"

The slabby-tablets of ice cream, chocolate and vanilla, came wrapped in white paper that students peeled away before spooning over runny marshmallow sauce. Sometimes, when they were given bowls instead of saucer plates, Sam would let the ice cream and marshmallow bleed together into a soup.

"I don't think he's coming," said Garrett.

Sam had now turned onto her stomach. She was cutting a block of 'ice cream' from the snow.

"No," she said, dropping her hand in a slow karate chop against the four edges of the rectangle. "And someday . . . " she began, headed elsewhere with the thought, "he will have two children and a striped necktie and gray in his hair."

"Huh?"

"And I will be some girl he knew when he was young. And you'll just be that girl's brother."

"Maybe." Garrett was now bouncing on the balls of his feet. "But he *won't* have a striped necktie."

"Probably not." She sat upright and brushed the loose snow from her back and shoulders. "It's hard to say." And then, because this was what she really wanted to know, "Do you ever miss something while it's happening?"

"What do you mean?"

"When you think what you're doing is absolutely right, and the next week or the next day or even the next minute you won't feel exactly the same. About anything."

"I guess."

Gloves shed, her hands disappeared into the pockets of her coat.

"Why?"

"I don't know." She removed a large silver lighter, massaging the lid with her thumb. "It just came into my head the other day when I was thinking about things. Mostly about Dad. How he always seemed—always *seems*—to be able to make those moments last longer. While he's painting or fixing something or even flaking out, he's got this focus."

As Garrett squirmed in the cold, she could tell she hadn't reached her brother.

"I'm not saying he's aware of all this shit. Just that some part of him runs at a different pace, notices what we don't. And that's maybe one of the reasons he doesn't always fit."

"Yeah, I can see that." And he did. "But I think there's a bigger part of him that's just gone sour."

When Sam didn't answer right away, Garrett raised his arm and asked for the cigarette lighter. He took a few practice strokes. She rose and walked to his side, lifting one of the red tubes. On the bottom end was a short wick, waxed straight. Garrett touched it with the flame and stood back, watching as Sam pointed the tube above her tiny town of ice and snow and sticks. From the mouth of the tube came orange and yellow fire followed by a wedge of smoke, accompanied by a low clap of sound and sparks like a rotary saw to metal. Then a green and red projectile shot deep into the sky. At its apex the projectile, a molded figurine, expanded and fell to the ground with an easy, rocking motion beneath a parachute of plastic and string.

The legs of the first figurine clipped the spike of a snow tower before landing sideways near the collected space of stones. Another figurine drifted left, catching its parachute on the exposed prong of a rusted nail. Others scattered about the area: in snow houses and tree branches and far against frozen soil. After each, Garrett lit firecrackers and tossed them at the descending toys.

The only differences between this peculiar evening Garrett and Sam were spending together and a similar night their father had once shared with his own brother, Hutch, in Wheeling, West Virginia, was that Kendall, who'd retold the story to his children, had wrapped a battery-powered model train set around his ice town and, instead of an abortion clinic, they'd chosen the barren land of a drive-in movie theater.

"Didn't Dad and Uncle Hutch get arrested when they did this?" asked Sam.

"No. But the cops made them go home and promise not to come back."

"I wish they'd make *me* promise not to come back."

They stared into the dark sky at the last of the parachutists on its fall, twitching with a metronome's steady rhythm. Having nothing left to ignite, Garrett held the flame to one of the hollowed tubes and watched the sizzle-'n'-spit of a few remaining grains of gunpowder.

The way one of the parachutes was pulled taut, tangled behind four cords of string, red plastic and white, Garrett's eyes were tricked into seeing something else. Caught quick from where he stood, blurred slightly, it resembled meat his mother used to buy through the mail. For special events, birthdays and holiday dinners, she sometimes ordered fine steaks and other beef products from the backs of magazines. The meat came shrink-wrapped and papered and boxed from Omaha, Nebraska. Always, Garrett and his sisters wondered what would possess a person to order beef, to order any perishable, by mail. A few years ago when one of the crates smelled strangely of linseed oil, Mercer refused to sign for it; she told the United Parcel delivery man to return the product. That was all. From then on, the only food that came by courier was the occasional fruit basket or selected chocolates sent by an appreciative patient.

"Let's leave this," said Sam, kicking at their mess.

"Why?"

"Big smile."

"No one's gonna think it's funny."

Sam walked to the half tower where the parachutist dangled, and stomped it, once with each boot. Near the fence was a wire-weave trash drum. Both Sam and Garrett wound the parachutes around the figurines, shooting them like wadded Kleenex. Discarded also were the cardboard tubes and shredded oats of firecracker and loose kindling. Once everything but the snow had been removed, Sam dropped to her side and did a barrel roll over the bumpy town. Back and forth.

Only a night before, awakened, Sam had entered her brother's bedroom after a horrific dream in which she'd paid a curious visit to some hospital where an entire floor had been devoted to undead fetuses (and their still-bleeding mothers)—disfigured bodies, frozen in time, wandering aimlessly from corridor to corridor under their own tiny strength. For Sam, there was the uncertainty of where images such as these would begin their gestation. Her own knowledge of Mercer's work was so clouded—pieced together from shortened conversations with her family, friends, and insults gathered from protesters and schoolmates. Theoretically, she understood what her mother did. But in truth, what was included among Mercer's daily tasks?

Speaking softly into darkness, she'd asked Garrett what the dream had revealed. Good or bad? Was it suggesting that the dangers of this procedure, when in dummied hands, would leave behind victims crippled and scarred and an inflated number of dead? Or was there something else?

Garrett was adamant in his support of their mother. This was simply a terrible nightmare. Not more. And then both agreed, no matter where the motivation took root, kids shouldn't have these thoughts—in their own homes, in their bedrooms. Before leaving her brother, Sam proposed, in a reasonable, curious manner, that they visit the clinic—even if it only meant a peek from the outside, a step or so closer to the looking glass. It was Garrett who, thinking of their father, decided on hauling along fireworks and the means to an imaginary town. A tiny sense of closure within the one place that to them would always remain open. Part symbolism, part the desire to behave only like children. Let their fantasies run wild, however briefly, so they could at least pretend to shed loose—*destroy*—all the roughness they were bid to carry throughout youth. The two could invent a pleasant thought as their mother had done years ago with the gingerbread factory.

In tandem, they departed the same way they'd entered from beneath the highest seam of the fence. To keep warm, Sam walked with her legs rubbing together, firing down and up like pistons; Garrett lowered a wool longshoreman's cap so it nearly covered his eyebrows. Both were hungry and tired and confused about the depth of an invitation that would've led them to muddle out on a night where there was only cold.

Some windows were illuminated with green and red and white lights no larger than gemstones. Hooked to windows and doors were wheels of pine branches and holly and leafy clippings from poinsettias. A freestanding birdhouse on someone's lawn, decorated in winking lights, seemed a ready target for snowballs. But Sam could hardly consider lifting her arm through the necessary motions of a throw: up, back, forward, across.

Hanging from telephone poles near a strip of stores was silver bunting that glittered in the streetlamps. A few of the poles were also wrapped in narrow bands of red and white crepe paper, angled, so they resembled enormous peppermint sticks. Peering from one of the store windows was a plaster snowman with an electric motor that yanked his right arm in a small wave and pushed clouds of transparent smoke from his pipe. Inexplicably, there was an assortment of yellow ducklings scattered at the snowman's base. Next door, the hardware store had taped to the inside of its window a poster of a sexy model dressed in a Santa's helper outfit, holding a huge wrench. At the end of the block, G & S Appliance had a mounted speaker above its door playing a cassette loop of holiday music.

"It's pretty close," said Sam, referring to the span of real estate between where they were going and where they had been. "But sometimes it seems like it takes forever."

"Just the weather."

"No." She zipped her coat to the top. "I think I'd feel the same way if it were warm outside."

"Like you just want to be home."

Bathed in lemon light below the church steps sat a thatched hut with porcelain statues arranged in a Nativity Scene. Because there had been thefts the previous few winters, baby Jesus had an eye screw drilled to the back of his head so he could be fastened to his manger with a combination lock. The Wise Men were not only linked by sense of purpose but also with bicycle cable. Oddly juxtaposed behind the makeshift barn stall, suspended from the stone face of the church, was a large cross holding a life-sized Jesus. Beginning to end, his whole life right there in the raise of a glance.

A blown tree branch had lodged itself along Christ's nearly closed right hand, like the plume to an old quill pen or the wide brush of a housepainter. Sam took a step nearer to gain clarity.

"Paint me, Jesus."

When Garrett continued walking, she called to him. "What do you think about Christ's high school years?"

"Huh?"

"How come no one ever talks about that?" She shuffled her feet in a trot to reach her brother. "There doesn't seem to be any recorded history of J.C. when he was a teenager. I mean, those way-cool tricks—walking on water, healing folks—would've earned him big points with girls."

Only a shrug from Garrett.

"Imagine him standing at the water fountain with some chippy," said Sam, now smiling. "He could just put his finger near the spigot for a little instant *vino*."

"Come on," said Garrett.

From the sound of his voice, it was difficult to tell whether he wanted his sister to quit with her peculiar hypotheses or if he was beckoning her to walk faster.

" 'I forgive you for that wedgie,' " she said, raising her arms.

"They didn't have underwear back then."

"Maybe not."

She still seemed pleased. Skittering with a sugar-jag quickness, they navigated their way through back streets. Nearer to the river they paused to watch a chunky ore ship float from dockside. Ants and honey and naval oranges were thoughts that pulled themselves across Sam's mind.

Fifteen years later . . .

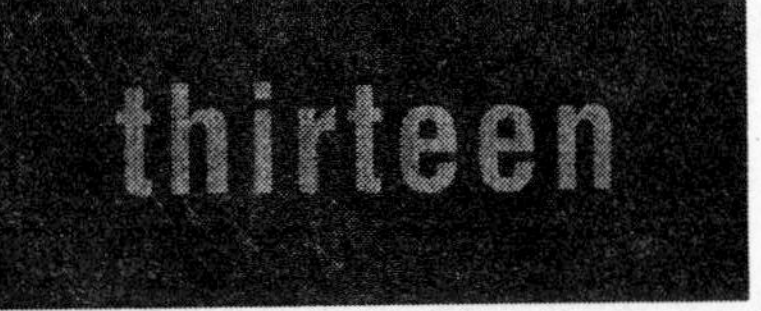

So many places to find the crawl of danger. In the swell and pull of water or the choke of sand. A kick. The sharpened mouth to a seashell. Dogs unleashed and unfriendly. Clem watched, one child against her breast and the other slapping a plastic spade to a plastic bucket. (They now came perpetually linked in kits.) Even, remarkably, the worry of great gulls swooping down for food. Literally being scratched from her arms. There was comfort, though, in knowing it had never before happened. At least not among the new mothers she'd known.

Something along the back of Clem's neck, horseflies, the heavy beads of sweat, forced her to remove a hand to wipe herself clean. With those so young, not quite ages four and one, the sun, too, was enemy. She had painted his skin white with zinc oxide; she'd also tied (after terrific struggle) a cotton golf hat to his head. Near her chest the youngest was wrapped, face to feet, in linen blankets. A bright red backpack sat at her side stocked bumpy with tools for childhood: putties and sauces for sun protection and sores; crust-free sandwiches; juice boxes with tiny straws sutured to their sides; diapers; gauzy towelettes marinated in their own (hygienic) broth; and always, napkins to rid stickiness and spills. She'd once told a friend that much of parenting was simply toting the correct supplies. If they need it, she said, I've got it.

Another month of hot weather remained. She'd been visiting this beach, which erased into the Atlantic, almost daily with the children. A short walk from their home in Bantam, Massachusetts, and only a forty-minute drive from her husband's office in Boston.

"Don't fling sand," she called to her son, Max. "It'll get caught in your eyes."

He was not listening.

"Well"—she sighed into the baby's shoulder—"he'll have to learn for himself."

Against the sky, couples walked together, some holding hands. When the spirit moved him, Max would lift his head and follow whoever was trudging past. He had the same chunky build, already, as his father. Once more a geyser of sand but, this time, too close. She thought there would be screaming, tears. Instead, simply a rough blotting with his forearm, spade still gripped.

"You okay?"

Answerless again.

It would not be long before days like these, which burned well after the dinner hour, had disappeared into autumn. She savored the quiet moments shared with Dixon, her husband, once the kids had gone to sleep, seated together on the front-porch glider, drinking gin and freshly squeezed lime juice, exchanging tales of their afternoons. Rarely came news that brought the raised eyebrows of astonishment. Dixon ran his own investment firm; Clem was on her second maternity leave from an editing job at a small book-packaging house. Life hummed predictably away. For him, there were new clients and frenetic (or sluggish) activity and bonds to trade; for her, Max wandering off (detrousered) to find the neighbor's dog, clickety sounds from the car, and baby Greer having trouble holding down food.

Since she'd given birth again, Clem's bladder had contracted to the size of a wristwatch. Sometimes she felt the urge to pee while she was tearing loose of a sheet of toilet paper after having just *peed.* On a beach painfully bereft of toilets, this day, she huddled behind waist-high saw grass and shrubs. She kept Max in her sights, Greer bundled in the sand at her side. She'd done this before and, always, she feared the sudden appearance of the beach patrol. It was not, she knew, the way a mother was expected to behave. Especially with her children so near.

"You're not setting a very good *example,*" she imagined the officer saying, his thick pad of citations waving above his khaki shorts as he prepared to ticket her for indecent exposure and public urination and whatever else.

So she pissed quickly, wiping herself with one of the baby's towelettes. Though curious, Max only once asked what his mother had been doing behind the bushes.

"Changing Greer," she'd said.

The response, reasonable, seemed to satisfy the boy, who'd continued raking furrows into the ground with his fingernails.

After finishing, now, she gathered all their things and led Max to a beveled slab of concrete. At its center was a small drain beneath a crooked lamppost of piping. They'd been here before. She threaded a piece of yarn, carried from home, through a chain that dangled above Max's head. He liked to control the water himself, but he was not tall enough to reach the cord. She fastened the frayed yarn around his right wrist.

"Okay," she said.

He gave a light tug, testing the tension against change from the previous day. Water spilled, a sloppy mouthful, across his head, shoulders, and back. He stepped away, still restrained, and then forward again for another pull.

"Cold?"

He nodded. Soon he was mostly cleansed of sand and tiny sticks and dried beach straw. She handed him a towel, which, after a few pats, dragged in a soft serpent at his side. Other times, she had reminded him to lift it from the ground.

"What do you feel like eating for dinner?"

A shrug, a shuffle.

"Squash?" she offered for conversation's sake. "Squishy squash?"

"No."

Then, because of the smell, his least favorite food. "Turkey?"

"No. I hate it."

"You *do?*" she said, as if this was a sudden discovery. "Imagine . . ."

"Those rolls."

"Ahhh." She lowered the visor on Greer's stroller to dull the sun. The path the three walked had twisted into brightness. "The whole-wheat ones? With pumpkin seeds on top?"

He shook his head. "No. The brown ones. Like this." He held up his index finger.

It took a moment. And then she knew exactly what he meant.

"Tootsie Rolls?"

"Yeah."

Now he was smiling.

"We don't eat Tootsie Rolls for dinner. They're only for special occasions. Because it was Melanie's birthday."

Two days earlier, Melanie Sirillo, a neighborhood friend, had been given a party.

"We could . . ." he began, struggling for something that would make eating Tootsie Rolls appear sensible to his mother. "We could have 'em with other things."

"Like salad?"

"Uh-huh."

"How else?"

His nose crunched with lines of worry.

"Maybe . . ." The peak of his chin lowered, then raised. "We could put 'em in buns."

"Now, that's thinking. Pile them up with mustard and hot-dog relish."

Behind this screen, Max needed to test his mother's sincerity. "Do we use the grill?"

She chuckled. "No, silly. They'll melt."

He looked up, head cocked.

"They're made of chocolate and chewy stuff. You want that dripping into the coals? Then every time Daddy makes hamburgers they'll taste like burnt Tootsie Rolls."

"That's okay."

Few children—none that she knew, anyway—would disagree with

her son. Given the opportunity for cheeseburgers or, say, beef patties topped with gooey wads of Tootsie Roll, they would choose the latter. Every time.

They reached the turn of their block, bordered on both sides by white fencing and small, finely hemmed lawns separating the road from homes. Each was similar: New England-style clapboards painted in muted grays and whites and weathered black trim. Almost all had porches with rocking chairs or swings. Decorative sea buoys striped in bright reds or oranges rested against railings or were bolted into the faces of the houses themselves. Two doors from Clem's, the Kalispells had recently converted an old wooden rowboat into a small garden of flowers and parsley and basil and mint. Alma Kalispell, nearing seventy, brewed "sun tea" in large glass pitchers she kept single-file (three) in the bed of her husband's seldom-used pickup truck. Once, having forgotten to remove them, he drove into town leaking a wake of broken glass and minty brown water.

Speeding ahead, Max unfastened the gate to his yard. It was a responsibility he took seriously, as city-dwelling kids might scramble to push the buttons of an elevator. If Clem forgot to let Max swing wide the gate, which sometimes, preoccupied, she did, they would all have to step back onto the sidewalk and allow him another chance. Near the stairs he stumbled, his feet tangled in the soppy towel.

"Be careful," she said.

And then she was tired, with immediacy, collapsing in the grass under the heavy hinge of day-to-day parenting. She lay on her back, arms outstretched, knocking a fist against the wheel of Greer's stroller to offer soothing movement. Finished for now. She could not creep any farther. So she stared at the sky and listened to the yaw-yaw of her daughter's carriage shaking above the sigh of ocean.

Something for dinner, she considered, still unprepared. Snap peas and broiled swordfish and a chopped salad of tomatoes and onions. Maybe, if there was time, she would squeeze fresh lemonade. She also had to remind Dixon that the garbage disposal needed repair—a day earlier she'd allowed its blades to clog with torn sponge. The astronaut night-light in Max's room needed to be replaced. And more oil soap for the living-room floor on her next visit to the grocery store. Then, from beyond her right shoulder, came the plucky clink of Max's music-box record player. Each disk, fat colored plastic with wide, toothy grooves, dropped neatly onto a turntable. Too often, the numbing notes of Claire de Lune (green) and "Michael, Row the Boat Ashore" (blue) and "Baa-Baa Black Sheep" (yellow).

Enough, she wanted to tell her son. But she did not. Instead, she remained prone for a few final minutes.

DIXON HAD CHANGED into a T-shirt and jeans. On Saturday, he would climb beneath the kitchen sink with his toolbox. For now, he was scraping the slop of their dinner plates into the trash. Because he possessed a peculiar aversion to any wet messiness—foods, footprints, coasterless cups—he was holding the dishes at an uncomfortable distance, by his latexed fingers. The room still smelled of fish and boiled potatoes. In her high chair, Greer struggled with a bottle; she could lift it herself but had difficulty raising the bottom once the milk had gone short.

"Did you talk to Steve?" said Clem, seated.

She was asking about a guy with whom Dixon worked.

"He said a seal coat works fine."

"That's what they did to their driveway?"

"Yep."

"And concrete?"

"Clem . . . " he said, abruptly flipping a pan into the dishwasher rack. "He says concrete tends to crack."

"Take that out."

"Huh?"

"The saucepan. Take it out of the dishwasher. It gets done by hand."

He removed the saucepan for a more thorough rinsing, and then dried it with a plain towel. Max skittered barefoot into the kitchen doorway. He stood watching his father, clutching a worn woman's pocketbook in his hand. Several months earlier he'd found the handbag, emptied, while walking with Clem. Oddly, it had become one of his favorite toys; he refused to let it leave his sight for more than a few hours. Now a stuffed bull poked its head from between the purse's unclasped mouth.

Having grown bored with the dishes, aching to move on, Dixon turned to his son. "What?" he asked.

"I wanna see a video."

Across the room, Clem was busy cleaning Greer and the space around her. Dixon flicked soapsuds at Max. "Go pick one out," he said.

"I did."

"Well . . . " As he spied a mixing bowl he'd forgotten to wash, his voice grew stern. "Sit on the couch. Hold the video in your . . . purse. And wait."

A clumsy pirouette and he was gone.

Upstairs, in the baby's room, the smell of powder and tiny bowels. Hunched above the changing table, Clem folded a soiled diaper twice. To her side was a canister resembling a miniature potbellied stove of plastic where used diapers could be plugged into a hole at its top and sealed individually in garbage bags. Tacked to the wall at Greer's left, in the stomach of a painted hippopotamus, was a narrow mirror. Often, she tried to touch herself—images of baby Greer reaching toward baby Greer. She was also fascinated with a brown electrical cord drooping from a desk lamp, which months earlier had been unplugged. Parents, overly protective, fearing the impossibility of shock rising from vulcanized wire.

Clem's skin appeared nearly stained against the whiteness of her daughter. So white, in fact, there was a bluish transparency to her hips, her thighs. New noise from below. Having finished in the kitchen, Dixon had followed Max to the den. There was a child's scream and, because it had happened before, just like this, Clem knew the details of the exchange. For Dixon, the desire to check the television news for a moment. This was not a concession Max could tolerate. He had waited patiently (for him) to watch a video of friendly foxes or singing children or, recently his favorite, Pooh Bear. From the space beneath Clem's feet came another raspy shout of protest.

"Dixon!" she called in her son's defense. "Leave him be!"

There was quiet, finally, and then the exaggerated high-low tones of children's music.

To no one, Clem said, "Better . . . "

She looked down, pasting the corners of a new diaper against itself with prepositioned adhesive strips. The baby was kicking: her legs flexing in a fury to some beat only she understood. A kiss from her mother between pencil-prick nipples.

"Time for bed, sweetie."

Because the evenings had been warm, Clem ignored clothing. Only the diaper to avoid muddied sheets. And beside Greer in the crib a stuffed cow (which came in a set with her brother's bull) and two pacifiers. Binkies, they were now called.

In the hallway, once she could hear just her daughter's gentle cooings and the television sounds banging up the stairwell, Clem removed four rolls of toilet paper, shrink-wrapped together, from a storage closet and carried them to the bathroom. She ran water, though not for herself. At day's end, Dixon needed to soak the muscles of his sore back; they tightened during eight, nine hours seated even in his posture-perfect chair. He found that salted baths—thirty minutes, with occasional nozzle twirls for fresh hot water—worked better than showers. The standing was excruciating. He needed to lie flat, as flat as their tub allowed.

She sat on the counter, near the sink, and let the steam rise against her. The weight of her own arms sometimes felt too heavy. Like now. Palms on thighs, faced down. To the left, a mirror which she contemplated touching, if only to emulate her daughter. She followed the break and bend of her profile. This body, she considered, had distorted beyond post-pregnancies. The edge of her ass, soft bumpers, spread too easily, pushed wide when she left her feet. A puffiness to her face, so slight, and a breadth of excess skin wagging along her upper arms.

She was still young. In her early thirties. But her body had been sacrificed, kicked and twisted, crowbared, stretched past what she'd thought physically possible. She wondered if she would always be doughy, a few pounds overweight. Never quite firm again. A fear one day—this day—of waking to find she'd been equipped with another woman's thighs and breasts and ankles. It was her mother's body on a sticky afternoon during summer break before Clem's junior year at college. Shopping for groceries together, Clem wandered loose. When she'd discovered what she'd been looking for (yogurts or bottled water or shampoo), she zagged back through the supermarket aisles to reach her mother. She had come upon Mercer from behind, slowly, khaki shorts (too-shorts) lifting further as her mother grabbed for something high. Those hips, those legs, had dimpled and veined and kneaded into unfamiliar parts.

She recalled thinking not so many years ago, What happened? Would Clem unsettle and shift, too? And now, in the bathroom alone, she had her answer. Though not yet as dramatically. More left to come.

THERE WAS A LONG, ROPY PILLOW from Clem's last pregnancy. It was designed for folding and fitting along (and between) a woman's newfound lumps and slopes. Recently Dixon had taken to snaking the pillow near his knees, upwards, until it curled against the small of his back. This was how he awoke, before five, Clem rocking Greer in a chair across the room.

"What?" he asked, startled.

He was ignored by Clem, who thought he might ease back to sleep for another hour or so.

"She's up?" he said, for real this time.

"You didn't hear her crying . . . "

"No."

"I fed her a little," said Clem. "Now she's just fidgety."

Kicking away the pregnancy pillow, Dixon sat with his shoulders against the headboard. He took a swallow from a glass of water on his nightstand. For a moment, he pondered turning on the light and reading the rest of a magazine article he'd begun just hours earlier. He decided against surrendering yet to the day. He didn't want to speak. He feared the light and the article might incite Clem because, strangely, one of her pet peeves concerned his reading material: he chose newpapers and magazines and pamphlets before books. She'd asked a group of his friends at a party, in all seriousness, why men didn't organize their own reading clubs—*magazine* reading clubs.

"You could meet once every three or four weeks like us," she'd said. "But instead of *Middlemarch* or *Light in August* you'd have—" and she'd pointed to a coffee table loaded with glossy newsstand titles.

When he moved, the bed tapped the wall, but not loudly enough to cause Greer to stir. He scratched his cheek, his arm, his balls.

"You gonna put her back down?"

"If she'll go," said Clem. "I just think"—she was whispering—"the minute we cross into her room . . . "

And Dixon watched his wife and daughter disappear through the door frame. Then he stared at his feet beneath the sheets, far enough from one another in distance so they each formed independent spires.

fourteen

It could not be seen from common roadways. Even the fencing and gates were hidden from the naked eye by closely planted jack pines and spruce and thick-weaved mattings of vine. The only thing visible was a stone-and-aluminum guard hut, windowed, large enough for two men. Along its left side, a paved twin-lanes street slithered back beneath a low mountain. Built partially into the earth itself like a copper mine, near the summit, was a gleaming bunker, enormous, of brushed steel and smoked glass and titanium, curved and cornered.

Hidden by more trees and blimp-sized sculptures of oxidation-proof cast iron, were a series of parking lots. In the lower right hand of each space, neatly stenciled in silver-sheen paint, were letters and numbers. A6, B14, C9, et cetera. A place for every car, a car for every place.

The lobby had an atrium ceiling, floors marbled and dark, and a horseshoe-shaped stainless-steel desk where employees scanned their I.D. cards (worn on neck chains or pocket clips or walleted) and visitors signed their names in logbooks. Near the elevator banks were showy, oversized girders and rivets and moon-shaped valves copied from vintage industrial plants. Dropped from an offshoot of the atrium ceiling, a simple banner, fantastically large, reminiscent in design and coloring (red and black and white) of Fascist-era motifs. Now the familiar X preceded by a significantly smaller '*sa*' and followed by the also reduced '*on*' saXon. The lower edge of the banner must have been weighted or tethered with clear nylon wire because there was no movement, no flap or ripple.

On the fourth floor, open and Bauhaus-y, were Plexiglased independent work stations for each designer. Self-styled. Throwbacks, these booths, to World's Fair pavilions of the 1930s. Product showcases. Except here, mostly, the products were all the same. Or similar. They were creating athletic shoes. Inventing, refining, improving. On other floors, track suits, T-shirts, collared shirts, caps (adjustable and fitted), sunglasses, duffel bags, even swimming trunks.

Near the far corner, along the bend of the L, was a carrel with walls busied by photographs and magazine clippings and rough sketches of footwear. Impaled on a ski pole, askew, the head of a Styrofoam mannequin. Faceless, save for a handlebar mustache someone had felt-tipped and a Cleveland Indians stocking hat. A rollered chair was propped beside a hockey stick, chipped and smudged and pilling where taped.

Sam was seated ankle to knee, barefoot, on her desk. A telephone headset—the kind worn by TV commercial operators ("Standing by now!")—was fitted across her ears so she could speak (and presumably listen) while completing other tasks. She was picking lint from between her toes. A co-worker waved to catch her attention; he lifted his hand to his mouth and said, low-voiced, "We're ordering Chinese."

"Eggroll," she said, apologizing to the person on the phone. She pointed to a mug filled with loose change.

On the opposite side of her cubicle was a table with piston-like devices that raised and lowered and shifted the angle of the drawing surface. Pink and yellow Post-Its hung in a neat row beneath the lower of two suspended bookshelves, colored spinnakers at a used-car lot. Toes cleaned, Sam shot a rubber band at a plastic gorilla, two feet high, wearing miniature saXon basketball sneakers. He'd been part of an old advertising campaign.

She finished her conversation and slipped the wiry headset from her ear. Sandwiched between the drawing table and one wall was a small, blocky refrigerator she'd purchased from a friend during college, so low to the ground she often pried open the door with her foot. It was half filled—Diet Pepsis and bottled water (carbonated and flat) and a carton of tomato juice. There was also a log of chocolate-chip cookie dough, peeled and gnawed nearly to its heel.

Outside, it was raining again, and she watched the water bust into rivulets against the window. She was standing, her forearms resting across the deroofed edge of her "office." She'd moved to the Pacific Northwest for college twelve years ago. The University of Washington. UW. Or, as locals pronounced it, "you-dub." The school farthest from home to which she'd been accepted. More rain, less snow. Same gray.

Now she lived with two roommates in a rented house in the Queen Anne section of Seattle. It was about a twenty-minute drive to work, most mornings, in a used Saab she'd bought the previous fall.

On a lark, as a freshman, she'd enrolled in an introductory art class to help fill some humanities requirements. By her junior year, she'd discovered it was something for which she had an affinity and, more important, which she enjoyed. Industrial design ultimately seemed a good fit. But as she completed her bachelor of arts and began applying to graduate programs, a recruiter from nearby saXon invited her for a series of interviews. Every spring the athletic-shoe company hired a handful of promising young design and engineering majors for its staff. Regular infusions of talent ensured fresh ideas, concepts. Newer, fancier, funkier shoes (and other synergistically linked products).

Most of the design team was male, which, not surprisingly, often fostered a near fraternity-like atmosphere in the "bullpen"—the slangy name given her floor at saXon. Sam was not bothered by the sometimes boyish behavior of those with whom she shared space. In fact, as with her hockey teammates during childhood and adolescence, these men held her in high esteem. She never backed down from ideas, from spirits, from challenges in a hybridized game of kickball played in the hallways mostly during late-night deadlines. On a company retreat, in her second year, she'd won an obstacle-course footrace with a then-record time which her officemates painted to construction paper and posted (for a full week) beside the elevator bank.

LOUNGING NEAR THE FIREPLACE in her home, Sam tested the spongy, sneaker-shaped peel with her fingertips. She was holding the prototype mid-sole to a new golf spike on which she was working. It was to be bonded with a graphite cushioning system.

"God forbid these tubby golfers actually develop heel spurs."

"Or grow a blister," said Callie, whose room was across the hall from Sam's.

On the table sat a half-empty pot of vegetarian chili that had been reheated a second time and served with crusty French bread, sour cream, and diced white onion. Both women were drinking beer from long-necked bottles; a third housemate, Lynn, was taking swallows of herbal tea between trips to and from the kitchen with dirtied dishes. Five compact discs—three jazz, one rock, one classical—were alternating softly on the stereo's shuffle-track deck.

Hooking the flexible mid-sole deep in her palm, bent against itself, Sam formed a puppet's mouth. "Is there any more ice cream?" she asked, squeaky-voiced, flapping her rubber-lined hand.

"Maybe the dregs of that almond fudge," said Lynn.

"No," said Callie. "Ate it yesterday."

"Well, then . . . " said Lynn, speaking now from back in the kitchen. "There's some freezer-burned vanilla."

"From those pies?"

The previous winter, they'd hosted a theme party where guests were asked to bring a home-baked pie of their own choosing. Each participant had been told to phone over a prospective selection so there were no duplications.

"Throw that out," hollered Callie. "It's not fair. Every time I open the icebox"—she liked to call it an icebox—"I get a rush of excitement, momentarily, thinking there's a gallon of ice cream I forgot about or someone's gone shopping."

Sam laughed, nodding in agreement.

"If you make an ice-cream run," she said, "I'll melt this in a saucepan"—she was waving the mid-sole—"for topping."

"Tempting as it sounds . . . "

"We've got this," said Lynn, returning from the kitchen with a quarter block of confectionary chocolate for baking.

They each took desperate bites, passing the slab from one to the next. Though not particularly tasty, it was enough to quell the urge for sweets. Together, they completed the dishes and the rest of the cleaning: Sam wiping the table, Callie sealing and stowing containers, Lynn beside the sink.

They had two telephone lines, and while Callie and Lynn spoke to people from the living room and den, respectively, Sam lay in darkness on her bed. Against her dresser was a portfolio of drawings, old and new, schematics of golf shoes with fringed tongues folded to cover the laces and hidden mid-sole wraps for stability and replaceable cleats of hard plastic. She could picture in her head the twin stipple marks, holes of perforation along the shoe's upper instep, to be removed because staying dry was of greater importance than breathability. Also, she knew, others would not share her belief in high-style colors—melons and silt and pewter. Instead, only, *always*, a black, a white, a beige, and a saddle (either white with black or beige with white).

Now she was tired.

The huff and clink and whir of this immense sneaker propaganda machinery. Hype of hype. Logos and symbols and names, stitched or tattooed or silk-screened to every available space. This is us—buy us, wear us, like us. Love us. A notion, a consideration that her line of work had become the next great American art form. To follow jazz and denim and fast-food hamburger patties. At trade shows they placed shoes she'd help design in transparent Lucite towers (Do not *touch!*) rotating slowly like the floors to microwave ovens, klieg lights shining from four evenly proposed directions. Overhead, there were video monitors of athletes wearing shoes—*her* shoes—in action; running faster, jumping higher, kicking or hitting or throwing a ball farther or more accurately or quicker than ever before. She'd made it possible. And later, on this very day, some basketball player barely twenty, who'd only recently signed his name to a contract *paying* him to wear their shoes, tracksuits, caps—paying him eight goddam figures—will sign his name, again, to anything chain-passed to him (Do not *touch!*) for the agreed-upon thirty-three minutes, so long as it bears the company seal.

She was tired.

Maybe, possibly—dare we dream it—on a cloudless fall afternoon two teams will compete against each other (in football or soccer or basketball or baseball) and every participant will be wearing saXon-logoed products on his feet and torso and head . . . And more important, so will every person in every seat in the stadium, and every vendor and parking-lot attendant and rummy pleading for coins. These people will drink colas and beer from appropriately sanctioned cups and eat hot dogs and spicy sausages from the right colored wax paper and napkins. Even tacked to once-naked space (gasp!), Greyhound-bus-length banners in support not of the teams but rather of the T-shirts and sunglasses and leisure wear.

Her eyes closed.

From beneath her bed came the prolonged sucking sound of the dishwasher.

THEY SIPPED STRONG COFFEE from tall, clear mugs. Peppery and powerful coffee, the kind squeezed of beans as shiny and dark as onyx stones. They did this sometimes when they both rose early, with distance between morning and work. Across the table Lynn pinched loose pieces from a cranberry-walnut muffin, still warm. She was a publicist for the university. During her first few months on the job she'd worn a school-booster pin on her lapel or sweater. No longer, though. She'd grown weary of sales, which, in truth, was most of what her position required. Putting a positive spin on all that's dubious.

"He won't call," said Lynn. "Not unless he wants something . . . else."

They were talking about a guy she'd met a few nights earlier at a nearby club.

"Maybe . . . " said Sam.

Lynn had brought him home; she'd had ragged, fitful sex with him on the floor of her bedroom, against her opened closet, pressing hangered clothing into the wall with her back.

"There's nothing so wrong with getting silly," said Sam, a euphemism for things they understood, "every once in a while."

"I guess."

"Listen, we've all got certain needs. Bing-bang. And it felt more good than bad. And you were cautious"—a nod from Lynn—"and you burned a few LB's. And you weren't gonna find your soulmate in a bar anyways."

"No . . . "

"Tomorrow he calls and you date for a while and a couple months later we sit in this exact spot"—Sam slapped her hand on the sugar dispenser for emphasis—"and you tell me what a jerk he is and how you've got to find some way to cut him loose because there's this *other* guy from work . . . "

"Right."

"Fuck him."

"Fuck him."

"And next time you'll listen to Callie when she says never sleep with a man wearing a belt buckle larger than his fist."

They both chuckled.

They watched two suits order lattes in takeout cups with corrugated sheaths to protect their hands from heat. Subconsciously Sam's eyes dropped to their feet, though she knew they'd be wearing loafers. Lowcut Italian ones. Bad for rain.

THE RUMBLING OF THUNDERHEADS came like a sound from the chest, leaky with fluid. Sam waited beneath the awning, a group of cigarette-smoking teenagers milling to her left. She pretended to be occupied, rummaging through her backpack for papers and binders and, finally, the focused study of her weekly planner. An appointment to be rubbed away, another affixed with tiny asterisks. Until, eventually, a voice from behind her neck.

"Have you been here long?"

She shook her head.

"I'm sorry." He was tall, with broad shoulders and long shaggy hair. "I got hung up at the office."

"No problem," said Sam, returning what had been removed.

They hadn't known each other long, only a few weeks. They'd met through work, of course, when he'd been commissioned to create a Web site for saXon. Though you wouldn't have guessed it from looking at him—ratty leather jacket, fat-soled construction boots, black jeans—Brett Tarver had recently been named to Seattle's "Hot Young Talent" list by a local magazine. He'd received recognition for the remarkably innovative Web page designs he'd developed at other corporations. He'd also padded his bank account by working with friends to program software for a computer game called Phiz, wherein the participants must master thirteen ever-changing stages using brainpower and unearthed weaponry. (The assault rifle slung across your shoulder won't fire against the zombie-Huns because, naturally, it hadn't been invented by the fifth century; likewise, you'd better reach for something more powerful than a slingshot when confronted by a villianous troop of SS soldiers.) The game had fostered a cult-like following complete with its own Internet site and code-breaking manuals for assistance during each level.

"You excited about this?" he asked.

She shrugged.

"I don't know much about them," she said. "Only that one of the guys who works for our courier service plays the drums."

"That's good by me."

Near the doorway was a sign listing the three bands playing that evening, and beneath the names, in red ink, the assurance that it was an "All Ages" show. This meant there was no minimum age limit, no alcohol was to be served.

"Not that I went to many concerts when I was young," said Sam. "But we didn't have anything called 'All Ages.' If we wanted to go we had to sneak past the guards."

He nodded, pushing away Sam's hand while he unfurled six dollars (for both) to pay for the tickets. Inside, it was loud and crowded and mostly filled with kids in their early teens. The two of them found a place to stand against the back wall, far from the chin-high stage speakers barking crunchy, distorted rock music like you might hear from a cheap car stereo. They both drank Pepsis.

"He's not bad," said Brett, lifting his head toward the band.

"That's not him."

"Huh?" He pointed to his ear with his free hand.

"That's not *him!*" she said, louder this time. "He's in the next group."

"Oh." He smiled, meekly. "Well, then . . . I was just trying to be polite. This guy sucks."

They both laughed.

There wasn't much more they could say to one another. They strained to hear the other's voice. Even between bands they struggled, thinking that any moment the music would begin again. They remained for five songs of the second set.

"I'm gonna suffer for this later," said Brett, walking from the club in the misty evening air. "My ears will ring for days."

"Okay, grandpa . . . "

"Right. I'd forgotten I was with a real experienced concertgoer. We'll see how *you* sleep tonight."

"There's a simple formula." She lowered her backpack. "I'll just turn the volume up on my clock radio. That way the ringing will be drowned out by more ringing."

"Nice."

She was now twirling her car keys—fastened to a ring which also held a tiny rubber sneaker—around her index finger. He asked if she liked sweet-and-sour chicken because, near where she'd parked, was a place with wonderful sauce.

"Not tonight," she said. "Maybe next week."

And he kissed her, lightly, at the fold of her lips—a spot not likely to be misinterpreted. They had pushed past friendship but not quite into what might come next. He was respectful, caring, wary of motion too rapid or clunky. He recognized Sam's apprehension and knew, soon, they would together become either more or less.

She drove him to his car, slowly, only a few hundred feet from hers, with the passenger-side door ajar and his right boot kicking against the moving pavement. She watched the lights of his car illuminate before departing, alone, a hurdy-gurdy whistling in the back of her head.

DEFLATED AT BOTH ENDS of the couch, bowls of seedy and picked popcorn between them, Callie and Lynn took turns with the remote control. At times the channels flashed past so quickly, stock-still images halted on-screen, it seemed as if they were searching for photo slides to discuss during a presentation. ("Now, where's that shot of us with the baby cheetah . . . ?") Sam stood over their shoulders, briefly, waiting for them to continue speaking. There was nothing but, on occasion, the call from Lynn to "Go back" or "I missed that" or "Iiiiick." When the screen went momentarily dark between commercials, Sam could be seen reflected against the bowed glass.

"What're you doing?" asked Callie.

"Nothing." She slipped her coat across the back of a chair. "No *thing.*"

"Want some popcorn?" asked Lynn, shaking a bowl of salty, burnt kernels.

"I'll pass . . . "

She sat on the arm of the couch.

"He called," said Lynn.

"What?" She let her head fall to the side, droopy with the hint of dejection. "I just left him."

"No," said Lynn. "Not Brett. *My* him."

"Oh," she said, quietly at first and then, once it connected, "*Ohhhh.*"

"Go away," said Callie. "Trust me. You don't want any part of this conversation. Just pick your little ass from the couch and march straight to your bedroom. Do not look back. Do not answer when spoken to . . . "

Because this was exactly what Sam had wanted, anyway, she collected her belongings and scaled the staircase. Behind, she only heard a heavy sigh from Lynn, then voices she could not understand.

RESENTMENT THAT THE CONNECTIONS NEVER SEEMED TRUE. Not for Sam. She sat on the toilet, nightshirt bunched along her waist, staring at the mildewy hem of the shower curtain. This man, she liked. Only she'd been flavored with the pessimism of failures past. There would be some slippage when they pressed close at the surface or deeper. The flatness of a single toggle-bolt thread, stripped of its teeth—its *tooth.* Biteless. And nothing else would matter because the detail would inflate to some disproportionate size. Each would ratchet onward until, finally, their directions cleaved. The long wait for settlement. The pitch and pull of cleansing agents all froth and grit and stingy to the nose. Later, still, the promise of something new.

ARM COCKED behind his head, suspended in time, he prepared to slam dunk a tiny basketball. The figure stood nearly three feet high, sculpted from goat cheese and detailed with withery pegs of sun-dried tomatoes and other vegetation. A closely cropped Afro of minced parsley. Concentric circles of seeded crackers and celery stalks and carrots cut for single bites began at the toe of his right sneaker, which, of course, had been reliably depicted with food coloring. The rest of the conference-room table was stocked with salads and sandwich meats and sliced bread stored in replica shoe boxes. There were also tubs of iced beverages.

The celebration of another walking billboard, signed only moments earlier, set to begin his second season of professional basketball.

Sam's boss, *the* boss, drank carbonated apple juice, his hand held at careful range from his turtleneck and lime-green blazer. Other executives bumped about his orbit. Tipped into a distant corner, dressed in a mustard-colored six-button suit and V-neck sweater (shirtless), the feted player spoke into the vicinity of a credit-card-sized cellular phone pressed against his ear. Only once did he move among the staffers, and then it was to jackknife his body across the buffet for a handful—his *free* hand—of pretzels.

Sam balanced a napkin of munchies in her palms, using her elbow to navigate a pathway from the room.

"I thought I might find you here," said Brett, from behind, as she'd nearly reached the door.

She rolled her eyes, lazily, as if to imply she wouldn't have missed this for anything. The turn and press of bodies moved them closer to each other. Brett had been chewing cheese and pumpernickel when he'd spied Sam, and there was still a smudge of dark food, like olive paste, below his upper gums.

"Going back to work?" he asked, because, really, there was nothing else.

She nodded. "I like to cart away as much booty as my tiny hands will carry." She lifted the edge of the napkin to reveal some crackers, veggies, and a crumbled peanut-butter cookie. "I take it all home and store it in Tupperware containers. I'm hoping after another few months I can throw a party of my own."

"Mmmmm. Count me in."

For an instant she stood in both places. She could see with a lucidness what her life might be like in the disordered moments after she'd told Brett they should consider a less taxing relationship; she also saw the glow to his face when she proffered that, perhaps, they had the potential to become more than only friends.

They walked to the elevator; Sam's office was two floors down.

And then he did the right thing. A decision of remarkable insight, intuitively correct. He remained stationary. He allowed Sam to depart alone. While the doors began closing he delivered a small salute, fingers to forehead. And she was gone. There was no pinkie-thumb gesture suggesting a later phone call, no fleeting words into the smooth pulleys and cables of the descending carriage.

She was kicked into curiosity, the loss of a few beads to confidence—which is everything two people need when they are trying to discover whether they belong. Something unredundant.

She sat parked in the driveway curled behind her house seat snapped down so it rested on the cushion in back. She stared through the parted sunroof looking for needles of light in the darkened sky. She remembered a time she'd snuck into one of Missy Reeler's father's limousines when she was young. There was a boy, though not Doak, and they had sex. Early sex but not the first. Then came the smell of something sweet gone overly ripe. And the stickiness of semen against her thighs, climbing dry along her belly so it felt like a sutured wound. She remembered a friend telling her she needed to pee immediately after intercourse to burn away any infection. But she didn't, and still, she'd been fine.

He'd spent the morning hauling lumber for a friend. Garrett's T-shirt, a BVD with the collar tugged sloppy, was yellowed by sweat and sawdust and prickly spines of wood. The sandy remains of a fried-egg sandwich on toast sat in front of him on a plate. He was drinking coffee and listening to Don Cape, stretched straight in a booth across from him, tell a story.

"The two guys looked like they'd been on a construction site. They wore work clothes, they had faces you could've passed on the street a million times." Don had a cousin from near Fort Wayne, in Indiana, who'd told him all this by phone only a night earlier. "They walked into this Italiany restaurant and took a real long time figuring what to order. Finally, they got, like, the house-specialty pizza—which was stacked with a lot of shit and wasn't easy to make. They both had salads and sides of spaghetti and garlic bread. Afterwards, they ate these big-deal sundaes: banana splits with three flavors of ice cream and three kinds of toppings, hot and cold, and nuts and whipped cream and cherry halves."

He removed his wallet and placed it on the table.

"Then?" asked Garrett.

"Then it was just like I told you before," he said, plucking a few singles from his billfold. "They walked over to the pinball machine, yanked the cord from its socket, and carried it out the front door. And they never planned on stealing the damn thing. They only wanted to play pinball in the sunshine. So they hooked the machine to some outlet at the bottom of a parking-lot light post."

"Nifty."

"The fucking *stones* on these two. I mean, to do this *after* the guy has gone to all that trouble making your meal."

Outside, in the hazy heat of late summer, Garrett rubbed a dead spider from the headlamp of his pickup, thinking it was a crack, and stepped onto the running board. He peered across the roof at Don, who was walking to his own car, slowly, lighting a cigarette with a book of matches.

"You want me to come with you this afternoon?" asked Don.

"No." He rocked for a moment, high above the smooth asphalt. "It's never bad on Wednesdays. Usually only the weekend. Saturday mornings when people got too much time."

They backed onto Route 14, moving in opposite directions. Passing beneath a stoplight, two, Garrett considered taking an afternoon skate at Thurmer Park—he loved the ice, alone, on warm days—but decided against it because his skates were at his mother's house. Instead, he would kill time with phone calls, a nap. Maybe a half hour at The Shed, where he'd buy a newspaper and watch truckers and salesmen and barely legal boys jockey for position beside the rack of pornographic magazines. He also liked to listen when people selected their lottery numbers; he enjoyed the stories of inspiration as the machine spit down their cards.

A muddled, tiresome swing through side streets left him only a few blocks from his apartment. It was the second story to a double-residence home. The staircase, which he'd built only a few months earlier, was fastened to the side of the house and allowed him access without disturbing the people who lived on the ground level. When the air was clear he could watch a bend in the Wayonga River from the roof. Some nights he liked to escape to his private patio with a lawn chair, portable radio, and six-pack.

Magnetized to the refrigerator door was a photograph of Garrett with his girlfriend, Lucy Kinter, taken not long ago at the bar where she worked. Their faces were illuminated by red-and-green light thrown from a neon sign advertising Genessee Cream Ale. A visitor could see in the mirror behind them, if he looked closely, a shift of workers from Gruman Powder entering from the street. One summer Garrett had worked for the blasting-powder company, loading product onto semi-trailers for delivery at various coal mines across the Ohio Valley.

He stripped to his boxer shorts and squeezed a damp washcloth into the back of his neck. He gargled with a capful of spearmint mouthwash, limy in color, that sat on a ledge above the sink. Fuzzy hairs not half the length of eyelashes grew from his ears, so, from time to time, like now, he used a periscope attachment to his electric razor to shave them away. He ate a few aspirin tablets in anticipation of a headache he felt beginning along the center seam of his skull. Above the couch in the living room, the curtains were pulled closed against a small window so the sun's glare wouldn't swallow the television picture. He let the cable news play absently while leafing through his mail, mostly bills and flyers and a coupon (which he tucked into another stack of papers) for a two-dollar dinner at the House of Pancakes.

The telephone, dimpled and decorated like a rubber football, had been sent as a premium from a magazine to which he subscribed. Sometimes if he moved his head too rapidly while speaking, the phone disconnected one party from the other. There was also a gritty static to calls of any significant length. He thought about the possibilities for work in the coming weeks. There was talk of building a patio behind some couple's house; he was waiting for them to consider the estimate. Another potential job to discuss: constructing a skeletal sleeve for trash cans behind a nearby Mexican restaurant where animals—raccoons, stray dogs—had begun tipping over the canisters when they dug for food scraps. And for Lucy's father, finally, he'd promised to lay new tile in his bathroom.

A ragged pile of old newspapers was stacked against the far side of the couch, in a spot one might typically reserve for an end table. Over the past few weeks, Garrett had been intending to tie the papers in manageable bundles and cart them, along with plastic sacks of bottles and aluminum cans, to the recycling plant. Now he let his eyes run across the counter surfaces in the room, and in the open-walled kitchen to his left, for a cone of twine. Nothing. Which, truthfully, was fine, because he didn't feel much like moving again until absolutely necessary.

Glowing in refracted sunlight, visible on the kitchen windowsill, was a small aquarium. The last fish had died eight days ago, but the tank still held cloudy water and artificial seaweed and a glass shipwreck punched into multicolored stones along the bottom. Both Garrett and Lucy knew that soon inspiration must seize them: while visiting the mall they needed to remember a pet store on their list of activities. Otherwise, the tank would grow darker and darker, eventually becoming a receptacle for leftover beer and table crumbs brushed from hand to water.

Noises from the street reached him in a hurry. The report of voices in the alley between houses, a rogue car alarm with second and third lives. He lay with his feet propped against the coffee table. Then came the stutter of a lawn mower and, in the warm afternoon breeze, the smell of sweet grass clippings.

BESIDES MEDICATIONS, the refrigerator also had a shelf for canned pop and brown-bag lunches and the occasional piece of fruit. Seated quietly on a folding chair, Garrett sipped from a Royal Crown cola. It was much too cold, so when he'd pulled down the tab a slushy film of ice formed in the can's mouth. He waited, he watched as gurneys with patients, covered to their armpits by white sheets, were wheeled past the open door toward the recovery room. Usually, by the time Garrett arrived, there were only one or two remaining. He heard his mother giving someone instructions. She shuffled across Garrett's vision, wearing avocado-colored surgical scrubs and matching paper slippers and cap.

"It won't be much longer," she called to him.

He glanced at the duffel near his chair. To varying degrees, this had all been a part of his life for a long, long time. A graph filled with spikes and pits. His mother had never blanched when, as a young OB/GYN, she'd been confronted with appalling tales. Women who'd been given potassium permanganate tablets for dissolution into purple, fizzy liquid so they might perform self-administered abortions with a douche. But many, misinformed, inserted whole tablets directly into their vaginas. The undiluted chemicals, abrasive, ate through their skin, left ulcers and sores and bleeding, which, oftentimes, was mistaken for a lost fetus. And other "remedies" for pregnancy: squirting a mixture of turpentine and salts with a meat baster; steaming over a boiling tub of coffee and toxins; rolling themselves down stairwells; and finally, prodding their uteruses with a sharp stick or knitting needle or wire coat hanger.

Worse still, the filthy spaces where men with limited or no medical background would twist a probe between the pregnant woman's legs to tear the fertilized ovum. These women were sent away, told to wait for a heavy flow of blood. And often the bleeding would continue for days, weeks, until it brought them death.

In truth, Mercer viewed abortions as only another piece to her practice. A neccesary one. She'd never considered *not* performing them, just as she had never thought about limiting her number of pap smears or deliveries. And though she believed in a woman's right to control her own body, on a less noble front she performed abortions for the income. Money. The patients paid her ahead of time, in cash. She was not ashamed to admit this when protesters waved baby dolls dangling from a hangman's noose with dollar signs painted to their chests. She gave quality care for a price.

Though she refused to proselytize, wishing instead to be a silent representative for choice, often she would slip trivial oddities into the course of conversation: "The Supreme Court's ruling on Roe v. Wade received limited newspaper coverage because it came on the same day L.B.J. died," or, "The decision overturned one statute outlawing nearly all forms of contraception put in place by a local New England official named P. T. Barnum." And, after a prolonged pause, "Yep, *that* P. T. Barnum."

There had been periods when his mother's professional life, and, by association, his own life, puttered along quietly. Other times they were not so lucky. Great swells of concern came randomly from those who opposed the practice of abortion, in the form of aggressively mounted demonstrations. On these days he came for her, watching nervously the motion around where she walked.

When she returned to Garrett, dressed now in street clothes, he unzipped the duffel and raised the black vest over her shoulders; he pressed closed the Velcro fastenings beneath her arms, along her waist. Formed of Kevlar and nylon fabric, the vest, which felt like the heavy bibs worn by X-ray technicians, was designed to halt the path of a bullet. Unless, of course, the gunman aimed for her head.

"Only a few," said Garrett, referring to the number of people marching outside the clinic.

"It'll get worse," said Mercer. "Next week. One of those groups—I don't know their name—has targeted us for a few days. They're going to bus people in."

Sometimes the act itself filled Garrett with alarm: fitting his *mother* in a bulletproof vest so she could walk to the car with peace of mind. Protected. Though, really, it was Garrett who worried more than Mercer. She had her job, Mercer reasoned, and they had theirs. The coyote sharing a moment with the roadrunner before another day of chase.

"Did you warn the police?" asked Garrett, tucking the empty duffel beneath his arm. "Do they know?"

"It's just noise." She saw his mouth drop. "But Tiff called them."

Together they moved to the back door. There had been inconveniences and, also, fear. Once, headed to the parking lot, she saw a flash of light as a strange man slid from the shadows. Though it was only a metallic ring on the binder of assorted right-to-life literature, she'd been convinced it was a gun. Another time a man jumped into her path while spastically waving his arms. "The blood of babies!" he shouted, aiming a plastic bottle of ketchup at her neck. More hostile still, a short-haired woman fastened herself with a bicycle chain and padlock to the rear bumper of Mercer's car. She drove away, slowly, dragging the woman for two blocks over sharp nuts of gravel before pausing at a stop sign, for sixteen seconds, she'd counted, allowing the woman to finally disengage from the automobile.

When Garrett was young they had come, on occasion, to create disturbances at the house. Not the first or second time, but later, when they had developed a strategy, a nastiness squawked from their collective rictus, he remembered his mother stomping through the kitchen after trying to reason with them to wait until her children had departed for school.

"Are they armed?" asked his father.

A sudden and reasonable query.

"They're armed all right," said Mercer. "They're armed with ignorance."

And always, Garrett thought of these people as being infused with some dangerous instability. Truthful or not, it was the impression left on a small boy and his sisters when unsettling displays of noise and color occurred so near the place in which they lived.

It used to bother Garrett more that those who'd chosen to demonstrate—in thoughtless, angry ways—didn't recognize that Mercer was a parent, too. Once, against the advice of peace officers and family members, a teenaged Garrett walked to the end of the driveway toting a leather-bound scrapbook. He flipped through it for the marchers, who mostly ignored him, providing fresh narration with each page: "This is my mother holding me on a water slide because I was too afraid to go down alone," and "The blue stuff in this picture is frosting from a birthday cake," and "We're all dressed nicely, here, because we're going out to celebrate my father having sold a real big painting."

Afterwards, scrapbook stories complete, Mercer met Garrett at the door, eyes moist from pride and, also, the shame of seeing her child so near the teeth of the thing she'd most wanted to keep him from. She wrapped her arm across his shoulder, already level with hers, and pulled him close. Spinning in her head, oddly, was the simple truth that there was only a single letter's difference between *protest* and *protect*.

Now, at the clinic, more noise from the public sidewalks connecting all sides of the building. The protesters knew from which exits Mercer and her staff would depart, and they kept their calls to an even pitch until the doors separated. Then the volume would rise.

"You have your purse?" asked Garrett, slowing momentarily until his mother revealed it had been hidden by the vest.

The walk was always the same with Garrett: head down, no eye contact. He held his mother along the bend of his shoulder, her face near his chest. When they reached his truck, she climbed inside with Garrett at her rear. There were others to lend assistance. Volunteers wearing uniform T-shirts who'd been present from early-morning hours to escort women through the front doors and here, later, the doctor out the back. Farther off stood law officers, whom Mercer knew by name.

During the drives home they rarely spoke of those brandishing signs and chanting. And when they did, it was usually about some innocuous detail like the look of a particular piece of clothing. If the sounds got too loud, Garrett would turn on his cassette deck. On this day, nothing abnormal. They stopped once on the ride away so Mercer could buy a few things from the market.

"I can't stay for dinner," said Garrett.

His mother was repacking a sack of groceries between her feet.

"I'm supposed to meet Lucy."

"That's fine." Even though she would be home in a few minutes, Mercer tied closed a Baggie of radishes. "Anyway, I don't remember inviting you."

They both smiled.

A head taller than his mother, Garrett could see down into her scalp, where a band of white roots had poked loose. Every six or so weeks, she allowed Tiff to color her hair over the bathroom sink. It was again time.

"Where are you two going?" she asked.

He shrugged.

The skin of her face was pale save for the gray beneath her eyes, puffy like pressed Chinese dumplings. Deep lines of worry framed her mouth, her nose. Along her hands and forearms, and, if one were to look, her breasts and shoulders, were speckles of brown. Though she had not gained much weight in the past eight or ten years, the very heft of her body had changed: it now tilted forward as if lightly spun on one of those saucer rides at amusement parks. She had aches in her lower back and neck and wrists from countless repeated patient examinations, exactly the same movements again and again.

Having stopped at a traffic light, both Garrett and Mercer watched an elderly woman pulling a wire basket on wheels. She was toting six empty bottles of ginger ale.

"We should offer her a ride," said Mercer, reluctantly.

The woman, rarely pleasant, lived three blocks from her.

"She won't come," said Garrett. "Besides, she's taking those bottles back. She waddles her ass out for a handful of pennies."

Still, Mercer rolled down her window and called to the woman. "Can we give you a lift?"

"Naw." She waved her hand, almost in disgust. "I'm fine, I'm fine."

Garrett tapped the gas pedal, not wanting to allow the chance for reconsideration.

A sigh, then another, and finally Mercer said, "She should have held more children."

It was, over time, a panacea she'd repeated with regularity. How can being near children—holding them in your arms—*not* make you feel better? Surely, for a moment or more, the act had the ability to brush away shallow troubles.

Beside the driveway, Tiff stood watering the flower beds with a garden hose. He was using a hoe, in his left hand, to rake channels for drainage. When the pickup doors opened, he set down his work and took the groceries from Mercer. They both climbed to the porch.

"All right," said Garrett, elbows across the truck's warm hood. "I'm going."

"You want I should announce it?" asked Tiff.

"Don't start with me, old man," said Garrett, playfully raising his fist.

On the ride to his apartment, he listened to an all-news radio station. He would shower, he would shave and dress in clean clothing. He was pricked by a curious desire for fried chicken.

ENOUGH LONG-NECK BOTTLES of Budweiser were abandoned between them to make the table resemble a giant chessboard. The beer had been consumed not only by Garrett and Lucy but by others at the Union Bar & Grill who'd stopped by to chat, standing over the two of them for a time before moving onward, leaving an empty reminder of the conversation. After taking their order, the waitress returned from the kitchen to inform Garrett that the deep fryer had surrendered to faulty wiring—the chamber of grease was tepid and still. He could have chicken, she'd said, but it would now have to be broiled or grilled.

Instead, he chose a meatball sandwich; Lucy had a tuna melt with tomatoes.

"I really wanted fried chicken," he said, after they'd already eaten.

She nodded, acknowledging she knew exactly how he felt—though she did not. She hated chicken.

They flicked a bottle cap back and forth between them, trying to make it sing off as many objects—bottles, flatware—as possible.

"Hey, *Daniel* Boone," said a voice behind Garrett.

It was Don Cape, still dandered with the morning's dirt. He removed his baseball cap, briefly, and ran his fingers through his limp, choppy hair.

"Get anything done?" asked Garrett.

"Some." He pulled over a chair, straddling it, with the back support across his chest. "We poured the foundation. But—Christ!—that Eddie's a talker. I had to blast the stereo to keep him from yappin' my ears off. Did you know his wife left him?"

Both Garrett and Lucy nodded.

"And I'm not surprised. Like a fucking washerwoman . . . "

"You know, Don," said Lucy, taking a drink of coffee. "Some people—and I'm not saying they're right—but some people actually think *you* talk too much."

His posture shifted, spine locked rigid. You could see, momentarily, as his eyes moved from Lucy to Garrett and then back again, that he didn't know if she was being sincere. He started to speak, but nothing came out.

"Oh, relax." Lucy raised her head. "I was kidding."

Part of a smile broke down his lips. His shoulders dropped, finding comfort against a slat of chair threaded through his armpits.

"Not funny." He lifted a soft pack of cigarettes from his breast pocket and knocked one into his hand. "But if it brings you joy . . . "

"It does."

At the bar, someone called out to tell Don his food had arrived.

"Well . . . "He stood again. He wanted to say more but was afraid Lucy and, worse, Garrett actually did think him a chatterbox. "See you later. Maybe this weekend or something."

Once they'd bid him farewell and he'd walked away, Garrett turned to Lucy. "You know, you're gonna have to apologize before we leave."

She tipped her head in agreement.

"I mean, *really* sell it. If not, he's gonna mope around for weeks. He'll ask me every damn time I see him whether or not you were serious."

They took turns with a wedge of peach pie until there was only a worm of crust remaining. Afterwards, Garrett waited by the door while Lucy spoke to Don, privately, in a far corner beneath the dartboard. Every few seconds Don would nod to a point beyond Lucy's shoulder, fearful of staring her too full in the face. Tucked into his collar, oddly, was a paper napkin to protect his already soiled shirt from food stains.

HIDING NEARLY AN ENTIRE WALL of Garrett's bedroom was a painting from his father's "gray" period. It had no frame, except the fringe of excess canvas along the edges. Age and moisture had warped the wood so the painting refused to lay flush at each corner. The bed had been given distance at all sides because once, during sex, the banging of headboard to wall knocked the painting from its hooks.

In only silky underpants and brassiere, Lucy sat on a steamer trunk beside the window. She was leafing through a catalogue of men's and women's sportswear while Garrett finished in the bathroom. He'd left the door partially opens and, amid gaps in his nightly routine (brushing teeth, washing face and hands, clipping jagged nails), he stole long glances in her direction. They'd been together for nearly two years, but only recently had the relationship found the heat of substance. One afternoon while walking to his truck from the hardware store, he'd caught Lucy's reflection in a picture window buying some shirts. She hadn't see him standing there, alone, on the sidewalk outside. So he watched her through the plate glass. In a moment, unexpected, he discovered the significance of his life with her: a thing to share between only them. The fleetingness of time spent as a couple. Soon, he thought, I will never have this chance again. With purpose, he rushed to kiss her neck—a warm twinkle of surprise—and confess his affection. And she knew, paper money still folded in her fist, the act was more than a simple sweetness. He did not need further explanation.

When they were both finished in the bathroom, they lay in bed covered only by a cotton sheet. She read a paperback, he encircled words with a pencil from a game in the morning newspaper. Because it was still warm and the window was parted halfway, they could hear voices from downstairs. One of the neighbors was toting bags of trash to the curbside even though garbage removal was two days away. Another person was filling his radiator with water by the light of his porch but kept missing the hole in the shadows.

"What're your plans for tomorrow?" she asked, once the lamp had been shut off.

"More wood." He folded a pillow against itself, giving his head a boost. "I'm supposed to take a load out to some Amish guy."

"Apple butter."

"Huh?"

"Don't forget to bring home some apple butter. They make it fresh out there."

The only things he knew of Amish country were that the drive was far and, always, the men didn't let him assist. They would leave him standing to one side while a group would unload his truck. Occasionally, someone would offer him a glass of lemonade or cold cider or well water, but that was all.

"One time," began Garrett, rolling to his side with his elbow bent awkwardly against his rib cage, "I went out there to get a bench this guy had made—they put it near the pond at the botanical garden and now it's all carved up with initials and graffiti. But when I was first driving out there I saw these two boys walking home from school. I slowed down because they were on this road where there wasn't much car traffic, only a horse and buggy traveling the opposite way. Anyhow, I lowered the window to ask them for directions to the right house. They both sort of jumped. They seemed startled and they moved their hands real quick, together, hiding something against their black jackets. In all the glare and bustle I only caught a glimpse of what they were holding. They'd been looking at some real hard-core porno magazine. Not like *Playboy* or *Penthouse* but real raunchy stuff. I only saw it for, like, a second. But I got a good look at a full-page photograph of a man having doggie-style sex with a woman."

"It happens."

For a moment, he paused. He wasn't sure whether the "it" to which Lucy referred was the act of sex or the two boys flipping through the magazine.

"Yeah," he said, responding to both. "But I remember I couldn't stop thinking about those kids. I mean, I drove off without asking them anything. And I kept wondering what it must've been like for them the first time they saw those pictures. Way different from what they understood in their lives. Not that sex existed, but that it could be sold in photographs at a corner store between milk and dish soap."

"I'm not sure." She kicked the sheet from her bare toes. "Think back. How much more shocked do you think those Amish boys were than any other boys the same age seeing a magazine like that for the very first time?"

"I don't know." His eyesight had now adjusted to the darkness and he could see the angles and shapes of her face. "As much TV and movie shit that's out there today, I guess most kids would be softened to the blow."

"Or not. Maybe it's like seeing a dead body. Do you think you'd be so desensitized by all the violence you've swallowed over the years that it wouldn't alarm you? Or would you be even more scared because you knew it was *real?*"

Both tired, they allowed the other's words to kiss around in their heads. Across the room a slight breeze tapped the drawstring of the curtains against the screen. There was something else from outside, but not loud enough to keep either of them awake.

Sam shuffled the car through the evening's beltway traffic, speeding or slowing (briefly) dependent on need. Eventually she reached her exit ramp and the vast, fat pavement narrowed to a single lane. Past the stop light, she was forced to travel below the speed limit when she found herself caught on the bumper of an octogenarian-driven Chrysler.

"Come on, bud," she said, aloud. "Dare to dream."

At another intersection she worked her way around the guy on the packed-dirt shoulder, turning momentarily to cut him a look of concern. But he was preoccupied with the road and continued staring straight ahead. Once she departed, motoring on, she glanced into her rearview mirror and saw the Chrysler's bright headlights, unnecessarily illuminated, already a significant distance behind. The rest of the ride took her only ten minutes.

High towers of toothbrush-shaped lights set the field aglow. There was a small pro-shop at the entrance. Sam had decided, on her own time, to watch real-live golfers smacking balls at a driving range instead of simply studying waves of computer-generated images. She took a few moments examining the selection of items they had for sale, spending most of her time with the meager offering of shoes. (All of which she'd seen before.) Then she found a place on a bench behind the stalls, laying a notepad across her lap. Most of the golfers chose to hit from a rubberized tee poking through a square swatch of artificial grass; a few moved their basket of balls to a carved hump of soil beyond the designated boxes.

Locked in concentration, she observed the motions of golf which mattered most to her work. The swing only as it related to the space on a golfer's body below his calves. She focused on the slant of their feet, the roll of their ankles. Did most golfers drag their toes? (Thus, the need for a protective glaze of polyurethane along the right and/or left toe cap.) Other concerns: Where did shoes need increased padding? What about using unconventionally patterned displays of spikes?

She kept lists on her unlined paper, each regarding another aspect of the prospective shoe. She watched a lumpy man, fiftyish, hack down on a golf ball; he was wearing a dress shirt, sleeves rolled to his elbows, suit pants, and white golf cleats. As he struggled, pausing for the occasional pull from a cigarette balanced on the overturned head of his driver, Sam filled with a sudden gloominess. She wondered what greater good came from designing improved footwear for this kind of suburban wonk. Lost in thought, she sketched a shoe with inverted spikes, freckling the once-cushy insoles so, with a secret button, they would telescope upward through the golfer's stocking feet. What can years of drawing athletic shoes prepare one for except drawing more athletic shoes?

Her trance was snapped by an electronic braying from her briefcase. Recently, many of the folks in Sam's division had been given cellular telephones (stickered with *Leave On At All Times* decals), to keep them only a toll call away. She lifted the tiny phone from her bag and shook it, instinctively, to consider whether something had broken. When the noise continued, she began pressing buttons until, finally, a voice spoke to her from within the earpiece.

"Sam? You there?"

It was Clem, who, technology be damned, sounded like she was calling from the pit of an abandoned missile silo.

"Clem? I can barely hear you." She stood, walking from beneath the driving range's aluminum apron into open air. "Can *you* hear *me?*"

"It's better now." Though the line cleared of static, there was still a slight echo behind both their voices. "Where are you?"

"I'm doing something for work. I'm watching golfers. How'd you get this number? Is everything all right?"

"A secretary in your office gave it to me." There was more crackling on both ends. "Yeah, everything's fine. I just keep missing you at home. We hadn't talked in a couple weeks."

"How're the kids?" asked Sam, still unconvinced.

"Good, good. Everyone's good. What about you?"

"Well"—she found a light post on which to lean—"there aren't many things less exciting than staring at weekend golfers flailing away on a driving range. But otherwise I'm decent."

They continued with the vagaries of their lives, back and forth. Every few minutes Sam was forced to adjust the tilt of her head for a sharper signal. A continent away, Clem sat in her living room, Dixon and the kids on the floor above. Finally the conversation neared its close.

"Have you talked to Mom or Garrett?" asked Clem.

"I spoke to her last week. But I talked to Garrett two days ago."

"I keep missing them, too."

"Oh, I really feel for you. Get Dix to buy you one of those cellular jobs and you can ring them from the beach."

"Sure." She looked over her shoulder, thinking she'd heard a car pull into the driveway. It was someone across the street. "How're things back home?"

"Seem fine. It's pretty lean workwise for Garrett." Two teenage boys in the last stall at the range were shouting because one of them plunked a distance marker with his ball. "He also said Mom's getting strange calls."

"What do you mean?"

"You know, protesters. They're calling at weird times."

"Saying?"

"What they always say. Shitty stuff. Some ask her to stop 'killing babies,' some are more obscene."

There were other questions Clem suddenly wanted to ask her sister, but the connection had again turned fuzzy; Sam thought the battery might have lost its charge. They promised to touch base in a day or two. With that, Sam lumbered back to the bench and returned her phone to its pouch within her briefcase.

Clem sat quietly on the couch, legs crossed, to her side a now-empty mug of tea on the end table. She considered calling her mother or Garrett, but she could wait until tomorrow, she thought, rising to finish in the kitchen before heading to bed. Over the sink, she rinsed the remaining few glasses and a dessert dish from angel cake she'd allowed Max after steamed cauliflower. She unexpectedly poured herself a finger of brandy and retreated with her checkbook to the breakfast nook. From the tall grass behind the house came the noise of cicadas and the clapping of leaves in the salty air.

Before filing the family's bills, Clem stored them in a swollen date organizer with checks and several sheets of postage stamps. She liked to unwrap the bills and complete all envelopes—return address, stamps—at once, saving payments for the end. Writing one check after the next. Always, she remembered without looking, without having been told "*Thank you very much for your last payment of* . . . " what the previous sum to any given bill collector was. Sometimes, after random visits to specialty shops in which she'd been persuaded to sign for a private line of credit, her memory ran back a few years.

The burden for the last of these bills was granted her after tremendous struggle. A monthly balance paid to the assisted-care home where her father now lived—the amount not covered by his medical insurance. After prolonged discussions, the three children—Clem, Sam, and Garrett—could not imagine their mother having to handle this responsibility alone every fourth week. It was not the financial weight of the twelve yearly checks of almost two hundred dollars each. Rather, they hated to think of her mood being drastically altered with unsuspecting visits to the mailbox. Another reminder she didn't need. One coming, perhaps, on a day when all was fine and clear.

The money came to Clem from her brother and sister in increments they could afford, like debt relief on a credit card. Still, she shouldered most of the load. There were also packets with itemized rosters of the medications Kendall was being fed. She and her siblings assumed it was all appropriate but, occasionally, she would ask a pharmacist friend about one thing or another. Years earlier, when Kendall had first been hospitalized, the diagnosis was schizophrenia. Drugs chosen to stabilize his condition left him logy, distant. As time passed, though, his station shifted and he began showing preliminary signs of Alzheimer's. It became increasingly difficult to know what part of his behavior was caused by the disease and what part was a side effect of the chemicals.

Paired with Kendall's early months at the assisted-living home was a new kind of worry for Mercer and the children. Some days he seemed nearly normal, tolerated small spans of lucid freedom to work on his art. Rapidly, though, his behavior began to deteriorate—not only in the course of an afternoon, but also from hour to hour.

Late one night, he was discovered wandering shoeless along the shoulder of the interstate. Another time he was found in a public park, trance-like, having carved a bowl of fruit into the trunk of a living tree. The worst episode came after he'd stolen the keys to a van: Mercer was on the phone with someone from the assisted-care staff when Garrett called her to the window. On the sidewalk of their house, amid a knot of protesters, Kendall was marching numbly in small, broken circles. Once brought inside, he seemed confused, recognizing only that he'd managed to travel back to a place he vaguely remembered.

Soon after, he was kept under near-constant surveillance. In the weeks that followed, Garrett told Clem he couldn't shake the picture of their father seated uncomfortably at the kitchen table, lost, as they all waited for a person in authority to take him away. Even then, Garrett accepted the parallels in his parents' lives: one needing protection from others, one needing only protection from himself.

Over time, the frequency of visits by family members had decreased. Of course, the distended proximity of Clem and Sam to their father's residence, hundreds of miles away, limited them. But even for those who were nearby, the hours shared had steadily declined. How hard when, mostly, he didn't recognize either of them. Indelibly seared into their minds was this image of a father or husband dribbling juice, painting with only his thumbs, grappling for words that made sense to someone other than him. Often Mercer would sit in her car afterwards, keys bunched and thorny against her palm, crying softly until the sadness passed and she had the energy to drive home.

Worst of all were reprieves, those thimbles of hope and cures. Random days when Kendall seemed suddenly only a few steps away from an illness they could understand. Sensical watercolors and sculptures in bright Play-Doh which chaffed and cracked like cold skin. Maybe connections could be made again: with his family, with his art. But nothing good ever lasted more than a wisp of afternoon.

Bills completed, Clem took a last swallow of brandy. She heard Dixon flush the toilet and return to the bedroom. She was no longer tired. Instead of sleep, she wanted to walk the beach with a blanket and a bottle of wine in search of a spot to lie, alone, pointed toward the line where the blackness of sky met the blackness of water. There were other nights when she'd had similar thoughts, but rarely had she acted on them. As now, she remained in the dim kitchen with her hands gripped to the sticky glass.

SUCH A STRANGE THING to enter her head, Clem considered the next day as she spread napkins along the coffee table. Dixon and Max were eating Thai food while watching the Red Sox on television. In a sudden declaration, Max claimed he hated shrimp. Or, as he called them, "shrumps." His newfound distaste for the crustaceans, which he'd been ingesting without prior incident nearly since birth, sparked something in Clem's mind, an event she had been unsuccessfully trying to keep sealed away in her powerful memory for years.

During college she had a friend named Liz Madan, a Catholic, who got pregnant after a brief "relationship" with a guy from her literature class. Once she'd decided, after careful consideration, to have an abortion, she spoke with Clem and another woman about the possibilities. Clem suggested they travel to Ohio; she explained that her mother actually performed the procedure. To the best of Clem's recollection, it was the first time she'd ever offered that information, unprovoked, to anyone. She'd allowed, finally, a time to turn this cumbersome weight back on itself—some good coming after years of struggle.

A week later Clem and Liz borrowed a car and drove the twelve hours, straight through, taking turns behind the wheel. When they'd finally reached Lukin the two were exhausted, mentally and physically, from the road, from this time in their lives. Together they sat on the floor of Clem's room sharing cartons of Chinese food. As with Max, now, Liz, too, decided she no longer had a taste for shrimp (which had come folded into fried rice). They ate silently, warm breath busting from their nostrils and busy mouths.

Late, when they were nearly ready for sleep, Mercer spoke to Liz in the hallway, with Clem lying in bed. Once Liz returned she only said, "Your mother's really nice." And the next morning they were again silent on the ride to the clinic. Standing on the sidewalk was a single picketer, a man resting a sign near his ankles.

Peculiarly, it was the first time Clem had ever stepped inside the building. When younger, the three children had on occasion visited their mother in her OB/GYN office a few miles away. Clem remembered once playing catch in the hallway with a gelatinous ball that turned out to be a silicone breast implant kept for demonstrations. Other days, she and Garrett and Sam would sit in the waiting room pawing through stacks of magazines or allowing water from the cooler spigot to fall directly into their mouths. When Clem was very young, she'd been permitted to crayon long murals against the crinkly paper that rolled across examination tables; the three of them were propped on wheeled stools, lifted to their highest setting, while they colored to the sounds of Mercer's dictation in the next room. During a game in which Garrett was pretending to be an invader from another planet, he'd used elastic bands to fasten a speculum to his head for antenna.

But this visit, obviously, was different. Clem was not introduced to anyone, proudly, as Mercer's daughter. Instead, she was a companion for Liz. And they sat together until a nurse beckoned.

Clem accompanied Liz into the operating room and then, if she wished, was allowed to wait just outside the doors once the process began. In hindsight, Clem wondered why her mother had granted such access. Was her purpose to frighten Clem from ever finding herself in a similar circumstance? Or perhaps Mercer believed Clem was finally old enough to glimpse a world that had surrounded her for such a long time. Not simply a response to actions, but a closeness to the actions themselves. A tight focus on something that had been seamlessly attached to her life, her family's lives, since she'd been a child. Though Clem never asked, she considered, in the days that followed, that maybe her mother wanted this to be seen no longer in only abstract terms. You brought Liz to me, went the rationale, so you must *understand* the consequences. In a reasonable, thoughtful manner I am willing to help you. But this is not like sewing a button to your blouse or calling an old chum for a favor.

During her time in the clinic, Clem's eyes swallowed information at a frenetic pace. There was so much she'd never before seen. Items, still nameless, to every side: trays of metal half tongs, dilators, each slightly larger in diameter than the next, for opening the closed cervix; small loops, called curettes, used to scrape residual tissue from the walls of the uterus; Betadine in squirt bottles similar to the one she used for watering houseplants.

While Liz was put under with a general anesthetic, Clem stood in the hallway gripping a rail for support. Though she tried to look away from the doors, there was an extended moment, too long, when they parted so a nurse could retrieve rolled gauze from a storage closet. The view came to Clem rapidly from a place above Liz's shoulders, Mercer seated on a rolling stool between stirruped legs, and on the slick linoleum floor, a machine that resembled a portable carpet shampooer with a coffee-can-sized canister screwed to its roof. Snaking upwards to the shadows of Liz's crotch was a clear plastic tube turned cloudy with blood and, as Clem would later learn, what clinic staffers called the products of conception. A hoarsy engine ticked along, damp and slurpy, similar in sound to the saliva vacuum a dentist hooks on a patient's lower lip.

Clem swung her head in another direction to rest her sight on something comfortable and reassuring. Before her vision had been cleared, she'd locked on a transparent jar of sodium-lime pellets fastened to an oxygen mask so Liz wouldn't rebreathe carbon dioxide. Not that Clem had any knowledge of what belonged in an operating room other than things she'd gleaned from television, but the pellets seemed too organic for common medicine. They were a better fit for a primary-school crafts class, beans pasted to construction paper.

She moved to the recovery room and waited, between other patients, for a nurse to roll Liz's gurney to a halt. When Clem finally saw Liz, she was surprised to find her lying face down. They were both told it was a more comfortable position. As the nurse adjusted a sheet along the gurney's frame, Liz began regaining consciousness.

"Don't do much over the next few days," the nurse said. "Let bleeding and cramping be your guide."

Lifting her mouth from the pillow, Liz tried to vomit. Instead, she only ran her tongue to a spot near her left cheek.

"Before you leave," continued the nurse, repeating what she'd said many other times, "let me know if you need a doctor's excuse. Nowhere on the note does it reveal what you've undergone. Only that you had a medical procedure performed."

In the half hour it took for Liz to gain back her strength, she did not say much to Clem. They remained quiet while Liz stepped into her clothing, Clem offering a hand for balance. While they were preparing to leave, Mercer paid another visit, introducing both women to a large man who would escort them to their car. "It's unfortunate," said Mercer, tapping the man on his arm. "But some people's beliefs are"—she tightened her ponytail—"different than ours. They want to make this even *more* difficult."

The creepy clumsiness of feeling like a trespasser seized Clem when she realized she'd waited nearly two decades for a peep behind this window shade. Not that she hadn't known there existed sobering realities to her mother's *other* job. But she was trying to sort through what things meant. It was almost like discovering one of your parents had been previously married. She hadn't figured the hidden text to her mother's life would be this way. Mostly, she longed for only hours earlier when there was simply the pepperiness of issues to digest and not what had become suddenly tangible.

Head down, Clem listened as her mother dispensed information to Liz while keeping a soft hand on Clem's waist. Then Clem locked elbows with Liz and they walked toward the doors behind a giant wall of a man. When they reached the parking lot, Clem made sure Liz kept her eyes planted firmly between the man's shoulder blades. To the sides, pressed against wobbly hurricane fencing, the single protester had now been joined by five others. They jeered, they shouted predictable epithets. But with her mouth near Liz's ear, Clem repeated, in her normal speaking voice, "Let's have pizza. Let's have pizza." It's what came into her mind, at that time, to distract a friend during trouble.

Once they'd reached the house there was not pizza but rather a vegetable soup in chicken stock prepared the night before by Tiff. In the days that followed, the two of them talked about other things and, except for an inquiry from Liz about payment (Had she been charged too little?) on the ride back to school, they never spoke of their visit to the clinic again. After more time passed, the girls drifted apart; they saw each other only on those rare occasions when they crossed paths walking to class or in the library or a campus coffee shop. Until, finally, their contact became so infrequent that when they did stumble into one another, Clem always wondered if Liz was thinking about Lukin even as they discussed the specifics of their current lives.

Many months later, in the warmth of summertime, Clem innocently asked Sam and, afterward, Garrett what knowledge they had of their mother's actual work. Both responses skewed toward Mercer's OB/GYN practice, late-night calls to deliver another baby. There were the recollections of protesters and sinister-shaped shadows beyond their front windows and heavy breaths coming from quickly answered telephones. It all seemed reasonable because, in truth, these would also have been Clem's answers had she not offered Liz assistance. Before Clem returned to school the following autumn, she spoke with her mother across a weathered picnic table in the yard.

"There's a part of me that thinks about it always," said Mercer. "Even when I'm with a young mother in a birthing room—*especially* when I'm with a young mother in a birthing room."

"Does it make you sad?"

"All the time." She lay her fingers flat against the wooden table as if presenting them for inspection. "I'd imagine no one wishes there weren't a need for abortions more than the doctors who perform them. It keeps me awake. But I can't just hide my eyes and hope it'll disappear. The only satisfaction—if that's even the word—I can take from doing abortions is knowing I gave the patients the best medical care I was capable. A proficient set of hands." She inhaled a mouthful of air. "It's hard not to sound preachy. These patients all have difficult choices to make. I'd like to believe I offered some dignity to their decision; they weren't forced to consider alternatives like the unsafe stinkholes that existed before what I was doing was legal. But, honestly, more times than not they end up hating me, too."

Both women took sips from tall glasses of iced tea.

"My only regret concerns you children. I've done my best to protect you three from what's out there. I've tried to control a part of our lives so things aren't that dissimilar from having a parent working in a machine shop or hair salon. But it seems silly that any of you might actually know how normal kids spend their days—without picketers on the lawns of their houses as they headed for the school bus. I mean . . ." Again she paused for breath because, she knew, the next words from her daughter might be hardest. "Do you resent me?"

"No." Clem shook her head slowly. "There are times when I wish things were different. But probably no more than any other kid does with her own life. Like, well, wouldn't it be great if we lived near the mountains or my father owned a movie theater."

Thinking back, Clem knew she hadn't been completely truthful with her mother. There had been moments when the three siblings asked only for what was nearly possible: a mother with one less responsibility, a father who wasn't lost.

A month earlier the T-shirt had come mailed in a box with a pair of running sneakers. Oversized teal cotton with a black, torso-sized "U" across the front and centered to its back, in smaller type, the word "GO." Above the hem of the left sleeve was the saXon logo, also in black. Though the sky had gone dark with storm clouds and fat fans of sulfur dioxide squeezed from nearby smokestacks, it was still warm outside. With the heels of his boots hooked to rain gutters, Garrett, dressed in familiar teal and black, sat on a hunk of roof facing the back yard. He was repairing a leak, tacking freshly cut shingles of tar paper. He had a view of the entire neighborhood; he could even see where a clearing of trees surrendered to the Thurmer Park ice rink.

This was a skill he'd learned, fixing roofs and ceilings, just as he'd been shown by others the necessary work it took to repair and build other things. In the years since college, which he abandoned early, he'd been able to piece together self-employment with odd construction-type jobs and plowing driveways and long days running snow-making machines at a local ski slope. The time in his life when he dreamed of the fantastic had passed. Not so many years earlier he'd considered illustrating comic books or inking layouts for advertising agencies. He still liked to draw. But he'd caved under the structure of university art classes designed, he believed, not to foster encouragement, but rather insecurity. And always, in strange contrast to his sisters, he had missed home. His desires, now, were realistic: a better truck, steak dinners on Saturday night, a week someplace bright during the slushy days of spring. There were obviously moments when he longed for more, but they rarely lasted.

Palms pressed to the gritty skin of the roof, he crawled backwards from the edge to take a drink of water. His plastic thermos was hung on a nail he'd only partly tapped down. Soon he would be finished. A ride home for his mother, then an evening alone. Maybe he would eat at the bar with Lucy while she worked. But he needed a second wind. More likely, a couple of takeout burgers on the couch with the television and morning newspaper.

As he loaded his gear into the truck, it began raining in long droplets that took the shape of arrowheads when they struck the windshield. He wiped his face with a wadded Kleenex. He was busier in the winter: he split time with Don plowing driveways after storms and worked as a snowmaker at Alpine Ridge. There was a camaraderie at the resort similar to when he'd played organized hockey. Together they drove SnoCats up the side of the slope, towing big fan guns in their tracks. It gave him purpose, painting the side of a skier's mountain with fresh snow.

In season, he worked four twelve-hour shifts a week, either from noon to midnight or vice versa. Noon to moon is what they called it. The fan guns had three-phase, 480-volt motors they fastened to power outlets hidden along the tree line; they were also hooked by firehose to underground water pipes. When the temperature was right, the fans blew sparkling raisins of water into the air, giving them the hang time necessary to freeze. After letting the piles of new snow cure for a day, they used SnoCats with plow blades, as on bulldozers, to push and pack the surface.

Garrett enjoyed running the (smaller) ground guns even more. These he could hitch to the back of a snowmobile, alone, and follow behind several other workers to cleared spaces. He also liked the manual labor. The guns were always pointed with the breeze at their backs, but sometimes, in changing weather, the wind shifted; the fresh snow swirled in place, burying the machines. It often took several men with shovels a couple of hours to dig them loose.

Afterwards, they would retreat to the locker room, one crew finishing while another prepared to begin its day. They sat around warming themselves, slowly removing clothing and drinking coffee and discussing conditions on the slopes. He didn't have that now. Infrequently, a partner joined him. But it wasn't the same.

HE SAT BESIDE DON in the bed of his pickup truck, legs locked straight, eating a pineapple sundae from the pocket of a miniature baseball helmet. The two were parked with the rear of the truck facing a winding, paved oval where, assuming you were of minimum age (fifteen) and height (62 inches), you could rent and race go-carts. The track was surrounded by bricks of hay, like giant coconut bars, and stacked tires designed to reduce the damage of crashes and spinouts. While the two of them talked, Garrett and Don, they had to raise their voices, slightly, to carry the buzz of the weed-eater-sounding engines.

"Didn't I tell them 'no nuts'?" asked Don, picking crushed almonds from his tacky fudge topping with a spoon.

Behind the track was a large hoop of netting pitched to resemble a circus tent. Spoked toward the netting's center were batting cages with coin-operated ball machines of varying speeds. In between the passing go-carts you could hear the ping of aluminum bats or, farther still, the shrill of couples playing Putt-Putt.

When Garrett finished eating, he poured bottled beer, cloaked in a brown paper bag, into his helmet and dumped the cloudy suds over the side of the truck. He wiped the helmet dry with his pants leg and placed it on his fist. "I hate the Twins," he said.

"They're better than the goddam Cubs," said Don, raising his own dish.

Together they nodded in agreement.

"We had this weird talk the other night," said Garrett, recalling a discussion he'd had with Lucy. "She's at this place where she isn't very sure about things. She doesn't know where she's going, where *we're* going."

Before Garrett continued, Don adjusted himself so he didn't have to twist his head to make eye contact.

"She's tired of tending bar and eating plastic-wrapped food and struggling to finish her degree, and, really, of living here."

"What's she want to do?"

"Well, that's the thing. She doesn't know. Maybe move somewhere nice, where the clouds break more than once a month." They both smiled. "Find a job she cares about."

"Like?"

"Mmmmmm." He shrugged. "You know what she told me? She said she's always wanted to own a shop that sells, like, lotions and creams and French soaps and bath salts and that kinda shit. Can you believe? I mean, Lucy?"

Considering the question rhetorical, Don remained quiet.

"But then we started arguing. Mostly, because I was getting really tired. And she was anxious and wired and needed some closure." Despite his own life choices, despite appearances, Garrett was not an unintelligent man. There were times when he had terrific insight: a device of blinking lights and trilling bells fastened to his brain stem that offered a capacity to see beyond a simple exchange and, whether by talk or touch, select the correct response. "So I walked to where she was standing and put my arms around her waist in this different way, like I'd seen on a Lamaze poster in my mother's office, and just held her for a while."

Stuck for words, Don only managed, "That'll work."

"And then . . . " began Garrett, pulling his knees close, "right before we were finally ready for bed, she said, kind of from nowhere, 'Tell me one thing you'd remember about me?' It was strange because, really, I knew exactly what she meant. A long time ago I'd asked Jessy Wicks, this girl I liked from high school, almost the same thing. And I knew, having been on the other side of the question, that there wasn't a *right* answer."

From Don, only silence.

"Just by responding you imply the two of you won't always be together . . . "

"I get it," said Don, even though he probably did not.

"I tried to kiss her but she wouldn't let me. Not for more than a few seconds. So, using whatever fucking sense God gave me, I said, 'I'd remember you as the love of my life.' "

"Really?" And they both felt awkward, the conversation tumbling to new territory. "Do you believe it?"

"I don't know. Maybe. But it worked, I guess, because we went to sleep. We haven't talked about it since." He kicked his legs out again. "She's too smart to think I was being totally sincere. She knows, on some level, I just said those things because I wanted to shut up for the night."

Feeling outgunned, uncomfortable, in his best friend's pickup truck talking about a depth to relationships he'd never experienced, Don tried to tug the subject away from specifics.

"It's hard to know what's really right about anything," he said. "I mean, not just with women and love but, also, with work and . . . and . . . life."

Garrett nodded, politely, lost with where his friend was headed.

"One summer, when I was helping my uncle out in the sheriff's department in North Carolina, they brought in two guys—*kids*—on a manslaughter charge. These boys had been hiding in the parking lot of some motel, smoking cigs and drinking malt liquor, when a fancy car pulled in—a Lexus or BMW or something—and the kids went to rob the driver. He struggled and they shot him once in the head. The idiots dumped his body in the bushes and took his car, driving it around for a day or so. They'd been talking all tough, telling anyone who'd listen about what they'd done. But when they were finally brought into the station they both went soft. Like suddenly they'd realized the consequences."

Close to where they were parked, a go-cart stopped and another one bumped it from behind. Both carts wobbled into a tower of tires.

"I remember standing in the hallway when they led the two boys to separate holding cells, and because it was big news down there, a few reporters from the local newspaper and TV stations were yelling questions and holding bright strobe lights. You could see the terror on these kids' faces, even as they tried to pretend they weren't afraid. And I guess what I'm trying to say . . . "

"What *are* you trying to say?" asked Garrett, and they both laughed.

"Well, that some decisions come to us slowly and others—huge, life-altering choices like whether to shoot a man or spend the rest of our lives with a person—can hit us instantly. Maybe it's fuzzy for a while but then, finally, you reach a point where you either pull the trigger or you don't."

A soft smile broke across Garrett's face because, in Don's own distorted way, he'd actually made sense.

"We've been together too long, pal," said Garrett. "I'm beginning to know what you mean."

They watched the two stalled go-carts drive away before Garrett continued.

"The other night with Lucy I was kind of reminded about that time you and I went to Kentucky a few Septembers ago. We'd stopped for sandwiches and Cokes at a roadside diner." Don's head bobbed with recognition. "And we were sitting on those metal tables in the back staring at all the crap they had scattered on the lawn. Burned-out cars and hubcaps and rotted wood and old appliances. Just before leaving we saw that sign bolted to the door of that discarded refrigerator reading. 'This is a land of peace, love, justice and *no* mercy.' "

"Yeah. We tried to fuckin' pry the thing off with a rusted bumper."

"Man, I thought that was *so* deep. I've got it written across the front page of my checkbook."

They didn't speak for a few minutes, their heads swiveling in tandem as they watched the carts speed past.

"Last week, I'd just dropped my mother off after the clinic and the radio was playing. I'd backed out of her driveway when this guy who comes on after the news, on some station near the low end of the dial, says, 'We are never promised justice, only mercy.' He'd quoted some Indian chief. And I let it bang around in my head until, like I'm having a fucking heart attack, I pulled to the side of the road. Which one do we believe? I mean, *really*. Wouldn't it change the way you lived? Justice or mercy?"

"Right."

Some part of Garrett knew everything he'd said after describing the trip to Kentucky had been lost on Don. It had only come so Garrett could hear how the words sounded out loud. He stuck his thumb in the mouth of his beer bottle and began plunking it, which, reasonably, set both men back at ease.

POSITIONED LIKE DRAPES across the upper edge of the window was a row of T-shirts, in various color combinations, alternating a frontside "U" with a backside "GO." Beneath was a collection of shoe boxes moored by padlocked bicycle chains. A wooden easel at the center of the window display held a hand-lettered sign announcing the release date of saXon's newest basketball sneakers. Though it was only nine-fifteen in the morning—forty-five minutes before the store opened—there was already a line of mostly teenage boys waiting along the sidewalk. Clem had errands to run, here in Boston, and she was wheeling Greer's stroller while Max walked to one side holding a loose strap of nylon designed for fastening diaper bags.

The three of them paused near the sporting-goods store to watch. About a year ago, Clem remembered having a conversation with Sam about the phenomenon of kids needing to own the newest and, presumably, best sneakers. Status symbols for their feet. Often the difference between one season's model and the next was only cosmetic: a changed color scheme, or a superfluous rivet, or once, Sam recalled, the stitching of a popular player's uniform number to the tongue. "We're exploiting these kids," said Sam. "Sometimes we stagger the release of basketball shoes so they'll hit the market four or five weeks apart. God knows where fourteen-year-olds are getting a hundred and twenty bucks for *athletic shoes* every couple of months."

Clem looked down at her own son's tiny sneakers, a gift last June from his aunt. "Forgive us, Max," she said. "You're no longer cool."

He didn't understand, of course. He was mesmerized by the collection of older boys leaning against the building—dribbling balls and shaking their Walkman-bound heads and, in one case, flashing a knob of cash.

"Let's go," said Clem, leading the stroller away. "This is how it all begins." She was speaking to herself. "They'll get you hooked early."

The three of them continued in the direction of a gallery where

Clem hoped to send a piece of blown glass to a friend who'd recently been married. But first they stopped at a small restaurant so she could feed the children, neither of whom had been particularly hungry before they'd left the house. In a side booth, with stroller and baggage pushed to the corner, they sat in semicircular fashion with Clem and Max at opposite arms of Greer's high chair. Clem arranged the food near both children: grilled cheese and carrots (cut into tossed-salad-style chips) for Max; bottled milk and jars of pureed pears and spinach for Greer.

"I don't like this," said Max, drilling his finger into the toasted bread.

"Yes you do."

"I want the *other* cheese."

At home, Clem fixed his sandwiches with mozzarella instead of American.

"They don't have that kind here." She lifted a spoon of pear toward Greer, who, at the last possible moment, turned her head, so it ran down her cheek. "You like this cheese, too."

"No." He watched as Clem wiped his sister's face. "I'll have a hamburger."

"You will not."

Again, she tried feeding Greer, who, this time, knocked the spoon from her mother's hand. Clem used a napkin to clean the spattered table; she surrendered a bottle, which the waitress had heated in a microwave oven. After taking a sip of coffee, she turned her attention to Max, who, predictably, was staring straight ahead with his arms flexed across his chest.

"I'll wait," said Clem, biting a corner of her tuna melt.

The two of them sat there, silently, with Greer chugging wetly away.

Clem watched a man several booths down. He was eating fried eggs and toast, alone, his fork held awkwardly in the crease of his fist. Near his place was coffee and water, but nothing else. No newspaper or magazine or book to occupy his attention. Strangely, this was how Clem pictured her brother sometimes back in Lukin. Always by himself, a businessman in a foreign city, incapable of casual conversation with the restaurant staff or the person seated at the next table. Lifting item after item of food to his mouth. Changeless. The same every day.

Though she knew many visions of her brother were fabrications, she still had trouble shaking them from her mind. They came one after another: pitched overwhelmingly with emotion and tragedy. Did he live in a room of soiled walls and chipped plaster and furniture with exposed girdles of spring? Allow for assistance, she imagined, sadly. From me, from your *family*. We once shared the same kitchen and bathroom and swing set. We once shared a life.

But she was usually able to talk herself down. On her last trip home she'd visited his apartment. And nothing was so terribly dismal. He had toothpaste and fresh milk and, more than she and Dixon, frosted mugs for root beer. Though she'd rarely seen her brother drunk, she believed, in part, he put himself to sleep nightly with the reek of hard liquor. This, too, proved false. As when she'd departed for college, she wondered what survived at home without a grease she'd once provided.

She was brought again to the present by the clink of flatware. Max was stretched across the table, his fingers smudging the edge of her plate.

"What do you want?"

"That one," he said, grabbing for her sandwich.

"This is tuna fish." She waved a half just beyond the reach of his hands. "It's got the same cheese that's on your sandwich."

"It's better . . ."

"Are you gonna eat it this way?"

He nodded.

She swapped lunches, watching her son chew a cautious mouthful of tuna melt as if considering whether he'd made an error in judgment before it was irreversible. Once they finished, Max managing only a few more bites, they continued with their list of chores.

The saleswoman in the glass store was nervous, Clem could tell, carefully setting vases and decanters on the counter while keeping a watch for Max.

"He's okay," said Clem, assuring the woman with a tap-tap to her thigh as though calling a dog.

Max had his face pressed to the side of a display case stocked with glass figurines of animals and birds and wire-supported balloons. For purposes of distraction, Clem rolled Greer into the saleswoman's line of vision;

she hoped a cute infant might suspend anxiety. Instead, the woman simply moved to another position. These kinds of people only liked children in the abstract, Clem thought. As when a valued customer spoke with distant affection of her grandson or niece. "Wonderful," Clem could imagine the woman saying, though truthfully meaning it was *wonderful* that the aforementioned child was living in remote environs where there was little opportunity they would ever cross paths.

Hurriedly, Clem selected a set of crystal candlesticks—discouragingly boring—and scribbled a short note. The three of them were so absently escorted from the shop that, upon reaching the crosswalk, Clem was stopped from behind by the breathless saleswoman waving the carbon receipt to her credit card.

They moved on, Clem and the children, making their way to Newbury Street to kill time until Dixon could provide a ride home; he was only working a half day because of new carpeting being laid in his office. There were dresses and handbags and houseware she wanted to examine but, with napless kids, her concern was keeping active. Max, she knew, would soon turn cranky. She had inexplicably forgotten the Snugli to carry Greer, which would've allowed her to adjust the stroller for her son. Now her morning was only a way to chew minutes until they could leave Boston. She'd be fortunate to gather visits for kids' clothing or a submitted order for new monogrammed stationery. For Max, the promise of his own BAG of Gummi cowboys.

"I could have them now . . . " he said.

"No. But later. If you're good."

"Maybe I could jus' hold them." He shook his hands excitedly near his chest. "I won't eat any."

"Later," she repeated.

After a few more steps, in the lapse where she expected Max again to plead for the candies, she was surprised to hear instead a weak-sounding yelp. He scrambled for shelter near the loose fabric of her slacks. He'd been frightened by a gargoyle-like dog, cut from stone, with spiked collar and long red ribbons of leash blowing into the line of passersby.

"It's not real," said Clem, leading Max around by the hand. "It's just a brightly painted statue."

She guided him to the sculpted creature, taking his fingers and rubbing them against its coarse surface.

"The people who own this store put it out for decoration," she said. "It's like a big rock."

"A rock," he repeated, quietly.

Turning away, she told him about a time when she was young and had wandered into the warehouse studio of her father—Max's grandfather—for an unsuspecting visit. The cavernous room had been mostly dark until the doors parted. Against the back wall were girders soldered together so, in the mind of a child, they resembled the skeletal frame of a dinosaur. But before even Clem could run for freedom came a sound and flash in the place where the iron beast's lowered head might be positioned. She saw a single greened eye and terrific wands of fire. A dragon, she thought, bolting for the house. There's a dragon in our yard.

Later, Clem explained, she was rescued from beneath her parents' bed and told how the dragon had only been a figment of her imagination. "A misunderstanding," her father repeated in a language meant for adults. There were no bones, only crookedly stacked pieces of industrial waste. And the lifeblood was her father armed with a blowtorch and welding mask.

"Did you see it again?" asked Max.

Though some part of his little brain had understood the story he'd just told, now her son was fixated on the notion of a "dragon" caged behind his mother's childhood home.

"Well, yeah," said Clem. "But it was never really a dragon. It was some junk and . . . " She pointed to him for a response.

"Gran-*pa*," he said, referring to a man he'd only met once.

"Right-o"

The rest of the morning passed without incident. They waited on a park bench outside the building where Dixon worked. Seated with one hand rocking Greer's stroller, Clem watched people search for unoccupied space to eat their bag lunches: other park benches, the rim to a fountain, soft hips of lawn for the daring. To her side, Max slapped his toy cars against a brick walkway. She had released the Gummi cowboys into his possession long ago.

"Who's that?" she asked, gesturing to the sky above his left shoulder.

He turned and, after a moment to adjust, recognized his father crossing the street.

"Dad." And then, as if maybe she hadn't heard him, the word was repeated.

Quick kisses were exchanged, patted heads and limbs. Navigating their way to a nearby parking garage between even more bodies escaping for an hour of midday sunshine, Max secured himself against the stroller and his father's right leg. Oddly, once they retreated to the hollow tunnels of asphalt and concrete, Max seemed liberated, racing down the curling ramps until he was corralled by his parents, concerned for his safety.

Upon exiting, Max was permitted to pay the attendant through the back window.

"And I *thank* you," said the man, cupping his cigarette so the smoke wouldn't leak into the car.

For the first part of the ride Max clutched the ticket stub, twice dropping hands to his lap when Dixon spotted him rubbing it near his mouth in the rearview mirror. They jerked through the busy streets, gas and brake, gas and brake.

"She's sleepin'," said Max, presciently, when Clem turned to examine Greer.

And soon, once they'd reached Route 24, Max, too, had nodded away. Every ten or so minutes, Clem would steal glances at the two children. She watched the scenery swim past. She remembered long drives with her own family, trips to Tennessee and eastern Pennsylvania. A station wagon her mother once owned had a window cut into the roof, behind the headrests of the front seat, so Clem and her siblings could stare into the sky. They liked to pretend they were strapped into fast-moving planes or space capsules; they even ate snacks from single-serve pudding cups, as they imagined the astronauts did. When bored, they used yellow markers to reveal answers in Hide-n'-Peek books.

There were times—not now, but during short stops to the market or dry cleaners—when Clem feared for her children. Perhaps their car seats were defective or ineptly fastened, a lax buckle or strap. She wondered whether her parents had had similar worries. Things were different then. Laws demanding youngsters ride belted in backseats were not yet passed. Drivers were left to their own discretion.

A soft sigh from Max, pleasant burbling from his sister.

And Clem could not contain her desire to touch them both, running her finger along the mushy skin of their arms and hands and chins. She'd had another kind of childhood. Neither worse nor better. The love of her mother and father was not less than her own. It was exhibited in other ways. There was a coolness to her parents with their kids. The relationship was one of efficiency. Within the domed snow globe of their little world, they did their best to make decisions they believed appropriate and honorable. Bestowed upon their three children, more important than unsheathed displays of emotion, was a sense of common responsibility. A day when Sam was made to weed a neighbor's garden in payment for a trampled flower bed, or when Garrett was led to apologize for flicking a classmate's ear in a school assembly.

Later, when Kendall began showing the first signs of mental illness during the children's teenage years, the burden of parenthood fell completely to Mercer. Though she finally lacked the hours she'd once hoped to spend with her children—cookie cutting and skating and teaching them to drive—she had done her best. Impart a wisdom, she'd told Clem during a recent phone conversation, so that decisions were not left to scattershot . . . unless that, in itself, was the most intelligent choice. There was an ephemeral quality to raising children, to the tools given them.

Clem considered the day when Max, with her knowledge, would select what was wrong. A lesson coming from his own hand. She let her mind run to whether it was easier watching this from a distance or in the fissure granted to those nearest.

"You would stand in the way of trouble to protect the kids," Clem said to Dixon, not in the form of a question.

"Of course."

He removed a pair of sunglasses from his breast pocket and slipped them onto his face, soothing a glare.

"But what would you *let* them do?"

"Huh?"

"If Max was riding a skateboard and you knew he might fall"—she licked her lips—"would you take him off? Would you *physically* remove him from the board?"

"I guess it would depend how fast he was going."

"You'd tell him to stop"—Dixon nodded—"and then . . . "

"There are worse things than Max skinning his knee."

The scrutinization of details. By one another.

"When Sam was young my parents gave her such room. Maybe because she was the third child and they were less apprehensive or maybe because it was just what her personality called for. But she'd come home with cuts and bruises from hockey or roughhousing. And most of the time no one said a thing." She peeled loose a breath mint from its roll. "I never had the same freedom."

Even now, Clem lacked a clarity for which part came first: the tight rein of parents or the dearth of adolescent friendships. Early in life she was bid to lend assistance in the kitchen or yard while other children—later, her own siblings—gathered on neighborhood lawns for games of kickball and smear-the-queer. Was this nurture or nature? Over the years, she wondered whether she'd dawdled near the house, avoiding contact with others—practically forcing her folks to provide a busying alternative—or was it they who wanted to keep tight their grip? A control that was lost, finally, for Mercer, when her attention gained focus in more troublesome directions. The business of keeping sanity afloat.

"Well, I can't imagine you wrestling with some boy at the playground."

"No, I guess not. It's just that how many of those 'being-lifted-from-a-skateboard' episodes would it have taken for me to be another person?"

"How much rope do we give *our* kids?"

"Yeah. I think Sam's a whole lot better adjusted than me."

"Would she agree?"

"Mmmmmm."

"Listen," he said, changing lanes to pass a truck. "We've got two kids. We can try it both ways."

"Cute."

"A contest. May the best child win."

"Speak a little louder," said Clem, checking the backseat. "I'm sure they'll want to remember every word for when they're working through this in therapy twenty years from now."

They didn't talk again until they'd left the main highways. Clem rolled down the window a few inches for the grit and smell of ocean air.

"One morning," began Dixon, unprovoked, "these kids will stare into the mirror and see your face or mine. Maybe both. They'll rattle in disbelief. Max will call his wife into the bathroom and ask, 'Do I look like my ol' man?' And because he'll have married a thoughtful, sweetly woman, she'll say, 'No.' He'll shave his cheeks and drink his coffee and, hopefully, think good of us more days than not."

"We're trying."

"Exactly . . . "

They were near home. Passing familiar landmarks they'd walked to with the children. Town road, general store. An antique anchor which Max liked to climb.

The tick and moan of wheels as Sam scooted along the lobby's polished floor. Behind the reception desk a security guard managed a reluctant salute, his acknowledgment that though rollerblades were not permitted inside the building, he was willing to look the other way with her. Sweat turned clammy against Sam's back and beneath her arms when she entered the structure's climate-controlled air. She had skated powerfully, inspired, during time meant for sandwiches or tinfoiled bowls of pasta salad. Earlier in the day she had been praised for the design of her golf shoes. The head of her division had, amazingly, liked the entire "package," from the selection of materials to the earthier-color choices. Of course there were questions: Was the staggered lacing system excessive? Did the heel counter need to be raised? But mostly, the presentation had been a terrific success.

In the elevator Sam wiped her forehead with the back of her hand. The chance for a quick shower, a cup of dry granola. She clopped her carpeted way to the office carrels. Three message Post-Its, ignored, were stuck to the chair where she prepared to sit and remove her skates.

"You've got a call," said a man whose job it was to answer them, from across the open hallway. "Third time."

This would need to be fast, thought Sam, lifting the telephone receiver instead of her headset.

"I've been trying for the last hour," said Clem. Her voice sounded reedy, anxious. "No one"—she slowed herself—"spoke to you?"

Bad to follow a morning of good.

"What's wrong?" Sam rifled through the phone message: two from Clem, one from Tiff. "I was away . . . "

Sam knew her sister was often likely to attach a disproportionate amount of drama to common events. This was not one of those instances.

"An explosion . . . " Clem could say nothing else before losing herself to wheezy swallows of breath, a race of distance completed.

"Take it easy, Clem. What happened?"

The words came stacked upon each other in rapid succession, so even after she'd heard them, Sam needed to take a moment for reexamination.

"There was an explosion." A smaller pause. "They don't know whether it was a bomb."

"What *bomb?* Where's Dixon? Where are the kids?"

"They're in the other room. I'm waiting to hear more."

"I still don't—"

In a cadence Sam could understand, Clem told her there'd been an explosion at the clinic in Lukin. Maybe a bomb. Both Mercer and Garrett were present.

The sticky vapor of confusion filled Sam's head, forcing her to grab the half wall of the cubicle for balance. She was still listing awkwardly on the narrow tires of her skates. Someone passed smiling, mouthing a phrase of good fortune in reference to the golf spikes.

"What else?"

"That's all I know." Clem let it break from her mouth as if accused. "I'm waiting for the other line to ring with something . . . "

"And you have no idea?"

She didn't answer right away and Sam felt nauseous, doubling over. But Clem had only been whispering to Dixon or one of the kids, who'd entered the kitchen, and when finished, she said she didn't have any other details.

They traded questions, back and forth, full of fear and insecurity.

They agreed to talk again the minute Sam got home, regardless of whether new information had come or not.

They were each at too great a distance from what mattered.

Later, Sam moved from bedroom to bathroom to hall closet without precision. She carried clothing, wrapped in cleaner's plastic, to the medicine cabinet before remembering it belonged folded in the suitcase on her bed; she wrote herself reminders of things to do only moments before actually doing them. She scaled the staircase three, four times. Unneeded items retrieved from the backs of drawers—cough drops, old rings—were stuffed into a zippered pocket of her shoulder bag. Sweaters and T-shirts, khakis and shorts. She had forgotten the weather in a place she once knew well. Warm or cool? Into a slot meant for shoes she wadded a windbreaker to repel rain.

She ran the shower, still barefoot and wearing workout clothes. She wriggled out of her spandex tights with the telephone cradled against her shoulder. From Clem, nothing more. They talked above the hoosh and spank of water as Sam adjusted its temperature. A desire to take action. Get there, *be* there. Another method of preparation for Clem, controlled and thoughtful.

Notes were scribbled to Sam's roommates as she wandered, toothbrush tucked into her left cheek. Couldn't this news arrive with more clarity? They were *her* relatives, mother and brother. She needed to know before others, before the firemen and police and rescue workers pawing through the crumbled building. Another call answered while she dug through a pile of dirty laundry looking for used underpants; a voice she recognized yammering about things lacking import. He hadn't expected to find her home; he'd intended to leave a message. Would dinner on Friday be out of the question? She told Brett Tarver, a name that arrived as she stuffed toiletries into a rubber sack, it was not a good time for her to make decisions. They would talk later. A different day.

She returned for her money. The car was left running in the driveway, door half parted. It took a second to remember she'd placed the wallet on the dining-room table. She would find a flight—a series of connecting flights—to get her back soonest. Through Denver or Chicago or Saint Louis even.

At the airport she parked in the first available space, a lot that required she ride a shuttle van to the terminal. She watched the gates raise and lower from her seat in the rear, a needle of traffic merging at her left and then again at her right. Suitcases and laptop computers were stacked awkwardly in the aisle between the feet of business travelers who all looked the same, dressed in neckties or polo shirts. While she jogged from the van she could feel beads of wetness from sweat and shampoo water hitched to the line of her scalp.

Inside, she let her eyes roam the green-hazed television screens, fastened together into a wall. She stumbled over her bags as she turned to take inventory of the airline counters; she was looking for a plane that would get her to Ohio without unbearable waits. After taking a few steps in one direction and then the other, she stood behind two people waiting before the American Airlines reservations desk. She nervously tightened and retightened her damp ponytail.

Then came a now-familiar bleating from the pocket of her shoulder bag.

When she crouched to retrieve the phone, her temples inflated with the swell of a beer headache.

She spoke rapidly, warble on warble, waiting for a response. This was not a place to talk, the staticky hub of an airport. She heard the crunching of microwaves looking to connect. A voice, high then low. She walked away from the ticket purchasers' line, lifting and lowering the angle of her head for cleaner reception. Finally, once she'd moved baglessly through the electronic doors, she heard Clem in the middle of a sentence. Sam stood in the broken sunlight with cars and minivan taxis pulling near the curb to unload passengers. Surrounded by people with the wide, glossy hope brought by travel.

Everything rotated in Sam's head pinned to the deep roar of jet engines. Always, she thought, the words were paired together in media reports: crude and bomb. She imagined a news anchor blathering about a crude homemade bomb built of leather scraps and analgesic tablets. The hide of a stuffed teddy bear. She found the realness of

Clem's speech, mumbled and cracking. This bomb had been built with gunpowder and steel pipes, the same kind the Boones had once used to construct the goals for their back-yard ice rink. There was now information, plenty, spit on slow crawls at the bottom of TV sets. One of the protesters, a regular who'd often lugged a wooden cross over his shoulder, had attempted to plant a backpack with an explosive device at the clinic's front door. The detonator was soft, poorly rigged. Damage intended to arrive when the building was vacated could not wait.

There had been no warning, no calls of good faith.

A technician whose responsibility it was to examine gelatinous fetal tissue in metal pie plates after abortions, poking through the nearly visible hands and feet of late-terms, had been killed.

Big haunted holes of blown-out glass left a sparkly residue on the sidewalk like fresh snow. Wind-scattered "Wanted" signs of Mercer, copied on Xerox paper, flapping in shrubbery and between the torn roots of trees. A smell from cordite and recently watered fire. Lanced by a toppled fence, hand-lettered, a placard reading, "Oh, Mommy, Mommy, Don't murder me!" Clothing in awkward shreds of fabric, a collar or pocket square, moist with the spray of blood. Exposed beneath the stairway were ribbed cables of steel, floured with concrete.

And when the first person arrived, a man who'd been passing in his car, he saw the wrecked bodies through the drift of smoke and called to his wife, "Don't come over!"

Already on TV screens at the airport, suspended above some bar with a cutesy name like The Cockpit, images from the blast seen repeatedly on all-news stations, video loops of the half-sunk structure. The muzzy overdub of sound in Sam's ears: something that resembled the nasally horn of a foreign automobile; the pesty whisper of many conversations pushed into one. And she made her way to the gate, now ticketed, with the phone warm against her cheek and her sister's voice weak then strong then weak again.

Sam chewed ice in her seat, jittery, spitting back into the plastic cup the pieces too large and cold for her mouth. The wait of departure: sealing the cabin doors; pulling from the terminal; a woozy roll to the airstrip.

It was not until they'd reached a comfortable cruising altitude, thirty or forty minutes later, that she spoke again to her sister, using a phone tethered to the headrest of the seat in front. And Sam knew from the way Clem answered, the dry rake of her throat, the next moments of their lives would be runted with sorrow.

She was dangled six miles from the ground with nowhere to go, really, except home. Locked tenuously to her sister, she concentrated on Clem's slowed language as her ears fought the ricky-ricky-ricky of a drinks' cart coming down the aisle. Sam's brother had lived; her mother had not.

The only other time she had been this close to death was when Barley, their dog, had been euthanized to spare him the remaining ravages of bone cancer. That night, the family gathered unexpectedly on the back porch, swapping stories about the dog to lift their spirits. The best came from Mercer, who told of a day when one of her patients following childbirth asked her to bury the placenta as part of some mystical ceremony. Mercer had granted the request, finding a peaceful place behind the warehouse in the yard. But the next morning, when she'd called Barley into the house for his food, the dog was carrying the burst placenta in his mouth. Sticky curlicues from the pouch had worked their way across the bridge of the dog's nose like the tentacles of a squid.

Motionless, Sam let the contraction of thoughts bloom and wither. A leaky emptiness to accept over time. This was not going to be all right. Some things don't get better in passing minutes and days. They change shape, they become distorted in other light. She took a breath, then another. She was left with the gilded knowledge that nothing worse could ever happen.

She rubbed her fingers against themselves as if polishing stones.

THE NEXT MORNING'S NEWSPAPERS were crowded with condemnations from both sides. Some stories contained the word "reprehensible" four or five times, jimmied into quotes from clergymen and activists and politicians. There would soon be investigators from the Bureau of Alcohol, Tobacco and Firearms. In a sleepy joke over the breakfast table, Clem said if the letters were shifted the agents could announce themselves as being from the Bureau of F.A.T. Dressed in sweatshirt and boxer shorts, Sam managed a smile of mercy. She covered her face, brief and childlike, with a napkin whose color and position gave it a chadory appearance.

Hunched over the stove, bandanna tied tightly to his head, Tiff prepared food. There were eggs and linked sausages and toasted hooves of rye bread. Neither sister was hungry.

What remained of Mercer's belongings, the items she had *on her person* at the time of the explosion, would be returned to the family once the investigation was completed. This had been queerly volunteered by a uniformed officer at the hospital late the previous night.

Without rest, Sam's eyes had turned quilty and dark. She listened to the pattering of feet as Max walked into the kitchen, unfamiliar, taking stock of his new surroundings.

"I'll have cereal," he said.

There were bran flakes and wheat squares and unsweetened pellets of oat. Nothing he would choose if the selections were unboxed, poured into a row of bowls with milk and sugar and diced fruit.

"You will *not* have cereal," said Tiff. "Sit down and I'll fix you a plate."

Clem nodded to her son, adjusting several of Mercer's medical books on a chair so Max could reach the table.

Pressed to the counter, Tiff drank coffee and nibbled on a blackened digit of sausage. With focused precision, using the pointy blade of a steak knife, Sam carved loose the seeds to a peeled tangerine. She collected them in piles and, when one oozed away, she batted it across the table at Max. He looked for it, half interested, beneath the curve of his plate and then turned his attention again to his food.

"They think we can get him this afternoon," said Clem to no one in particular.

It was difficult using words like "lucky" and "fortunate" when considering a detonated bomb, *this* bomb. But Garrett had only suffered lacerations to the head, face, shoulder, and a sprained wrist from falling to the ground. They had been permitted to speak with him, quickly, in the broken hours of early morning before a newly injected sedative ran through his veins.

"There'll be lots of questions," said Sam. "From the investigators, from the press."

Many of the same neighbors who for years kept Mercer at measured distances had, unanticipatedly, dropped off condolence bouquets or dishes of cellophaned baked goods. Missy Reeler's mother had left a lemon-poppy Bundt cake on the porch swing. Reactions which, to a vocal Sam, smacked of guilt and hypocrisy. "They're happy she's gone," she said. "Believe me. They know what someone different does to the value of property."

"It's not like this place has fallen apart," said Clem.

"Doesn't matter." Sam took a swallow of juice. "I'm not saying they wanted her dead. Just moved."

Max left the table for the living room.

"You were off at school," said Sam. "But there was a collective sigh of relief when Dad was carted away."

It had seemed to Sam and Garrett—and maybe even Mercer—that after Kendall's departure everyone in the neighborhood became just a bit friendlier. A nod of greeting from Mrs. Haynes down the block, the offer of a ride home in the sleety rain from Mr. Dexley. These people didn't like the Boones any better, only now they recognized there'd be one less problem to worry about coming from "that house." And of course, the goodwill didn't last very long; it dissolved, piece by piece, each time a new batch of protesters unloaded from their van.

With Mercer's death, the showy displays of kindness—the flowers and potted casseroles and handwritten notes—were offered by neighbors who hadn't bothered to speak a thoughtful word during all the time Mercer was living only a few lots away.

Now Sam and Clem, hardened by their histories in Lukin, had been able to restrain emotion. There were no gulpy fits of crying, no dizzied shouts in the morning's leanest hours. Tears, of course, but only the kind you could wipe away with a hankie or the back of your shirtsleeve. Even for Tiff, who had seen more than any of Mercer's children, there were the busied movements of taking final care, of cleaning and cooking and sponging egg grease from Max's chin.

Both sisters confessed a near-immobilizing loss to reality in the wake of this madness. Everything hitched surreally together at proximate distances. They conceded that, indeed, when younger, they some-times imagined harmful attacks on their mother, their home.

Worse than any of it until now. Ball bats and pitched stones and the destruction of property—more also than the split porch post coming the year Clem departed for college. But never, even when reading newspaper accounts of other clinic protests and shootings and bombings, had they believed this degree of danger would find its way into their lives.

Strangely threaded to the relief of knowing it was all nearly finished came a sigh of regret for something important suddenly gone. A final bond for the three of them, to their home, now rubbed away.

After Sam excused herself to shower and dress, she sat on the toilet in the upstairs bathroom, the one she'd shared during childhood with her brother and sister. She stared through the smudgy window at the brown grass and the strip of sidewalk where pirouetting bands of protesters had once marched. She remembered police cars and colorful signs. Fleet noises from Max and Clem and Greer, awakened, seemed caustic against the floor tile.

A bolt of long days was unfurled before them. Futures faced from a new and peculiar release point. Life during times of war, she thought. How to behave? What decisions would they make? Please, she repeated to herself, allow this one thing to pass without great difficulty.

She leafed through an old magazine, letting the lower regions of her legs turn tingly. There was a photograph of a carnival in Philo, Illinois. Her mind spilled to a time when they were all young and had visited some fair in a nearby county. Her parents were not much beyond Clem's current age. How odd. Like passing the seniors during your freshman year of high school and imagining, throughout the autumn months, you'd never be that old. She remembered celebrating maple syrup or the blossoms of springtime, riding a vintage carousel with Clem and Garrett. Her parents stood beside the gate, eating square-cut pizza, waving after every revolution. She and her siblings remained seated for five, six tickets' worth of rides until, finally, they were pulled away. Deep into the night, and the ones that followed, she and Clem and Garrett spoke of their carousel horses with outsized affection. They told one another the horses, named by each, were stabled at a local raceway. Months later they still called to them from the backseat of the car when driving past the track.

Sam could no longer invoke their names. She shouted for her sister into the heating duct at her feet, which cryptically linked her to the kitchen.

"What were the names of our horses?" And more, unnecessary for Clem. "From when we were little. On the carousel."

Downstairs, Clem pulled her chair closer to the wall so she could speak into the pleats of the vent without raising her voice.

"Lancelot Larry, Bluey, and Victor Vanilla Coke." She lowered her head. "Mine, Garrett's, and yours."

"Yeah," said Sam, returning the magazine to its wicker holding stall beneath the sink. "Victor Vanilla Coke."

A strange satisfaction bristled across her memory, rising with a newness each time she repeated the name. Victor Vanilla Coke. Said with joy, only to herself, in the warm shower water.

SEATED BETWEEN enormous whitewashed columns on the porch, Sam and Clem rocked in chairs normally occupied by residents of the Dover Mills assisted-living hospital. Aged and infirm, aged who were also infirm. On the lawn, some played a painfully endless game of croquet with extended mallets (to minimize bending) and liberal scorekeeping. Others wandered aimlessly into fencing and tree brush until, righted divinely by attendants, they were again pointed in impediment-free directions. They were surrounded by enough green so the random crescents where leaves had already begun to wilt with reds and tans appeared, from afar, to be the half-hidden siding of curiously painted houses. Near the curve of the property rested a decorative fountain, emptied of water for obvious reasons of safety. Rising from its center was an elaborately carved tower of fish and sea vegetation and prickly coral. Sunk low in the earth along the fountain's stippled shadow was a chair-and-table set of perforated iron. There, fiddling with the lid to a peanut-butter jar, sat Kendall.

He was wearing a metallic-gold jogging suit, sent by Sam, tucked into tube socks and slippers. His hair had been combed away from his face with a gleamy gel. Whiskers stubbly from two, three days without shaving formed map shapes at his jaw, lips, and chin. He spun the lid against the table with his index finger to the same bite-and-climb rhythm of open-field oil pumps. With his mouth hanging low, his tongue, exposed, seemed dry and salted.

It had been Garrett's wish to visit his father before returning home. He'd been seized during this fragile time by the need, immediate, for a parent—half a parent even. He sat to his father's right, hands folded quietly in the seam of his thighs. He waited for a certain stillness to begin speaking. Explanations, he figured, only a parent would understand.

He told his father he'd arrived at the clinic late, by no more than four minutes. The doors were locked and he walked away, intent on trying the front entrance. As he moved again down the pathway he passed the man with the backpack, someone he vaguely recognized; he told him the place was shut closed. But the man continued. And Garrett, too, was several steps farther when he heard the steady tapping on the glass of his mother calling him. She was standing with another woman, a technician, when Garrett made a motion with his hands as if to say he was going to bring the truck around. In the wink of the second it took to turn toward the street, only partway, came a white-light flash and diesel thunder he felt first in his feet. The heat and wind spilled him flat; he was pecked and bitten by splinters of metal and exploded concrete. A second gust rolled across his back in a combustible ball of oranges and yellows that lifted past the darkened rooftops. There was the noise of settling: a steamy hiss and tinkling glass and the crunchy shift of cinder blocks and steel. Soon he heard a man stepping heavy-footed through the debris and then, once he'd reached the door, shout back to his wife, "Don't come over!"

Struggling to rise, Garrett expected the man would've sounded like those sluggish audiotape voices you hear in movies during times of hardship. A beat too slow. But, instead, it was perfectly normal; the same speed and tone used to call someone from across an empty playing field.

Garrett reached his knees, palms pressed into the sharp dust, and swung his head to the right like a swimmer taking air. Other protesters had been knocked to their butts, on the lawn, looking pensive and confused; they were spattered with their own blood across laps and chests and necks. A ringing wave of nausea inflated in Garrett's throat, in his gut. He fingered the busted line of his forehead, stopping when he felt something stiff and nervy and foreign. Half hooding his left eye, parallel to the ground, a scrappy coin of sheet metal that had tomahawked into his skull. He tripped; his mouth filled with the peculiar tastes of sodium and ginger. And when he remembered trying to talk, not so many minutes later, he was riding in the back of an ambulance with a black man screwing an IV into his arm.

"How do you *not* think about this?" said Garrett, letting his gaze fall to where his sisters were seated along the horizon. "Predictable for me . . ."

What he meant, what it would have taken someone with a significantly keener mind than his father to recognize, was that much of Garrett's life had been spent in shiftless anonymity. Middle child, maybe. But more, he had learned—expected!—while playing hockey goalie that the only times people really noticed him was when he screwed up. Missed the save. He had spent too many sleepless nights as a boy running over mistakes, *his* mistakes. Slightly stunted anticipation, his leg or arm an inch too short for reaching the puck. And everyone always remembered. He stowed each failure in a heavy sack.

Unexpectedly, Kendall lifted his hand toward his son's face; he touched Garrett at two points of damage. A connection, perhaps. More likely, though, he was struck by the severe whiteness of the gauze and bandages taped to Garrett's forehead or the shiny strawberry chafing at the slope of his cheekbone. Bright colors in his sea of familiarity. Garrett let his own hand meet his father's. Skin to skin, Kendall pulled away and cradled his arm, as if injured, against his rib cage.

Still, the initial gesture was enough to bring more from the son. For Garrett, one butaned day burning longer and cleaner than others. He began telling his father, who showed few signs of attentiveness, about something buckling a hard crease in his memory. A single afternoon when he was fifteen playing hockey at Thurmer Park. That rare game when his entire family had been in attendance: Sam sharing ice time; Clem working a bake-sale table in the lobby; his parents in the stands. The other team was from Medina. Late, with a one-goal Lukin lead, Sam started skating sloppily at center ice; she had the puck stolen by a competing wing. It all happened so fast—a remaining lifetime reduced to several rapid seconds. The crowd rising in near-unison to its feet as the Medina forward slashed toward Garrett, alone, on a breakaway. Rushing left with a feint, another, before slapping a backhand top shelf—above Garrett's shoulder—to the right.

As though the puck were suspended on a string, within Garrett's reach, he plucked it from the sky with his gloved hand.

And there was applause for only him.

Stonewalled, they sometimes called it when a goalie stopped a breakaway. Stonewalled.

The next morning's newspaper had a photograph of Garrett stretched into a wide X before the mouth of the goal. Years later he still kept a copy of the article, bleached and fringed with age, in the drawer of his bed stand. On nights when he had trouble clearing his head he spread the story and accompanying photograph across his blanket.

The moment belonged to him, fully, he thought in the afternoon's waning light.

Kendall slid the peanut-butter lid across the table at Garrett, who tapped it back. They continued with this graceless game of catch while Garrett spoke more. He explained, not simply for his father but also for himself, how he would often take great pleasure in reading the tiny agate-type box scores and four-sentence accounts of their hockey games in the papers. Better than the local newspaper were the ones from neighboring counties, where they wrote the team's entire name in splendid redundancy. Town, sponsor, and nickname. Lukin Briar Gears. Sometimes they left Ben Briar's name out, choosing only Lukin Gears.

He liked the way the words sounded pressed in such close proximity. Lukin Briar Gears. Joined words whose meanings you wouldn't know if you didn't know their meanings. They fit together. It made him think of more than hockey. The way things had once also fit together with his sisters, like gears, when everyone was living beneath the same roof. And trouble was never so wide as it seemed.

A male nurse came to take Kendall inside for a bath and dinner. The man was wearing white trousers and a white, open-collar shirt. Looped to a thin chain around his neck was the slanty wedge of a shark's tooth.

When Garrett asked about it, if only for conversation's sake—he was ready to hear someone else talk—the man said, "Just a trinket I found during a vacation in the Florida Keys." He helped Kendall to his feet by holding his armpits. "Makes me seem like I've got a history."

Both men smiled.

Sometimes people ran out of things to think, important things. So they created them by speaking about homemade jewelry or moments from the past that were once too great to imagine living without.

Now his head hurt. Too much for one day, for a year of days. He saw his father led up the stairs, and stop without visible knowledge beside the two women who were his daughters.

THE THREE OF THEM DROVE in Sam's rented car. All silent except for the occasional question asked of Garrett in the backseat. When did they replace that tailor's shop with a video store? Was this street always so deserted?

Nothing now about either parent. Time remained for that.

They stopped at the Dairy Freeze so Garrett could drink a Seven-Up with his pill. There had been messages and phone numbers left for all of them, for *any* of them. People who wanted to know: What do *you* think? And Garrett could say whatever he chose, giving birth to countless other newsclippings. The kind he wouldn't save.

Clem and Sam split an order of french fries. They ate them from a cardboard boat smashed behind the gearshift at their knees. Greasy prints pressed into the vinyl of the dashboard and steering wheel.

A generation ago came impending worry from the Atomic Bomb, squeezing people together with the threat of blowing them apart. Now, it seemed, those same people (and their progeny) had scattered in fear of many bombs. Little, unannounced. The type your neighbor's son could build in his garage with ignored plumbing supplies and fertilizer.

Because each Boone needed something kindly to remember during so much grief, Garrett used the final blocks home to offer his sisters a few tokens he had taken unexpectedly from his childhood. Applied in recent days. "These will not seem that great," he said while touching his head. "But they're from you—and Mom."

During Lucy's birthday a couple of weeks earlier, Garrett had prepared dinner. One of the dishes was freshly chopped fruit salad he'd seen his mother fix for a picnic. She'd told him, back then, to stir in lemon juice to prevent the fruit from turning brown while left sitting in the refrigerator. And it had worked. Later, while waiting for Lucy, he gift-wrapped a pair of earrings with a trick he'd picked up from Clem: he folded over the frayed edges of the paper for smoother lines.

"Not so amazing," he said. "But something I wouldn't have known without watching Clem with Christmas presents."

Smiling into the rearview mirror, Sam knew whatever her brother said next, whatever he may have learned from time spent with her, would not involve the kitchen or techniques for neater gift presentations.

"You'd just finished college," he said, stabbing his straw down and back through the plastic lid of his cup. "You were dating that real estate guy, the one who helped you find your last apartment."

A nod from Sam.

"And you two were gonna break up. You'd just had a fight about something or other."

"Water glasses. He hated when I left my water glass beside the sink. He thought I should put it away every time."

"Well, whatever." Garrett checked the nicks and cuts along his forearms. "But you and I were talking on the phone. It was late. Late here, anyway. And you told me this thing I've tried to keep in mind with Lucy, with anyone. You said men have a desire to instantly fix something when it breaks, even a relationship. But women simply want the damage recognized. They don't need all the answers."

After a moment of extended silence, Clem spoke in a playful tone. "I sure feel cheated," she said. "That's a lot better than folding poorly trimmed wrapping paper."

"Oh, I'm not sure," said Sam. "Depends on the circumstances."

Nearly home, Garrett lowered the window to release the stink of fried vegetable oil. He let the wind hit him square, so the bandage above his eye became dimpled and flossy with air.

THE FIRST THING that caught Sam's eye was a horseshoe-shaped wreath of flowers tied to the fence. Angled across the arrangement was a white sash, like those worn by beauty-pageant contestants, reading *You'll Be Missed.* Other offers of condolence were also propped and fastened to the fence around the clinic where Mercer had worked. There was a pink teddy bear and various greeting cards and hand-painted signs and lesser bundles of daisies and miniature roses.

"They're from her patients," said Clem, who'd moved in for a closer look once the car had been parked.

Strangely, none of the Boone children had given much thought to all the women who relied on their mother for care. In the past, it had all seemed so abstract, so faceless. The late-night calls that would carry Mercer to the bedside of someone who was sick, or ready to give birth, or only scared.

"See this?" asked Sam, calling her brother and sister to her side.

She was pointing to a row of hastily mounted photographs, each showing a child—or children—at various stages of their adolescence. Something about viewing one of the pictured infants, swaddled against fierce weather, caused Clem to begin weeping softly. To wipe her tears, Garrett offered the fabric of an Ace bandage wrapped to his wrist. Mostly, Clem had been slugged by sadness—the way meaningful thoughts leap from quiet places—when she realized her children would never know their grandmother.

Behind the fence, streamers of yellow crime-scene tape flapped in the breeze. Several police officers met Clem, Garrett, and Sam at the mouth of the gate, leading them up the scarred pathway. Federal agents, wearing navy windbreakers with oversized white lettering across the back, were scattered purposefully into small groups that each concentrated on a specific aspect of the investigation. In the distance, the Boones saw a crowd of photographers and television crews jockeying for position inside a pen roped and guarded by police officers.

Along the walls of the building's badly disfigured entrance were great bands of black bomb soot, concentric circles that faded as they pushed farther away. The air still smelled of smoke and chemicals and charred clothing. Against the seat cushion of a damaged chair was a dark spill, resembling chocolate syrup, and Clem, imagining the stain must be blood, turned her head.

"In here," said Garrett, nearly whispering as he guided his sisters into the room where clinic staffers dressed and ate and waited for escorts to take them to their cars.

A bulletin board on the far wall was crowded with items meant both to offer a break in the seriousness and, also, to provide sobering warnings. There were political cartoons, TV listings, restaurant menus, bumper stickers, and articles on other clinic protests and suggestions about how staffers could change the patterns of their days so they would become more difficult to follow.

Seated in the corner, Garrett unzipped his duffel bag—the same one he used to store Mercer's vest. (Though she'd been wearing the body armor when she died, it only served to keep her torso clean of shrapnel and splintered wood.) He kicked a locker that belonged to their mother. Tacked at various heights along the inside of the locker's door were pictures of both grandchildren and, from long ago, a photograph of her own children and Kendall standing beside the family station wagon.

Clem carefully removed the pictures, rubbing off tiny balls of Scotch tape. Together, the three of them folded a pair of trousers and two shirts and a lab coat. On the top shelf, there was a hairbrush, a stethoscope, a box of apple candies, and a cylinder of roll-on deodorant that Sam uncapped and held near her nose to see if she could still find her mother's scent.

"I remember this," said Clem, after inexplicably discovering against the back of the shelf a keyless lanyard she'd braided for Mercer in day camp.

There was a certain order to putting the final pieces of their mother's life in place—a sudden responsibility that came to them not after the ravages of a long illness or the shock of learning some organ had failed. Even something other than the horrible surprise that seized individuals after hearing a loved one had been in an accident. To them, the order arrived linked not with the loss of life but, instead, with a life violently taken away. A life, a family of lives, splashed with poison.

When finished, they walked down the hallway with Sam carrying the duffel filled with their mother's belongings. It was the last physical evidence connecting Mercer to the clinic—unless the blood and skin fragments on the seat cushion near the entrance tested as hers. Several staff members expressed their sorrow; they told Clem, Garrett, and Sam how much everyone who worked at the clinic respected and loved Mercer. Then, because the wheels must continue to grind forward, once the Boones had moved almost far enough away, the staffers began talking—in hushed tones—about a doctor from some neighboring county who had agreed to fill in two days a week until a permanent replacement could be found.

While preparing to depart from the clinic for a final time, both sisters paused beside the open doorway to one of the procedure rooms. Sam, moving with the weight of hesitation, took several steps toward the empty table; she ran her fingers over a tray of instruments. Deliberately, she eased herself around to the fork of the stirrups—standing, now, in the space so often occupied by her mother.

"I wonder," she said, speaking as much to herself as to her sister and brother across the room. "If I had seen all this when I was young, how it would have stayed with me."

She let her eyes swallow items slowly. Everything seemed so innocuous: the canister of pellets, the boxy vacuum, the spear-shaped dilators. She lifted a flexible curette, stabbing it against the air like a switch of maple.

"Having been in this room," she said, turning to face Clem and Garrett, "what if you were told, 'Remember something from your childhood, something important.' " She raised her arms. "Would this be it?"

Clem shrugged; Garrett, who in recent times had visited the clinic more than both sisters, massaged the soreness in his wrist.

"I hope not," he said, finally.

Taking another long look, so it would all catch against her memory, Sam walked to the door. The three of them headed outside. The cluster of journalists had grown both in size and in restlessness. Several police officers, stationed near the entranceway rubble, led the Boones to their car. As Clem guided the car at a crawl's pace through cameras and extended microphones and federal agents and a collection of people who'd come only to watch, Sam propped herself on her knees, staring out the back window at what remained of the clinic, until all she could see were the tiny figures of the crowd like smooth pegs in a cribbage board.

YOU ARE HERE, read the sign. There was an arrow pointing to a dot in the middle of a cross-hatching of lines which represented paths at a Lukin nature preserve. Except, really, here was home. The sign had been unearthed in the back yard, near the warehouse. Something Kendall had once stolen (or "borrowed") for use in a future sculpture or painting. Clem brushed off the dirt and leaned the sign, green and white and black, on the fencing of the porch.

She waited for her brother and sister to return, in weather much too cold for late September. Already she could see great fists of breath. Inside, her children were asleep; Tiff was fixing a fresh pot of coffee, warming a braided walnut ring. Clem swept the stairs with a push broom, hooking dirt away because the rows of raky bristles, perpendicular to the handle, would not fit completely on each narrow step. Earlier, she had made phone calls and read through magazines and fed both children. They had rolled back an area rug and played games on the smooth wooden floor of the living room.

Once afternoon had nudged to evening and then night, she heard the humping of heavy machinery and the biting squeal of strained brake shoes as Garrett's truck slowed in the driveway. It would take the three of them, and maybe Tiff too, for the lifting and movement. The trailer hitch was the same kind used for towing powerboats to water landings. Walking to the back, Garrett wore a stocking cap which covered his bandage; the only visible sign of injury was the purpled blood drained to crooked wings beneath his eyes.

In floodlight, the carted object of steel and shiny coils and bolted O-rings resembled something dunked low in the ocean for research or propelled to another atmosphere for intercepting radio signals. Boards of pine were used to slide the ornate capsule down on runners so no one would blow a hernia under its weight. Giving instructions, Garrett surveyed the land to the side and rear of the house.

Earlier that morning, Sam had closed her eyes and pleaded for a single wish. Impossible and inappropriate. Not for another five minutes of her mother's life, not for a sudden and brief lucidity to fill her father's head. She'd wanted ice in autumn. A nearness to miracle her brother could actually provide. No tight-stamped molecules for skates but, close enough, prickly clouds of snow belched across the lawn. Promised, even, to a skeptical Max that when he awoke there would be whiteness from his window.

The fan gun was finally dragged and rocked to the border of the vacant, wobbly hooped skating rink. And they listened to Garrett, linking electrical extension cords and adjusting beams of flashlights and clearing scattered timber. Binding a despouted cooking funnel with duct tape, Garrett attached it by garden hose to the water outlet behind the house. There were two tanks of liquid nitrogen strapped to the gun for times, like now, when the temperature was still ten or so degrees from the freezing mark. Feeble water pressure would slow the process in a machine designed for the high-powered rush of fire hoses. And the noise was loud: the strummy wizzle of a lawn mower stuck mulching loose sticks.

Both sisters sat with Tiff on the porch. They drank coffee and watched Garrett turn nobs and pace along the wet ground. Soon came tails of snow, strong then weak, loomed to points in the sky like confetti shot from a cannon. Several times, Clem thought she saw drapes parted on the second floor of a house down the street. She shook her head when Garrett began walking in her direction.

"Ridiculous, huh?" he said, hiking himself onto the railing beside his sisters. "Just a bunch of gearheads making snow. In the back yard. In fucking September."

It had been a long while since Clem or Sam had heard the word "gearhead." Often, during youth-league hockey days, the Lukin team and its fans were taunted by boosters of competing teams with the chant, *Gearheads! Gearheads!* It was a jab at the mostly blue-collar backgrounds of Lukin's players.

Eventually, Tiff grew tired and retreated to the living-room couch. The other three remained bundled outside for the final hours of night, taking leave only for warmed coffee or visits to the toilet. Every forty minutes, Garrett would call upon his sisters for help in changing the angle of the gun to prevent drifted snow from concentrating along a single direction. Taking pride in proper work, he disappeared into the darkness of the warehouse.

"I wonder what he's gonna do?" asked Clem.

"He's looking for tools."

"No." She balled her hands at the palms of her gloves, away from the finger slots. "I mean in general. Will he stay here?"

"Probably," said Sam. "Where else would he go?"

"Anywhere."

They let their thoughts subside: Above the consistent rumble of the fan gun came a series of tinny clanks from wherever Garrett was now.

"And you?" said Clem. "Do you think if Garrett left for Colorado or California or Canada . . . ?"

"Someplace that begins with a 'C'—"

"Or not." She collected herself. "But do you think if he left here, moved away, *you'd* ever come back?"

"Maybe. To see Dad."

"But after that. Later."

The two of them watched Garrett carry a few of their father's things into the yard.

"Mmmmmm." Sam licked some moisture from her lips. "What about you?"

"I can't imagine coming here just to come here. I guess if we were taking a road trip we might pass through. For a night."

The snow had stacked itself in crooked piles, shaded gray, images of lunar landscapes. Using a steel-bladed shovel, Garrett bulldozed the hills and craters into even valleys. He stomped with his boots. He gathered water in a peach tin, sprinkling it where the lumps wouldn't easily collapse. For those places demanding more care, near the rink's wooden and brass-bracketed frame, he folded snow with a squeegee once used on ice. Sticky flakes nested on his shoulders, in the fibers of his stocking cap.

"The best we can do," said Garrett, jogging past his sisters into the house.

When he returned, hands filled, he sat on the cold planks of the porch. He slipped two layers of plastic baggies over his boots and fastened them above the laces with rubber bands. Then he trudged to the rink, skidding nearly the moment his shrink-wrapped feet met snow. The bags were more for reducing friction than keeping dry. He pushed hard with his right leg, sliding a few steps before doing the same with his left leg.

"It's kind of slushy," he said above the purr of machinery. "But better than sand."

Less enthusiastically, Clem readied herself next to Sam. They both joined Garrett, testing the wet-packed snow with blousy, makeshift skates. Movement worked best, it seemed, when they gained momentum by taking stutter steps built into a tiny leap slide. The way one might gather steam before hopping onto a sled.

They each took turns, waving the other two aside for the chance at longer skid marks. Several times, during aggressive runs by Sam and Clem, they tumbled onto their pants seats and hips. Crawling beneath the elastic of their sleeves and the collars of their shirts, the snow had the grainy texture of grated ice.

In sudden silence, Max appeared across the yard. He stood mesmerized between bars of the porch railing.

"Snow," he said in a disbelieving voice.

A smile came to Clem's face when her son began moving heedfully in her direction.

"Snow," he said again, patting the insides of the rink with the tacky feet of his Spider-Man pajamas.

She fixed Baggies below the bulbs of his knees. She tapped him on the butt, only fingers, and whispered into his ear. Skateaway, she said. Two words bunched as one. And seized by some act of defiance and pleasure, he wobbled into the cripply space between his uncle and aunt. He flapped and kicked. He felt the very earth squish beneath the tender slopes of his toes. Tiny hands raised to claws beside his chin, mimicked by Sam and Garrett and then Clem. A muted light turned their shadows long, narrow, hinged queerly into the spokes of a wheel. The look of objects easily defined. Everything that was white and airy and weightless.